PRAISE FOR *DIRECTED VERDICT* AND OTHER NOVELS BY RANDY SINGER

"There is plenty of room in evangelical Christian fiction for fresh voices, and debut novelist Singer is a promising one."

PUBLISHERS WEEKLY
ON *DIRECTED VERDICT*

"A riveting courtroom drama . . ."

CBA MARKETPLACE
ON *DIRECTED VERDICT*

"Realistic and riveting, *Directed Verdict* is a compelling story about the persecuted church and those who fight for global religious freedom."

JAY SEKULOW
CHIEF COUNSEL, AMERICAN CENTER FOR LAW AND JUSTICE

"Randy Singer's novel of international intrigue, courtroom drama, and gripping suspense will challenge readers to examine anew issues of faith and ethics."

JERRY W. KILGORE
FORMER ATTORNEY GENERAL OF VIRGINIA, ON *DIRECTED VERDICT*

"After a string of suspense-filled nights and bleary-eyed mornings, I can personally testify that Randy Singer writes a better legal thriller than even John Grisham. *Directed Verdict* grabs you on page one and never lets up."

SHAUNTI FELDHAHN
BEST-SELLING AUTHOR, SPEAKER, AND NATIONALLY SYNDICATED COLUMNIST

"Randy Singer never disappoints. The plot builds, the pages turn, and the message is always right."

HUGH HEWITT
AUTHOR, COLUMNIST, AND RADIO HOST OF THE NATIONALLY SYNDICATED *HUGH HEWITT SHOW*

"Singer hits pay dirt again with this taut, intelligent thriller. . . . [He] is clearly an up-and-coming novelist to watch."

PUBLISHERS WEEKLY

ON *DYING DECLARATION*

"[*Irreparable Harm* is] an accomplished novel. Randy Singer combines edge-of-your-seat action with a powerful message. Highly recommended."

T. DAVIS BUNN

AUTHOR OF *MY SOUL TO KEEP*

"In this gripping, obsessively readable legal thriller, Singer proves himself to be the Christian John Grisham."

PUBLISHERS WEEKLY

ON *FALSE WITNESS*

"At the center of the heart-pounding action are the moral dilemmas that have become Singer's stock-in-trade. . . . An exciting thriller."

BOOKLIST

ON *BY REASON OF INSANITY*

DIRECTED VERDICT

TYNDALE HOUSE PUBLISHERS, INC., CAROL STREAM, ILLINOIS

RANDY SINGER

Visit Tyndale online at www.tyndale.com.

Visit Randy Singer's website at www.randysinger.net.

TYNDALE and Tyndale's quill logo are registered trademarks of Tyndale House Publishers, Inc.

Directed Verdict

First printing by Tyndale House Publishers, Inc., in 2009.

Previously published as *Directed Verdict* by WaterBrook Press under ISBN-10: 1-57856-633-9.

Designed by Dean H. Renninger

Published in association with the literary agency of Alive Communications, Inc., 7680 Goddard Street, Suite 200, Colorado Springs, CO 80920, www.alivecommunications.com.

Library of Congress Cataloging-in-Publication Data

Singer, Randy (Randy D.)
   Directed verdict / Randy Singer.
     p. cm.
   ISBN 978-1-4143-3154-6 (sc)
    1. Persecution—Saudi Arabia—Fiction. 2. Missionaries' spouses—Fiction. 3. Actions and defenses—Fiction.
I. Title.
   PS3619.I5725D47 2009
   813'.6—dc22
                                                          2008053387

Printed in the United States of America

19   18   17   16   15   14   13
8   7   6   5   4   3   2

For Rhonda, Roz, and Josh.
You're the best. Ever.

PART 1

PERSECUTION

1

"SARAH, THE MUTTAWA FOUND US! They're coming. Maybe tonight." The caller paused, his voice trembling. "Arrests. Interrogations. Executions. They'll stop at nothing," he whispered rapidly in Arabic.

Sarah tried to answer, but the words stuck in her throat. She clenched the receiver so tight her knuckles turned white. She was suddenly out of breath, yet she knew she could not allow the man on the other end of the line to sense her fear.

"Sarah, are you there?"

"Is this Rasheed?" she asked in her own low murmur. She too spoke in Arabic.

"You must cancel the services tonight. And, Sarah?"

"Yes?"

"Get the kids out of the apartment."

The kids. Twelve-year-old Meredith. Ten-year-old Steven. Of course she would find a place for the kids. But what about her . . . and Charles? They couldn't just run and hide at the first hint of an investigation. But if this were not a false alarm . . .

"Sarah? Remember, we are not given a spirit of fear but of power and love and a sound mind."

"Um, okay . . . we'll be all right." As she spoke her voice grew steadier, but she still whispered. "Pray for us."

"I will," he promised, and the line went dead.

Sarah kept the phone against her ear, not yet ready to hang up and face Charles and the kids. A million questions screamed for answers. It was Rasheed's voice, but how could he possibly know about the Muttawa? And if they were coming tonight, what did they know? Who told them? And why?

She tried to gather her thoughts, calm her fears, stop the spinning sensation in her head. She lowered the phone and stared down at it.

"Is everything all right, hon?" Charles asked. He crossed the kitchen and began massaging her shoulders. She closed her eyes and felt his fingers penetrate the knotted muscles. They did not relax. "Hey," he said gently. "What's got you so tight?"

Sarah turned and let Charles embrace her. She trembled in his arms, then stood on her toes and whispered in his ear. "The Muttawa have found us. They may be coming tonight."

Tilting her head to look at him, she searched his eyes for the comfort and strength she had found on so many occasions during their twenty-three years of marriage.

Instead, she saw nothing but terror.

◁▷

There were few empty seats in the cavernous courtroom, and the marshals were on full alert. The middle aisle divided the spectators into two camps. They had nothing in common.

The left side, behind the prosecutor's table, was jammed with the local defenders of a woman's right to choose. Employees of the Norfolk Medical Clinic were there, as were leading pro-choice advocates from across Virginia. Joining them, so as not to be associated with the fanatics on the other side, were court personnel who had taken time off to see the defendant get what he deserved.

The other side of the courtroom—the right side—was populated with members of Chesapeake Community Church. Many kept their heads bowed in silent prayer as their pastor, the Reverend Jacob Bailey, came to a critical point in his testimony. The church members were joined by some hard-core veterans of the pro-life movement, men and women who had served time for chaining themselves to each other or to abortion clinics. They had seen some irate judges and pit-bull prosecutors in their day. But, as they eagerly told any reporter who would listen, they had never seen a judge as biased as this one—the Honorable Cynthia Baker-Kline. And in this case, with no jury, she had the sole power to convict or acquit.

Two sketch artists, drawing fast and furiously, sat with the reporters on the left side of the courtroom. The woman wearing the robe was easy, a sketch artist's dream. Behind her back, the lawyers called her Ichabod Crane.

She had angular features—a long pointed nose, wire-rimmed glasses, accusatory bony fingers, a perpetual scowl, and a jutting jaw—the quintessential schoolmistress. She had not smiled the entire case.

The Reverend Jacob Bailey would prove more difficult for the artists. Try as they might, neither had succeeded in making the defendant look like a criminal. His face was thin and pale. Twenty days of a fluids-only fast had rendered him gaunt. Static electricity charged his wispy and unmindful blond hair, and he slumped forward as he testified, his bony frame engulfed by the witness chair. He talked so softly that Ichabod had to keep reminding him to speak into the mike.

The man presently questioning Bailey was defense attorney Brad Carson. He fared better with the artists. He was thin, possessing a runner's build, a chiseled jaw, deep-set and expressive steel blue eyes, and jet-black hair. He had the comfortable bearing of a man without pretense and a quick and easy smile that charmed both witnesses and spectators.

The artists put down their pencils as Carson got to the crux of the matter.

"What were you doing outside the abortion clinic on September 13, Reverend?" Brad addressed the witness from behind the podium. Yesterday his efforts to pace the courtroom had generated a stern lecture from Ichabod on proper decorum.

"Praying," the reverend said, softly and simply.

"Were you talking to God or talking to men?"

"I pray to God," the reverend answered, "in the name of His Son, Jesus Christ."

Brad had not put that last part in the script, and he shot Bailey a reproving look. "Did you have your eyes closed as you knelt to pray?" Brad emphasized that the reverend was on his knees; it would make his conduct seem less threatening.

"Yes, of course."

"Did you even know whether anybody else was around?"

"Not really," the reverend said. "When I pray, I try to focus on God and block out everything else."

Another bonus answer. Brad got the impression that the pastor was juicing it up a little for the congregation.

"Were you within one hundred feet of the clinic?" Ichabod asked sharply, leaning forward so she hovered over the witness.

Her question, though an easy one, seemed to startle the witness. He looked up meekly at the judge. "Yes, ma'am," he said.

Brad watched Ichabod make a check on the legal pad in front of her. The criminal statute applied to any speech or activities within one hundred feet of a medical facility.

He moved quickly to regain the initiative. "May I approach the witness, Your Honor?" Brad started walking toward the witness box.

Ichabod glared at Brad and waited a few painful seconds. He stopped. "Yes," she said, when she had his full attention. Brad sighed and moved forward. Out of the corner of his eye he watched Ichabod return to doodling on her legal pad, doing her best to look bored.

"I'm handing you a copy of the criminal statute in question," Brad said as he extended a single sheet of paper to the reverend. The paper trembled as Bailey held it. Brad knew this would happen. It was part of his plan to generate sympathy.

"Look down at the second paragraph," Brad continued, moving back to his own counsel table and pulling a pair of reading glasses from his suit coat pocket, "and follow with me as I briefly read the things this statute prohibits. Did you try to obstruct, detain, or hinder anyone from entering the facility?"

"No."

"Did you knowingly come within eight feet of any patients for the purpose of passing out a leaflet or handbill?"

"No."

"Did you knowingly come within eight feet of any patients for the purpose of engaging in oral protests or persuading the patients not to proceed with an abortion?"

"No," the Reverend Bailey said, his voice picking up some confidence even as his hand continued to tremble. Brad was pleased with the witness; it had not been easy to convince the pastor to answer so succinctly.

But Ichabod was not through.

"When you pray," she asked, looking thoughtfully out toward the audience, "does your religion require that you pray at a certain spot?"

"No, Your Honor," Bailey admitted, looking befuddled.

"So you can pray anywhere in the country, and God will still hear?"

"Yes, of course. He's omnipresent."

"And can your God hear you whether you pray out loud or to yourself?" the judge asked, still staring off into the distance.

"Sure," Bailey said. He had leaned too close to the mike, and it squealed. He jumped back as if it had bitten him.

"On the date in question, were you praying out loud or to yourself?" Ichabod queried.

"Out loud."

"Loud enough for others to hear?"

"Yes."

Ichabod made a few more check marks on her pad. Then she turned and gave the witness an icy stare. He shifted uncomfortably.

Brad felt like he was watching a train wreck develop in slow motion and was powerless to stop it. He took off his glasses and began gnawing on them.

"Then do you expect this court to believe that you just *happened* to pick this spot to pray and just *happened* to pray out loud, but really had no intention of persuading the women who might just *happen* to walk by?" Ichabod raised her inflection and eyebrows in a show of disbelief.

"Your Honor," Brad said quickly, drawing attention away from the witness box. "I find myself in the unusual position of objecting to the court's own questions." He flashed a disarming grin that the judge did not return.

"While I've got a suspicion that my objection will be overruled," he continued, "it does seem improper for you to be asking argumentative questions of this witness. Particularly when the question implies that this statute prevents someone from praying out loud on a public sidewalk. My reading of the statute does not suggest that interpretation."

"Is that your objection?" Ichabod turned her icy stare to Brad.

"For now," he added quickly.

"Overruled. The court is entitled to develop a full record. Now, Mr. Bailey, answer the question."

Reverend Bailey hesitated and exhaled deeply. "Honestly, Your Honor," he said in a soft-spoken plea, "I felt burdened to pray about this." He paused and looked down at his folded hands, his voice softening even further. "This sin that is plaguing our nation . . . this killing of unborn children. And I felt led by God to do so in front of the clinic, regardless of the consequences."

Attaboy, Brad thought. *Show a little spine.* Brad jumped on the chance to regain control.

"Why did you feel so burdened?" he asked, leaning forward, feigning interest.

The question elicited a quick response from the prosecuting attorney, a severe-looking woman in her midforties named Angela Bennett, who rose immediately to object. She could have saved her energy, because Ichabod, the self-appointed guardian of the Norfolk Clinic, was all over this one.

"Mr. Carson," Ichabod hissed, staring at him over the glasses perched on the end of her nose, "that question's improper, and you know it. I've told you before, we are not going to get into the reverend's personal views on abortion—"

"But, Judge, motivation is key. The statute requires that Reverend Bailey intentionally come within eight feet of abortion patients for the *purpose* of persuading them not to—" The judge held up her hand and Brad stopped in midsentence.

"Mr. Carson!" she snapped. "I am not finished!"

"Sorry, Your Honor," Brad said, without the least hint of remorse.

"You *will not* inject the issue of motivation into this case. This is basically a trespass case. He either violated the law, or he didn't. His purpose for being there—and whether it was to persuade women not to have an abortion—can be determined from his actions. His motivation for being there does not concern me. Is that clear?" She gave Brad her most intense federal judge stare.

He wanted to tell her she was splitting legal hairs, that she was a disgrace to the bench. He wanted to tell her off the way he had in his dreams, the way he had while driving to work, the way he had a thousand times this morning in his own mind. He felt the heat rising in his neck, and he knew how good it would feel to unload. But he also knew it would be pointless.

His plan called for a far different approach. And his client's future hinged on Brad's ability to keep his cool and execute the plan.

So he just glared back, his eyes flashing with equal intensity.

"Mr. Carson, I'm speaking to you," Ichabod said, her voice nearly cracking.

"Sorry, Judge," he replied at last. "I just wanted to make sure you were finished this time."

His impertinence caught her speechless. Her eyes were mere slits, with the nostrils on her enormous nose puffing in and out. When she finally did speak, it came in short, staccato bursts.

"Don't you ever . . . treat this court with such disrespect again! Next time . . . I'll hold you in contempt. And, Mr. Carson?"

He raised an eyebrow, determined not to speak.

"Get back behind that podium and resume your examination from there." She watched warily as Brad retreated to the podium. "Your juvenile shenanigans do not impress me."

Brad shuffled his notes on the podium, then leaned down to whisper in the ear of the heavyset woman seated at the counsel table, his longtime assistant, Bella Harper.

"Watch that vein on her neck," Brad whispered. "I'm going to make it explode." Even as he spoke, the prominent vein on the right side of Ichabod's neck was pulsing visibly, in and out with every heartbeat.

"Don't be a hero," Bella whispered.

But Brad realized he no longer had a choice. He could not win this case in front of Ichabod. She had already made up her mind and would not be confused by the facts. His best chance now was to demonstrate her bias and set her up for reversal on appeal.

To do so, he would have to provoke the full fury of the judge and put his own reputation at risk—a reputation that had taken twelve years to build. It would make matters unbearable at trial but give him a shot on appeal. As an unpleasant by-product, it would make him the poster boy for the Christian Right, a martyr for a cause he did not embrace.

He would do it anyway.

He would do it because he had taken an oath to represent his clients zealously. He would do it because it was the right thing to do.

Brad paused for air and braced himself. Ichabod had not heard the last about motivation.

It was time for Plan B.

◁▷

On the other side of the world, a warrior stalked his prey.

Ahmed Aberijan was a holy warrior, and he was in a holy war. His official title was director of the Muttawa, the Saudi Arabian religious police. His colleagues called him the Right Hand of Mohammed.

His agency was the last bastion of religious purity in a society ravaged by the cancer of Western culture. For Ahmed, Islamic law was all that separated his country from the degradation of the West. Without it, Saudi Arabia would become America's puppet, its Arab slave. America sickened him—the haughty women, the crass materialism, the arrogance of the weak Western politicians. He had secretly gloated when the Twin Towers of the World Trade Center collapsed, watching with pleasure as radical Muslims danced in the streets. Like the infidels in the trade towers, all Christians would one day face the fierce wrath of Allah and answer for their transgressions.

In the meantime, they would have to deal with him.

He lived for nights like this one; he could feel the blood racing through his veins, each nerve-ending fully alert. His target was the underground house church of an American missionary named Charles Reed. But his ultimate goal, as always, was purity for the people of the Kingdom.

Prophet Mohammed himself—peace be upon him—had declared that there should be no religion but Islam on the Arabian peninsula. It was holy ground. Sacred. Not to be desecrated by Western infidels.

For that reason, non-Islamic sects were prohibited from holding public meetings or worshiping. And converting from Islam to another religion was still punishable by death.

A young Ahmed had cringed when the Muttawa enforced religious purity with unfeeling brutality, torture, even beheadings. But as he grew in strength and fervor, Ahmed began to understand that advancing the cause of the Great Prophet sometimes required the shedding of blood. He still remembered the first time he had personally exacted revenge for Allah. He was overwhelmed with a euphoric sense of passion and peace. He experienced, like never before, Allah's pleasure. And that day, he dedicated his life to advancing the cause and punishing the infidels.

Tonight, that mission required Ahmed's presence on the other side of town at a run-down apartment complex. Though he could easily have done so, he never dreamed of delegating this task, of sending someone else to do the hard work for Mohammed. And as his caravan sped through the dark side streets of Riyadh, he sat alone in the backseat of the first unmarked car, interior lights on, reviewing the file and savoring his plan.

The Reed file was thin, the information sparse. Page one contained the summary. Dr. Reed's official occupation in Saudi Arabia, as listed on his visa application, was that of a private school teacher. His wife, Sarah, posed as a school administrator. But Ahmed knew the Reeds were, in fact, American missionaries, sent to deceive and proselytize the Muslim people.

According to his source, a loyal Muslim who had feigned conversion and joined the Reeds' church, the combination of Dr. Reed's passionate teaching and his wife's administrative skills had proven effective in leading more than a few Muslims astray. Tonight he would put an end to their crimes.

Page two of the Reed file contained the affidavit from the source. The Reeds and their followers crammed themselves into the stuffy family room of the Reeds' apartment every Friday night at seven o'clock, the source said, forming one of Riyadh's fastest-growing underground churches. The Reeds were passionate about converting those who attended and equally passionate about the secrecy of the service, which lasted about two hours.

But it wasn't the Friday night service that bothered Ahmed. The names and addresses of those worshipers could be—in fact had been—acquired from his informant. One small church gathering did not merit a minute of Ahmed's valuable time. But the affidavit alleged that the Reeds were also the catalysts for a network of underground churches. They would pray for these other churches on Friday night. Some were led by the Reeds and worshiped at other places. Some were led by other pastors who were in turn mentored by Reed. They never used names, and the informant did not know the leaders or locations of these churches.

But Reed knew. And if he cared about his wife and children, tonight Reed would tell.

Ahmed stared at the passport photos of the couple. The years of pastoring had not been kind to Charles Reed. Ahmed smirked at the pale and pockmarked skin of the pudgy American, the thick glasses, the receding hair, the deep wrinkles that spread like vines from the American's eyes. He would be easy prey. Soft. Pliable.

Sarah Reed had aged more gracefully. Her short, wavy blonde hair framed a face of gentle lines and smooth skin. High cheekbones complemented deep blue eyes that glistened with life even in the photograph. Ahmed was surprised that Sarah Reed made no effort to accentuate those features with the detestable makeup or jewelry of the West. Her looks communicated a natural and comfortable warmth, a woman who would become an immediate friend and confidante to the unsuspecting Muslims she was leading into heresy.

He was sure, just from looking at the photographs, that Charles Reed would love his wife deeply and do anything to protect her. He was also sure that the men he had brought for this raid, with their lust for subjugating Western women, would give Charles Reed sufficient cause for concern.

◁▷

Hours after the phone call, Sarah was beginning to think it was a false alarm.

Shaken by the call, she had first suggested leaving.

"Where would we go?" Charles asked. "Who would we stay with and place in danger?"

Sarah looked down and did not respond.

"Sooner or later, if we're going to stay in this country and reach these people, we'll have to face them," Charles said softly.

Without another word, Sarah picked up the phone and started making calls. She called some trusted friends to take care of the kids. She called every family in the church, explaining the situation, telling them the service was canceled, and asking them for their prayers. Only three members of the church were not home, and though it was against every rule of the fledgling underground movement, she left a vague warning on their answering machines.

When Meredith and Steven were safely out of the house, Sarah and Charles went about the job of sanitizing the apartment of all things religious. Charles started on the computer. He deleted Bible software programs, e-mails, files, and backup files. He transferred lists of church members to flash drives.

Sarah collected all the CDs, Bibles, song sheets, address lists, and papers from the mission board and put them in two large green garbage bags. She even took down the refrigerator magnets with the Bible verses on them. She wrapped the bags in a second bag for safekeeping, then carried them outside.

The Reeds' apartment building was in a forgotten part of the bustling city of Riyadh. It housed hundreds of residents, mostly foreign nationals, in look-alike apartment boxes distinguished only by the apartment number. The place smelled like stale urine. The apartments had not seen a fresh coat of paint in many years, and the Dumpsters in the parking lot were overflowing. Ignoring the full bins, Sarah walked past them and carried her heavy trash bags to a Dumpster in a complex three blocks away.

By the time they were done with their "spring-cleaning," the apartment could just as well have belonged to a couple of atheists.

It was time to pray. And for the next few hours, Charles and Sarah sat beside each other and talked—to each other and to God. "Lord," Charles said quietly as he held Sarah's hand at the kitchen table, "if it be Your will, deliver us from the Muttawa and keep us safe. But if it is Your will that we suffer, give us the same power and courage through the Holy Spirit that You gave to the apostle Paul. And give us the grace that allowed Paul to say he counted it a joy to suffer for Your name's sake. Above all else, put a hedge of protection around Meredith and Steven and keep them safe."

Charles squeezed Sarah's hand. She squeezed back.

"In the name of Jesus, amen."

Sarah stood to survey the apartment one more time. It was getting late. Maybe they wouldn't come. It was nearly eight o'clock. Maybe the Lord had already answered their prayers.

She looked at Charles and forced a small smile. He was trying to act calm, but Sarah had felt the sweat on his palms as they prayed, and the look of terror had never left the depths of his eyes.

As she stood, she jammed her hands into the pockets of her jeans. Then she felt it. Her prayer card. The daily list that reminded her to pray every time her fingers reached into her pocket. She smiled at the way the Lord had just reminded her to get rid of it. She had gone over the house with a fine-tooth comb and totally forgotten about the list in her own pocket.

She pulled it out to read the names one last time as she headed for the door. It would go in the trash bin with the other stuff. But first, she would try to remember. *Pray for salvation,* the list read, *for Hanif and for Khartoum, who has attended, but never—*

She stopped reading midsentence and froze midstep. A noise—maybe a shuffling—from the landing outside her door. Her eyes darted over to Charles, who put his index finger to his lips. She reached inside her blouse and stuffed the list in her bra. Another noise, muffled words . . .

By 8:02, Ahmed and his thugs had crept up the stairs and assembled outside Apartment 3C. He gave his orders in low and hoarse Arabic.

In the next instant, he and his men crashed through the wooden door of the apartment and unleashed the fury of Mohammed on Sarah and Charles Reed.

2

FOR SARAH, EVENTS BECAME A BLUR, jumbled images on a screen that changed so quickly the eye could not focus.

Without knocking, two large Muttawa agents blasted through the wooden door, destroying the dead bolt and shattering the door itself. Two others quickly followed, guns drawn, orders flying in Arabic.

An older man entered next, walking quickly through the splintered door, clearly in charge, his eyes blazing as he assessed the apartment. He was not a tall man, but he had a linebacker's build with a dark complexion and a darker scowl. Deep wrinkles creased his leathery face, and a thin and wiry beard covered his chin. His penetrating eyes stared straight through Sarah until she diverted her gaze.

The man unleashed a vicious stream of Arabic curses. Sarah couldn't catch it all, but she got the gist. He expected a worship service. He had been double-crossed. They would pay. The traitors would die.

The other men began moving toward her and Charles.

Sarah instinctively backed away toward the family room adjoining the kitchen, her empty hands raised over her head. She glanced at Charles, who still stood at the kitchen table, frozen in time. He had placed his own hands behind his head, like they did in the movies. His countenance quickly changed from consternation to calm, and he shot Sarah an almost imperceptible nod. For some reason the terror was gone. His reassuring look calmed Sarah.

A slender agent with small, dark slits for eyes and a scar that ran down his left cheek began shouting orders in English at the Reeds. "Hands on your head! Spread your legs and face the wall!"

Sarah immediately turned to face a wall in the family room, craning her neck slightly sideways toward the kitchen table and Charles. He was slower to move, and she saw another man jam a forearm into Charles's back and slam

14

him into the wall. His nose hit hard, and blood started trickling to the floor. Charles kept his hands on his head, with the agent standing right behind him, fists clenching and unclenching.

Sarah took a quick look over her shoulder at the apparent leader. His hooded eyes were red and wild with emotion, like a badly developed photograph. Though she immediately diverted her gaze back to the wall, she knew those eyes had been etched into her memory forever, tattooed as a grim reminder of this horrible night.

She wished she had never looked.

She could sense the man moving slowly and purposefully behind her. Within seconds, she smelled the stale breath coming from over her shoulder and felt the callused hand squeeze the base of her skull. He exerted pressure, and the pain shot through her head. She wanted to scream but could only whimper.

"Do not defy me," he whispered hoarsely. "Do not look me in the eye." The other men in the apartment stopped moving. Sarah heard nothing but the man's heavy breathing in her ear.

He closed the vise again between his finger and thumb. Her knees buckled from the pain, and she groaned pitifully in submission. He released his grip and took one step back.

Sarah took an uneven breath and let out a slow groan. She tried to focus on standing, leaning heavily against the wall. The room spun, and the throbbing at the base of her neck would not let up.

She would not look at them again.

Someone began to pronounce the charges. Perhaps the man with the scar; the broken English sounded like his.

"We have reason to understand you are leaders in a criminal—how do you say?—plan or conspiracy," he announced. "We have reason to know you sell cocaine through a group of people who, uh, pretense to act like church. We have papers of arrest and search."

"Let me see your credentials." Sarah heard fear in Charles's words. His voice, an octave higher than normal, sounded more like a whimper than a command. But he bravely stammered on. "These charges are ridiculous."

A sickening thud caused Sarah to glance at the kitchen. Charles's face and bloodied nose had been crushed against the wall, his glasses knocked to the floor. Charles moaned in pain as a thick agent ground the glasses with his heel and pressed Charles's face harder into the wall. The blow had opened a gash above Charles's left eye, and more blood trickled down his face and splattered on the floor.

Sarah shrieked at the sight of the blood; then she stopped abruptly when the barrel of a gun touched the back of her own neck. She began to shake and quietly sob. She closed her eyes to erase the images. But all she saw in the darkness was the face of Charles covered in blood. And the vicious eyes of the Muttawa leader.

In the next few moments, the men began ransacking the apartment. Sarah tried to fight off the pain and fear, her slender body convulsing silently as she sobbed. She kept her eyes closed as she listened to the agents move from room to room, dismantling, destroying, searching.

She prayed for courage.

A commotion in the bedroom indicated they had found something. The men huddled briefly in the hallway and then began turning the rest of the apartment upside down with renewed vigor. The man behind Sarah jammed the gun harder against her skull, a warning not lost on her, and then pulled it away as he joined the others in the search. Sarah finally mustered the courage to look discreetly over her shoulder as the men attacked the family room. Her heart skipped a beat as the agents cut open the cushions of the couch and withdrew packages filled with a powdery white substance.

We've been set up, she realized. *What now?*

The search complete, the small apartment looked like a war zone. The agents marked and stacked the plastic bags neatly on the family room coffee table.

"Ahmed!" The agent with the scar called to the leader and pointed to the stack. "Ten kilos," he said with a cruel smile.

Sarah questioned Charles with her eyes, the silent language that flows from years of marriage.

What do we do?

Peace continued to fill his steady gaze, a coming to terms with the reality of being persecuted for his faith. His composure was her strength, and for a moment she believed they would actually be all right.

The man called Ahmed dished out more orders, and the agents jumped into action again. They turned a kitchen chair to face the family room, threw Charles into it, then wrenched his arms behind it. Ahmed leaned over in front of Charles, his face inches away.

"We find ten kilos of coke," Ahmed bragged. "You will soon be famous drug king. But you are also an American missionary—yes?"

Charles Reed did not speak. He locked his eyes on the floor.

"Do not ignore me!" Ahmed demanded. He grabbed Charles's hair and jerked his face upward. "Look . . . at . . . me," he growled.

Charles narrowed his bloodied eyes and glared back. Defiance filled his look in a way that Sarah had never seen.

"I want names and addresses of other church leaders." Ahmed spoke in a low and gruff voice.

Without thinking, Sarah slowly started shaking her head from side to side. Her husband could no longer see her, his view blocked by the bulky body of his interrogator. But Sarah willed her husband to defy this evil man. *Just hang tough,* she pleaded silently. *Don't give even one name!*

"I see," Ahmed snarled as he let go of the hair and watched Charles resume his stare at the floor. "You make this difficult."

He turned to the agents in the family room. "Continue the search," he commanded in Arabic, but this time he gave the orders slowly, enunciating the words carefully so the Reeds could comprehend. "Remove the woman's clothes and search her for drugs, every hiding place on her body. Enjoy yourselves."

Sarah went numb.

As if fueled by his wife's fear, Charles reacted with the desperate impulse of a man who had nothing to lose. He jumped from the chair and shook off one agent just as Ahmed turned again to face him. Charles lowered his head and drove himself forward. He landed a perfect head butt, driving his forehead as a battering ram into Ahmed's chin.

Ahmed reeled backward, spitting blood, but quickly regained his footing. With the fluid motion of a martial arts expert, he spun and landed his foot squarely against the side of Charles's face, the sound of cracking bone a testament to the blow's force. Charles's head snapped to the side, and his body hurtled against the kitchen wall, collapsing helplessly on the floor.

Sarah dropped her face into her hands and screamed.

A large agent instantly jerked her around and clamped his hand over her mouth. She bit. Hard. And she brought up her knee with all her might. He yanked his hand back, doubled over, and cursed.

But now two more agents were up against her, pinning her to the wall, stuffing her mouth with some type of cloth. Her small frame was no match for these men. They were in her face, pinning her arms and legs. Then they went after her clothes with a vengeance, ripping open her cotton blouse, gawking and grinning stupidly.

The prayer list, she remembered. *They'll see the prayer list!*

This thought energized Sarah, and with an adrenaline-fueled explosion she slipped away from one assailant and lunged at the other. He barely averted her wild swings, wrapped her in a bear hug, and threw her backward to the floor, landing squarely on top of her. Her neck snapped back, and her head bounced hard on the thin carpet.

Everything went black.

◁▷

Brad checked his notes and his nerve one more time. Ichabod would never let the witness answer these questions, but still he had to ask. When you try a case with one eye on the appeals court, you have to preserve the record. Make the judge rule. Demonstrate her bias.

"Do you believe that human life begins at conception?" Brad bluntly asked Reverend Bailey.

"Objection."

"Sustained," Ichabod ruled. "That question ought to be taken out and shot."

"Do you have a basis in the Bible for your belief that human life begins at conception?" Brad persisted.

"Objection, Judge," prosecutor Angela Bennett whined. "That question assumes that the witness answered the prior question, which he didn't."

"Sustained," Ichabod snapped. "Mr. Carson, move on to something relevant."

"Do you believe abortion is murder?"

Bennett stood but had no time to object. "Mr. Carson—" Ichabod's voice had a hard edge—"do you understand English? The reverend's personal beliefs about abortion are not relevant. *Not relevant.* Now move on to something that is or sit down so the witness may be cross-examined."

"May I at least explain the basis for asking the questions?" Brad asked, a trace of sarcasm in his words.

"No."

Bennett smirked and sat down.

Brad's eyes locked on Ichabod as he planned his next line of attack. His next question dripped slowly from his mouth, but he kept his stare fixed on the judge, daring her to rule the question out of order. "The statute requires that you purposefully try to persuade a woman not to enter the clinic and have an abortion," Brad explained. "What was your *purpose* in praying on the sidewalk in front of the clinic?"

Ichabod frowned but did not speak.

"To petition God for mercy," the reverend said.

Brad returned his attention to the witness. The man looked paler and more fragile than ever. "And why did you choose to have this prayer meeting in front of the abortion clinic?"

"Because that's where the evil was happening," the reverend said softly.

"Speak up," Ichabod demanded, "and move closer to the microphone."

"Because that's where the evil was happening," the Reverend Bailey repeated. "That's where the babies were dying."

"Is the front of the abortion clinic the only place you have conducted this type of prayer meeting?" Brad asked.

The prosecutor was on her feet, but her objection was forestalled by a quick look from Ichabod.

"Don't bother," the judge said testily. "Don't bother objecting, because I'm going to let it in. I'm going to give Mr. Carson all the rope he needs to hang himself."

Bennett shrugged and sat down.

"No, it's not," the reverend said, leaning into the mike.

"It's not what?" Brad asked.

"It's not the only place we have petitioned God for mercy and to halt evil. My congregation and I have prayed over the last few years in front of our local pharmacy when they started dispensing the RU-486 pill, and in front of some of the bars down on Military Highway, and, you know, places like that . . ." His voice trailed off, and he leaned back from the mike.

Brad gave him a sideways look of reproach. "Any other places you can think of . . . where you have petitioned God to end some perceived evil?"

"How can this be relevant?" a frustrated Angela Bennett asked.

"Because it shows the Reverend Bailey didn't go to the abortion clinic with the purpose of persuading pregnant women as prohibited by the statute," Brad answered. "His purpose was to petition God, and that's not prohibited. And it shows he has prayed with his congregation at other places where he perceives evil influences exist, also for the purpose of petitioning God. In short, it demonstrates a pattern."

Brad looked at the judge and waited for her ruling. He knew she didn't like this line of questioning, but neither did she like getting reversed on appeal for making bad evidentiary rulings.

"Go on," Ichabod said, without hiding her impatience. "Is there anyplace else you have done this prayer meeting thing?"

"Just one other place," the Reverend Bailey said meekly. He paused. The entire courtroom waited.

"The steps of this courthouse."

"That's ridiculous," the prosecutor said sharply.

"I agree," Ichabod barked. "The remark will be struck from the record." Her face flushed and the vein pulsed.

She had taken the bait.

3

CHARLES REED TRIED TO FOCUS. His mind swirled in a rage of anger, pain, and helplessness. Two muscular agents forced him into the kitchen chair again and pinned his arms behind his back. Ahmed was in his face. Sarah lay motionless on the family room couch.

She was alive, he knew. And by the grace of God, she had not been molested. After she blacked out, Ahmed started barking orders. Check the pulse. Lay her on the couch. Grab that list from her bra. Leave her alone.

Charles did not know the reason for the last order. Maybe they were waiting for her to regain consciousness. Maybe they could get whatever they needed from him. Maybe even these men had limits on what they would do to American citizens. Maybe it was just a miraculous answer to his prayer. Whatever the reason, it gave Charles hope.

"Who is Hanif?" Ahmed demanded, reading from the list.

Charles stared at the floor. His face throbbed. The taste of blood trickled through his mouth.

"Who is Khartoum?" Ahmed continued.

More silence.

One of Ahmed's men removed a sleek black stun gun from its holster. He held it inches from the base of Charles's neck and looked at Ahmed, apparently waiting for his cue. Ahmed grinned at Charles and boasted about the weapon. It would immobilize any man, Ahmed told him, with two hundred thousand volts of electricity. And the best thing, Ahmed claimed, was that the instrument left no marks on the victim except two small burn spots where the probes of the gun contacted the skin and unleashed the electricity. Only the central nervous system would suffer permanent damage, and the cause would be difficult to prove.

Charles wondered for a fleeting instant how bad it could be.

He soon learned. And for the next twenty minutes—for what seemed like an eternity—his hope for survival faded with every passing question, with every mind-searing jolt.

"I need names of the leaders of the other church groups you have started." Ahmed spoke deliberately and calmly, as if he knew Charles was beginning to have trouble understanding the words. "Don't play games with me."

The waiting was the hardest part. Knowing what was coming—the surging current of the stun gun—and being powerless to stop it. How many times had they been through this? How much more could he take? How long ago had Sarah gone down? And what would happen to her now? His mind raced, chasing questions with no answers.

Charles sensed movement behind him and convulsed at the thought of another jolt from the hated gun. "Please . . . I'm begging you." He trembled, struggling for breath. "You've got to believe me. . . . I don't know what churches you're talking about. . . . These names on the card are just friends—"

"Shut up," Ahmed snapped. He grabbed Charles's hair and jerked his head backward again, demanding eye contact.

Charles prayed for strength.

Ahmed slowly raised the corner of his mouth, a small and sick smile, then spit in Charles's face, letting go of his hair. Charles's head dropped hard against his chest. The saliva dripped from his cheek.

"You think you are strong," Ahmed whispered through clenched teeth. "But you are stupid. You will talk, my friend." Ahmed paused, letting the words hang in the air. "You will talk."

Ahmed held out his palm to stop the agent with the stun gun. This time Ahmed himself would do the honors. He took the gun and jammed it furiously against the base of Charles's neck.

Burning flesh, surging electricity, searing pain. Charles shook and yelped as his body twitched involuntarily, the pain affecting every nerve ending, the electricity jolting his brain. His body was on fire from the inside out. His screams did not seem to belong to him, and he jerked uncontrollably in the chair, unable to escape the gun or to bear this new round of torture.

Finally, mercifully, Ahmed disengaged the gun. Charles's seizure continued, blood and saliva flowing from his contorted mouth into his lap. The smell of burning flesh filled the kitchen.

Charles was losing his will to endure. He prayed for strength for the next minute, nothing more. He tried to focus on Sarah and the kids. He would make it one more minute for them, for the church members, for his Lord.

Images flashed through his mind in rapid succession. Images of his wife and children, of baptisms of church members, of the face of Christ as it had been portrayed in his childhood picture Bible. Ahmed's voice brought the parade to a stop.

"We are just beginning," Ahmed said gruffly, without emotion. "Do not be a fool. My men are anxious to finish what they started. On both you and your wife. Your wife needs help, and I need names. Let us make a deal."

The threat to Sarah brought Charles back to reality. He raised his head, looked out toward the living room, then locked eyes with Ahmed. *What does he mean?* Charles wondered. The eyes told him nothing. *Can you deal with the devil? God, give me wisdom!*

Sudden clarity came over Charles in the midst of the pain, an immediate answer to a desperate prayer. *This man is just keeping Sarah safe so he can use her as leverage against me. If I give up the names, he will have no reason to let either of us live, no reason to protect Sarah from his men. The informant must have told him the names of the Friday night worshipers. But the other names he does not know. My silence keeps Sarah alive.*

Ahmed narrowed his eyes. Charles was sure the man could read his thoughts. As Ahmed reached again for the stun gun, Charles mumbled a sentence and dropped his chin to his chest.

"Again," Ahmed demanded. "Say it again."

As if possessed by a force greater than himself, Charles repeated the words, slowly, and in a barely audible whisper. "'He was led as a lamb to the slaughter—'" he paused, taking a labored breath—"'and as a sheep before its shearers is silent, so He opened not His mouth.'"

Ahmed's silence caused Charles to raise his head. When he did so, Ahmed turned and looked at Sarah sprawled on the couch, the only sign of life in the heaving of her chest. "Some men need a little extra persuasion," the Muttawa leader growled. He turned to Charles again and, with great force, pulled Charles's right arm from behind his back and grabbed Charles's wrist. He pushed hard against the back of Charles's hand, nearly bending the wrist in half as he forced the hand toward the forearm. Charles flinched and ground his teeth, swallowing the scream that welled up in the back of his throat. Surely his wrist would snap in two.

The pain returned. Searing, debilitating pain. And then Ahmed backed off slightly on the pressure but continued to hold the wrist. "Speak to me," Ahmed said simply. "Or you will beg me to stop, and there will be no end."

Once again Charles summoned courage he did not know he had for another symbolic act of resistance. He gritted his teeth and made a futile effort to yank his wrist away from Ahmed's iron grip. Charles knew immediately that he had made an awful mistake.

Ahmed reasserted the pressure with a vengeance. This time he did not let up as Charles begged for mercy. Ahmed pushed harder; the pain intensified. It shot up Charles's arm and engulfed his brain. And then it happened—the sickening snap of the wrist bone as his hand went limp.

His bloodcurdling scream echoed throughout the apartment.

◁ ▷

"When did you hold a prayer meeting on the steps of this courthouse?" Brad asked innocently.

Angela Bennett bolted from her seat, hands spread in protest.

"Mr. Carson, that's not relevant," Ichabod said gruffly, leaning back and folding her arms.

"Judge, it *is* relevant. If you give me a few minutes, I'll link it up," Brad promised.

The judge hesitated, then scowled. "Go ahead, Mr. Carson. But it better be good."

Oh, it will be, Brad thought.

"Reverend Bailey, when and why were you praying on the courthouse steps?"

"It was in the summer of 2000," he said, "after the *Stenberg v. Carhart* Supreme Court case in which the Court sanctioned partial birth abortion. I just couldn't believe that in this country our courts would defend a procedure like that—a procedure where a viable fetus is delivered into the birth canal, and then . . ." The reverend paused, pursing his lips and sadly shaking his head. "And then the skull is torn open with scissors, and the brain material is extracted to reduce the head size and ensure the child dies before delivery."

He did not look at Brad as he finished his answer. Brad chose to let the silence linger.

"God help us," the reverend mumbled into the silence. "I knew then it was time to pray."

Ichabod appeared unmoved except for the telltale vein, now a bit larger and pulsing a bit faster than before. She had been duped; Brad saw the realization in her eyes. The volatile issues she had worked so hard to keep out of the case were now cascading around her, and she was powerless to stop them.

"Did you read the opinion in *Stenberg* before you went to the courthouse to pray?" Brad asked, pushing the point.

"Yes, I pulled it off the Internet."

"Was there anything in the opinion that surprised you?"

"Yes. I had heard so many news reports about the gruesome procedure referred to as partial birth abortion. But until I read the *Stenberg* decision, I had never focused on what really happens during a normal D and E procedure, not a partial birth abortion but the kind of abortion performed every day right here at the Norfolk Clinic."

"And is that what motivated you—," Brad began.

"Stop! Right there!" Ichabod demanded, her harsh words echoing off the courtroom walls. "You are flaunting this court's rulings, Mr. Carson." She clenched her teeth and hunched her shoulders. "Move off this line of questioning."

"Doesn't the prosecution have to make her own objections anymore, or are you just—"

"Don't push it, Mr. Carson," Ichabod snapped. "Don't push it."

Brad pulled a copy of the case from his counsel table and turned to the dissenting opinion of Justice Anthony Kennedy. "Do you recall these words from the opinion?" he asked the reverend. He began reading as if Ichabod had never spoken. "Are these the words that caused you so much anguish that you went first to the courthouse and later to the clinic for the purpose of begging God to stop these procedures?"

Ichabod looked stunned, but Brad could sense the wheels turning. Would she dare rule out of order, as being too emotionally charged, the very words from an opinion of the U.S. Supreme Court?

"'In a D and E procedure,'" Brad read, "'the fetus, in many cases, dies just as a human adult or child would: it bleeds to death as it is torn from limb to limb. . . .'"

The prosecutor jumped to her feet again. "I strongly object to this inflammatory tactic," Bennett shouted in an effort to be heard over Brad's reading.

"'. . . The fetus can be alive at the beginning of the dismemberment process and can survive for a time while its limbs are being torn off. . . .'"

Ichabod started banging her gavel. "Mr. Carson! Mr. Carson!"

The prosecutor continued objecting, and a loud murmur rose from the left side of the courtroom. The Reverend Bailey's eyes widened.

Brad increased his volume and continued over the rising din. "'. . . Mere dismemberment does not always cause death. Dr. Carhart knew of a physician who removed the arm of a fetus only to have the fetus go on to be born as a living child with one arm.'" The gavel was still banging, Bennett objecting, and Ichabod was repeating the word *sustained* over and over. "'At the conclusion of a D and E procedure, no intact fetus remains. In Dr. Carhart's words, the abortionist is left . . .'"

"That's enough!" Ichabod screamed. The intensity of it stilled the courtroom. Nobody moved.

"'. . . with a tray full of pieces,'" Brad said into the silence.

All eyes turned to the seething form of Ichabod, still hunched forward, wild-eyed, her face crimson.

"That comment, Mr. Carson, will earn you contempt of court and a ten-thousand-dollar fine," she said coldly, straining every muscle to keep control. "I have never, in twenty-six years on the bench, seen such obnoxious behavior." As she spoke, her voice shook, the anger etched deeply on her face. "In addition," she continued, "your contempt citation will carry a five-day prison term . . ."

An audible gasp went up from the right side of the courtroom. Brad averted his eyes.

After an exaggerated pause Ichabod continued. ". . . to be suspended on the condition of an apology to this court and good behavior befitting a member of the bar throughout the remainder of this case."

She glared at Brad. "Does counsel wish to make a statement or comment?"

Brad knew the drill. She was waiting for a humble and contrite Brad Carson to grovel and apologize, and then she would probably consider some leniency. Even Ichabod was not in the habit of sending lawyers to jail. The ball was in his court.

For this moment, Brad was ready. He had done his homework. He had mulled this scenario over in his head during the prior sleepless night. He knew that only one word could have the desired effect and consummate his plan. He weighed his response carefully.

Then he shrugged.

"Whatever" was all he said as he turned to take his seat.

"Get him out of here!" Ichabod barked to the marshals, her voice thick with emotion. "Cuff him and get him out of my sight! You have five days minimum, Mr. Carson. And you will stay behind bars longer than that unless and until you apologize to this court and promise to show this court proper respect in the future. This case is hereby suspended until Mr. Carson can finish serving his time."

She slammed her gavel.

Two hefty marshals grabbed Brad and placed handcuffs on his wrists. The Reverend Bailey looked aghast at the sight of his lawyer being treated like a criminal.

The church members prayed.

Brad turned and caught Bella's eye as he was being escorted from the courtroom. He stared at her for a second, and then he winked. These were not the actions of an unbiased judge. Perhaps now the appellate judges in Richmond would understand.

Plan B had worked to perfection.

◁ ▷

Charles Reed had no plan. He simply wanted to die.

He curled on the floor in a fetal position, left arm wrapped tightly around his legs, his broken right wrist dangling at his side. Nausea had overcome him. The thought of more torture, the shooting pain from his wrist, the throbbing of his temple and face—it all seemed to lodge momentarily in his stomach. The vomit was the least of his worries. He made no effort to clean himself.

He had given names. He couldn't bear the thought of another jolt from the gun. But the names were just the Friday night worshipers, names that Ahmed already knew, and so the ordeal continued. Other names had not yet crossed his lips, but he knew they had broken his will; he was ready to talk.

Instead, he prayed.

Lord, take me home. Let me take these names with me. Take me home before I talk.

It was all so confusing now, so dark. The images morphed into one another with increasing speed. He tried to focus on the kids, on Sarah, on the suffering of his Lord. He remembered the cross, the nails driven into those hands of mercy. And then the nails became a needle. A needle Ahmed drove deep into Charles's left arm. There was talk of cocaine. Then his arm became Sarah's, and he saw the needle again. They made him watch. She didn't even move as they emptied the contents of the needle into her arm.

The images blurred, the pain became distant. And then he felt it. The cold touch of the two metal prongs on the base of his neck. The voice of Ahmed in the background, demanding more names. The involuntary tightening of every muscle as the current began its deadly course. He squeezed his left arm tighter around his legs. He tried to scream.

This time the pain stuck in his chest, as if he had been stabbed. He struggled for air, but the tightness overwhelmed him.

Jesus loves you, he said to his tormentors. But the words clung to his vocal cords and reduced themselves to a gasp.

His last thoughts were of Sarah and the kids. He subconsciously committed them into the hands of his Lord, and then prepared his soul to die. In the distance, he could hear Ahmed barking orders to his men.

◁▷

Ahmed looked down at Charles Reed in disgust. The American was ghostly white, his chubby face distorted by pain. He gasped again and went still.

As his victim succumbed, Ahmed felt himself begin to relax. The adrenaline that had been fueling his body slowed, the savage vitality of the torture gone.

"Scrape his knuckles against the wall," Ahmed ordered. "Make it look like a fight."

He glanced at Sarah, still motionless on the couch. He saw the lust in his men's eyes.

"Don't touch the woman," he ordered, "except to put another shirt on her. These are American citizens, and every injury will be endlessly investigated."

Ahmed motioned to one of the officers who had been holding Charles Reed. The officer approached Ahmed and stood in front of him.

"Did the American not try to resist us in his drug-induced state?" Ahmed asked.

The officer nodded in nervous agreement.

"And did he not break his wrist as he lashed out at us?"

"Yes."

"Then we must have more evidence of a fight," Ahmed said. And with lightning quickness he drove his powerful fist into the cheekbone of the agent. A gash opened and blood flowed.

The man reeled backward, clutching his face, fear in his eyes. He did not raise his hands in defense.

"You," Ahmed said, "are Exhibit A." He rubbed his fist and smiled. "Now call an ambulance."

He turned to one of his officers and asked for the two lists of names they had compiled. He compared the first list, provided by the informant, with the list that they had coerced from Charles Reed. Reed had coughed up twenty-one names. All but two had been previously divulged by the informant. Their efforts had fallen woefully short of Ahmed's expectations.

"Deal with the infidels on these lists," he said as he handed them back to the officer. Such common church members did not merit a personal visit from Ahmed Aberijan.

Even without giving an explicit order, Ahmed knew exactly what would happen. The Muttawa would combine with local authorities to handle the more prominent members of the church. Drugs would mysteriously appear at residences. The church members would be arrested, threatened, then released after they signed detailed confessions. They were the lucky ones.

Islamic radicals from the Wahhabi sect would be dispatched to handle the lesser-known members of Reed's group. No arrests would be made. If the church members recanted, they would be severely beaten and released. If they did not recant, they would not survive the night. Their gruesome deaths would serve as a graphic warning for anyone inclined to doubt the Great Mohammed.

4

A FEW MINUTES AFTER MIDNIGHT, the U.S. Embassy in Riyadh began making calls. The embassy had been alerted by a friend of the Reeds, the pastor of another church the Reeds had helped start. The pastor and his wife were taking care of Meredith and Steven. Just before midnight, the couple went to the U.S. Embassy and breathlessly told their story.

Sarah Reed had called earlier in the day and asked them to care for the children. She was worried about a surprise raid from the Muttawa. The pastor began phoning the Reeds' apartment a few minutes after nine o'clock, but nobody answered. After almost an hour of phone calls, he assumed the worst and headed to the Reeds' place. The apartment looked like it had been hit by a hurricane. There was blood on the kitchen floor. He had photographs to prove it.

He had already called the Muttawa, but the Muttawa said they were not in the business of giving out confidential information about arrests and pending investigations.

The embassy officials did not fare much better. They confirmed, through the Muttawa, that the Reeds had been arrested. In fact, the Muttawa claimed the Reeds had resisted arrest and were being treated for injuries. Dr. Reed and his wife were not school workers, as they claimed on their visa applications. Instead, they were drug kingpins, and tonight their tawdry enterprise had been quashed. It was a major drug bust for a nation like Saudi Arabia, netting an estimated two million dollars worth of cocaine. The Reeds themselves were high at the time of the arrest, and tests would soon confirm the levels of cocaine in their blood.

The Muttawa wanted to be helpful but could give no further information. No, the embassy officials could not speak to the Reeds until the investigation was complete. No, the Reeds did not have legal counsel and had not requested counsel. No, the Muttawa were not willing to make an "educated guess" about the possibility of bond or how the process would unfold. And so it went, one governmental bureaucracy stalling another, the Muttawa getting the better of the exchange.

The situation escalated throughout the morning. Higher-ups in the embassy contacted higher-ups in the Saudi government. First one department, then another. Officials who were needed to make decisions could not be reached. Those who could be reached had no authority to decide.

Late Saturday morning, the embassy officials finally learned that the Reeds were in the King Faisal Specialist Hospital in Riyadh. Charles Reed was in critical condition. Drug charges had been filed.

The potentially explosive situation had international implications. Both sides were motivated to deal. The Saudis wanted the drug lords deported. The Americans wanted the missionaries safe. And so they agreed, early in the afternoon, that the two Americans would be transferred to a military base hospital thirty miles from Riyadh. American specialists would assume their care. The Reeds would surrender their visas, and the charges would be dropped.

Charles Reed was transferred against the medical advice of his surgeon. He was post-op, and his prognosis was not good. His heart surgery had been complicated by the cocaine racing through his bloodstream, the delay in treatment, and his preexisting heart condition.

Surgery had taken more than three hours. Ventilators, tubes, monitors, and other gadgets kept him breathing and his heart beating. But it would be a stretch to say he was alive. His surgeon's prognosis was dismal. A transfer would only hasten the inevitable.

The embassy, however, desperately wanted to get Charles under the care of American physicians. They ignored the Saudi surgeon's advice and authorized the transfer.

◁▷

Brad awoke Saturday morning to the smell of coffee. He was groggy and disoriented—that brief moment between being fully asleep and fully awake—and he couldn't quite make sense of his surroundings. He rubbed and squinted his eyes as the bright sun streamed through the barred windows toward his cot. The warm rays cleared his head. *That's right,* he remembered. *A federal holding cell. A prisoner of my own government.*

Brad beamed at the logic of his plan. Sure, he would have preferred to plot his appeal in a place where he could use the bathroom unchaperoned, but for the pure brilliance of the legal strategy, Brad was sure he had outdone himself. Yesterday his case was going nowhere fast; today he had a serious issue for appeal. It was a long shot, but it was a shot.

It had dawned on him late Thursday night: Quit trying this case against the government in front of the judge; try the case against the judge in front of the government. Put the judge on trial. Aggravate her in such a way that the record would unmistakably reflect her bias. Appeal based on judicial misconduct. Ask the appellate court for a new trial in front of an unbiased judge. Trade what little chance you might have for a trial-court verdict for a much better chance at a successful appeal. Roll your dice with the boys on the Fourth Circuit.

To Brad's surprise, he was now something of a folk hero among the federal marshals who ran the Norfolk detention center. They confided in him last night that they couldn't stand the brooding arrogance of Baker-Kline either. She was impossible to please, they said. And the marshals, who were occasionally assigned to her courtroom for the judge's own protection, were some of her favorite whipping boys. Brad got the distinct impression that his captors dreamed of spouting off to the courtroom despot just as he had.

The night before, Brad had been allowed a private shower. He had his own holding cell—small, dank, and musty, with only one cot and an open toilet sitting against the far wall—but at least it was private. No drug lords as roommates. And now, at 7 a.m. Saturday, his day started with hot coffee.

"Mornin', Brad." It was Clarence, one of the marshals who had swapped stories with Brad the prior night. Clarence stood outside the cell holding two Styrofoam cups. "This ain't the Hilton, but we make some mean coffee."

"Thanks, man."

Clarence grunted something, carefully placed the two steaming cups of black coffee on the floor, and went about the business of unlocking Brad's cell. "You got a visitor, Brad. She's pushy. If she were visitin' somebody else, I woulda told her where to go. But I figured you might need to hear from her this mornin'."

Brad couldn't resist a grin. He knew who it was.

"But hey, tell her to chill out or next time she's not gettin' through. And, if she works for you, put her on a diet." This said by a man who had obviously devoured more than his share of doughnuts.

"You try telling her that," Brad said, stretching his back. He was not surprised that Bella had come so early. "Is there some kind of private conference room where we can meet? It won't take long."

"Well, technically it ain't visitin' hours." Clarence handed Brad the hot cup. "But I'll see what I can do." He turned his back, left the door unlocked, and lumbered slowly down the hall.

Brad took a sip of the scalding coffee. Terrible. Twice as strong as the stuff at his law office, and no cream. As soon as Clarence disappeared, Brad flushed the powerful black liquid down the grungy toilet. He sat gingerly on his stained cot, resisting the urge to simply walk out the door.

◁▷

For a lady who stood only five feet two inches, Bella Harper was imposing. The source of her stature was her personality, definitely not her looks. She was a bulldog in every sense of the word.

She packed some serious weight on her short frame. Nobody dared ask how much. Nor did anyone have the guts to ask her age. Bella didn't celebrate birthdays.

Bella featured a butch cut for her salt-and-pepper hair, precious little makeup, a pack-a-day cigarette habit, and a constant scowl that let people know she was not a woman to be trifled with.

She was also the world's best legal secretary.

Bella had been with Brad since he hung out his shingle after graduating from William and Mary Law School. Her outward personality aside, she had been a tough-loving mother to Brad, particularly when Brad's wife divorced him, claiming she could no longer compete with the law for his attention. Bella, however, was fiercely loyal, both to Brad and to her own ailing mother, whom Bella cared for with the attentiveness of a master gardener.

And today Bella was a sight for Brad's sore eyes. She was booting up her laptop when he entered the room and slouched into the bolted-down chair on the other side of the bolted-down metal table.

"You look like death on a bad day," Bella said in her New York accent without looking up.

"Thanks." He rose from his seat and started pacing on his side of the conference table. "You don't look so hot yourself."

Brad was not lying. Bella's eyes were more bloodshot than normal. Because it was not an official workday, she was not dressed in "professional" attire. Her black stretch pants seemed two sizes too small.

"I've called the three largest law firms who have the most federal court experience." Bella wasted no time. As if Brad had important places to go that day. "None of them will handle this emergency writ of mandamus. They've all got the same lame excuses—too busy, schedule conflicts; you know the routine. Everybody's scared to take on Ichabod."

This part of the plan had always worried Brad. He knew he couldn't contact lawyers to represent him before he pulled his little stunt. It would look too calculated. Now he was at the mercy of the local bar as the wagons circled. None of the usual federal court firms would take on a sitting federal court judge. Brad had lots of friends who would do it in a heartbeat, but he wasn't about to ask. He would not poison those friendships just to get out of the can a few days early.

His pacing intensified. He ran his hand through uncombed hair.

Bella rambled on, "Harris, Clark & Yarbrough; Day & Adams; Kilgore & Strobel. They're all runnin' scared. I offered to pay full hourly rate. You could almost hear 'em laugh through the phone. Brad, you've already sued half their clients. Representing you would be suicide."

"Somebody needs to tell them not to take those suits so personally," Brad muttered.

"Right."

Bella absentmindedly reached into her purse and pulled out a pack of Camels. As she lit up, the rancid smoke filled the poorly ventilated room. Brad continued pacing in silence, altering his path and cutting Bella a wider berth.

"By the way," Bella said between puffs, "I had to fire Tina."

Brad stopped midstride and let out a groan. "C'mon, Bella. We're already shorthanded. Tina was doing a good job. How many times have we discussed this?"

"Tina was a parasite," Bella snapped. "She'd come in late, take two-hour lunches, and be gone by five. Should have fired her a year ago. I'd rather do her work myself."

"She wasn't even with us a year ago," Brad protested. "And now you *will* be doing her work yourself."

He waited for Bella to respond, but she just puffed in silence.

"Put in the usual classified ads. Make sure you hit the legal periodicals," Brad said. He really needed some caffeine to clear his head. "And this time, Bella, I want the paralegal reporting directly to me. I hire them, and only I fire them."

He looked at Bella again and waited for confirmation. She ignored him and pulled some more files out of her briefcase. It was no use getting mad at her now. He would deal with her attitude later. At least she was here, first thing on a Saturday morning. And they had more important things to talk about than office management.

He switched gears. "We've got to get a brief and petition for a writ of mandamus hand-delivered to Judge Baker-Kline and a Fourth Circuit judge by the end of the day to have any chance for a hearing on Monday. We'll have to write it ourselves. I'll need you to help with the research. I'll sign it and argue it in front of the Fourth Circuit."

In response, Bella took another long draw on her Camel, then tossed a manila folder and an extra pair of reading glasses onto the table in front of Brad. He put on the glasses, opened the folder, and was not entirely surprised to find a twenty-two-page brief and accompanying petition. Bella couldn't suppress a grin. Her bloodshot eyes twinkled.

"I stayed up all night drafting this baby," she said proudly. "I had a little help."

Brad sat down and started reading, ignoring the smoke that came in waves across the table. Ichabod sounded like the Ayatollah. The brief was fat with applicable case law—precedents where more egregious conduct by other lawyers was found insufficient to justify contempt. By page eleven, Brad was ready to sign.

"That won't be necessary," Bella said. "You know what they say. A lawyer who represents himself has a fool for a client."

"Somebody's got to sign it."

"Why don't you check the last page before you go startin' another argument you can't win."

Brad looked and his jaw dropped.

The signature belonged to Jay Sekulow, renowned constitutional law expert and lead counsel for the American Center for Law and Justice. Sekulow had the personal reputation and legal firepower to get the attention of the Fourth Circuit judges. The smell of victory began to replace the stale fumes of Bella's cigarettes.

"I didn't even have to beg," Bella said curtly. "Turns out he's been following the case closely. His group is big on religious liberty cases. All I had to do in return—" her voice lowered as she mumbled the rest—"was to promise you'd appear on *Jay Sekulow Live* when you get out."

"You *what*?" Brad cocked his head sideways, as if eyeing Bella at a new and skeptical angle would change this news. "Just what I needed. A nationally syndicated radio show. Brad Carson, the new lapdog for the Christian Right." He took off his glasses and placed them on the table.

Then he hunched forward, narrowed his eyes, and locked in on Bella to make his point.

"Whatever," she said with a wry smile.

◁▷

By midafternoon Brad was sitting in the regal chambers of the Honorable Cynthia Baker-Kline. It was a surreal scene and a humiliating one. The judge sat behind her large oak desk, dressed in a black pin-striped suit. Assistant district attorney Angela Bennett sat next to Brad and also sported a power suit, even though it was Saturday afternoon. Brad wore his orange jail jump-suit, his feet adorned by the standard-issue jail flip-flops.

Brad knew the fix he was in when he got to Ichabod's office on time and discovered that the judge and the ADA were already meeting. Such ex parte meetings were technically improper—a judge should never discuss a case with only one lawyer present—but when Brad entered the office, the two women started chatting aimlessly about everything but the law. The message was clear: we were not discussing the case, so don't even bother complaining.

Ichabod pretended not to notice his jumpsuit. But Brad sensed a per-petual smirk on the lips of Bennett, who seemed to be enjoying herself way too much.

"How's it going?" she asked snidely.

"Better if I'd remembered to bring my toothbrush with me to court on Friday."

Ichabod did not smile. She began laying out a proposal that Brad was sure she had already discussed with ADA Bennett. It was damage control and face-saving time for Ichabod. She clearly did not want this case appealed. Now that she had calmed down, read Brad's brief, and seen the name of Jay Sekulow, she was apparently willing to do everything within her power to keep the appeals court in Richmond from considering the case and evaluat-ing her conduct.

"This is a no-win situation," Ichabod was saying, her elbows on her desk, fingertips tented together. She was looking back and forth at Brad and Angela

Bennett. "I've been giving this a lot of thought. Mr. Carson's ill-advised actions have escalated the emotional nature of this highly charged case and created a difficult situation for everyone."

Brad suddenly noticed there was no court reporter present to record their conversation.

"I have every right, and half a mind, to keep you in jail for as long as you stubbornly refuse to apologize for your childish conduct," she continued, giving Brad her holier-than-thou look.

Brad spread his palms—*bring it on.*

"But I won't," Ichabod announced, "because I refuse to let counsel drag me down to his level."

Bennett's smirk widened.

"Instead, I want to propose an agreement that could turn this into a win-win situation." Ichabod shuffled her papers and began reading from some notes.

"I strongly suggest that counsel consider a plea bargain in this case, and I have given some thought to the types of terms I would accept. Let me be frank with you, Mr. Carson. Your client has no chance of being found innocent."

She said it and paused, as if it were some shocking pronouncement. In truth, Brad knew this from the moment he drew Ichabod to hear the case. Years earlier, when she first ascended to the bench, some pro-life senators had delayed her confirmation hearings for more than eighteen months, digging for dirt they never found. It was common knowledge around the courthouse that Ichabod had a long memory and painted those responsible with a broad brush.

Brad had spent a long time kicking himself for suggesting to his client that they waive their right to a jury trial and take their chances with a judge.

"I assume the Reverend Bailey's conscience would not allow him to plead guilty to this charge, so I would be willing to accept a plea of 'no contest.' It would have the same effect, of course, except he wouldn't have to admit guilt. You will withdraw any defense and any rights to appeal, and I will find the reverend guilty. I will sentence him to serve only four days in jail, to be done on four consecutive Saturdays. No overnight stays. I will also sentence him to a total of six months in jail but will suspend that part of his sentence conditioned on good behavior for the next year, including no more protests or prayer meetings within one hundred feet of any abortion clinic."

Ichabod quit reading and looked at Brad. He sat absolutely stone-faced, determined not to give her the satisfaction of a reaction. It *was* a good deal. And he knew it was motivated by Ichabod's desire to avoid looking bad in front of the appellate judges in Richmond. But he didn't want to look too anxious to jump on it. Better to make the judge sweat a little.

"I'll have to discuss it with my client," Brad said, thoughtfully rubbing his unshaven face.

"Judge, I don't know if I can agree to this," Bennett blurted out. "It's very lenient. But this case is getting out of hand, and I would love to put this matter behind us." She paused for effect.

All part of a carefully choreographed show—with me as the audience, Brad thought. He was flattered.

"I'll agree to it," Bennett finally said, trying to sound reluctant, "but only if we can wrap it up by 5 p.m. I'm not willing to spend all weekend wondering about what we're going to do. I've got a closing argument to prepare for this trial . . . assuming, that is, that Mr. Carson will find the good sense to apologize."

"Oh, that's another thing," Ichabod said, looking back at her notes like she just remembered something. "If we can all agree to this plea bargain, I will release Mr. Carson from custody on Monday morning."

What a surprise.

"So, Mr. Carson, what's it going to be?"

He was tempted to say "whatever" again. He was tempted to tell Ichabod how much he liked jail, and how much the marshals liked him because he had stood up to her. Instead, he just stared down at his flip-flops. It really was a good deal for his client, and he didn't want to say anything to jeopardize it.

"My client is a man of strong convictions," Brad said solemnly. "And I'm not sure he'll go for it. But I'll talk to him, and I'll recommend it. And I'll let you know by five o'clock."

"Thank you, Mr. Carson," Ichabod said, sounding both sincere and smug at the same time. Then she looked at Bennett. "I'd like a moment alone with Mr. Carson, please."

The government lawyer quickly excused herself. Brad studied his flip-flops some more, knowing what was coming. No court reporter, no witnesses. Ichabod was going to lower the boom.

"Mr. Carson," she began, her voice low and even as she measured each syllable, "you may think that you are clever. And, I will admit, you have done well for your client by your little stunt in this case. But the most important thing any lawyer brings into my courtroom is his or her own credibility. And once you lose it, you can never, ever, reclaim it. You have lost every ounce of your credibility with this judge, Mr. Carson. In my courtroom, you are a marked man. And I have a very long memory."

Brad felt a deep breath leave his body, and with it went some of the pride of his cunning achievement. He had indeed done well for his client, but at what cost to his own career? Did he really want to be known as a lawyer who couldn't be trusted, even by someone as petty as Ichabod?

He began to carefully choose the words for his response, but Ichabod didn't give him a chance. She simply pushed a button under her desk, and a marshal appeared at the back door.

"Clarence," she said, "give Mr. Carson a half-hour leave from his contempt sentence so that he can go buy a toothbrush."

Brad stood and flashed Ichabod a puzzled smile. He waited for her to look up so he could offer to shake hands. *No hard feelings?*

But Ichabod began reading some more papers, not bothering to stand or extend her hand or even look at him.

"Good day, Mr. Carson," she said without taking her eyes from the page in front of her.

◁▷

"What did he say?" Bella asked.

She was sitting in the muggy, dank jailhouse conference room with Brad. He had recounted the plea bargain offered by Ichabod, then called the Reverend Bailey on a cell phone that Clarence allowed Bella to bring into the conference room.

"He said if I recommend it, he'll take it."

"The man is clearly a poor judge of character," Bella offered.

Brad ignored her sarcasm and pensively stared at the floor. He was pretty sure he had won this case. He just didn't think winning would feel this bad.

◁▷

Sarah Reed tried to open her eyes, encountered blinding lights, and closed them again. Her head was throbbing, and she could not seem to get out of the haze. She heard voices in the distance but couldn't make out the words. She tried to speak, tried to scream and tell someone about the pain, but the noises just tumbled out of her throat, making no sense.

She tried to sleep, but sleep would not come. Her mind swung in and out of consciousness, while nightmares blurred the lines between reality and dreams. She tried to reach out and grab something real, to get her bearings, but her arms would not respond. *Where am I? Where is Charles?* Then the haze became darker, and she floated away, voices mocking her in the distance.

"Sarah?"

A disembodied voice cut through the thick fog engulfing her. A touch on the arm, an insistent shaking, then the same kind voice.

"Sarah, do you hear me?"

It was a man's voice. *Maybe Charles?*

She reached out for him, finding comfort in the soft and understanding tone. He moved closer, bringing a peace and order to her thoughts. Without even knowing why, she took comfort in his presence, pictured his face. She couldn't remember what had happened, but she had a feeling of great danger and great loss. And then . . . he changed. The face hardened before her eyes, transforming into the leathery image of the Muttawa leader, the eyes turning rabid. Sarah heard his heinous laugh . . . She recoiled, fear wracking her.

"Sarah."

Another gentle touch. This time she opened her eyes, then squinted to protect them from the lights' harsh glare. She could make out the silhouette of a figure standing over her.

"Sarah, my name is Dr. Rydell," the soft voice said. "Do you know where you are?"

Sarah nodded her head ever so subtly. At least she tried to. She didn't know if she actually succeeded. She tried to focus. She could feel the sleep coming back and somehow knew she didn't have long to get an answer about Charles.

"You're in a naval base hospital outside of Riyadh. You took a pretty nasty blow to the head, but you're going to be all right. You're going to need some rest."

Even as the haze started closing in, Sarah felt the images cascading around her. The Muttawa. Charles. Blood dripping from his face. The men coming at her. She closed her eyes and felt a stream of tears running down her face and toward her pillow.

She had to know.

She struggled to form the words, to fight off the fog for one last critical moment, but her tongue was thick and uncooperative. Still she managed to mouth a single word, inquiring with her eyes and lips.

"Charles?"

The doctor reached out and touched her arm again, bending forward and nearly whispering. "I'm afraid we weren't able to save him," the man said. "We tried everything we could, but he passed away a few hours ago from massive heart failure." He paused for a beat as the awful news penetrated the fog and pierced her heart. "I'm sorry, Sarah."

No! she wanted to scream. *Bring him back! It can't end like this! Not for those who love God and are called according to His purpose . . .*

More images flashed into her mind—unheeded—of their last struggling moments together. She remembered now. Vividly. The way Charles courageously refused to give up the names of other pastors. The brutal reaction of the Muttawa. The pain and the blood.

She needed to hold her husband one more time . . . say her good-byes . . . tell him how much she loved him . . . how hard it would be without him . . . how much he had taught her about the love of Christ.

But Charles was not there, and even in her drug-induced state she understood with awful certainty that he would never return. She found herself clutching the arm of this doctor, her lips forming one final haunting question as she slipped back into the darkness.

"Why, God? Why?"

PART II

THE LAW

5
Six months later

LESLIE CONNORS LOOKED DOWN at her watch and could hardly believe it was already 11:30. The law library would close in thirty minutes. As usual, she had run out of time before she ran out of work.

She leaned back in her chair and stole a quick look around. Not surprisingly, she was the only one left on the basement floor. Most students avoided the loneliness and despair that seemed to linger in these parts of the catacombs. No windows, no noise, no socializers, no distractions. Just the way Leslie liked it.

She put in her time at this same carrel night after night, grinding away and chasing her dream. She owned this carrel, not in a legal sense, but through the personal effects she had scattered around the small cubicle and her chastisement of any intruders. After all, she was a second-year law student and already a bit of a legend. She was on track to graduate second in her class. That feat alone would take her one step closer to her goal of becoming one of the top international law practitioners in the country. The world was shrinking, and the global village was becoming a reality. Leslie loved the thought of the travel, the prestige, the intellectual challenge, and yes, the money. For a girl who grew up in a double-wide trailer, a career representing multinational corporations seemed like the perfect ticket to a better life.

There was no sacrifice she was not willing to make.

Her carrel was lined with law books across the back. Pictures, yellow Post-it notes, and to-do lists filled the sides. One of the faded color photos reflected the happier times in her life. It was a picture of Leslie and Bill, her late husband, with their arms around each other, standing on the steps of the U.S. Supreme Court.

At the age of thirty-three, Bill had been diagnosed with an aggressive form of prostate cancer that had already metastasized. In the bittersweet nine months that followed, a nostalgic Bill made Leslie promise to pursue the legal career that she had sacrificed in the real-life compromises made by a young couple trying to make ends meet. And so, at the age of twenty-eight, and without Bill for the first time in eight years, Leslie enrolled at William and Mary Law School. She had been tearing the place up ever since.

"Ready for Friday?"

Leslie jumped and turned quickly around. Her friend Carli was smiling. "Little edgy tonight, aren't we?"

Leslie shook her head and returned the smile. "Didn't know you were sneaking up on me."

"Just stopping by to see if maybe you had died down here or needed a sleeping bag or something."

"Very funny."

Carli surveyed the casebooks and legal briefs scattered around the carrel. "So . . . you ready?"

"Not yet, but I will be."

"Right," Carli teased. "No pressure, but the law school bookies have you as a five-to-one underdog. They're sayin' you'll wilt under Strobel's withering questions."

"And what do you say?"

"That Strobel will be so amazed, he'll offer you a plum job in his international law practice on the spot."

"Just in case," Leslie said, "you might want to put down a few bills against me."

Carli laughed and gave Leslie a playful push as she walked away. "You kidding?" she said over her shoulder. "I already did."

Leslie's thoughts lingered for a moment on Maximillian Strobel, the managing partner of the largest law firm in southeast Virginia. Strobel was one of three moot court judges who would hear and decide the finals in two days. More important, he also headed the only thriving international law practice outside of Washington, D.C., New York, and Los Angeles. Because Leslie had promised herself that she would never live in those mammoth cities, Strobel was her only chance at a serious career in international law with a quality of life she could tolerate.

She glanced again at her watch. It was now fifteen minutes until midnight. Six in the morning would come quickly. She reached into her backpack and popped a couple of sleeping pills. They would kick in about the time she got back to her little studio apartment. In the meantime, she would use fifteen minutes wisely. She picked up a brief and began reading through it for the third time.

◁▷

The next morning, Sarah Reed walked into the law offices of Carson & Associates, not at all confident she was doing the right thing. She had a nagging conviction that Christians should avoid lawyers in general and lawsuits in particular. Still, the insulting letter she now carried in her purse had overridden her feelings, and the Reverend Jacob Bailey, her pastor in Chesapeake, suggested she come here. She knew of no other attorney she might be able to trust.

But as she got off the elevator at the fifth floor of the Tidewater Community Bank building on the outskirts of a Virginia Beach shopping mall, she started to have second thoughts. She had never been in a law office before. She would rather be going to the dentist.

She followed the signs for Carson & Associates to the end of the hallway. She hesitated in front of the oak door with the name of the firm emblazoned in gold letters. Then she took a deep breath, said a quick prayer, and entered the waiting area.

The receptionist did nothing to put her at ease.

"Yeah," the squat woman said. She didn't bother to pause her typing. The nameplate on the desk identified her as Bella Harper. Smoke wafted upward from the ashtray next to her, where a half-gone cigarette smoldered.

"I'm here to see Mr. Carson," Sarah said timidly.

"Do you have an appointment?" Bella asked.

Sarah immediately felt stupid. She knew she should have called and scheduled in advance. But that would have locked her in. She needed the freedom to bolt if she got cold feet. Like right now.

"No. Reverend Jacob Bailey referred me. I was hoping I could get just a minute of Mr. Carson's time. I'll come back later."

"Honey," Bella said, finally deigning to look up, "we don't take drop-ins. I can get you an appointment, but it'll probably be about three weeks before Mr. Carson can see you. He's in court this morning on a trial that will last a week. Then he's got back-to-back appointments for two weeks after that."

Three weeks!

Legal matters were something Charles would have handled. The thought of it made Sarah's eyes fill with tears, which made her feel even more self-conscious. It didn't help that Bella was eyeing her up and down. Sarah had become so emotional since Charles died, and waves of grief would wash over her at the most inopportune times.

"I'll just make an appointment some other time if I can't get this resolved on my own," she said to Bella, swallowing hard and forcing a plastic smile.

"Suit yourself." Bella resumed her typing.

Sarah stared at Bella for a moment, dumbfounded. *No wonder lawyers have such a bad reputation.*

This was obviously God's way of telling her to drop the matter. She shouldn't have come in the first place.

As she turned to leave, a slender, well-dressed man burst through the thick oak door and nearly ran over her.

◁ ▷

"Sorry," Brad said, stopping just short of a collision. He gave the woman a quizzical look. "Do I know you?"

She shrugged her shoulders. "I don't think so."

"I'm Brad Carson," he said, sticking out his hand. *She looks so familiar.*

"Sarah Reed," she said softly.

Even her name sounds familiar. Brad noticed a trail of smoke from the ashtray where Bella had just stabbed out her cigarette.

"What happened?" Bella called out. "I thought you were in trial."

"We settled."

Then it hit him. He had seen this lady on the news. The missionary whose husband had died in Saudi Arabia. CNN had run live coverage of her testimony before the Senate Foreign Affairs Committee. The government of Saudi Arabia had denied Sarah's allegations of murder. They claimed her husband died from a heart attack unrelated to the injuries he received from resisting arrest on drug charges.

In the end, the importance of the vast Saudi oil reserves won out over the testimony of a missionary. The committee authored a scathing report but avoided any real sanctions against the government of Saudi Arabia, and the Saudis agreed to conduct an internal investigation and punish any renegade police officers. The Senate placed the Saudis on probation for a while, and the Saudis agreed to diligently protect human rights.

The oil kept flowing.

"I remember now. I'm sorry about your husband," Brad said earnestly. "And I'm sorry about the way your case was handled by the government."

Sarah shrugged and seemed to relax just a little. "Thanks. I'm just trying to move on. One day at a time."

"Can we help you with anything?" Brad asked.

Bella shot him a look. "She was referred by Reverend Bailey," Bella said, as if that explained everything. Reverend Bailey's church members had not given up on their abortion protests, and many had tried to solicit Brad's representation.

Once had been enough.

But Brad could sense that Sarah had not come for that reason. He saw something else etched in the soft lines of her face. She looked tired, older now than she had seemed just a few months before when he saw her on television.

"Well," Brad said, "as fate would have it, my day just cleared up. Come on back to the conference room, and we'll talk." He turned to Bella with a playful smile. "Bella, could you get a couple cups of coffee?"

Bella grunted and stalked down the hallway to the kitchen. Brad ushered Sarah into the conference room.

◁▷

"This is ridiculous," Brad said, slapping the letter down on the large oak table. "Unbelievable."

The letter came from Charles's life insurance company and denied Sarah's claim for one hundred thousand dollars in death benefits. Brad glanced down to the operative paragraph:

> The investigation of Trust Indemnity has revealed that, according to tests performed at the hospital and during the autopsy, the Insured had a lethally high dosage of cocaine in his bloodstream on the night of his demise, and the Insured's heart attack was precipitated in part by this self-induced overdose of cocaine. Accordingly, Trust Indemnity cannot honor your claim for insurance proceeds in light of Exclusion 4 Section A(2).

Brad stood and began to pace, still holding the letter. To line their own pockets, the insurance company had chosen to disregard Sarah's version of the facts and to conclude that Dr. Reed had died from a self-inflicted drug overdose. And, Brad knew, this was par for the course with Trust Indemnity. He had sued them twice in the last year alone for bad faith.

He looked at Sarah's expectant expression. She was just sitting there, engulfed by the deep leather swivel chair, her hands folded on the table, concern etched deeply into her brow.

"We'll sue," Brad promised. He said it with that air of authority that clients loved. "This is outrageous. We'll sue for every penny of the hundred thousand; then we'll sue for bad faith and punitive damages. I've had lots of run-ins with these folks, but this is the worst." He paused for emphasis. "It's time to teach these guys a lesson."

Brad was surprised that the look on Sarah's face did not change. He didn't get the same sparkle in the eyes, the you-tell-'em look he was used to receiving from other clients when he uttered the magic words "punitive damages." If anything, the creases of concern on Sarah's forehead burrowed deeper.

"Couldn't you just send a letter and see if we could handle it that way?"

"A letter won't do any good, Sarah. The boys at Trust Indemnity understand two things: lawsuits and punitive damages. Nothing else gets their attention."

Sarah shifted uncomfortably and looked down at her hands. "I don't want to file for punitive damages, Mr. Carson."

Brad tried not to look at her as if she were some kind of freak. *Doesn't want to file for punitive damages? Does God still make people like this?*

Still looking down, Sarah continued softly. "I really don't want to even file a suit. But I've got two kids to think about, and the money . . ." Her voice quivered, then broke off.

Brad leaned forward on the table, looked directly at Sarah, and lowered his voice to its most comforting tone, perfected by years in front of the jury box. "Okay, Sarah, listen to me." She looked up, and Brad continued. "There's nothing wrong with filing a lawsuit." He said it with real conviction, his voice comforting and steady. "Sometimes it's the only way in our society to obtain justice. These guys owe you a hundred thousand. To let them get away with that is to admit that Charles committed suicide and died from a self-inflicted overdose of cocaine. And I know you don't want that."

Sarah forced her lips into a thin smile and shook her head.

"Then here's what I'm going to do. I'll draft a lawsuit and have it served on Trust Indemnity. My guess is that they'll pay immediately once they know you've got a lawyer involved. If not, we'll talk about a fee agreement at that stage. I won't charge anything for drafting and sending the lawsuit."

It was not good business, but every once in a while Brad believed he owed it to the profession to take on a case pro bono. If ever there was such a case, this one was it. At least that's the way he saw it; Bella probably wouldn't speak to him for a week.

"Reverend Bailey said it would be just like you to take this case for free," Sarah said. "I don't want that. I want you to take your normal fee. In fact, I insist on it, and I'll go to another lawyer if you refuse."

Brad gave Sarah another sideways look. Where did she come from? It was hard not to be charmed by this lady. "I seldom see clients so insistent on giving me their money. But if you insist, I'll sic Bella on you, and we'll have you sign our retainer agreement."

Sarah paused before answering. "If I've got to deal with her again, maybe I'll reconsider." She smiled, and her moist blue eyes lit up for the first time.

Brad laughed politely, struck by the warmth of her smile. He stood and shook hands with his new client, walked around the table, put an arm around her shoulder, and gave her a squeeze. They chatted for a few moments; then he ushered her out of the conference room and into the clutches of Bella.

Brad watched Bella attack the fee arrangement with gusto, placing one form after another in front of Sarah for her signature. Carson & Associates would receive one-third of any money recovered "against Trust Indemnity or otherwise" as a result of the death of Charles Reed. Brad knew Bella had another form that actually placed the fee at 40 percent, but apparently even she could not spring that form on a grieving widow like Sarah in such a simple case.

◁▷

Rasheed turned over and reached out to stroke his wife's hair. As he touched her cheek, he felt the warm tears. He leaned up on one elbow and tried to focus in the dark.

"What's wrong, Mobara?"

He sensed a slight movement, perhaps a shudder, perhaps a shrug of the shoulders. "Nothing," she said.

Rasheed knew better than to accept that answer.

"You just decide to start crying in the middle of the night for no reason? Come on, you can talk to me."

Mobara wiped the tears away with the palms of her hands. "I feel so guilty," she sobbed. "I've felt this every day and every night since the Muttawa came . . ." Her voice faltered.

Rasheed reached over and drew her to himself. He held her softly as she cried.

When she regained control, she spoke again in a desperate whisper. "We denied our Lord, Rasheed. I can't live like this."

He squeezed her tighter in the silence. "Nor I," he said at last.

"What . . . are we going to do?" Her sobbing intensified.

Rasheed gently released his wife, then drew her out of bed to kneel together. "We must pray . . . ask forgiveness . . . trust God to give us another chance."

Mobara joined him and put her hand on his. "What if they come back, Rasheed? I'm so afraid."

"I know. Let's pray. Remember, God has not given us the spirit of fear."

Mobara looked intently at her husband. "I love you, Rasheed. And I'll be okay if you're with me."

Rasheed put his arm around her again and drew her close, still kneeling, preparing to pray.

"Are you afraid?" she asked.

Rasheed thought for a moment and looked down. He couldn't lie to Mobara. She would know. "Yes," he admitted.

Together, they began to pray.

6

LESLIE TOOK ANOTHER SIP from the glass of water on her counsel table. It was half-gone, her mouth was still dry, and she hadn't even started her argument yet. She tapped the sides of the typed pages in front of her, perfectly lining up the edges of her notes, then surveyed again the panel of accomplished lawyers who would act as judges for the moot court final.

Seated on her left was Professor Lynda Parsons. She was rumored to be tough, fair, sarcastic, and witty. Leslie had skillfully avoided taking her classes, but now she had to face her as a judge in the moot court final.

In the middle, and acting as chief justice because of his experience and reputation in international law, sat Mack Strobel. He was already staring down the litigants.

Leslie stared back.

She had read the book on Strobel. *Don't let him intimidate you. He's from the old school—blunt and full of bluster. Respect him but don't trust him.*

It was hard not to look away. Strobel's eyes became piercing. His clean-shaven head, close-cropped goatee, and fierce scowl gave him a draconian look—like some type of WWF wrestler dressed up in a business suit. His leathery skin and bald pate were well-tanned, though summer was months away. He had broad shoulders, was above average height, and he seemed to dominate the courtroom without trying.

After making her point with Strobel, Leslie diverted her gaze to Brad Carson, who sat to Leslie's right. Carson shuffled some papers and looked absentmindedly around the courtroom. He caught Leslie's gaze and smiled. Compared to Strobel, Carson was not an imposing figure, but he seemed so sure of himself and so natural in a courtroom setting that he, too, commanded respect. He also seemed bored and ready for some action.

"Be seated," Strobel barked, obviously ready to get down to the business of beating up the litigants.

◁ ▷

The sizing up went both ways. Brad had already decided that Leslie would win if points were awarded for style.

"Is counsel for appellant ready?" Mack asked.

"Ready, Your Honor." Leslie stood and flashed a nervous smile.

"Is counsel for appellee ready?"

"Yes, Your Honor."

Brad studied the young man opposing Leslie. Stiff posture, short-cropped hair, and precise movements. Probably active duty military, attending school on a JAG scholarship. Long on discipline, short on creativity, Brad figured.

Leslie was more of a mystery. She was attractive but trying hard to look more like a lawyer than a beauty queen. She wore her shoulder-length auburn hair in a tight braid, and her traditional dark blue suit camouflaged a tall, thin frame. Intense sky blue eyes seemed to sparkle with anticipation. She had the high cheekbones and long neck of a model, but none of the makeup that would accentuate or draw attention to those features. Her pale skin had probably been weeks without seeing a ray of sun, and red blotches marked her neck where she had probably scratched nervously. Brad pegged her as a hardworking overachiever who was taking this event way too seriously.

She stood and addressed the panel.

"May it please the court, my name is Leslie Connors, and I represent the appellants—the former Taliban regime and the nation of Afghanistan. The issue in this case is whether a U.S. federal court has the jurisdiction to hear the case and award damages to certain female Afghanistan refugees against the Taliban and the nation of Afghanistan for the alleged torture of these refugees. Let me make myself perfectly clear. The issue is not whether the Taliban abused these women and should be punished for their heinous conduct; it is whether a U.S. court should usurp the role of the international community and set itself up as the final tribunal to judge that conduct."

"Counsel," Strobel interrupted, "would you agree that your clients committed some of the most despicable and far-reaching human rights violations since the atrocities of Hitler?"

"Your Honor, that is for the international community to decide, not this court."

"But, Counsel," Strobel drawled, "do you deny that the Taliban regime deprived women like yourself of the most basic human rights?"

"No, we do not deny it." Leslie appeared uncomfortable making even this obvious concession. Brad watched as she shifted her weight from one foot to the other, then nervously tucked an imaginary strand of stray hair behind her ear.

"Do you deny that the Taliban beat and tortured women if they attempted to run away from an abusive husband? Do you deny that the Taliban treated women as something less than human, as property of their husbands?"

"No. But the international community addressed that in removing the Taliban from power—"

"Counsel," Strobel interrupted, immediately silencing Leslie, "this court has now been petitioned by a group of refugees to grant redress for these terrible acts of torture. Are you suggesting that this court just sit idly by, refuse to take jurisdiction over this case, and let the Taliban get away with rape, murder, and torture?"

"We are a nation of laws," Leslie responded, slowly and evenly. "And on this point the law is very specific and very clear. All nations have the privilege of sovereign immunity, a basic and fundamental privilege that prevents them from being hauled into the courts of another nation as a defendant. We must respect the sovereignty of other nations and not drag them into our courts as if they were just ordinary American citizens, especially since a new government in Afghanistan has replaced the Taliban—"

"I'm well aware of the law, Counsel." Strobel used a tone a parent might reserve for scolding a young child. "So let's talk about the law for a minute. Under the Foreign Sovereign Immunities Act, there are certain exceptions. For example, a foreign nation can be hauled into our courts if that nation causes harm associated with a commercial activity, such as breach of a contract. Is that right?"

"Under some circumstances."

"And a foreign nation can be hauled into our courts if an agent of that nation causes injury on the high seas, right?"

"That's correct."

"And if an agent of a foreign nation injures someone on American territory, then that nation gets hauled into American courts?

"Yes, in most cases."

"So let me get this straight." Strobel stroked his goatee as if he were deep in thought. "A foreign nation can get hauled into American courts if they hurt us in the pocketbook, or if they injure someone on the high seas, or if they breach a contract, but there is some overwhelming reason that says we can't drag them into American courts if they systematically torture, rape, or kill innocent civilian women. Is that the way you read the law?"

Leslie shifted her weight. The red blotches grew. She pushed at more imaginary hair.

For his part, Brad was growing weary of the bullying. He was always one to cheer for the underdog. Especially an underdog as pretty as Leslie.

"That's not exactly the way I would phrase it," Leslie said. "There are important foreign policy reasons—"

"Counsel," Brad said, coming to the rescue, "did you write this law? Justice Strobel seems to think you did." He shot a sideways glance at Strobel. No love lost there. "Last I checked, Congress wrote the law, and it was the job of courts like this one to apply it."

Leslie looked relieved to get a pitch she could actually hit. "Congress had to balance numerous important factors in drafting the Foreign Sovereign Immunities Act. There are delicate foreign policy issues at stake—there is a new regime in Afghanistan, put there by our own country, and that regime should not be undermined and held accountable for the actions of the Taliban. Plus the governments of other countries must be respected by the courts of the United States, or those other countries will reciprocate by hauling the United States into their courts as a defendant. The role of this court today is not to question the wisdom of the Sovereign Immunities Act passed by Congress, but to apply the law even if we don't necessarily like the result."

Brad looked at Strobel and nodded.

"The court should not open this can of worms," Leslie concluded. "Otherwise, plaintiffs' lawyers will clog our courts with all manner of bogus claims against foreign governments, just trying to get lucky and hit it big."

Brad winced. Now Strobel smirked.

Brad was fully engaged. The game was clear: it was Brad against Strobel, head-to-head. The litigants were just allies—pawns to move around the chessboard. Brad thought it worked out nicely to have the attractive one on his side. Strobel could have the drill sergeant.

"You are aware, Counsel—" Strobel's voice boomed again—"that all civilized nations acknowledge certain generally accepted principles of international law?"

"Yes. These fundamental principles and values common to all mankind are called *jus cogens* laws and are considered binding."

"These are the highest forms of international law, is that correct?"

"Yes, they are."

Brad leafed through his materials for a copy of the Foreign Sovereign Immunities Act. He could not put his finger on it, but this moot court argument was giving him a strange sense of déjà vu.

"And one of those norms widely recognized as a *jus cogens* norm is the right of people everywhere to be free from torture at the hands of their own government, right?" Strobel asked.

The trap was set. Brad could see it about to snap.

"Basic human rights, such as the right to be free from torture, would be considered *jus cogens* laws," Leslie admitted.

A mirthless smile formed on Strobel's lips. "Well then, if a nation violates a basic human right, like the right to be free from torture, they have violated one of the most basic tenets of international law. Shouldn't a nation that breaks one of these most basic tenets of international law, a *jus cogens* law—" Strobel let his deep Southern drawl lengthen the phrase like some religious incantation—"by torturing and killing its own citizens be seen as waiving the protection of sovereign immunity?"

Strobel leaned forward, elbows on the bench, waiting for an answer. The phrase *jus cogens*, majestically Latin in its origin, seemed to echo around the courtroom.

Leslie cleared her throat. "If we start weighing violations of international law and decide that some violations are worthy of the protection of sovereign immunity while others are not, then we will find ourselves in an ambiguous area. If nothing else, international law requires certainty and predictability—"

"But aren't we already making exceptions?" Strobel insisted. "It's just that now we make exceptions for commercial cases, and I'm suggesting that the far more important cases for exceptions are violations of basic human rights—violations of *jus cogens* laws."

Leslie let the question hang in the air. She looked at Brad—an appeal for help.

Brad and Mack each started a question at the same time. Brad raised his voice and continued. "Ms. Connors, you are an American lawyer representing the Taliban and Afghanistan, is that right?" he asked.

"Yes," Leslie said tentatively.

"Do you remember when the American jets were relentlessly bombing cities in Afghanistan and there were numerous reports of civilians being killed during the bombing raids?"

"I believe so," Leslie answered, apparently hedging her bet.

"Would you say that killing innocent civilians violates one of those, how do you say it?" Brad wrinkled his forehead, a picture of naiveté and perplexity.

"*Jus cogens* laws," Leslie replied.

"Yeah," Brad said. "Would you say killing innocent civilians with a military jet would qualify?" He took off his reading glasses and began chewing on them.

"You bet."

"Do some of the people in your client's country, including some of the judges, still dislike the American troops who bombed their cities and killed their civilians?"

"I think it's accurate to say that some detest Americans," Leslie volunteered.

"If an Afghan court, which as I understand it is still governed by Islamic law, were allowed to put the United States on trial for the bombing of those civilians—in other words, if the shoe were on the other foot—do you have any prediction as to the amount of the judgment that an Afghan court might render against the United States in such a case?"

Brad expected the answer was obvious to everyone in the courtroom.

"I'm sure the judgment would be in the billions," Leslie answered enthusiastically. "The U.S. courts would then retaliate with a judgment against Afghanistan for billions more. Pretty soon we're heading down a slippery slope of retaliation—nations slapping each other with billion-dollar judgments and throwing international law into total chaos."

Leslie looked thankfully at Brad and, for the first time during the argument, flashed a relaxed smile.

◁▷

Driving home it hit him—the reason for his déjà vu. The case of the Afghan refugees reminded him of the abuse that Sarah Reed had endured at the hands of government officials. Slippery slopes aside, why should foreign governments be allowed to torture innocent civilians, then hide behind the doctrine of sovereign immunity? Why should the Saudi Arabian police be allowed to torture and kill an American citizen and not be held accountable in an American court?

Brad was not familiar with the vagaries of international law, but he had a keen sense for justice and fairness. And in the case of Sarah Reed, justice demanded that the Saudi police pay for what they did.

He picked up his cell phone and dialed directory assistance. He needed an international law expert who could exhaustively research this potential cause of action. He knew just the person.

◁▷

Leslie could not stop fuming. She had lost the final round of the moot court tournament and spent her drive home ruthlessly critiquing her own performance. She second-guessed every word and every gesture, replayed the entire argument in her mind, thought of things she should have said, and hated herself for not having said them.

She lived twelve miles from the law school in a quaint studio apartment above a detached garage in the country. A law school professor owned a majestic estate about two miles off the main road on the banks of the scenic Chickahominy River. Because the professor had taken a two-year assignment at another law school, she'd hired a contractor to build an apartment in the attic space of her three-car garage. She'd offered the apartment to Leslie rent-free so long as Leslie kept an eye on the estate.

Leslie's friends thought she was insane for living alone in such an isolated setting. But Leslie loved the seclusion, the scenery, the wildlife on the riverbanks, and the price of the apartment. Besides, Leslie practically lived in the law school library. Her apartment was just a way station for sleeping, showering, and licking her wounds.

By the time Leslie turned off the main road, she had pretty much concluded that she would always be second best. She had also decided that she had no desire to practice international law at the firm of Kilgore & Strobel. She dreamed of a day when she, a big-city lawyer, would try cases against Strobel and his small-town law firm. She would crush him with superior resources and clever lawyering. She had a sudden hankering for the Big Apple, where she could plot her revenge.

Leslie parked her car in the garage and slowly climbed the steps to her apartment. The sun was just beginning to set over the Chickahominy, and the light show was spectacular. She planned to microwave dinner, grab a law book and a bottle of wine, and sit on the dock until the sun completely disappeared.

She had struggled with dependency in the days following Bill's death, and she had therefore not allowed herself even one drink since the start of the semester. But after a day like today, she had earned it. She would indulge just this once. As she popped a Lean Cuisine into the microwave and poured her first drink, she also checked her phone messages.

The first caller had not left a message. The second one was a consolation call from Carli. "You did great. You should have won." Sweet lies to make Leslie feel better. The third call made her quickly forget the other two.

"Hello, Leslie, this is Brad Carson. Listen, great job in moot court today. I know this sounds a little strange, but I'm actually investigating a real case that is similar to the hypothetical case we were discussing. I need someone familiar with international law to do some research and help me determine if we've got a cause of action. Uh . . . I'm willing to pay enough to make it worth your time, and you can work around your school schedule. Anyway, if you're interested, give me a call, and my secretary will set up a meeting."

Leslie replayed the message twice, wrote down the number he left, and weighed her options. She didn't have time for this. She needed to stay focused on school to maintain her class ranking. Good offers from top firms would follow. Besides, it was March, and Leslie planned on spending the summer abroad as part of the William and Mary study program in Exeter, England.

But as Leslie walked down to the dock, the lawyer in her couldn't help but argue the other side. She owed Brad a favor since he had saved her from complete humiliation. Maybe this would be her big break in international law. She was tired of studying concepts and arguing hypotheticals. The thought of a real-life case with a real-life client was intoxicating. Besides, she needed the money.

She debated with herself vigorously until the sun finished its descent and she had polished off the tiny helping of Lean Cuisine lasagna and two glasses of wine. By then she had rendered her verdict. She would call Brad first thing Monday morning.

After another glass of wine, she finished critiquing her performance and decided maybe she hadn't done such a miserable job after all. She was ready to practice some real law and work with a real lawyer. Forget Monday. She would go to the library first thing tomorrow morning. She would call Brad tomorrow afternoon and sink her teeth into a real case by the beginning of the week.

It was a beautiful night, and her head was starting to spin. She lay on her back on the dock and watched the stars as they circled the sky. A chorus of bullfrogs serenaded her, accompanied by the steady rhythm of small wind-blown waves lapping against the bank. She felt her nerves relax as exhaustion overwhelmed her weary body. Before long, she closed her eyes and drifted away.

She dreamed of humiliating Strobel.

7

MILES OF TREE-LINED SIDEWALKS snaked their way among the tall and stately brick colonial buildings, each adorned with beautiful white columns, that made up the City of Virginia Beach municipal complex. The sprawling office park boasted plenty of green space and immaculate landscaping, adding to its bucolic appeal.

The courthouse building was always a beehive of activity. And on this Friday morning, as on most Fridays, large crowds crammed themselves into the courtrooms for "motions day," the weekly cattle call where lawyers hashed through all their motions on their cases so they could reserve the other days for trial work.

Two weeks after her moot court argument, Leslie walked into the weekly melee of Virginia Beach Circuit Courtroom No. 7 and took a seat in the back. Brad had told Leslie he didn't know what time he would be done with his motions, but afterward they would have lunch and discuss her research.

She decided to come a few hours early to see how motions and other important legal issues were decided in the real world. Her valuable time bought a study in mediocrity that made Leslie thankful for her class ranking and more determined than ever to avoid the slosh pit of mundane law where most lawyers wallowed.

The cases of Billy "the Rock" Davenport dominated the morning's hearings. Leslie immediately recognized the name. The widely known senior partner of Davenport & Associates was the genius behind his firm's irreverent and ubiquitous television ads: "When trouble rolls, call the Rock." It was the kind of advertising Leslie detested, the kind of exposure that gave all lawyers a bad name. Turn the television to Jerry Springer, and the breaks would be accented by a tough-sounding and mean-looking lawyer with boxing gloves ready to deck the insurance companies. Watch ESPN, and another lawyer, this time fit and in jogging shorts, told you how to avoid the insurance company runaround. Tune in to your favorite soap, and a young and handsome lawyer assured you that Davenport & Associates literally feels your pain. Of course, none of the lawyers on television looked even remotely like the short, bald, pudgy man who meekly took his place behind the counsel table in Courtroom No. 7.

For forty-five minutes, defense lawyers of all stripes took their turns pummeling the Rock. The cases were different, but the themes were the same—the Rock had not answered interrogatories in a timely fashion, the Rock had failed to provide required medical reports, the Rock had failed to show for a scheduled deposition, the Rock had failed to name expert witnesses in a timely manner, and so on and so on. The lawyers asked for sanctions against the Rock, or that the cases be thrown out, or that the Rock be forced to concede major points in penance for his failure to comply with discovery rules.

The Rock was clearly on the defensive, shuffling papers, mumbling lame apologies, trying to survive the morning with some of his cases still intact, and above all, avoiding eye contact with the judge. By the end of his time on the hot seat, Leslie couldn't help but feel a little sorry for the hapless Rock and desperately sorry for his clients. She sighed with relief when Brad finally got his turn at the counsel table.

By 1:15 the judge had ruled on the last case, and Leslie was ready for lunch. Brad insisted that they eat at one of his favorite restaurants on the Lynnhaven River. He offered to let Leslie ride with him. They could talk business on the way.

She was not looking forward to this. Leslie's initial enthusiasm for this assignment, which waxed so strong in the beginning, had been decimated by her sobering research into the black-letter law. Sarah Reed had no case. And now it was Leslie's job to ruin Brad's lunch and explain to him the harsh realities of sovereign immunity law.

◁▷

The three adults waiting anxiously in the dimly lit apartment had little in common except a dangerous faith. They had all been members of the church in Riyadh formerly led by Charles and Sarah Reed. They had been severely beaten by the Islamic radicals unleashed by Ahmed Aberijan. To their great shame, they had recanted with their lips, if not with their hearts.

But now Rasheed and Mobara Berjein had boldly reinstated the weekly prayer meetings. These two young schoolteachers were joined by Kareem Bariq, another former member of the Reeds' church, who drifted from one construction job to another and was presently unemployed. The Berjeins were doing what they could to help Kareem both financially and spiritually, with mixed results on both fronts.

The Berjeins had been overjoyed to reunite with Kareem and to learn that he had struggled with the same feelings of guilt and conviction. The tiny church of three rededicated themselves to the cause of Christ and the study of His Word. Over time, forgiveness replaced guilt, and courage began to take the place of fear.

The Berjeins became so emboldened that on this night they had invited another couple from school, close personal friends and spiritual seek- ers. When Rasheed heard the special knock at a few minutes past ten and welcomed his friends to the meeting, he was expecting nothing short of a miracle.

But now that the guests were there, Rasheed didn't really know where to start. He looked at Mobara with rising panic in his eyes and asked her to share a little about her own spiritual journey. Mobara smiled warmly and launched right in, as if it were the most natural thing in the world. Before long, she was fully engaged, passionately telling of her own feelings and faith. She talked about her life as a devoted Muslim, as an ardent follower of Mohammed and the teachings of the Koran. She talked about how much she had learned from her time as a Muslim and what great respect she had for other devout Muslims. But she also shared about an emptiness, a longing for something more than the discipline and sacrifice of the Islamic faith. She longed for peace; she longed for joy; she longed for assurance of eternal life. In a word, Mobara said, she longed for a Savior.

Without realizing it had happened, Rasheed found himself entranced, on the edge of his seat, as if he were hearing his wife's story for the first time. He loved to watch Mobara's ever-changing expressions as she took her listeners through a gauntlet of emotions, every feature on her face going all-out to accen- tuate her words. And then Mobara seemed to notice this as well—that she had become the center of attention—and she suddenly seemed self-conscious about it. Perhaps only Rasheed, who knew his wife so well, noticed the slight change in her countenance. And he was not at all surprised when she turned to him and flawlessly asked him to tell how they had found the answers to all their spiritual searching, to all of their many questions, in the Bible.

Rasheed swallowed hard, cleared his throat, and suddenly realized how thick his tongue had become. He said a quick prayer, licked his parched lips, and opened his Bible. He began sharing some stories that were not found in the Koran. He started with some of the great teachings of Christ, common ground for Muslims and Christians. As he talked, with his guests listening politely and Mobara nodding her agreement, he grew bolder. He felt a power not his own, an eloquence he did not know he possessed.

Oh, he still stammered around some, and he couldn't remember half the Bible passages he wanted to explain, but he was now ready to hit the issues head-on. He explained how Christ had suffered and died on a cross. How Christ had paid the price for sins. He knew this was a major sticking point for Muslims; it had been his own greatest obstacle.

"I couldn't believe that a God of love would actually let His own Son die on a cross," Rasheed admitted, looking at his guests. He saw the same question register in their eyes. "If God is all powerful, why did He allow this to happen?" A long pause. "But then I realized that the very love of God required this—that He loved us so much He was willing to pay any price, including the death of His own Son, to provide us with a way to be brought back into relationship with Him."

He couldn't tell if he was getting through, but there was no stopping Rasheed now. He talked about Christ's resurrection and the historical evidence for this miracle. He said that new life in Christ was available to everyone—Jew and Muslim, male and female—that God was the Father of all.

"In the Christian faith," Rasheed explained earnestly, "salvation does not come from sacrificial living, faithfulness in prayer, or following a certain set of rules. Christ obeyed all the rules, kept the entire Law, something we could never do. And He did it for us.

"Salvation comes through faith in Jesus Christ."

It was time to put the choice squarely to his friends, Rasheed could feel it. And he knew that these words were not his own, that somehow the Holy Spirit prompted them. "Christ cannot be regarded as just another good man, or even another great prophet in a long line of prophets culminating with Mohammed. Christ claimed to be God and wants to be Lord of your life. We must either accept Him on those terms or reject Him as a liar or a lunatic."

Rasheed put down the Bible he had been holding in both hands and looked squarely at his guests. "Does that make sense to you?" he asked.

There was a long and uncomfortable silence as his question hung in the air. His guests looked down, quietly studying the floor, and Rasheed had no idea what to do. He had blown it. He had gotten so excited that he had overwhelmed them. He had not communicated clearly. He had turned them off. Here he was, a trained teacher, and for some reason he couldn't explain the most basic thing in the world—the simple gospel of Jesus Christ.

And then the woman looked up. Rasheed saw the tears welling in her eyes. Her husband reached over, gently taking her hand. He nodded his head ever so slightly, almost imperceptibly. He was saying it all made sense!

"It does?" Rasheed asked, more surprised than anybody else in the room.

The man just nodded his head again. "What do we do now?" he asked softly.

Startled, enthused, bewildered, and excited, Rasheed looked at Mobara. She smiled and turned to the guests. "Rasheed will lead you in a prayer," she suggested. "A prayer that can change everything."

Hesitantly at first, then with great enthusiasm, Rasheed led the couple in a prayer that ended their separation from God and started their relationship with Christ. They talked for an hour afterward.

That night the small church grew by two. That night Rasheed became a pastor.

They ended, as always, in another prayer. And their prayer ended, as always, with the petition that God would help them to remain faithful to Christ, "no matter the cost." They did not have the option of the cheap and easy Christianity of the West. Their faith, with its great reward, would also demand great sacrifice.

◁▷

Brad didn't spend one minute talking about the Reed case on the way to the Lynnhaven Mariner. A master storyteller, Brad entertained Leslie with improbable tales of quirky lawyers, convoluted cases, and irascible clients. After they arrived, he made the long wait longer by insisting they hold out for a table on the dock overlooking the bay, and Leslie surprised herself by not minding any of it. At one point she laughed and realized her anxiety about this bad-news meeting had faded.

Brad didn't get down to business until their lunches sat before them.

"So, Counsel, do we have a case for Sarah Reed? Don't pull any punches."

Leslie hesitated for just a second. "It doesn't look good, Brad. I wouldn't say impossible, but the next thing to it." Her eyes met his. He stared at her intently, and she felt her throat constrict. "I've got a complete memo in my car, but I can give you the nutshell." Was that her voice? Was she going hoarse?

"Go for it." He continued staring.

She took a quick drink of water and collected herself. "Sarah would have a potential cause of action against both the individuals who tortured her as well as the government of Saudi Arabia for the actions of government officials. There are different laws and procedures for each. With regard to the individual police officers, there is a cause of action under the Torture Victim Protection Act.

"That part of the case is pretty straightforward," Leslie continued. "We would have to prove that Sarah and her husband were tortured by official representatives of the Saudi government. We could recover against those persons who performed the torture and against any higher-ups who authorized, tolerated, or willingly ignored these acts."

"Sounds good to me," Brad quipped. "Where do I sign up?"

Leslie risked looking Brad in the eye again. "As you know better than anyone, the issue is not whether you can get a verdict, but whether you can collect against the defendants. Even if you can pinpoint the police officers who were involved, they probably don't have a dime to their names. And you can't even try to collect against them unless they have property in the United States or enter the country personally."

"What about Prince Asad?" Brad asked. "There's no one I would rather sue . . . with the possible exception of Bill Gates."

"There is no indication that the prince either authorized or sanctioned this conduct," Leslie said in her best professional mode, trying hard to burst Brad's bubble. "The real issue is whether you could win a judgment against the government of Saudi Arabia for the actions of their agents."

"I'm pretty sure the Saudis have the bucks to satisfy any billion-dollar verdict we might get." Brad shooed away the waiter who was coming to refill their drinks. "So what's the answer?"

"I think it's a loser, Brad." Leslie knew it was not good news, and she liked him too well to sugarcoat it. "Foreign countries and their agencies have enjoyed immunity from suit in American courts since 1812 with only a few minor exceptions. And none of them apply here." She stopped abruptly. Brad was leaning forward, chin propped on both hands, looking directly at her. She found it hard to read his eyes. "Is this boring you?"

"Not at all," he said, then smiled. "I was just thinking how much I could use someone like you to help research some of the issues I'm constantly running up against. You sound like an encyclopedia."

"Thanks. I think." She couldn't help but blush. She felt like a schoolgirl with a wicked crush. *I don't even know this guy!*

She cleared her head of these distracting emotions—purposefully, clinically, she willed herself to disregard them—and continued with her rehearsed synopsis of sovereign immunity law. "In 1976 Congress codified the issue of sovereign immunity with the Foreign Sovereign Immunity Act. That law basically provides that foreign governments cannot be sued in U.S. courts unless one of five exceptions applies."

Brad's eyes lit up. "Loopholes are my specialty." He smiled playfully.

Leslie maintained her game face. "Maybe so, but I doubt any of these exceptions would apply. The Reeds are not the first U.S. citizens to be tortured by another country. Let me put it this way: if the Nazi holocaust victims could not successfully sue under this act in New York City, it's hard to think we could do it here in the conservative federal courts of Norfolk, Virginia."

Brad fell silent and stared pensively at the ships motoring slowly by on the Lynnhaven. Leslie thought she perceived a slight sag in his shoulders.

Brad turned from the horizon and picked at his food. "If you had to file suit on the Reed case, if you had no choice but to file suit, what approach would you take?"

Leslie furrowed her brow and took her turn staring at the river. "I would argue the implicit waiver clause—that when other nations torture U.S. citizens in violation of *jus cogens* norms, they waive their immunity from suit. This theory has never been squarely addressed by the U.S. Supreme Court. I would stress the fact that Charles and Sarah Reed were U.S. citizens tortured for religious reasons and that our courts have a special role to play when the fundamental rights of U.S. citizens are involved."

Brad thought about this for a moment. "Oh, you mean the Strobel argument."

Leslie winced. "Yeah, I guess so. But I'd prefer not to call it that."

"Call it anything you want, as long as it works."

"I didn't say it would work. Only that it was our best argument."

"What are our chances?" Brad asked. He sat up straighter, taking a big bite of a crab-cake sandwich. "I'm ready."

"What?"

He chewed for a minute, then swallowed hard. He chased the sandwich with a gulp of tea. "I said . . . I'm ready. I just want to know what our chances are."

Leslie put down her fork. This was not going as she had planned. "Nearly impossible. Didn't you hear me? Brad, every effort by every lawyer to haul a foreign government into court based on human rights violations for the past hundred years has been unsuccessful. And there are lots of cases with facts every bit as horrible as yours."

She said it with an edge. And either the tone or the bluntness of the assessment caused a long silence between the two. Leslie became uncomfortable and resumed working on her meal. Brad gazed down the river some more.

After what seemed like an eternity, he spoke. "There's got to be a first time," he mumbled.

"What do you mean by that?"

"Leslie, with every new breakthrough for justice, there's got to be a first time. How do you think we got our civil rights laws? Some lawyers were sitting around, just like we are today, knowing they had justice on their side, but not the law. That didn't stop them, because they knew the law was meant to serve justice, not the other way around. I know this may sound corny, but it's true. Ninety-nine percent of the lawyers in the world see the law as it is, but the few really great ones see the law as it ought to be."

Brad spoke as if the law were a sacred thing. He leaned forward, his voice reverent, barely above a whisper, and suddenly Leslie saw Bill leaning toward her, his voice coming out of the past full of captivating idealism. She gasped before she could stop herself.

"What is it?" he asked.

Leslie felt her cheeks grow hot. "Nothing," she murmured. "You were saying?"

Brad now focused on the horizon and continued in the same passionate tone. "Most lawyers think the laws are written in law books, but a few lawyers understand that the fundamental laws of justice are carved deep in the human spirit, that the law books just try to capture those transcendent laws that are already there. And when the laws on the books don't match what justice requires, you change the laws on the books, not the definition of justice.

"You wait your whole career for a case like this. There's got to be a first time, Leslie. And I think this case just might be it."

Brad finished his impromptu speech, and more silence followed. He fixed his gaze on Leslie, beseeching her with his steel blue eyes. It was, without a doubt, one of the most intense looks she had ever experienced—one of the most intense feelings she had ever felt.

She couldn't look away.

Get a grip, Connors, she told herself. *It's just a case. It's not a crusade, and it won't bring world peace. He's just another guy.*

Yeah, right.

"If I decide to go tilting after these windmills," Brad was asking, "will you join me? I could really use your help on the research. And I'll pay twenty bucks an hour."

Leslie had predicted this scenario. She had practiced saying no the entire trip from Williamsburg to Virginia Beach. She had finals coming up and the trip to England. It was not a good time.

"Thanks for the offer, Brad. But I just can't . . . I don't have time." She looked down at her food; it had not moved. "I promised myself I would study abroad this summer, then slow down some my third year and enjoy law school. I just . . . I don't know . . ."

Her voice trailed off, and she knew she had left the door open, cracked ever so slightly. It was not part of the plan.

Brad apparently sensed it too. "Law school will always be there. England can wait. But this case—" He paused. "A case like this comes around once, maybe twice, in a lifetime. Don't you see it? The moot court argument. Sarah Reed just walking into my office on another matter. It's destiny, Leslie. You can't say no to destiny."

Brad was playing hardball, but Leslie had steeled herself. Sure, she would like nothing more than to work on a potentially groundbreaking case. But she had already decided. She had other plans. Plans that had been two years in the making. Plans that would cause less pain than working on a case for another widow—a case that would remind her every step of the way of the devastating loss of her own husband. And she couldn't throw out her plans just because some irresistible man across a lunch table asked her to.

Could she?

"Okay," she said, stunned by her own words. "But I'm worth at least fifty an hour."

Brad smiled broadly, white teeth flashing, and lifted his tea glass for a toast.

"Deal," he said. "You can start Monday."

Leslie touched his glass gingerly with her own, convinced she had just made a huge mistake.

◁ ▷

The driver of the large rig had been at it for twenty-two straight hours. His logs would say differently, of course, so that his company would not be cited for violating FTC regulations. The money was good, but he was getting too old for this. He would dump his load at the depot on Military Highway, then push on through to a rest area outside Richmond.

It was warm for an April night, so he kept his windows down. The fresh air would help keep him awake, keep the heavy eyelids open, and might even help him shake off those brews he had thrown down at the truck stop in Suffolk. He was pretty sure he had stopped after two or three, nothing he couldn't handle, nothing he hadn't handled before.

Blasts from a car horn stunned him awake. He jerked his head up just in time to see the driver of the car, wide-eyed, looking out the driver's side window in horror at the truck careening toward him . . . felt a jolt, heard the surreal sound of shattering glass and smashing metal and the sickening thud of a car under the truck chassis.

◁ ▷

Nikki Moreno heard it on her police scanner. A bad accident, possible fatality, at the intersection of Military Highway and Battlefield Boulevard—less than four blocks away. With any luck, she could beat the police to the scene.

She wasn't dressed for this. It was Friday night, and she had gone straight from the beach to the parties. She was wearing shorts, a bikini top, and sandals. It would have to do.

She reached under the seat and pulled out a half-empty bottle of Jack Daniels. She made a mental note to replenish her stock. You never knew when opportunity might knock.

"Hang in there, pal, you've got to pull through," she mumbled to herself as she gunned the engine. "You're never worth as much dead."

8

EVEN BELLA HAD TO ADMIT the case sounded good. The caller was Ralph Johnson, who had first come to Brad five years ago after losing two fingers in a saber-saw accident. Bella remembered how Brad had parlayed those two fingers into a nifty structured settlement with a total payout of more than $150,000. After Brad took his third, Johnson would have had enough for a down payment on a new home. In his euphoria, and without even consulting his wife, Ralph decided to get a new pickup, stay in the run-down shack they lived in, and have a little money on the side to party.

Five years later, the party money was gone, and the house was feeling cramped, but the pickup was still going strong. Like a rock. Ralph never regretted the way he spent his windfall.

Now Ralph called from the bedside of his brother Frank at Norfolk General Hospital. Misfortune had again visited the Johnson family, and Ralph was hoping Brad could find another pile of cash to ease the pain. Frank had had the bad luck of navigating an intersection at the same time a sleeping drunk driver in an 18-wheeler blew through a red light and demolished Frank's vehicle. Ralph was sure this was a case for Brad Carson.

Upon learning the facts, Bella transformed herself into a sugary-sweet grief counselor. But she had a hard time disguising the glee in her voice as she offered Ralph and his brother her deepest condolences. She assured them that Brad would be on the way immediately. Justice would be done. The jerk who caused this terrible tragedy would pay. Dearly.

She talked of justice, but she thought about cash. The case was a gold mine. By the time she hung up the phone, she was practically drooling.

◁▷

Brad took the call from Bella on his cell phone and was at the hospital in a flash. He waited briefly for the elevator, lost patience, then bounded up the stairs to the third floor, where Frank Johnson was being treated. He took the stairs two at a time, his feet barely touching the floor, the adrenaline pumping. He always felt this way when he landed a promising new case.

This feeling, this sense of excitement at someone else's misfortune, always prompted a bout of guilt followed by the same Brad Carson pep talk. The practice of law was so competitive, he reminded himself, there was nothing wrong with feeling good about landing a new case. After all, the damage had already been done, and *someone* needed to help the man get the money he deserved to get on with his life. Brad was convinced that nobody could do that better than he could. Apparently Frank's brother agreed. Brad worked hard and got an honest referral. No need to feel bad about that.

Brad put on his best look of professional compassion and stepped inside the door to Frank Johnson's room. He surveyed the small crowd of people and immediately sensed that something was wrong. Frank was lying uncomfortably in traction, hooked up by tubes to a computer contraption that monitored his vitals and fed him intravenous fluids. Frank's wife sat by his bedside, holding his hand. Ralph stood next to her with downcast eyes. All of this was typical of the hospital room of an injured client. But the woman with her back to the door was the source of Brad's discomfort. She was clearly not medical personnel, and Brad sensed trouble.

Ralph sheepishly introduced the stranger as Nikki Moreno, a paralegal for Billy "the Rock" Davenport.

Brad extended his hand to Nikki. In her other hand, and clearly visible to Brad, was a typed contract for legal services. At the bottom of a full page of small print was a signature that Brad assumed belonged to Frank Johnson.

Brad gave her hand a menacing squeeze. Nikki lifted an eyebrow.

She did not look the part of a professional. She was thin—too thin for Brad's taste—and all legs, which she showed off with a tight miniskirt and three-inch heels. Nikki apparently believed that the gods of style required her to lavishly decorate and puncture her smooth olive skin with a small tattoo on her ankle, a more prominent one on her left shoulder, a pierced navel clearly visible under her cropped blouse, and numerous holes in her ears. Despite her over-the-top presentation, Nikki's face had an exotic Latino allure that came from sharp, angular bones, deeply tanned skin, long black hair, and dark brown eyes—accentuated with generous amounts of dark eye shadow.

Brad immediately determined he would not be outhustled by a legal assistant for a second-rate ambulance chaser like the Rock. "What are you doing here?" he asked bluntly.

"Our firm represents Frank Johnson. What are *you* doing here?" Nikki fired back.

Brad shot a glance at Ralph Johnson. Ralph pinned his eyes to a spot on the floor.

"Mr. Johnson—" Brad pointed to Ralph—"called *me* to see if I could help his brother the same way that I helped him. I didn't know that you were tailgating the ambulance to the hospital."

"It's not my fault you're a day late and a dollar short," Nikki retorted. She turned to Mrs. Johnson. "Brad's a pretty good lawyer who could do a pretty good job if this were a garden-variety personal injury case. But he works alone. In a complicated case involving serious injuries, you'll be better off with the resources of a firm like Davenport & Associates."

Brad snorted. "Your boss doesn't know the first thing about trying cases." He turned from Nikki to Ralph. "Tell your brother about our case, Ralph. Tell him how a real lawyer operates."

All eyes turned to Ralph, who was still mesmerized by the spot on the floor. He stood silent and unmoving, like a statue.

"A real lawyer," Nikki interjected, "does not act up so bad in court that he gets thrown in jail in the middle of his client's case. It's hard to be effective for your client when you're sitting in jail."

"I wasn't talking to you," Brad snapped.

The statue cleared his throat. "It's like this," Ralph said haltingly. "Ms. Moreno, here, brings some things to the case that no other firm brings. She can help us prove the other driver was drunk. She's an eyewitness to his drinking—"

"I can always subpoena her," Brad interrupted. "I'm telling you, Ralph, you don't want Davenport trying your brother's case. The other side will laugh all the way to a defense verdict."

"You can't subpoena me if I'm representing the truck driver," Nikki said, raising her voice. She waved the paperwork under Brad's nose. "And believe me, if Mr. Johnson reneges on this contract, the truck driver will hire me in a heartbeat."

Brad rolled his eyes. "If you're a witness, I'll subpoena you. And why would the truck driver hire *you*?"

Brad knew this argument between him and a second-class paralegal was totally undignified. *But what are my options? Let her steal the case so the Rock can sell out Frank for a quick and easy settlement?*

Not in a million years.

A nurse wearing the most severe scowl imaginable stepped between Brad and Nikki—*where did she come from?*—and unceremoniously asked them to leave the room. "My patient has enough trauma in his life right now," she said scornfully. "Why don't you take your little disagreement into the hallway?"

Chastised and feeling like a total idiot, Brad murmured an apology to the family, flashed another angry glare at Nikki, and walked quickly from the room.

Nikki followed.

"What a coincidence," Brad lectured, "that you just *happened* upon this accident and *happened* to witness the other driver slamming down a few drinks. What do you do, spend all night listening to a police scanner, waiting for some poor soul to get killed or injured? I ought to report you to the bar."

Nikki just stood there, staring at Brad.

"Are you finished?" she said at last.

"For now."

"Good, because then maybe you'll listen. We were doing just fine here until you showed up, hotshot. If you don't mind, I'm going to go back in there to confer with my client. You, by the way, are not invited." She turned on her heel.

Brad saw his window of opportunity closing quickly. He could not stand the thought of a hapless lawyer like the Rock representing Frank Johnson. He had to do something. Fast.

"Wait," Brad said. "We've both been called on this case." He paused. He was having difficulty forcing out this next sentence. "Let's work as co-counsel and split the fee."

Nikki stopped at the door and turned. She brushed her long dark hair back over her shoulder. If it was designed to impress, it didn't. Brad was already starting to hate himself for suggesting this pact with the devil.

Nikki glanced around the hallway and took a step toward Brad. "Okay, here's the scoop," she said in a hushed voice. "If you want a piece of this case, you hire me. It's a package deal. The case and I come together."

Brad was stunned. Slack-jawed. If he told her off, he would lose the case for sure.

"I did hear about this accident on the scanner," Nikki whispered. "I got to the scene before any help arrived. The other driver smelled like a brewery. I asked if he was okay. Somebody else was already helping Mr. Johnson. I looked into the truck and saw an open bottle of Jack Daniels. I told him I worked for a lawyer and suggested he have a drink to calm his nerves."

She paused, allowing the audacity of what she had done to sink in.

"I've been hanging with the Rock long enough to know the protocol. You tell a drunk driver at the scene to drink some more and then not talk to anyone. The blood-alcohol test will not be able to distinguish what percentage is due to alcohol consumed before the accident and how much is due to alcohol consumed after the accident and before the police arrived. The only person who knows how much the truck driver drank after the accident, as opposed to before the accident—" Nikki again paused and checked the hallway, looking this way and that—"is me. That's why both you and Mr. Johnson need me on this case."

Brad just stood there, shaking his head, condemning her with his eyes. He had never seen such outrageous conduct.

"Of course," Nikki continued, "I didn't want to see the guy get away with drunk driving, so I came over here as soon as Mr. Johnson could have visitors. I told Mr. and Mrs. Johnson that if they retained our firm, I would be happy to testify on their behalf."

"That was big of you," Brad huffed.

"If the Johnsons decide to use some other firm—including yours," Nikki continued in her conspiratorial whisper, "I'll just give the truck driver a call, and he'll retain us. That way any information I have will either be protected by the attorney-client privilege or I'll just conveniently forget it."

"You've got no morals," Brad said, stating the obvious.

"Says the man who purposefully baits a judge and gets himself thrown in jail."

"That's different."

Nikki shrugged. "Whatever." She smiled. "My morals are beside the point. I'm not stupid. I've got a case you want, and you need a good paralegal." She looked down the hallway one more time. The coast was still clear. "And if you repeat this, I'll deny I ever said it—but I also know you're ten times the lawyer Davenport ever dreamed of being. Take the deal, Carson."

Brad did some quick math in his head. Even if he gave Nikki a huge salary out of his one-third contingency fee, he would still turn a handsome profit. If he didn't like her work, he could fire her. If she was good, he did need a paralegal, and he could sure use a hustler like Nikki. But he would lay down some strict ethical guidelines on acceptable behavior in soliciting cases.

"Here's the deal," Brad said. "I can't give you a percentage of the case because it's unethical to give a nonlawyer a percentage for bringing a case to the firm. And despite the way you operate, some of us still believe the ethical rules that govern lawyers ought to be followed every once in a while. But if you bring this case to our firm, and you agree to abide by our code of conduct, I'll give you a one-year contract for fifty thousand dollars." He frowned to emphasize his displeasure at making such a distasteful offer.

Nikki scoffed. "This case alone is worth half a million to your firm. And I can bring in a bunch of other cases like it. But I'm willing to prove myself in the first year." Nikki furrowed her brow and glanced at the contract in her hand, as if she were trying to calculate the combined worth of the contract and her own brilliance. "I'll come for a mere seventy-five thousand, plus a bonus if we do well on the Johnson case. We can talk about the amount of the bonus when we negotiate year two."

Brad pushed a sharp breath out through his nose, like she had just asked him for the Grand Canyon. He shook his head. "Sixty thousand."

Nikki didn't hesitate or blink. She just turned on her heel again and headed straight for the hospital room.

"Okay," Brad fumed. "Seventy-five."

She turned. "Plus medical benefits, parking, and a 401(k) plan."

"You're hired," Brad said quickly.

The two new partners walked down the hall to the waiting area and drew up a short contract on the back of the paper that Johnson had signed. The knot in the pit of Brad's stomach reminded him he would have to break this news to Bella. He prepared himself to offer her a raise.

"One more question," Brad said to Nikki as he signed the makeshift agreement. "Where did that truck driver really get the Jack Daniels?"

"If you want the answer to that one," Nikki said, smiling, "you'll have to give me a raise."

Just as Brad expected. He made a mental note to keep an eye on Nikki Moreno.

9

"I CAN'T DO IT," SARAH SAID. "I won't do it. It might endanger the members of our church still worshiping in Riyadh. It may hinder the efforts of the World Mission Society to send other missionaries. But most important, it would probably mean I could never go back to the Saudis again—never return to the people I love."

Brad shot a sideways glance at Leslie. He had not anticipated this reaction to his proposal that Sarah file suit against the Saudis as well as the insurance company. Brad had predicted Sarah would balk at the prospect of risking any money on the case, so he offered to take the case on contingency and fund the expenses strictly out of firm reserves. Sarah would pay absolutely no fee unless they recovered. But Brad never dreamed that Sarah would still object for philosophical reasons. Clients never objected to the potential for a huge recovery when lawyers took all the risks.

"Well," Brad said after a long silence. He stared at his legal pad on the conference room table. "Nobody is going to force you to file this case. But it seems to me that there are times to turn the other cheek and times to fight back." Brad made a desperate mental search for some biblical arguments, but his repertoire was limited to what little he could remember from his Sunday school days.

He vaguely remembered that Christ Himself got angry a time or two and beat up on some guys in the temple—he could recall the picture from his Bible. "I mean, even Christ turned over the tables on those men selling pigeons in the temple." He looked up and noticed Sarah trying to suppress a grin. Maybe he should stick to logic. "I think it all comes down to the greater good. You could go back into Saudi Arabia and reach dozens of people, maybe even hundreds, as a missionary. But what if this lawsuit resulted in real religious freedom in Saudi Arabia? How many Sarah Reeds could minister in the country then? And not under cover of darkness, but in the light of day. And what if this case results in similar cases against China and other repressive countries? Could it be that God is calling you to take this stand, at this time, to pave the way for thousands of others to go where they could never go before?"

Brad finished talking and waited patiently for Sarah's response. She was deep in thought, not smiling at all now. Leslie fixed her eyes on Sarah as well.

"Brad, I just don't know," Sarah replied tentatively. "I've got to have some time to think about it, pray about it. What you say makes sense, but only if we win. If we lose, it's not just a case, and it's not just money, it's my calling at risk. I could never go back. You can shake off the dust and move on to your next case. But I couldn't live with myself if I made it any harder on the converts in Saudi Arabia."

"What would Charles want?" Leslie asked softly.

Sarah studied her folded hands. "What would Jesus do? If I knew the answer to that question, then I'd know what Charles would want."

More silence followed. The threesome eventually agreed that Sarah would take a few days to think and pray. Leslie would start drafting the lawsuit just in case. Brad made a note to get his hands on a Bible and muster some support for the proposition that Jesus would have filed suit. But he had to admit, it seemed odd to imagine the Man who went without objection to His death on a cross filing suit over a human rights violation.

Brad didn't have the foggiest idea what Jesus would do. But he did know what he wanted to do. He had to get Sarah's permission to file this case. And he had to find a way to win.

◁▷

Nikki enjoyed the first five minutes of her new job. She spent the time unpacking her personal belongings in her new office, waiting for Brad to arrive with instructions.

But at 8:35 Nikki's solitude was shattered when a thick woman in a foul mood parked herself at Nikki's office door. She stood there with one hand on her hip, the other handling a cigarette, while she huffed and puffed about the traffic, the miserable weather, and the other evils of living in Tidewater. "You must be Nikki Moreno," she finally said, her voice filled with scorn.

"Yep," Nikki replied. "Do you mind putting out that cigarette while you're standing in my office?"

Bella pointed out that she was not technically in Nikki's office, and even if she were, she'd put the cigarette out when she darn well pleased. Nikki pointed out that Bella was the only person she knew who was big enough to be technically in Nikki's office at the same time that she was technically in the hallway and technically in the reception area. The conversation went downhill from there.

They argued about the evils of smoking and the danger of secondhand smoke. They argued about whether Bella would do Nikki's typing and answer her phone. They argued about whether miniskirts were appropriate office attire. Bella told Nikki she was so thin she looked sick. Nikki said at least nobody had mistaken her for a beached whale lately. In honor of Nikki's tattoos, Bella called her "the Dragon Lady." In turn, Nikki dubbed Bella "Willy," in honor of the famous orca.

◁▷

By the time Brad arrived, the two women were almost at blows. "I see you two lovebirds have met," Brad said. "Bella. My office—now!"

Brad spent the rest of the morning talking both women out of quitting. By noon he was nursing a splitting headache. As expected, Bella demanded and received a raise, even though she was already probably the highest-paid legal secretary in all of Tidewater.

Even after the raise, Bella told Brad she just couldn't understand why she should be making less than the arrogant and inexperienced Nikki Moreno. Especially, Bella claimed, since her mom was in a nursing home and Bella had to single-handedly pay all the bills. Bella had used the same sympathy ploy for the last two years.

Later that afternoon, Brad heard Bella calling the office-supply company and ordering a brass nameplate for Nikki's office with "the Dragon Lady" etched in black. When he poked his head into Nikki's office, he saw her hanging up framed pictures of dolphins and whales that she had picked up on her lunch break at the mall, as if she had always been an ardent fish lover.

The psychological warfare was well under way.

◁▷

Sarah plopped down on the worn recliner in the small family room. It was nearly 10:30, and there was still so much to do before she could crawl into bed. Two more loads of laundry, dirty dishes all over the kitchen, lunches to get ready for school tomorrow, bills to pay that should have been sent yesterday—well, actually last week.

This was not the way she wanted to end her day. Meredith had just copped an attitude and been sent to her room. The walls were thin in this single-story ranch house, and now Sarah could hear the music from Meredith's CD player infiltrating every nook of living space. Before long, Steven would probably come out of his room and complain he couldn't sleep. Then there would be another battle with Meredith, who had grown increasingly distant and rebellious since Charles's death.

Sarah didn't know if she could take one more battle. Not tonight.

She sighed heavily and reached for the worn Bible—Charles's old Bible—sitting on a small coffee table, right where she had left it two days ago. When Charles was alive, they had devotions together nearly every morning, when they were fresh. Now she struggled to get out of bed in the morning, already running behind, and she would not get to her devotions until the evening. She often couldn't stay awake for the duration.

Before she began, she prayed the same little prayer she always did. "Lord, show me something from this Book tonight that is just for me . . . as I live for You."

She picked up her reading in the book of Acts. Chapter by chapter. The difficulties that Paul faced and his obedience to his mission in the face of extreme trouble inspired Sarah and made her long for the mission field again. She would go back some day. She loved the Saudi people so much.

She started relaxing as she read God's Word, and her eyelids became heavy. Paul had been arrested, for about the third or fourth time, for preaching the gospel, and he was being tried in front of some Roman governor named Felix. As usual, Paul was giving the governor fits, as he defended himself and witnessed about Christ and the Resurrection. Sarah's mind started to wander, imagining the bandy-legged little Paul, dwarfed by the grandeur of this Roman tribunal, wagging his finger at the great Felix and telling him about the resurrection of the dead. She could see the astonished looks on the faces of the Roman dignitaries as this ornery little Jewish man made his case. Sarah's eyes were blinking more slowly now, the music from Meredith's room drifting into the background, and the words on the page in front of her blurring into a sea of black ink.

And then a tiny phrase jumped off the page. "I appeal to Caesar," Paul said. The words pierced through the fog of impending sleep and slapped

Sarah awake. "I appeal to Caesar," Paul insisted. And then Festus answered, "You have appealed to Caesar? To Caesar you shall go!"

She sat up straight in the chair, her eyes wide.

The words spoke to Sarah, shouted to her from two thousand years ago and half a world away, as if Paul himself were in her family room at that very moment. "I appeal to Caesar."

Suddenly, Sarah was energized. She couldn't read fast enough. Why did Paul appeal to Caesar? Didn't he just want to get back to the mission field? Didn't he know that appealing to Caesar could take years away from his work? Why was this man, who rejoiced when he was abused for the sake of Christ, suddenly so insistent about his legal rights?

She stood up from the chair, gathered a pen and tablet, and cleared herself a place at the kitchen table. She made some quick notes and outlined the history of Paul's legal troubles and options. She read earlier chapters to put it in context. More notes. More excitement. She was onto something. The answer was here, somewhere.

Some time and several pages of notes later, she found the answer in the ninth chapter of Acts, right after Paul had been converted from a persecutor of the church to a missionary. She had read it so many times before, but she had never seen it. At least not like this.

The Lord called Paul a "chosen vessel" and said that Paul would "bear My name before Gentiles, kings, and the children of Israel. For I will show him how many things he must suffer for My name's sake."

There it was! Her answer. God had given Paul a threefold mission. To share with the children of Israel, which Paul did when he preached at Jerusalem. To share with the Gentiles, which Paul did when he planted churches all over Asia Minor. But Paul also had a mission to share with kings. And how did Paul do this? Through the court system! The Sanhedrin, Governor Festus, King Agrippa, and ultimately to the leading ruler himself—Caesar!

Paul's plea wasn't about winning or losing. He wasn't plotting some kind of legal strategy. In fact, Acts ended with Paul imprisoned in Rome, ready to testify before Caesar. How that trial ended, who knows?

But Paul fulfilled his mission.

To the children of Israel, Sarah thought, Paul's own people. In her case, these would be the Americans. To the Gentiles, foreigners despised by Paul's people. These would be the Saudis. And the kings, the court officials. They would be the federal court judges, the world's media, and the leaders of nations as they followed this international case through the eyes of the world's press.

A threefold mission.

"I appeal to Caesar," Sarah said solemnly.

Without bothering to check the clock, she picked up the phone and dialed Brad.

10

LESLIE FILED THE SUIT PAPERS when Norfolk Federal Court opened for business on Good Friday. The timing was Brad's idea. The press would be looking for some good religious news on Easter weekend. Brad was more than happy to oblige. The poisoning of the jury pool had begun.

The suit was a whopper. It spanned an impressive fifty-six pages, encompassing seven separate causes of action and containing enough *whereas*, *heretofore*, and *hereinabove* clauses to choke a horse. Leslie's masterpiece contained impressive citations of various international human rights laws as well as graphic references to specific acts of torture inflicted on the Reeds that would be good grist for the papers.

The suit named the nation of Saudi Arabia as a defendant and at least nine separate John Does, references to the unknown individuals who had assaulted Sarah and killed Charles.

After detailing the heinous conduct of the Saudi officials for more than fifty-five pages, Leslie demanded, in capital letters, the handsome sum of ONE HUNDRED FIFTY MILLION DOLLARS as compensatory and punitive damages.

The suit requested trial by jury on the counts against the individuals and trial by judge on the count against Saudi Arabia. Brad insisted they file in Norfolk, home of the famed "rocket docket," where cases were always tried within six months of filing. Brad also wanted to file in Norfolk because the court had a legacy of gutsy judges who made tough calls on racial-integration cases. Although those judges had since retired, Brad hoped to tap into this legacy of pioneering civil rights decisions.

While Leslie filed the suit, Nikki hand-delivered courtesy copies to the local newspapers and television stations. Both women returned to the office to help answer the phones. Leslie smiled as she listened to Nikki act surprised at all the media attention.

By noon, the phones were ringing off the hook. Local network affiliates wanted interviews; the newspaper wanted a comment. Even the Associated Press called with a few clarifying questions. It was heady stuff for Nikki and Bella, but poor Brad was mired in a medical malpractice deposition with a cantankerous defense lawyer paid by the hour who had no intention of finishing early.

At 12:30 the defense lawyer came up for air, and Brad sprinted out of the room to claim his rightful place in the spotlight. He called the newspaper first and spent the next thirty minutes explaining the case and waxing eloquent about the importance of international religious freedom. His opening statement in this case would start long before the jury ever assembled.

Brad ran out of time in his lunch hour before he ran out of interview opportunities. He told Leslie he was going to make her a star. He had Bella schedule a press conference for the local television stations for 4 p.m. Leslie would experience media baptism by fire.

Brad was right. Good Friday was a slow news day. National networks picked up Leslie's earnest face and lawyerly remarks from the local affiliates. Soon the cable networks picked up the story, and Leslie's face could be seen both at her apartment in Williamsburg and around the world on CNN.

Leslie watched her debut with Brad that evening on the local network affiliates. A few friends called to say they thought she came off cool and sophisticated. A professor left a message suggesting next time she should clarify she was only a law student. Brad heaped praise on her and toasted her brilliance.

Later that night, Leslie took a tape of the newscasts back to her apartment and replayed it several times. She was brutal in her analysis of her own premiere. She promised herself to do better next time.

◁▷

Frederick Barnes, a short bowling ball of a man who ran a Washington-based "consulting firm," made a small fortune from his Saudi account alone. Barnes took great pride in representing a stable of unsympathetic clients with deep pockets and a willingness to pay almost any price for services and information that fell just short—in Barnes's opinion—of espionage or treason. He knew how to navigate the seedy underbelly of Beltway politics in a way that generally pleased his clients and lined his pockets.

Not all his clients were satisfied customers. Ahmed Aberijan had not been on the phone long before Barnes concluded he would have to find satisfaction in taking Ahmed's money even as he endured the Saudi's verbal abuse. One of Ahmed's men had seen reports on CNN of a lawsuit filed against the nation of Saudi Arabia. The suit alleged that the Muttawa tortured and killed an American missionary. All lies, according to Aberijan.

Incensed and derisive, Aberijan spent most of the call railing at Barnes as if Barnes himself had filed the lawsuit. When he finished venting, Ahmed outlined several schemes designed to quash the lawsuit in its infancy. Even with Ahmed's invectives ringing in his ears, Barnes tried to focus on the merits of the plans Ahmed outlined. Barnes had to admit he was impressed with both the complexity and temerity of the plans hatched by this Saudi Arabian hothead on such short notice.

◁▷

Ahmed hung up and placed a call directly to the office of the crown prince. Prince Asad agreed that the case must be contained. The prince had no desire to dirty his hands in the details of the case. Ahmed would take the point. The official statement from the crown prince would reiterate his confidence in and support of the Muttawa. The crown prince would again express his sorrow that an American citizen had died after an unfortunate but unavoidable arrest. Prince Asad would make no other statement about the case and had no intention of answering questions from anyone.

Ahmed was instructed to keep the crown prince informed as the case progressed, and Ahmed knew how to read between the lines of that order. His job was to win the case at any cost, and it would be better if the crown prince did not know the details of what that might entail.

The first phone call between Ahmed and the crown prince on this subject would also be their last.

◁▷

Within twenty-four hours, Barnes called Ahmed back with his first task accomplished.

"I found just the lawyer," Barnes reported. "He knows international law, he's ruthless, and he's rumored to play dirty when necessary."

"Perfect," Ahmed replied.

11

THE MONDAY OF HER SECOND WEEK at Carson & Associates, Nikki burned up the phone lines talking to friends. As usual, she closed her office door, both to keep Bella from prying into her personal business and as a buttress against the cigarette smoke that wafted in whenever Bella came within spitting distance.

The phone calls were, of course, done on company time. Nikki believed it critical, for a variety of business reasons, to stay plugged in to the paralegal rumor network.

"No way!" Nikki exclaimed. She wore a headset and spoke into a small mike hanging on an attached wire, freeing both hands to type an e-mail to another friend. "Who told you that?"

"I heard it from Jessica, that new paralegal at the Jones firm. She's good friends with Marisa, who, as you know, has a thing going with a certain unnamed partner at Kilgore & Strobel."

"You mean a certain unnamed partner with wavy dark hair, broad shoulders, two BMWs, and a cute little tush?"

"You didn't hear that from me."

"Hear what?" Nikki laughed.

Her friend cackled, then started off on another story of romance and intrigue. But this time Nikki wasn't listening.

She was already formulating a plan.

◁▷

By the time he finally touched down in Norfolk, Ahmed was irritable and exhausted. The flight from Riyadh to Norfolk took a full nine hours. Even on board the Saudi government's luxury jet, he felt cornered and caged. At least he wasn't flying with the unwashed masses on a cramped commercial airline.

The unimpressive size of the Norfolk airport surprised Ahmed. He found it hard to believe that the mighty government of Saudi Arabia was being forced to answer groundless legal allegations in a city like this.

The palpable decadence of the American people threatened to smother him. He could see it in the magazine and bookracks, in the billboards lining the concourse, in the spring dress of the women. In his country, women saved themselves for the pleasure of their husbands. Here the women seemed to strut, to advertise themselves, to dominate the men. Surely it was only a matter of time before Allah judged this pagan culture.

Ahmed would spend as little time here as possible. And he would hate every minute of it.

Tidewater was hot, but he could handle hot. The humidity, however, threatened to undo him. Though it was nearly ten in the evening in the first week in May, Ahmed's short walk caused him to break a sweat. He enjoyed nothing about America. Except, perhaps, the ease with which he might successfully execute his plan.

◁▷

At five minutes after ten, Nikki's cell phone rang. The caller identified himself as Johnny, the desk clerk at the Marriott.

"He's here," Johnny whispered. "His name is Ahmed Aberijan, and he has checked in for just one night. As we discussed, I cannot give you his room number."

"You're a sweetheart," Nikki said, also in hushed tones. "Did he sign the paperwork?"

"How 'bout that!" Johnny exclaimed. "It seems I forgot to have him sign the rate sheet."

"I'll be there in twenty minutes."

Nikki hung up the phone and grinned at her luck.

Eighteen minutes later she entered the spacious lobby of the Marriott and glanced in Johnny's direction. After she caught his eye, she crossed the lobby to the winding, open staircase on the other end that ascended to the second-floor restaurant and bar. She climbed the stairs and crouched behind the railing, where she could inconspicuously observe the first floor and the check-in desk. She winked at her new friend behind the desk, and he picked up the phone.

When Johnny finished his call, he gave her a thumbs-up. She crouched down, eyeballed the elevator, and waited.

A few minutes later, the elevator door opened, and Ahmed stepped out, heading straight for the front desk. Nikki watched an animated discussion between Ahmed and the clerk, voices raised, hands expressing frustration. Finally, Ahmed leaned over and signed the cards with a flourish, threw his pen down on the counter, and turned around. In one quick motion, he glanced around the enormous lobby and then up, looking straight in Nikki's direction. She ducked, hugging her knees behind the railing.

Even as she held her breath, not daring to look, she realized how much she loved this element of risk and danger.

Ahmed would be out of range in a matter of seconds. If he saw her, she was history. If he didn't, she must work quickly.

She exhaled quietly and raised her head just over the railing. He had leveled his gaze and was crossing the lobby. She raised herself up a few more inches. He kept walking, unaware of her. *There. Keep going. Don't look up now, buddy.* A few more steps and he would be in the crosshairs.

She focused, aimed, squeezed her finger, and took three shots head-on.

◁▷

Rasheed Berjein responded quickly to the secret knock. The special sequence and rhythm always made his heart beat faster. His mind raced with expectancy and with dread. It could be another visitor, any one of a number of people he had mustered the courage to tell about this worship service. Or it could be the Muttawa. They had infiltrated the church once. There was no guarantee they would not do so again.

Rasheed looked through the peephole.

To his great surprise, the eyes that greeted him belonged to his brother, Hanif. Rasheed had shared his faith with his family and mentioned these meetings, but so far they had responded with only scorn and ridicule. Still, he prayed for his family morning and night. And now this! With tears welling in his eyes, he flung open the door, threw his arms around Hanif's neck, kissing each cheek, and invited him in.

As Rasheed introduced his brother, he thought about the phone call many months ago that had already meant so much to the struggling Christian churches of Riyadh. Hanif, a police officer for the city, had learned about the planned raid by the religious police. Though Hanif detested the church his brother attended, he was still family. Hanif reluctantly tipped off Rasheed, who in turn called Sarah. It was the only thing that kept the Muttawa from discovering records in the Reeds' apartment exposing a whole network of churches. It was no stretch to say that Hanif had saved them.

And so, tonight, Rasheed wanted to return the favor. He wanted nothing more in life than to show his little brother a very different type of salvation.

◁▷

The Berjeins' living room boasted only sparse furniture—one old couch, a recliner, a rickety coffee table, and a wooden chair. Most guests sat on the floor. None noticed, or could even see, the small electronic listening device that Ahmed's men had placed on the underside of the couch. Nor did they notice a similar device stuck to the bottom of the kitchen table. Nor the device embedded in the receiver of the phone. As soon as Ahmed received word of the lawsuit, he'd instructed his men to plant similar devices in all the homes of the former members of the Reeds' small church.

Tonight's service would be special not only because Rasheed's brother was present, but also because the listening devices would transmit every word by shortwave radio to a nearby van where two of Ahmed's men would join the worship. The church in Riyadh now had an unplanned media ministry, but there was no chance that the sinners in the van would think of repenting. Instead, they recorded the service on state-of-the-art digital equipment and smiled. Ahmed would be pleased.

◁▷

On this night, with a family member present, Rasheed was more nervous than ever as he started preaching. His voice was hoarse and high, hardly recognizable in its nerve-induced tone. *It's so hard to share these things with my own brother. He knows me too well—knows every character flaw and shortcoming I have. How can I have any credibility with him?*

But as Rasheed talked, with the faithful church members spurring him on and muttering their *amen*s, he gained confidence and began focusing less on himself as the messenger and more on the message. He kept it simple and delivered it with a genuine sense of humility—one sinner to another, one blind beggar telling another blind beggar where to find bread.

Hanif responded immediately, with tears flooding his cheeks. Rasheed embraced him again with a huge bear hug of acceptance, making no effort to stem the tide of his own tears. Others formed a close circle around Hanif, reaching out to touch him as Hanif prayed a prayer of repentance and committed his life to Jesus Christ. By the time the last *amen* was uttered, there was not a dry eye in the place.

Rasheed felt like he was floating, and he couldn't stop himself from slapping Hanif on the back and exclaiming, "Unbelievable," over and over. *My brother! My own brother!* Rasheed thought, shaking his head. The entire group seemed caught up in the enthusiasm and soon broke into spontaneous praise songs. Nobody sang louder than Hanif, though he obviously didn't know the tunes. The service lasted thirty minutes longer than normal, and even then, Rasheed had to practically force the people out the door.

Hanif was the last to go. As he stood in the doorway, Rasheed grabbed him by both shoulders, squeezed tight as if making sure that this whole scene was real, then looked him square in the eye. "I love you, Brother," Rasheed said for the first time in his life.

The new convert glanced down at the floor. "Thanks," he said softly, fighting back more tears. Then he kissed Rasheed on both cheeks, smiled broadly, and disappeared into the night.

The door had hardly closed before Rasheed dropped to his knees in grateful prayer.

◁▷

The phone's harsh ring woke Sarah. She sat straight up in bed and tried to focus on the clock. It was nearly 11 p.m. She picked up the receiver before the phone could ring again and wake the kids.

"Hello."

"Sarah, this is Nikki Moreno, Brad's new paralegal. We spoke on the phone last week. Brad's out of town doing some depositions, and I've got something real important I need to discuss with you about your case. I can't talk about it over the phone. Can you wait up for another half hour or so?"

Sarah was bewildered. She could tell Nikki was calling from a cell phone. She didn't like the idea of this lady she had never met coming to her house in the middle of the night.

"Can't this wait till tomorrow morning?"

"It really can't, Sarah. When I explain it, you'll understand. It's like, you've got to trust me on this one. I promise I'll be there before midnight, okay?"

After a long pause, Sarah agreed. She hung up the phone and headed to the kitchen to fix a pot of coffee. She wondered what she had gotten herself into.

◁▷

Just before midnight, Nikki arrived at Sarah's home in a quintessential Chesapeake suburb, located on a small postage-stamp lot on one of the hundred cul-de-sacs in this residential neighborhood. Standard-issue beige vinyl siding and blue and red trim lined the "Great Bridge Special," so named because it had the same floor plan as a thousand other single-story ranch houses in the Great Bridge community. As she pulled into the driveway, Nikki reminded herself that she never wanted to live like this.

Sure, the houses here were a step up from the shacks in South Norfolk, where Nikki had spent her childhood. But inside the four walls, inside the *home*, the struggles would be the same—single parents, dysfunctional families, constant friction. As she walked from the driveway to the front stoop, Nikki found herself wondering how Sarah was really doing. Nikki knew how deceptive appearances could be.

Forbidden thoughts of her own childhood flooded forward, unleashed by subconscious forces beyond Nikki's control. But as she knocked quietly, she banished those thoughts completely. That was behind her. Ancient history. She had overcome.

"Hi," Sarah said, sticking out her hand and forcing a smile. She answered the door in some worn-looking pajamas, with a housecoat thrown over top. "Come on in."

The two women settled in at the kitchen table and got right down to business. Nikki declined coffee. What she really needed was hard liquor, but Sarah said she didn't even have beer.

"As you know, when we filed this case, we sued Saudi Arabia and nine John Does," Nikki explained. "The John Does were named to represent those men who actually abused you and killed your husband. We didn't name specific individuals because the U.S. courts would not have what lawyers call 'personal jurisdiction' over someone who had never actually been inside the United States. Under our Constitution, individuals can generally be served with a lawsuit only if they actually appear on U.S. soil. Does that make sense?"

"Not really," Sarah admitted. She looked bewildered and only half-awake.

"Anyway, here's the bottom line. I took some pictures tonight at the Marriott hotel in downtown Norfolk of a guy from Saudi Arabia who is here to meet with some lawyers. If you can identify him as one of your torturers, we can legally serve him with an amended complaint tomorrow while he's still in this country. That way, even if the judge throws out the case against the nation of Saudi Arabia, we can still proceed against this guy and the other John Does."

Nikki slapped the photos down on the table, proud of her handiwork. The zoom had worked nicely; you could see every wrinkle on the man's leathery face. You could see the hatred in the bloodshot eyes, the wiry black beard, the broad nose, and the dark eyebrows.

"The clerk said his name is Ahmed Aberijan," Nikki said. "Isn't he the head of the Muttawa?"

Sarah picked up the photos, and her hands began to tremble. Tears started rolling down her cheeks. She made no effort to stop them.

"Are you all right?" Nikki asked.

The question seemed to jar Sarah back to reality. She nodded a yes and took a few deep, jagged breaths.

"He was the leader," Sarah offered. "He's the one who told his men to strip me and search me." Her voice was hoarse with emotion, her gaze far away. "I'm sure he's the one who ordered Charles killed. I can't believe he has the audacity to come to this country as if it never happened."

"Then he would be John Doe number one in the lawsuit," Nikki said softly. She shifted in her seat, never taking her eyes off Sarah. "Here's what I'm going to do," Nikki said, as reassuringly as possible. "I'm going back to the office right now to rework this lawsuit. We will substitute Ahmed Aberijan for John Doe number one and file the amended complaint first thing in the morning. By noon, we will personally serve the amended complaint on Mr. Aberijan, and there will be no question as to whether he is subject to the jurisdiction of this court."

Sarah looked at Nikki with hollow eyes. Nikki dropped the professional demeanor and lowered her voice again. "Are you sure you're okay?"

Sarah pursed her lips, nodded her head slowly, and promised she would be fine.

◁▷

After Nikki left, Sarah slouched over the kitchen table and stared at her coffee. She was suddenly so very tired, so very lonely. The man in the photos had reached out and delivered a gut punch that knocked the wind out of her, destroying all of her heroic efforts to put this behind her.

She needed, at this moment perhaps more than any other, to be held by Charles. She missed him so very much. She could not go to bed, because closing her eyes would simply bring back the face of Ahmed Aberijan. The flashbacks would overcome her: the shattering front door . . . the men hitting Charles . . . the blood pooling on the kitchen floor . . . the stench of the man's sweat and breath as he manhandled her . . . the heinous laughs as they ripped off her clothes . . . the struggle . . . the blackness. The nightmares were always the same. The faces of the Muttawa, the bloodied face of Charles, his hand reaching for her but never quite connecting, then visions of the casket.

She gently whispered Charles's name, while the tears dripped off her chin and onto the table.

◁▷

Nikki called Bella on her cell phone as soon as she pulled out of the driveway. It was now after midnight.

"What?" Bella answered, always the charmer.

"I need you to come into the office right away. I'll meet you there in about fifteen minutes."

"Fat chance." Bella slammed down the phone.

Nikki hit Redial.

"What?"

"Bella, don't hang up; this is serious. It's about the *Reed* case. A guy named Ahmed Aberijan is in town—" Suddenly Nikki was listening to a dial tone. She hit Redial again. She would have slapped Bella if they were in the same room.

Bella didn't answer, but after five rings her answering machine kicked in. Nikki punched *1* to leave a message.

"Listen, you lazy slug. We have less than nine hours to prepare an amended complaint in the *Reed* case, file it, and have it served tomorrow on one of the jerks that tortured Sarah and killed her husband. I can't get access to the documents I need because they're on your hard drive. If I have to, I'll go in alone and retype everything, even if it takes me all night. But, Bella, I could really use your help. I wouldn't call you this late at night if I wasn't desperate."

When Nikki arrived at the office fifteen minutes later, Bella was already at her desk. One cigarette smoldered in the ashtray; a second hung from Bella's lips. She looked worse than usual, and for a fraction of a second, Nikki felt sorry for her.

"What took you so long?" Bella asked.

12

AT SEVEN THE NEXT MORNING, Nikki and Bella camped out in the Marriott lobby's overstuffed chairs with strong coffee and the local paper. Every twenty minutes or so, Bella slipped outside for another cigarette. Nikki was grateful to see another desk clerk in Johnny's place. She didn't want to start the day by breaking his heart.

At ten minutes before nine, Ahmed came out of the elevators carrying his briefcase. Nikki and Bella watched Ahmed go straight out the front door of the hotel, then followed him across the street, where he disappeared into the rotating door of the twenty-story office building immodestly labeled One Commercial Place. They entered the lobby just as Ahmed elbowed his way onto an elevator that serviced floors eleven through twenty. As the elevator doors closed, Ahmed and the other grim-faced office workers stared straight ahead.

Once the Saudi disappeared, Bella headed straight to federal court to file the amended complaint and obtain a service-ready copy to be handed to Ahmed. In the meantime, Nikki hunkered down for a stakeout in the lobby. She determined from the directory that Mack Strobel's office was on the twentieth floor. Though she couldn't be positive, the bigger-than-life Strobel was an obvious choice from the many lawyers at Kilgore & Strobel to handle such a high-profile case. She called the commercial airlines, posing as Ahmed's secretary, and determined that he was not flying commercial. With nothing left to do but wait, she bought a magazine from a small deli and studied the latest fashions, leaning against the wall but always keeping at least one eye on the elevator doors.

Less than an hour later, Bella returned with the necessary papers.

The two women would wait patiently for the chance to slap a $150 million lawsuit into the bloodstained hands of Ahmed Aberijan.

◁ ▷

Twenty stories up, Mack Strobel suddenly felt cramped in his large corner office. Despite its spacious decor and expensive Persian rugs, it did not come close to being big enough or plush enough to comfortably handle the egos that now filled the room. Mack had suggested just talking over the phone, but Frederick Barnes wouldn't hear of it. "The client wants to meet his lawyer face-to-face," Barnes had insisted.

Mack strategically suggested they work at the small round conference table in one corner of his office, immediately under the expansive picture of Strobel's alma mater, the Virginia Military Institute. He made the suggestion to Barnes, who translated the request to Ahmed, who nodded his assent.

As Mack warily took his seat, Barnes reached into his suit-coat pocket and pulled out a small plastic cylinder containing an expensive Cuban cigar. Barnes removed the cigar from its case, gently licked one end, and placed it in his mouth as he patted down his other pockets in an apparent search for a lighter.

Mack looked on in disgust. He would have let it slide if Barnes intended only to chew on the nasty thing. But Mack was a reformed smoker himself and considered it his mission in life to keep others from lighting up.

"The air breathers would appreciate it if you would refrain from smoking in here. That stuff'll kill ya, you know."

"I don't inhale," Barnes replied as he finally found his lighter and flicked it to life. "Besides, I didn't think I'd get any flack from the firm that represents Phillip Morris."

"If you don't inhale it, we'll have to," Strobel growled.

Barnes ignored him and watched with detached satisfaction as the cigar's sweet, putrid smell quickly engulfed the room.

Client or not, Barnes knew how to push all the wrong buttons. Mack pushed politeness aside. "Either put that thing out, or go find yourself another lawyer. If you represented Phillip Morris, you'd stop smoking too."

Slowly and deliberately, cigar hanging out of one corner of his mouth, Barnes stood and walked nonchalantly to the office door, opened the door, still puffing on his stogie, and smiled at Strobel's young assistant sitting at her desk.

"Got an ashtray?" Barnes asked.

"No, sir, but I can get one for you," Mack heard his assistant say.

Barnes just nodded and leaned against the doorframe, his eyes following the woman as she raced off down the hallway. She returned with a clear glass ashtray and offered it gingerly. He took it, turned to face Mack again, and begrudgingly ground his stogie into the glass. Barnes closed the office door, then slowly returned to his seat at the table, chewing on the cigar, and smiling broadly at Strobel.

In that moment, Mack resolved to cut Barnes out of the loop at the first opportunity. He would earn Aberijan's exclusive loyalty as the case progressed. Mack had seen it happen a thousand times; he could always earn the grudging respect of even the most hard-to-please clients. When he did, Barnes would become expendable, and Mack would set him up.

"You ought to try one," Barnes said, eyeing the unlit stogie as he twirled it around in his fingers.

"Let's get started," Mack replied gruffly. "Mr. Aberijan didn't call this meeting so we could discuss cigars."

For the next two hours, the men talked legal fees and strategy. Despite the rocky start, Mack soon negotiated a premium hourly fee for himself and the host of other lawyers who would work the case. Four hundred dollars an hour for Mack. A new record. A new cash cow. There would be excited whispering over the phone lines and in the hallways as Mack's legend grew. There would be joy at Kilgore & Strobel.

◁▷

In the lobby, Nikki fretted. Ahmed had disappeared into the elevator more than two hours ago. She knew his luggage was still at the hotel, and she was pretty sure he would have to come back through this lobby on his way out, but still the possibilities kept bubbling up in her brain.

What if someone from Kilgore & Strobel had seen her and Bella hanging out in the lobby? What if Ahmed took the stairs and slipped out one of the stairwell doors? What if he took the elevator down to the loading dock in the basement, where a car was waiting for him? What if, somehow, he just avoided Nikki altogether and made it back to Saudi Arabia without getting served?

How could she ever explain it to Sarah if Ahmed got away?

For reasons Nikki could not yet put her finger on, she knew the case had now become personal. Something had snapped in her when she saw Sarah's distressed reaction to Ahmed's photo. She had to serve this man. He had to be brought to justice. He must pay for what he had done to Sarah and undoubtedly to hundreds of others like Sarah.

He would not get away with it again; not on her watch.

Two hours was too long. She explained her plan to Bella, who immediately shook her head in protest.

◁▷

Twenty stories up the phone rang. Barnes watched Mack answer it in a huff. He enjoyed seeing lawyers flustered.

"I told you to hold my calls. You know I can't be interrupted in this meeting." Mack listened and frowned. "Okay, put her through." Another long pause while he listened some more. His voice dropped, but not out of Barnes's hearing. "Bring me a copy immediately. Thanks for the heads-up."

He put down the phone and looked at Barnes.

"We've got some trouble here," Mack said. "One of our paralegals just returned from federal court. It seems an amended complaint naming Mr. Aberijan as an individual defendant has been filed. The plaintiffs also requested process papers so that Mr. Aberijan can be served personally with the suit while he is on American soil. This is the very thing I was talking about earlier when I explained that Mr. Aberijan should stay out of the country from now on. We've got to get him back to his plane before the plaintiffs serve him."

Barnes spoke to Ahmed in Arabic. Ahmed nodded his head and responded vigorously.

"He left some items at the hotel," Barnes explained. "I can go pick those up if you can get him to the airport."

"I'll call a limo to meet us in the basement. We'll be at the airport in twenty-five minutes."

◁▷

Nikki got off the elevator at the twentieth floor and stepped onto the thick Persian rug of the reception area. Lavish testaments to the prowess and wealth of the boys at Kilgore & Strobel surrounded her. Polished oak floors, mahogany trim, stylish antique furniture. Even the receptionist, barricaded behind a beautiful oak workstation sporting the firm's gold logo, looked like she had just stepped off the cover of a fashion magazine.

She flashed Nikki a blinding white smile and asked with sickening sweetness, "May I help you?"

Nikki returned a smile with her own lips closed—no sense trying to compete with those teeth. "I've got an appointment with Mr. . . . um . . ." Nikki shook her head in frustration at her own stupidity. "I can't believe I forgot his name. . . . I was just in his office a few weeks ago."

The receptionist gave her a wary look.

"Oh, you know," Nikki continued, "I've got his name in here somewhere." She started opening up the manila envelope she was carrying. She read a few lines of one document. "Here it is . . . that's right. The guy I originally came to see was a Mr. Strobel—" she pointed down a hallway toward her left—"but then he hooked me up with the guy whose office was right next to his, and I can't remember his name . . ."

The receptionist checked some papers in front of her. "Actually, the office right next to Mr. Strobel is one of our female associates, Andrea Gates."

Of all the luck—the Kilgore firm couldn't have more than a couple female lawyers total, and one of them had to be next to Strobel.

"Are you sure—," the receptionist began.

"Which side of his office?" Nikki interrupted. "His office is in a corner, right?" *That's a safe bet.* She motioned to an area behind her, on the northwest corner of the building. *Where is Bella? What's taking her so long? Can't she even do a simple thing like—*

"Right, but it's this corner over here," the receptionist said helpfully, motioning to the southeast corner. Nikki gave her a puzzled expression and an innocent shrug.

"Okay . . . right," Nikki said, turning a half circle as if getting her bearings.

"And the guy next to him on the other hallway is Brett Aikens," the receptionist said. "I'll give him a call."

Don't bother, Nikki wanted to say. Instead, she forced out a thanks. Still no Bella. She'd kill her later.

"Your name?"

"Oh." The request caught Nikki off guard. She'd forgotten to plan an alias. In the pressure of the moment, she said the first thing that came to her mind. "Bella Harper."

"Thanks."

The receptionist called the lawyer, and to Nikki's great relief, he was not in. But Nikki insisted on waiting for him to return. It was a very important meeting, Nikki said. So she took a seat in the reception area, checked her watch, and began silently cursing Bella.

Five minutes later, precisely seven minutes behind schedule, Bella stepped off the elevators. Nikki picked up the manila envelope lying next to her on the floor.

The receptionist was on the phone and lifted a finger, indicating to Bella that she would be right with her. Bella glanced over at Nikki, who glared back, jaw clenched, showing her displeasure with the timing. Bella responded with a quick roll of her own eyes and a little headshake that just made Nikki steam even more.

"May I help you?" the receptionist asked.

"Yes, I'm Bella Harper, and I'm here—"

Nikki nearly jumped out of the chair. *What kind of idiot gives her own name when she's part of a scam and hasn't even been asked her name?*

The receptionist's puzzled look lasted only a moment, for in the very next instant a bigger problem demanded her immediate attention.

Bella clutched her chest and groaned loudly. The eyes of the receptionist widened. Bella's face turned red, and she began staggering, fighting for air. With a fitful gasp Bella collapsed in a heap on the floor, falling thunderously and gloriously on the Persian rug, then flopping on her side, still clutching at her chest.

The receptionist put a hand to her mouth, stifling a scream. She looked down at Bella and frantically dialed a number. "Are you all right? Are you all right?" she kept saying.

Nikki wanted to watch this drama play itself out, but that was not the plan. "I'll go get help," she called out and bolted for Strobel's office.

She had taken no more than five or six steps down the long hall—a virtual gauntlet of secretaries at computer terminals and open workstations— when three men emerged from the corner office at the end. She recognized one of the men as Mack Strobel and one as Ahmed Aberijan. The third man she couldn't place. They huddled outside the doorway momentarily, talking to each other, no more than eighty feet away.

Nikki fixed her gaze straight ahead and quickened her pace.

She was halfway down the corridor when Mack Strobel noticed her coming and took a step in her direction. The shorter man grabbed Ahmed's arm and steered him down the perpendicular hallway, away from Nikki.

"Who are you?" Strobel demanded, walking toward her. Some secretaries stopped typing; others put a momentary freeze on their phone gossip; almost all of them glanced up. "What are you doing here?"

When she was just a few steps away, Nikki started speaking rapidly, motioning wildly with her hands to emphasize the urgency of her message. *"Dónde está la oficina de Señor Aiken?"* she blabbered. A puzzled look crossed Strobel's face; they were now standing no more than two feet apart. *"No entiendes ni una palabra que he dicho verdad, tonto?"*

Strobel gave her a blank stare, and the muscles in his face relaxed ever so slightly. "Anybody know Spanish?" he asked, glancing around.

Sensing her chance, Nikki exploded past him, shoving him slightly with her free hand, deftly sidestepping the startled lawyer. She broke into a sprint, quickly turning the corner.

"Stop her!" Strobel yelled.

The shout got the attention of Ahmed and his sidekick, who were still half a hallway ahead of Nikki, ready to turn a corner down another adjacent hallway. They both pivoted on their heels, a brief look of astonishment on their faces. Nikki locked eyes with Ahmed and ran straight toward him.

Before she reached Ahmed, his burly sidekick barreled into Nikki with a force that sent her crashing against a wall. Nikki gasped as the air left her lungs, and she collapsed to the plush floor. Pain shot through her left shoulder, which had hit the wall first, bearing the main brunt of the brute who assaulted her. He stood over her now. Her world spun, and she blinked to fight back the converging blackness and stars.

Dazed but still conscious, Nikki realized she still held the envelope containing the suit papers. She threw the envelope across the floor so that it slid within inches of Ahmed's feet.

"Congratulations," she gasped. "You've been served."

Ahmed sneered, his lips curled ever so slightly into an arrogant little smile, and the eyes sent an unmistakable message of their own. She had seen the same eyes before, the same pent-up fury, the same smoldering violence. It was the look of her own father, remembered across a decade of time, as if it were yesterday. It was the look she remembered from that split second in time before he would strike out at her mom . . .

"Get up," the stocky man barked as he yanked Nikki to her feat. Mack Strobel was telling shell-shocked secretaries to call security.

"Get your hands off me," Nikki shouted back. "You're hurting me. Someone call the cops!"

But the man just twisted her arm tighter, and with pain shooting through her shoulder, Nikki stopped resisting. One gawking secretary found the presence of mind to get security on the phone and hand the receiver to Mack Strobel. With the envelope still lying unopened on the floor, and Mack Strobel preoccupied on the phone, Ahmed came over to Nikki and leaned so close to her that the hot stink of his breath brushed across her face.

"You will pay," Ahmed said slowly and emphatically.

The words shot through Nikki's rattled nervous system, putting her flight instincts on full alert. Yet her sense of bravado never betrayed her.

"Promises, promises," she snapped back.

She stared hard at Ahmed, unblinking, until his friend yanked her back down the hallway and toward the lobby, ignoring her threats to sue the pants off him. He marched Nikki right past Bella, who was now sitting in a chair, wet paper towels plastered on her forehead, breathing fitfully. Nikki glanced sideways at her compatriot, who in turn acknowledged Nikki with an almost imperceptible nod of the head, then resumed her tortured performance as a heart attack victim and her loud complaining about how long it was taking the ambulance to arrive.

Ahmed Aberijan had been served.

13

A SPECIAL SENSE OF RELIEF washes over the body of a law student as she puts down her pen at the end of semester exams. Sagging shoulders straighten, a smile replaces a furrowed brow, and a bounce in the step replaces the exam week shuffle.

For Leslie Connors, this invigorating relief was underscored by the anticipation of spending the evening with Brad. He had asked her to dinner, ostensibly to discuss her work on the *Reed* case. But Leslie believed—and hoped—that the real reason had more to do with personal motives. Leslie had not seen Brad since she started exams two weeks ago, and she did not look forward to spending the summer away from him in England, separated by the Atlantic Ocean rather than the Chesapeake Bay.

Leslie was nearly thirty years old and experiencing emotions from her schoolgirl days. She felt a bit guilty for craving his attention so much. Though her tidy life plan left no room for a relationship with Brad, her emotions suggested such a relationship was exactly what she needed.

Tonight she vowed to throw caution to the wind and enjoy herself. Brad had insisted she choose the restaurant. It was an easy choice. The most romantic restaurant around was The Trellis, a quaint and elegant throwback to another era in the heart of Colonial Williamsburg. The Trellis sat on prime real estate, fronting on Duke of Gloucester Street, strategically located in the middle of Williamsburg's historic district.

Duke of Gloucester Street, or "Dog Street" in the parlance of the locals, was a passageway to a simpler time. The colonial architecture, the gravel road, the manicured lawns, the authentic historical costumes of the workers, and the exact replicas of the colonial buildings, all combined to make visitors a part of history. Any tension remaining from exams left Leslie's body entirely as she strolled down Dog Street, killing time. It was the perfect setting for a promising night.

◁▷

Like all drivers in Tidewater, Brad despised the bridges and tunnels that surrounded Norfolk and Virginia Beach. He hated them most when, like tonight, he was running late and heading north, because traveling in that direction meant crossing the Chesapeake Bay through the mother of all traffic jam generators: the Hampton Roads tunnel. The tunnel *never* backed up on those rare occasions when he was on time. But somehow, the desperation of his personal situation seemed to trigger the most gnarly jams. Tonight, with Brad running late, a stalled car performed the honors of backing up traffic for nearly a mile.

Inching his way along, Brad whipped out his cell phone and dialed.

"Strobel here." The words blasted. Strobel was on his speakerphone, and the echo made him hard to understand and louder than life.

"Take me off the box," Brad said.

"Who's this?" Strobel bellowed. He had the tone of a man who was not used to taking orders from a stranger.

"It's Brad Carson, returning your call, and I'm not going to talk to you if you don't take me off that blasted speakerphone."

"Bradley, thanks for calling back." Strobel was still on the speakerphone. Brad simmered. Nobody called him Bradley. "Look, old boy, as you obviously know based on that cute little stunt your paralegal pulled, we've been hired to defend the *Reed* case, and I thought I owed you a courtesy call before we file the kinds of motions we're preparing. You still there?"

"Yeah, I'm still here," Brad responded. He had now put his cell phone on speaker mode and laid it in the seat next to him. Two could play this game.

"What types of motions are you talking about?"

"Say what?" Strobel shouted.

"I said, what kinds of motions are you going to file?" Brad said it slower and louder, emphasizing each word.

"Well, Bradley, I've been practicin' law a long time, and you're a good lawyer, but I've never seen a case more desperate than this one, except maybe some of those *pro se* cases filed by prisoners complaining about jail food. Unless I'm missing something, you don't have squat. Am I out in left field here? Are you aware of some case law or authority I haven't stumbled across?"

Strobel was obviously on a fishing expedition, trying to flush out Brad's best arguments so he could address them in his opening brief. Brad was not about to bite that hook.

"You're the expert on international law. You tell me."

An audible sigh. Strained patience. "All right, Bradley, I will tell you. Your claims against Saudi Arabia are barred by the doctrine of sovereign immunity. In addition, the only witness you have to support your claim of torture is your own client. And her credibility is—how shall I say this?—shaky at best." Strobel paused, apparently wanting the thinly veiled threat to sink in.

"Our only choice, under these circumstances, is to file a motion to dismiss and to also ask the court for Rule 11 sanctions against you and your firm for filing a frivolous claim. I don't like filing such motions against my colleagues, Bradley. That's why I'm calling. If you voluntarily dismiss the case by week's end, we'll forget the motion for sanctions. We all go home, on to the next case. Your choice, Bradley, what's it gonna be?"

◁▷

Mack stopped pacing and yakking long enough to listen. Only then did he realize that the sound on the other end of the phone line was a dial tone.

Mack had his answer. This case was about to get personal.

◁▷

Leslie arrived ten minutes before seven o'clock and verified the reservation. By 7:15 there was still no sign of Brad. Leslie knew Brad typically began meetings and appointments by apologizing for being late. Tonight would be no exception.

As the minutes clicked by, she felt the magic of Dog Street waning. Leslie and Bill had eaten at The Trellis just once, a few months after the diagnosis. The evening was quite possibly the first since the disease became part of their lives that they spent the entire evening without mentioning it. Bill had resolved not to spoil a perfect date, and Leslie had followed his lead.

Now, as she sat here waiting for Brad, the memories of that night—the smells of fresh bread from the ovens, the sounds of laughing tourists, the sight of William and Mary undergrad just a few blocks away, the very feel of this area of Colonial Williamsburg—simply overpowered her. She felt a sudden need to be alone, to savor one more time the special relationship she had had with Bill, the one man who knew her completely—warts and all—and accepted her totally. She stood up to go home, pour herself a nice glass of wine, and unwind on the dock overlooking the Chickahominy.

She sighed and sat back down. All at once, tonight felt like such hard work, like it would be her job to impress Brad with an outgoing and fun-loving personality. She would have to guard against lapses in the conversation, against saying anything that might betray this building sense of depression eating at her. Why was it so hard to enjoy a night with someone she liked so much? Why did she suddenly feel so much pressure to make this work? And why, on tonight of all nights, was it so hard to get Bill out of her mind?

By 7:30, when Brad finally came jogging over from a nearby parking lot, Leslie's anxiety was in full bloom. As he approached, she felt her pulse quicken, but she put on her poker face and did not smile, a little psychological punishment for being late.

"Hey, Leslie. Sorry I'm late," Brad said, catching his breath. "Hope you haven't been waiting long."

They faced each other awkwardly as Brad seemed to vacillate between a quick hug and shaking hands. Leslie stuck out her hand as further punishment, and Brad took the cue. She immediately felt silly. She decided to put him at ease. Her poker face disappeared, replaced by a bright smile. She followed the handshake with a quick hug. She congratulated herself on her studied act of spontaneity.

"Don't worry about it. For the first time in weeks, I've got no deadlines." She was keenly aware of her unenthusiastic tone and wondered if Brad noticed. "But I am starving. Let's see if they've still got a table for us."

"I really am sorry," he repeated as they walked into the restaurant. Brad opened the door and placed a gentle hand on Leslie's shoulder as she passed through. The spontaneous touch sent chills through Leslie's entire body. The ghosts of Bill again. The gentle hand on the shoulder as she entered a restaurant, the soft spontaneous touch—these mannerisms belonged to Bill. Leslie had never realized how much she missed them, these little habits, until this moment.

"We should have something in about twenty minutes," the maître d' promised.

Brad leaned close to the man and whispered intently, as if the two were lifelong friends. Two minutes and twenty bucks later, the host seated Leslie and Brad at a remote window for two that overlooked Dog Street.

The conversation started slowly, weighed down by Leslie's melancholy.

But before long, her queasiness began to melt away in the face of Brad's relentless determination to have a good time. He put his personality on overdrive. He had quips and stories galore, and he even managed to strike up a nice conversation with the waitress, whom Leslie suspected of trying to hit on her date. But that was one of the things she liked most about Brad—his ability and desire to put people at ease. To make them feel good about themselves.

Despite her formidable defenses, Leslie found the Carson charm working. The conversation flowed more easily through dinner, time disappeared, and suddenly the server asked if they wanted dessert. Brad allowed the flirting waitress to talk him into Death by Chocolate. Leslie passed.

Brad didn't mention the *Reed* case until after his first bite of the life-threatening dessert.

"I talked to Mack Strobel today," he said out of the blue.

"You know how to ruin a perfectly good meal."

"He's going to file Rule 11 sanctions against us." Brad said it matter-of-factly, then took another bite of the rich, dark chocolate cake with chocolate icing and smothered in chocolate sauce. "Wants to give me another taste of jail food."

"Speaking of which, how's Nikki?"

"Bella didn't call you?" Brad pushed the dessert toward her. Leslie started to push the plate back, then caught herself. She shook her head in answer to his question and sliced off a small piece with her fork. No telling what this one small bite would cost her—probably three pounds, directly to the hips. But it tasted great . . . actually, beyond great, though the guilt of the calories hit before she swallowed.

She pushed the plate back.

"Four hours in jail, and we pleaded her out on misdemeanor trespass. I did the whole thing over the phone. Six months' probation—no time. I think the prosecutor actually thought it was funny."

Leslie eyed the chocolate. It was disappearing fast.

"But then this assistant U.S. attorney gets involved," Brad continued. "Angela Bennett—colder than ice—and threatens to file charges for assaulting a foreign dignitary."

"What'd you do?"

"You mean after I peeled Nikki off the ceiling?"

Leslie grinned at the thought of Nikki's reaction.

"Bennett was in our conference room, making these accusations face-to-face." A smirk curled across Brad's lips as he recalled the scene; then he chased the smirk away with another bite of chocolate. "So Nikki flashes her bruises, then stomps over to the phone and starts dialing a friend at a local television station. 'Let's just give the media a call,' she says, 'and let them know that this *foreign dignitary* beat me up, threatened me, and now you're going to pile on by filing charges.'"

Brad smiled broadly. He held his fork up with another bite of dessert, as if toasting Nikki's brilliance.

"Case dismissed," he said, then devoured the forkful.

"Was she hurt?" Leslie asked.

"She's pretty bruised, still threatening a lawsuit, but she'll be fine. She said that jerk from Saudi Arabia threatened her, but Nikki doesn't scare easy."

"She's got to be more careful."

Brad suspended his fork in midair and seemed to ponder this offhand comment.

"No," he said, looking serious. "The practice of law is the art of taking risks. You prepare and calculate the best you can, but at the end of the day, you just roll the dice, and your client's entire life is changed by what comes up. You can't be effective if you're not comfortable with risk."

Leslie thought about this as she watched Brad devour the remaining dessert. Risk was not her thing. Perhaps it was just Brad's style, or perhaps he was right. She would force herself to take a few more risks. She would start now.

She picked up her fork, thought about the calories again, and set it back down. She wondered what risk-taking Nikki would do with this dessert.

And the thought of Nikki behind bars suddenly struck her as funny.

"Did you ever think about doing lawyer ads featuring you and Nikki in jail?" Leslie reached out her hands and grabbed the imaginary bars. "Carson & Associates, it takes one to spring one."

"Very funny," Brad said. But he couldn't help smiling.

◁▷

An hour later they walked in silence down Dog Street, enjoying the brisk night and basking in the tradition of Colonial Williamsburg. Brad had stopped his running commentary, sensing a comfort between them that did not need to be broken with makeshift conversation.

While they strolled, Brad quietly fought his own inner war. He had mixed business and pleasure before with disastrous results—including devastated feelings and a lost case. The pressures of litigation had ways of forging romances that never lasted under normal circumstances. He had long ago established a hard-and-fast rule that he would never again date a lawyer involved in one of his cases.

Besides, his lifestyle left little time for meaningful relationships. At times he regretted that fact. More often, he realized he was still not ready to trade the thrill of pursuing the big case for the mundane life of a suburban husband and dad. But tonight his heart told him he should allow himself a loophole for a romance with this beautiful law student, a loophole that seemed particularly compelling as he glanced at Leslie's auburn hair shimmering in the soft moonlight. What made her even more beautiful, Brad decided, was that Leslie had no idea how pretty she was.

◁ ▷

Her earlier anxieties entirely gone, Leslie desperately wished the night had just begun. She stood in the shadows of Dog Street, facing Brad, inches apart. Brad reached down and took her hands in his.

"I had a great time," he said. "I really wish you weren't going to England. It could be a long two months."

"I know," Leslie said, surprised by the intensity of her inward response to the warmth and strength of his hands. She could not move or think; she could only shudder.

"Can we do this again when you get back?" Brad asked. He released one hand and gently brushed her hair back over her shoulder.

She hadn't felt this way in so long. "I'd like that."

Brad gently drew her close, and she did not resist. The warmth of being held by him, the security of his arms—she had forgotten how special the nearness could feel. She breathed deeply, filling her lungs with the presence of Brad Carson. And then, suspended in time, she closed her eyes and gracefully tilted back her head. Their lips gently touched. Dog Street spun; the passion flowed. It was, in Leslie's considered opinion, an awesome kiss. One that lasted longer than she intended. One that surprised her with the intensity of her own passion, the tingling of her skin, the release of pent-up emotions. It was at once tender and exhilarating. It was only a few seconds, but it completely carried her away.

Dog Street was indeed magical.

But for Leslie, it was also confusing. She pulled slightly away from Brad, thoughts racing through her mind too fast to process, a jumble of emotions and feelings from past and present colliding.

"I can't do this, Brad. I'm not ready; it's still too fresh." Even to Leslie, it sounded crazy. How could she not be ready to move on after three years? When would she be?

But it was also true. She needed more time. The emotions she had just felt, that she hadn't felt since she lost Bill, she had believed she would never feel them again. It was just too raw. Too overpowering. And Leslie cared too much for Brad to tell him anything but the truth.

"I lost a husband to cancer three years ago," she whispered. "I'm sorry." She took a half step back, looked down, and shuffled her feet. Her guilt was magnified by the knowledge of what she was doing to Brad.

"Leslie, I didn't know . . . I would have never . . ." He paused and gently took her hands. "You've got nothing to apologize for."

His kindness only made her feel worse. She could think of nothing to say, completely embarrassed by the unfolding events she was powerless to change.

"Do you want to talk about it?" he asked gently.

Leslie shook her head.

"If you ever do, just let me know."

She nodded.

"C'mon," Brad said. "I'll walk you to your car."

14

HIS THREATENING OVERTURES to Brad Carson aside, Mack Strobel was a sensible lawyer and would not file a Rule 11 motion lightly. He wanted nothing more than to see Carson taken out to the proverbial legal woodshed with a whipping stick, humiliated by the sanctions. But since the courts used the Rule 11 woodshed sparingly, Mack would have to exercise caution to prevent his request from blowing up in his own face. As he always did when he needed advice, Mack summoned the other members of the firm's informal brain trust.

Though Kilgore & Strobel had an official executive committee, everyone knew it was the four men assembled this day at the Norfolk Golf and Country Club who called the shots. They gathered informally to plot strategy on every major case or business deal the firm ever handled. It was their way of rewarding each other with easy billable hours at the expense of clients who would never notice the difference. Today, after a grueling eighteen holes in the heat of a May afternoon, they were paying off bets and throwing down a few cold ones to lubricate their brain cells.

Mack polished off his second glass, surveyed the group, and found himself silently shaking his head. *If this is the A team,* he thought, *it's a wonder that our firm can function at all.*

Seated directly across from Mack was a wrinkled man with sad, droopy eyes, stooped but still vigorous, with a pointed face and tufts of gray hair on the sides of his head. Nothing grew on top and had not for as long as Mack could remember. His name was Theodore "Teddy" Kilgore, the grandfatherly patriarch of the firm and the only lawyer who outranked Mack. He no longer actively practiced law, but he was still the firm's premier "rainmaker," snagging well-heeled clients so the young bucks could work on their cases.

To Mack's right at the small table was Melvin Phillips, a brilliant Harvard

graduate and a first-rate tax attorney with no social graces. The boys at
Kilgore & Strobel valued his big brain and frequently came to him with their
thorniest problems, but they also kept him well hidden from the clients. He
never combed his thick gray hair, and he wore ill-fitting suits that looked like
hand-me-downs from a traffic court lawyer. Melvin housed his huge cranium
inside a round head, precariously perched on a round body with not one
discernible muscle. He had an enormous chin and small beady eyes, shrunk
further by the magnification of thick glasses, so that he always sported an
out-of-touch look.

On Mack's other side was the member of the brain trust with the best
pedigree, a man whom Mack personally despised because of his genteel arrogance and condescending ways. Winsted Aaron Mackenzie IV came from
good stock. His father was a prominent Virginia politician, his grandfather
an appellate court judge, and his great-grandfather, the original Winsted
Aaron Mackenzie, fought for the Confederacy. "Win" was the pretty boy of
the firm—tailored suits and monogrammed shirts, silk ties and wavy brown
television-evangelist hair that never moved, even in the stiffest breeze. Win
was fifteen years younger than Mack, but already he had a reputation for
hard-nosed trial tactics that rivaled Mack's folklore. There was no small
amount of professional jealousy between the two.

"The issue I need this group's help on," Mack finally announced, "is
whether we should file for Rule 11 sanctions against Carson."

"I would," Win said predictably. "This is one of the most outrageous
claims I've ever seen. We aren't aggressively serving our clients if we don't
go after Carson. It's a no-brainer."

Melvin Phillips nodded his approval, then raised his hand to flag down
a waitress. "What's the deal? All the waitresses on strike? I'm dying of thirst
here!" Everyone in the room, including the waitresses, ignored him.

"I don't know," Teddy said. "This whole Rule 11 business is bad for lawyers.
We file against Carson on this case, some other lawyer will file against our firm
on the next one. Pretty soon cases just become personal wars between attorneys. We oughta be able to disagree on a case without getting personal."

Mack knew the old man would be cautious and reluctant to file. In many
ways, Teddy still lived in a bygone era inhabited by gentlemen lawyers. He
was not in touch with the age of Rambo litigation.

"Teddy, things have changed," Mack said dispassionately. "Carson would
slit our throats in a heartbeat if we gave him the chance, and so would half the

other lawyers in Tidewater. Litigation is not a gentleman's game anymore; it's war. And in war, you take no prisoners."

"I agree, Teddy," Win said. "If we don't file Rule 11, we're just enabling guys like Carson to file more junk lawsuits."

Melvin finally flagged down a waitress. "Anybody need another?" he asked. He replenished his drink, and the skull session continued. This time Melvin was engaged.

"What are the chances?" Melvin asked.

"What do you mean?" Mack countered.

"Exactly what I said. What are the chances that you'll win on Rule 11? To my thinking, it's purely a tactical call. If you have a fair chance of winning, file the motion. It will send a signal to the judge that you really believe this case is nonsense. It makes it more likely that the judge will throw the case out. It also gives the judge a compromise. He can deny your Rule 11 motion, thus throwing a bone to Carson, but then grant your motion to dismiss and get rid of the case. Judges like to play Solomon and split the baby like that, and you like it because you get what you are really after—a dismissed case." Melvin stopped for a long gulp of beer.

"But if your chances are bad," he continued, "the judge will just hammer you, because judges hate Rule 11 motions. What's more, you'll encourage Carson to make all kinds of other frivolous motions. Like Win just said, you become the enabler of his conduct."

The others thought about Melvin's comments. For a long time nobody spoke.

"I think Carson's claim against Saudi Arabia is totally bogus and Rule 11 has a good shot," Mack said, sensing that the others were waiting on his analysis. "But his claims against Aberijan and the individuals are based on a different set of laws and may have some merit. At the very least, he could avoid Rule 11 on those claims."

Melvin finished another long gulp and set his glass down hard on the table, as if banging a gavel. "That's your answer then. You file Rule 11 but limit it to Carson's frivolous claim against Saudi Arabia."

"Makes sense," Mack conceded, though he was actually hoping for a broader and more aggressive filing.

"Let's not make this a common practice of the firm," Teddy said. "I don't want a reputation as the firm that always files Rule 11."

The other partners nodded their approval. Mack would humor the old man for a few more years. Even Mack was not willing to take on Teddy just yet.

"Let's talk about Sarah Reed for a minute," Melvin said, rolling his huge head around to survey his audience. "Have you looked at the case from her perspective? If her allegations are true, what are her weaknesses and how can they be exploited?"

"Of course I've considered that," Mack said. Of course he had not, but he could not concede as much to this bunch. "We've looked at this from every possible angle."

"Since our last session, I've been putting myself in Sarah Reed's shoes," Melvin continued, as if Mack had never spoken. "There's one thing she fears worse than losing this case." He paused, apparently trying to create a little mystery. He took another long swallow of his beer. This was one of Melvin's annoying habits that Mack particularly despised. Start a sentence, then take a bite or a drink while others sit in suspense. "And that is revealing the names of the church leaders in Saudi Arabia. According to her own allegations, her husband died rather than reveal those names. She would undoubtedly dismiss this suit, rather than expose these people, for fear they would be persecuted. That's her weakness; figure out a way to exploit it."

I waited for that? "That's a great theory," Mack scoffed, "but impossible to implement. I intend to push for those names in discovery, but Carson will object. The judge will probably not think they are relevant to our defense of the case."

Melvin smiled, squinting his beady eyes. "Figure out a way to make them relevant, Mack. You're the litigator. Make them a central issue in the case. Force her to chose between revealing the names and dropping the case. Now, if you'll excuse me, I've got to take a little trip."

With that, Melvin staggered off toward the rest room, leaving the others shaking their heads.

"Old Melvin—frequently wrong but never in doubt," Win said.

But Mack just sat there, staring after his quirky partner, his mind a thousand miles away. Abruptly, Mack turned to the two remaining members of the group. "Maybe so, but he may be onto something this time. I've got an idea."

For the next half hour, they discussed and refined the details of Mack's plan. The entire meeting lasted two hours and cost the nation of Saudi Arabia $3,225. It would prove to be worth every penny.

◁▷

Brad pretty much neglected the *Reed* case during the two months that Leslie spent in England. To be sure, the case proceeded, but Brad himself was too busy with other matters to devote his time to the file. His primary concern during the summer months was a tricky product liability case that went to trial during the last week of July. The case settled while the jury was deliberating, but preparing the case decimated Brad's summer.

While Brad deposed engineers and scrutinized product-testing reports on this other case, the trickle of paper from Kilgore & Strobel became a flood. Every day, the mail would be littered with pleadings, motions, or discovery requests from Strobel's minions. Brad didn't pay much attention to the growing mountain of paperwork. He knew nothing major would occur until after the court conducted a hearing on the motion to dismiss in late August. Fortunately, Leslie would be back in the country a few weeks early to help him prepare.

◁▷

All summer long, Leslie and Bella wore out the FedEx planes between Virginia Beach and Exeter. Leslie attended class in the morning, worked on legal pleadings all afternoon, then reviewed her FedEx packages for more presents from Kilgore & Strobel. She was thankful her coursework was light but resentful that she had no time to tour the country. She could not take time off while there was work to be done on the *Reed* file, and there was always work to be done on the *Reed* file.

◁▷

For Bella, it was just another lonely day in the office. Brad was in court, and Nikki and Sarah were huddled in the conference room working on answers to interrogatories. As usual, Bella held down the fort, answering the phone and doing the firm's filing. The clock on her desk barely moved, the morning stretched on forever, and she found herself counting the minutes until lunch.

At a few minutes before twelve, Bella put her phone on forward, rushed down to the firm's small kitchen, closed the door behind her, and lit up her fifth or sixth cigarette of the morning—she had lost count. She turned on the small fan strategically placed in the corner of the countertop and pulled a plastic chair up to the small table. She grabbed her bag lunch out of the refrigerator and picked up her sappy romance novel. The plot was all too predictable, but she had bought it for the picture of the strapping young gladiator on the cover with the long dark hair and the come-hither look. She settled in for another solitary lunch hour. It was, she supposed, the price you paid when you exercised your freedom to smoke.

There were no windows in the kitchen, just white walls stained yellow, a tile floor, a counter area, sink, refrigerator, microwave, and coffeepot. To Bella, it was as cramped as a jail cell. But thanks to some tense negotiations with Brad a few years ago, it was also the one place inside the office where she could still officially smoke. Until Nikki came, she could also sneak a smoke in the women's rest room or light up when Brad was out of the office, but now even those minor luxuries had disappeared.

Bella indulged herself in a little self-pity. Discrimination against smokers seemed to be not just legal, but downright fashionable. It was not like she could control it. Someone ought to do something about this. Smokers have rights too.

As she worked her way through a salad and another unimaginative chapter of the book, the door burst open, and Nikki darted through. As usual, Nikki held her breath and went straight for the refrigerator to retrieve her lunch. She waved snidely at Bella and gave her a tight-lipped smile. Then she waved the smoke away from her face, neither talking nor breathing the entire time she was in the room.

"Hope you choke," Bella said as the door closed behind Nikki.

A few minutes later, three pages and two long, passionate kisses later, to be exact, the door opened again, but this time more slowly. Sarah Reed stuck her head in the kitchen and walked in with her own bag lunch.

"Hi," she said. "Mind if I join you?"

"Um . . . no." Bella put the book down and gathered her Tupperware a little closer to her own place, making room for Sarah. "That'd be great."

She watched Sarah spread out a sandwich, some carrot sticks, and an apple. Bella suddenly felt self-conscious about the cigarette smoking away on the ashtray in front of her. She liked Sarah—after all, no one else had dared join her for lunch in this smoking dungeon. But Bella decided not to put out her cigarette yet, as a matter of principle.

"What're you reading?" Sarah asked.

Would a missionary approve of a romance novel? "Just something I found lying around," Bella said. She gave the book a suspicious and unfamiliar look, as if somebody had just switched her book of choice when she wasn't looking. She turned the book over so it was lying with its cover facing down.

"It's probably a nice break after all those legal pleadings," Sarah said. "I don't know how you do it, day after day."

"Yeah, it is." Bella took a short puff on her cigarette and blew the smoke over her shoulder. "The other stuff does get pretty dry."

Sarah nodded. "Can I get your advice on something?"

"Sure."

"How do you keep everything around here straight? I mean, I'm finding as a single mom that I just can't keep up with everything. Seems like I'm always showing up late or missing something or not getting something done. Yet here you are, single yourself, and basically keeping this whole firm running on schedule." Sarah leaned forward and tilted her head a little. "How do you do it?"

It was, Bella thought, a good question. She pushed the novel aside. She was just thinking this morning about how she could see the strain showing on Sarah's face. Maybe this would help.

After a few minutes of time-management coaching, the conversation turned to other matters. Bella finished her salad, but still she kept talking. She seemed to mesmerize Sarah, who kept her eyes glued on Bella, asked the most insightful questions, and seemed enthralled with the answers. Before long, Bella found herself snuffing out her half-finished cigarette and laughing with Sarah, in spite of herself. She couldn't remember when talking to someone about nonlegal matters had seemed so natural.

"Tell me about your family," Sarah said.

Bella hesitated. The first noticeable pause in the conversation. What was there to tell? *I'm not married. Never been married. An only child whose parents are divorced. The only person who ever loved me—my mom—can hardly recognize me. Tell me about your family.*

What family?

"There's not much to tell," Bella said, looking down at her Tupperware. She began packing up. "Dad and Mom divorced when I was in college. No sisters or brothers. And Mom, well . . ." She could feel the tears forming in her eyes, the words catching in her throat. "Mom's not well." She sniffled. "Sorry."

Bella stood to leave and threw her trash away. She felt stupid, tearing up about her mom, but she couldn't help it. She knew it would be better to change the subject and get back to work.

But there was something about Sarah. "She's in a nursing home," Bella heard herself say, "with Parkinson's."

Sarah stood now as well and reached out gently to touch Bella's arm. "Do you see her much?"

Bella nodded.

"Maybe I could go with you sometime," Sarah said softly.

"You'd do that?"

"Sure. And there's something else I'd like to do."

"Okay."

"Would it be all right if I prayed for her?"

"Right now?" Bella couldn't imagine praying right here, right now, in the middle of the smoking room. Was it legal? It seemed so . . . well, so unclean. So . . . unnatural.

"Sure. What's her name?"

"Gertrude."

And before Bella knew what was happening, Sarah was praying for her and Gertrude right there in the middle of the smoking room, her hand gently rubbing Bella's arm. Sarah was so sincere about the whole thing, this sweet missionary who had lost her own husband, passionately praying for Bella and her mom, that Bella felt guilty when she realized she had not once directed the conversation Sarah's way.

Bella never closed her eyes, for fear that Nikki would blow through the door. Still, she somehow felt God couldn't help but hear Sarah's prayer on her behalf.

"Thanks," Bella said when Sarah was done. "That's one of the nicest things anybody's ever done for me."

Then she hustled out of the small kitchen area before the tears could start in earnest.

◁▷

Nikki spent most of her summer on the road, touring the continental United States, talking to potential expert witnesses, hunting down doctors who had treated the Reeds at the military hospital in Riyadh, and spending money on clothes. She hit real pay dirt with a young intern stationed at Fort Bragg, an Army doctor named Jeffrey Rydell, who had been one of Charles Reed's treating physicians in Riyadh. Nikki sat in a chair right next to Rydell, rather than across the small conference room table. She was wearing one of her stock-in-trade tight black miniskirts, and she crossed her legs provocatively, hoping the handsome young doctor would notice.

"How's Mrs. Reed doing?" he asked Nikki with genuine concern.

"If you mean physically, she's doin' great. On the other stuff, give her time. She'll be okay."

"She seemed like a fighter. I really hope she can get through this. I'll help any way I can."

"You can start by telling me your opinion of the cause of Dr. Reed's death."

Nikki placed her mini digital recorder on the table. She leaned forward and struck a pose, placing her elbow on her knee and her chin in her hand, letting the doctor know she was interested. She tried hard to ignore the wedding band on his left hand.

"Cause of death was cocaine injection by the Muttawa that in turn led to an acute myocardial infarction. Even before this happened, Dr. Reed had advanced coronary artery disease, and as a result, the flow of blood to his heart was severely restricted. The cocaine, in my opinion, probably stimulated the formation of a blood clot in a man who was already in extreme distress from being tortured. The blood clot might not have been fatal in the arteries of a normal man, but in Dr. Reed's case, it led to total restriction of the flow of blood to the heart, causing massive damage and ultimately death."

"You seem so sure that the cocaine was *injected* into his bloodstream, Doctor."

"I am."

"Based on?"

"Well, first, the word of Sarah Reed that she and her husband never even experimented with the stuff. Second, neither Dr. Reed nor his wife had any of the telltale signs of drug abusers, and I've been involved in the management of hundreds of critical care patients with abuse problems. Third, the toxicological testing confirms that the concentration of cocaine in Dr. Reed's blood actually showed higher levels at the second hospital he was in, the base hospital, than it did from the first hospital, the King Faisal Specialist Hospital."

There was a pause, and a mesmerized Nikki realized it was her turn to speak. "What's the significance of that, Doctor?"

"Well, it actually means that the cocaine must have been injected fairly close in time to when Dr. Reed was admitted to the King Faisal hospital, and that the cocaine was still being absorbed into his bloodstream while he was hospitalized. I was also shocked by the levels of cocaine found in the toxicological reports. They are not levels typically associated with snorting cocaine. When cocaine is snorted, it narrows the blood vessels in the nose, which in turn reduces the flow of blood, which results in a slower absorption rate. The types of elevated readings we saw in Dr. Reed's case typically come from either injecting cocaine directly into a vein or from smoking crack."

"Fascinating."

"And finally, and perhaps most important, a very peculiar aspect of the toxicological report that I didn't notice at first makes me certain the drug was injected." Rydell paused for a second. "But if I tell you, then you have to reveal it in discovery or make sure that I mention it in my deposition, is that right?"

The question hung in the air for a while, as Nikki realized she didn't have the foggiest idea what he had just asked. She had been too busy looking deep into his eyes, fishing for a sign of mutual interest.

"Huh? Oh, well, sure you would . . . What's your question again?"

"If I tell you this hunch I have about the lab report, do you have to tell the other side about my opinion prior to trial?"

"Yeah, we have to tell them about any of the opinions you intend to testify about at trial, and then they will ask you questions about those opinions in a deposition prior to trial."

"And then they will go out and hire sixteen other doctors to come and testify as to why I'm wrong. Isn't that the way it works?"

"Something like that. I can tell you've done this before."

Rydell looked pensive for a moment, perhaps conflicted on whether he should share his hunch with Nikki. "One more question," he said after a pause.

Nikki raised her eyebrows.

"If it really isn't my opinion yet, if it's just a hunch and I don't research this 'hunch' until just before trial, and if I can't really form an opinion until I've had a chance to research the 'hunch' further, then would you have to reveal it?"

"There's no rule that says we have to reveal a hunch," Nikki answered confidently.

"Good. Then let's just say I've got a strong hunch—" Nikki heard a vibration, and then Rydell looked down and checked his beeper. He looked worried. "I'm sorry, Ms. Moreno, but I've got to go. Like I said, I'll help how-ever I can. . . ." He was already up and out of his chair, heading for the door.

"Maybe I could come back for a follow-up interview. . . . There's lots of stuff to cover," Nikki offered.

"I'd be happy to talk further anytime you need me, but don't feel like you've got to come out here. Just give me a call, set up a time we can get together by phone." And with that, Dr. Rydell was out the door, off to save another life.

Nikki looked wistfully at the conference room door. She turned off her recorder and stuffed it in her briefcase. She worried that she was losing her touch. As she stood to leave, she caught sight of her own reflection in the conference room window. She straightened her posture, sucked in her stom-ach, and smiled.

That boy must be blind, she said to herself.

15

BY THE FIRST WEEK OF JULY, Nikki was preparing to take her investigation international. It had not been an easy trip to arrange. For starters, a visa to Saudi Arabia was impossible to obtain without a sponsor from within the country. And obtaining a sponsor was not easy when the purpose for entering the country was to investigate a high-profile case against its government.

Nikki started with the large multinational law firms that advertised a stable of English-speaking lawyers. Her goal was to hire a lawyer who would later help with depositions in the country and on this initial visit could serve as a translator and consultant. No respectable firm, however, was anxious to bite the hand that fed them.

After three days of phone calls and three days of rejections, Nikki gave up her insistence on a respectable law firm with specialists in international law. She would settle for any semiliterate Saudi lawyer who could speak passable English. And she finally found her man in Sa'id el Khamin, a sole practitioner obviously hurting for clients and ready to make a quick buck. She agreed to pay him the exorbitant sum of twelve hundred Saudi riyals per hour, the equivalent of more than three hundred U.S. dollars. Somehow the amount felt like a bribe rather than a legal fee.

With el Khamin's sponsorship, Nikki finally obtained her visa and prepared to prove her worth in Saudi Arabia. With el Khamin at her side, Nikki would interview former neighbors of the Reeds and the members of the Friday night church group.

Nikki arrived at the King Khalid International Airport in Riyadh late in the evening on July 8. She was bone weary after the brutal flight from Reagan National Airport, during which she sat sandwiched between two large Europeans who both slept soundly while encroaching mightily upon her shrinking space. When she arrived in the Kingdom, customs took forever, the process slowed by a shortage of agents and the fact that she was a single unaccompanied female.

She was finally rescued by her sponsor, a rumpled and bearded Sa'id el Khamin, who convinced the authorities that she was harmless and would behave. They allowed her to pass into his custody.

"Here, I bring gift for you.... Wear this abayya please." Sa'id presented Nikki with the ugliest garment she had ever laid eyes on, an enormous all-covering black cloak. To Nikki, who had seen similar garments in news coverage of Afghanistan, it was the very symbol of chauvinistic oppression. She held the thing at arm's length, as if it contained the germs for some incurable disease.

"Change . . . here," Sa'id suggested, pointing to a ladies' bathroom. "No need to cover—" and he made a sweeping motion over his face. "But, please, Mees Neekie, put on over other garments."

Nikki smiled and graciously headed into the bathroom, wondering why she was doing this. Mumbling to herself, she wrapped the cloak around her until she felt like a mummy, then looked at herself disapprovingly in the mirror. She immediately began to sweat. This would be a long week in the Kingdom.

When she came out of the rest room, her peculiar little host bowed deeply and thanked her enthusiastically. Sa'id himself was dressed in a white floor-length shirt that looked like a dress. He called it a "thobe." As they walked through the airport, he pointed out items to Nikki and named them in Arabic, as if she were going to learn the language in the week or so she would spend in this place. Nikki had only two immediate goals: get to a nice American hotel room and get out of the oppressive abayya as soon as possible.

On the forty-five-kilometer drive from the airport to the Hyatt Regency in Riyadh, Nikki sat in the backseat and gawked at the sites while Sa'id chauffeured. Nikki was told emphatically that women did not drive in the Kingdom.

Sa'id made some lame attempts at conversation, but Nikki was more interested in admiring the sights in this strange and foreign land. She expected a backward and dirty city. Instead, Riyadh was a high-tech oasis of glass, steel, and concrete rising up from nowhere in the desert. It boasted freeways, high-rise office towers, big hospitals and hotels, and modern-looking houses that stretched beyond the horizon. She was struck by the cleanliness of the city and its modern, glistening architecture. She was equally amazed by the glut of vehicle traffic and the absence of pedestrians. The roads looked like rush hour in L.A., but the sidewalks looked like a ghost town.

Nikki also noticed, much to her relief, that not all foreign women wore the stifling black abayyas. She decided that tomorrow she would not be wearing hers. Sa'id would just have to get over it.

◁▷

By her third day in Riyadh, the city had lost its charm. There was absolutely no nightlife, and alcohol of any type was strictly prohibited. All restaurants and stores closed during prayer time, and most closed for the day at 1 p.m. Nikki's favorite pastime, shopping for clothes, might as well have been illegal. Many of the shops actually prohibited female shoppers, and she wouldn't dare wear any of the styles offered by those that didn't.

To her consternation, the culture rigorously enforced a strict separation between men and women. Families ate together in special sections of the restaurants, some of which refused to serve women at all. Women rode in the backs of buses, and a taxi driver refused to give Nikki a ride one night when she was unaccompanied by Sa'id. According to Sa'id, custom restricted women from looking men in the eye, a custom that Nikki enthusiastically violated by glaring at all sorts of Saudi males. Her behavior invariably resulted in loud arguments between Sa'id and the victims of Nikki's rude behavior, reprimands from Sa'id, and threats to get Nikki a veil.

Contrary to her earlier intentions, Nikki reverted to wearing her hated abayya. It was the only way she and Sa'id could avoid unwanted attention as they traveled together, pretending to be husband and wife. Sa'id seemed to enjoy this fantasy, his body language and mannerisms belying the huge crush he had on Nikki. She did not know if Sa'id was married. She was afraid to ask.

The first three days of the trip had been a total bust. Nikki and Sa'id could not locate several of the former church members, confirming the rumors about a general crackdown on the church the night the Reeds were arrested. Those members they did find steadfastly refused to talk to either Nikki or Sa'id, with many refusing to even answer the door. Nikki was hot, discouraged, and tired of being insulted by men whose language she did not understand.

On the evening of the third day, Sa'id and Nikki found their way to the small apartment of Rasheed and Mobara Berjein and knocked gently on the door. A hesitant woman cracked the door and looked suspiciously at the couple in the hallway. Sa'id began a rapid explanation in Arabic about the purpose for their visit, but the woman did not move, and the crack did not widen. Nikki did, however, detect a slight widening of the eyes when the name Sarah Reed was mentioned, and for the first time since landing at the King Khalid International Airport, Nikki allowed herself a glimmer of hope.

Impatient with Sa'id's slow progress, Nikki butted into Sa'id's polite inquiry and produced a photo of Sarah and her kids. To Nikki's surprise, the woman reached through the crack, took the picture, and studied it carefully. She murmured something to Sa'id in Arabic.

"She asks how she can know we speak the truth," Sa'id translated.

"Tell her Sarah sends her love and a message," Nikki said. Her words were translated by Sa'id.

Nikki could hear the woman speaking to someone behind her; then she peeked back through the crack and asked Sa'id another question.

"She wants to know what the message is."

"This is the message from Sarah Reed: 'God has not given us a spirit of fear, but of power and of love and of a sound mind.'"

Sa'id translated the message. To Nikki's astonishment, the woman slowly and cautiously opened the door. She smiled timidly, introduced herself as Mobara Berjein and the man standing next to her as Rasheed Berjein, and bid the visitors come into her home.

After Nikki and Sa'id took their seats in the living room, Rasheed and Mobara offered them some Turkish coffee. Nikki had already learned from Sa'id that it was extremely impolite to refuse such an offer. Etiquette, Sa'id had said, must be carefully followed. Patience would receive its reward in due time; impatience would arouse suspicion. Nikki wondered how much of this was true, and how much was motivated by the fact that Sa'id's patience was being rewarded to the tune of three hundred bucks an hour.

Mobara served the coffee in a tiny, handleless cup that held only a half-dozen sips. Following Sa'id's lead, Nikki asked for her coffee to be served *mazboot*, which apparently had something to do with the amount of sugar. Nikki had to muster every ounce of her self-control not to make a face as she drank the thick, gooey liquid in her cup and listened to the others chat in Arabic. She dutifully drank every ounce, right down to the pile of grounds left sitting in the bottom.

After ten minutes of pleasantries, the Berjeins were apparently ready to talk church. They began asking some questions about Sarah, and as Sa'id started translating, Nikki's paranoia took over. She thought it strange that no other members of the church would even talk to her and Sa'id. She worried about the ever-present eyes and ears of the infamous Muttawa. Her instincts told her the place might be bugged. She therefore suggested, through Sa'id, that Rasheed and Mobara join them in the car and talk about these sensitive matters where they could not be overheard.

They parked on an out-of-the-way side street in the city, then turned the radio up to an annoying level. The four of them huddled together in the middle of the car, Rasheed and Sa'id leaning back from the front seat while Nikki and Mobara leaned up from the back. After two hours of intense questioning, Nikki got what she was after. The Berjeins agreed to testify on behalf of Sarah Reed, no matter the consequences. To confirm their testimony, Nikki hand-printed an affidavit for Sa'id to translate and the Berjeins to sign. As Nikki drafted the affidavit, Mobara quickly wrote a letter to Sarah, telling her about the phenomenal growth of the surviving church, the conversion of Rasheed's brother, and Rasheed's valiant attempts to fill Dr. Reed's shoes. She folded it carefully and handed it to Nikki.

As they returned to the apartment, Nikki notarized the affidavit bearing the Berjeins' signatures and placed it in her briefcase. She laid out a plan that would secure the Berjeins' testimony in an American court of law while minimizing the risks to them personally.

Before getting out of the car, Mobara extracted yet another promise from Nikki to make sure that Sarah got the letter. The women parted with hugs and Nikki's promise to tell Sarah of Mobara's continuing love.

◁▷

Rasheed held Mobara's hand as they walked back into their apartment, head held high. He was grateful for this opportunity to redeem himself and stand tall with Sarah Reed for the cause of their Savior. He locked the door behind him and immediately embraced his wife. No words were necessary, and no words could stop the trembling of Mobara in his arms.

They had done the right thing, but they would undoubtedly face consequences. After holding Mobara for the longest time and quietly stroking her hair as they embraced together just inside the door, he began to softly pray. It was only then that he felt Mobara finally stop shaking. And as soon as she did, almost as if events had been carefully choreographed and synchronized, a loud knock sounded at the door.

Rasheed turned calmly to the peephole, looking through as the impatient visitor knocked again, even louder than before. Four men stood outside his door, but Rasheed's attention went immediately to one. He had seen the face on television, seen the hatred in the eyes. And now, only inches away, the eyes were even more intense, causing Rasheed to shudder involuntarily.

"It's the Muttawa," he whispered over his shoulder as he reached to unlock the door. "And Ahmed Aberijan is with them."

16

LESLIE HAD ANTICIPATED THIS DAY for two months. Time crawled during the flight across the Atlantic. Leslie could think of nothing but Brad. There were so many things she would tell him when she saw him at the airport. Two months of thinking had cleared her head and calmed her mind. She was nervous but ready to pick up where they left off. She had dreamed for weeks of spending time with Brad, an afternoon at the beach followed by dinner and a long stroll on the boardwalk. She was determined not to compare Brad to Bill, since she was not at all sure who would win if she did.

There would be no handshakes this time. They would start with a hug. She was almost running as she approached the end of the concourse where he promised he would meet her. Two months of waiting. It would be worth it.

"Welcome back, Rhodes scholar," Bella said.

"Thanks, Bella. Where's Brad?"

"Great to see you, too," Bella said.

"I'm sorry, Bella. I just wondered if something was wrong."

"I'm parked in a metered spot out front, so why don't you grab your baggage and meet me at the curb. We've got trouble in the *Reed* case. I'll explain on the way to the office."

Leslie had not planned to go to the office, but she didn't complain. It sounded serious.

◁▷

Leslie found Brad, Sarah, and Nikki waiting for her in the main conference room. The conference room table and floor were cluttered with law books, notebooks, legal pads, briefs, miscellaneous papers, and half-filled coffee cups. The phones were ringing unmercifully, but Brad and the others seemed oblivious.

After warm greetings for Leslie and a hugfest that included everyone but

Bella, Leslie pulled out a document she couldn't wait to share with the team and placed it on the table. It was labeled "Preliminary Game Plan for *Reed v. Saudi Arabia*" and contained Leslie's best thinking for the case—witnesses to call, experts to use, evidence that would hurt and evidence that would help. It demonstrated her trademark attention to detail. The others did not know that it was in the works—she wanted to surprise them with it and use it as the framework for preparing the case.

Brad didn't notice Leslie's document and tossed another on top of it. It was an affidavit in support of Rule 11 sanctions, signed by Mack Strobel. It had been filed earlier that day. Leslie picked it up and began reading.

> On May 11, I had a telephone conference with plaintiff's attorney, Mr. Bradley Carson, for the purpose of explaining our firm's intent to file a Rule 11 Motion against Mr. Carson based on the frivolous nature of this case. I called Mr. Carson, as a courtesy, in order to give him an opportunity to explain whether he had any cases or authorities that would support the unprecedented claims that he makes in this case.
>
> In response to my question of whether he was aware of any cases or other authority that would support the filing of this case, Mr. Carson indicated that he was aware of no such authority. He also acknowledged our firm's greater expertise in international law and questioned whether we were aware of any authority that would justify the filing of this case. In this regard, his precise words, to the best of my recollection, were, "You're the expert in international law; you tell me whether you think there is any law or case authority to justify our filing." I responded by telling Mr. Carson there was no legal basis for this case. I waited several weeks, fully expecting Mr. Carson to either drop his suit or provide me with legal authority that would justify the filing of this case. I have not heard back from Mr. Carson and accordingly file this Motion for Rule 11 Sanctions based on the enormous waste of judicial time and resources occasioned by the filing of this suit.
>
> My client, the nation of Saudi Arabia, has incurred legal fees and expenses to date to defend this suit in excess of one hundred forty-five thousand dollars ($145,000) and, accordingly, requests sanctions in that amount against Mr. Carson.

Leslie's face turned one shade darker than her auburn hair. She cursed Strobel, then noticed the disappointed look on Sarah's face. "Sorry, Sarah. I just don't understand how any officer of the court can just flat out lie like this in an affidavit. It's outrageous."

"Welcome to the real world," Nikki said.

"This one's my fault," Brad said. "I thought he was fishing for information about our case, so I didn't give him any. From now on, if anyone talks to Strobel or another member of the defense team on the phone, follow it up with a letter confirming the substance of the conversation. We can't afford to have them misrepresenting us to the court."

"It's ridiculous that you can't trust the other lawyer any more than that," Leslie said.

Brad flipped his glasses on the table and picked up another document. He stood up to pace as he explained its legal import.

"This is another motion filed today by Kilgore & Strobel. It's a motion to compel answers to interrogatories. They have noticed it for a hearing on the same day as the motion to dismiss. Before I get into the details of this motion, let me make one thing clear." He paused and looked around. "This motion to compel is nobody's fault, and it won't do any good to beat ourselves up over this. There will be no finger-pointing on this team."

He then turned to Sarah. "As leader of this team, and the lawyer who you personally retained, I take full responsibility for any issues raised by this pleading."

Leslie's stomach began to churn. What was Brad talking about? Interrogatories were part of the typical discovery process in any lawsuit. One side would send a group of questions, or "interrogatories," to the other side asking about witnesses or exhibits or any other relevant facts or circumstances. The interrogatories would then be answered under oath, or objections would be lodged and a judge would determine whether the interrogatories had to be answered.

Leslie and Nikki had answered the defendant's interrogatories nearly a month ago. Leslie provided the legal objections, and Nikki provided the factual information. The objections and answers were full and fair. Leslie couldn't imagine what the defendants were complaining about now, but her instincts told her she had missed something. Something big. She tucked her cold and clammy hands under her legs.

"The motion to compel requests that the court overrule all of our objections as untimely, then require us to answer every interrogatory. Some of these interrogatories request information that is clearly protected by the attorney-client privilege. They are claiming that we missed the deadlines for filing objections—"

What?! "That's ridiculous," Leslie interjected. She'd heard enough. "We filed all of our answers and objections within the thirty days allowed by the rules." She grabbed a code book and thumbed through it.

"I hand-delivered the objections myself," Nikki added.

"Here it is," Leslie announced. "Rule 33(b)(3): 'The party upon whom the interrogatories are served shall serve a copy of the answers, and objections, if any, within thirty days.'" She closed the book and placed it back on the table.

"If you two are done, let me finish." Brad was still pacing. "Under federal procedure, each district court can pass some of its own local rules to supplement the federal rules. Leslie, they don't teach you this in law school, and you had no reason to know it, but the Norfolk courts, in their infinite wisdom, have passed a local rule requiring that all objections to interrogatories be filed within fifteen days, not thirty." He paused for just a second, but to Leslie, it stretched out endlessly. The awful consequences of this blunder immediately numbed her brain and set her stomach on fire. She could barely hear Brad's next words for the ringing in her ears. "That's why I'm saying this motion is my fault. I should have warned you to read the local rules."

Leslie felt the blood drain from her face.

"Won't the court cut us some slack?" Nikki asked. "This must happen all the time."

"It does happen all the time. But the court has a history of not being very forgiving on these matters."

Leslie forced herself to move and to think. Fighting off rising panic, she pawed through the local rules in the book that Brad had dropped on the table. She read the rule three times and still couldn't believe it.

"There are lots of problematic interrogatories," Brad continued. "But none as bad as number three. It requests the name of 'every alleged church member who ever worshiped with Charles and Sarah Reed during their tenure in Saudi Arabia.' Of course, we objected to this interrogatory, but now our objection may not hold up because it wasn't timely filed."

"What does that mean?" Sarah asked. It was the first time she had shown any interest in the legal issues.

"It means if we lose on the motion to compel, we must provide the names of every church member who ever worshiped with you and your husband

and pray that they are not persecuted by the Muttawa, or . . ." Brad's voice trailed off.

"Or what?" Leslie insisted.

"Or drop the case in order to protect these innocent church members," Brad concluded.

"We can't give them the names," Sarah said firmly. "Dozens met with us on nights other than Fridays that the Muttawa do not know about. Charles died rather than divulge those names. I would do the same."

Sarah's uncharacteristic bluntness generated a long silence. A sickened Leslie was unable to speak.

"Then we'll have to win the motion to compel," Brad said at length, "and talk the court into granting some mercy on this one."

The scene unfolding before Leslie's eyes was surreal, a lawyer's worst nightmare. The case would be lost, not on the merits, but on a technicality. Just like that. Justice perverted.

"So it all comes down to one judge and whether that judge will allow us to file objections late?" Leslie exhaled sharply. "No matter what the law says, it all just comes down to the discretion of one judge, thumbs-up or thumbs-down, and the case is over just like that?" Her voice was full of disdain, her pristine view of the law crumbling by the second.

"That pretty much nails it," Brad said.

Silence took over, the weight of this precarious position sinking in. Tears of frustration and guilt welled up in Leslie's eyes.

"This is all my fault," she said, her voice wavering. "I was the one responsible for filing the objections. I sweat out every detail of this case. I dot every i and cross every t, and somehow I missed this. I spent the last four months of my life working like a dog on this case and the last two weeks working around the clock on a detailed game plan for the case, and now it's all just wasted work because of some idiotic local rule that nobody knows about.

"The law isn't about this stuff," she said, and with her left hand she made a clean sweep of the table in front of her, knocking law books and documents, including her beloved game plan, onto the floor. "It's about clever lawyers like Strobel taking advantage of fools like me."

Then, in front of her speechless colleagues, Leslie stood and bolted from the room, leaving the others staring in disbelief.

◁▷

Brad had a strong urge to run after Leslie, talk to her, somehow calm her down, and make everything right. But something else told him to stay put. Leslie would have to learn to respond like a professional. Running to her would not help.

Sarah stood and looked at Brad. "Let me talk to her."

"Good luck."

As soon as the door shut behind Sarah, Nikki started in.

"Leslie's got to get a grip. But I don't see why we've got to drop this case if we get a bad ruling. I mean, let's just ask the judge to allow us to produce the names to Strobel under a court order that says he can't share them with his client. That way, we can buy some time and settle this baby."

"Right," Bella scoffed. "Let's put our trust in Mack Strobel, Boy Scout that he is. Even if he doesn't tell the Muttawa, he'll want to take depositions, and how do you hide the names then?"

Brad sat back in his chair and turned toward Nikki, interested in this budding debate. Maybe it would help him sort things out. Right now, Bella had a point. *Advantage, Bella.*

"All right then, we just run a bluff," Nikki responded. "You give them phony names, which still buys you enough time to settle, then you get something out of this deal. You don't just cave."

Shaky, Brad thought. *Bella will smash this one.*

"Brilliant. The only difference between that and highway robbery is that we wouldn't be using a gun." Bella snorted. "Let me get this straight. We run a scam on the court, lie under oath, and try to obtain money under false pretenses in the meantime."

Match point.

"Well, what's your bright idea?" Nikki shot back, her voice rising in frustration. "Just let the creep go? Let him laugh at us all over Saudi Arabia?"

"Drop the case!" Bella scowled. "Cut your losses! Don't be stupid!"

Nikki didn't respond this time; she just glared straight ahead at Bella. She looked ready to pounce.

In an act of studied defiance, Bella whipped out a pack of cigarettes, shaking one loose, and lit it up in the middle of the no-smoking conference room.

"Nice," Nikki said, chasing the smoke away with a wave of the hand. "Black-lung cases, Brad, what do they go for these days—for an overweight single secretary with limited earning capacity?"

Bella stood.

"Sit down," Brad said sharply. He turned to Nikki. "That's not necessary." Then back to Bella. "C'mon, put it out." She sighed, dropped her cigarette into a half-full coffee cup, and plopped into her seat. Brad felt like he was lecturing a couple of kids. "Nikki, we don't handle cases that way here. If the client says drop it, we drop it."

Nikki snorted out a derisive little laugh. "Oh yeah. I forgot. Let's see . . . *Lewis* case, two weeks ago. Client wanted 150K; insurance company offers 100; you said, 'Take it.' *Pardee* case, last week. Defense attorney says 75K; client says 90; you take 85. *Migliori* case—"

"They're different," Brad argued. "Every one of those cases is about a greedy client, unrealistic demands. You agreed with every one of the settlements. It's our job to make the client see reality. Sarah . . . well, she's different."

"So it's our job to just sell her out, drop the case—"

"You don't get it, do you?" Bella interrupted. "Nobody's selling out. If we take this case all the way, it could bankrupt us. It's a dog, Nikki. And if we go bankrupt chasing this dog, then all of your well-intentioned crusading won't do anybody any good."

"Nobody's selling out," Nikki repeated, mocking Bella's tone. "Then what do you call it?"

"I guess if anybody would recognize selling out, you would," Bella responded. "It's how you got here in the first place—"

"Enough!" Brad barked. He wondered if the two women would ever get along. "If we have to give up the names," he said softly, "we drop the case. I'm sorry, Nikki. But that's the way it's got to be."

Nikki began to calm down. "Shouldn't we at least get Leslie back in here and let her vote?"

"No votes," Brad replied.

"Oh, I see. And no respect either, huh?"

"C'mon, Nikki. You know that's not the way it is here."

Nikki pursed her lips and stared straight ahead, apparently not convinced. Bella, her victory secure, got up and headed for the door, a thin trail of smoke still slithering in her wake.

"Satisfied?" Nikki asked.

"Get over it," Bella said and slammed the door behind her.

◁▷

Leslie felt a gentle hand on her shoulder as she stood on the sidewalk in front of the office building and looked out over the parking lot.

"This isn't really about the case, is it?" Sarah asked.

"It is about the case," Leslie said, desperation in her voice. "It's about not letting Aberijan and the others get away with murder. It's about making your husband's death mean something."

The two women stood quietly for a moment.

"Listen, Leslie, I don't harbor any hatred toward these men. I miss Charles so much, but I know that if I don't forgive, it only eats me up and causes more pain. I trust God to take care of justice. That's His job, not mine."

Leslie could not fathom this forgiveness that Sarah so easily embraced. She loathed Ahmed for what he did to Sarah. She loathed Mack Strobel for being his hired gun. And right now was not a good time for the platitudes of a missionary.

You're sweet, Sarah, but you're not me. I'm not put together that way. I never will be.

Leslie turned and faced Sarah but did not look her in the eye. "I don't know how you can forgive these men—God either for that matter. I've been in a feud with God ever since He took away Bill."

"Maybe that's the difference," Sarah said softly. "I don't blame God for taking Charles away. I just thank Him for giving me Charles all those years."

The words struck Leslie like another blow. Though they could not have been more kindly delivered, they brought to the surface a lingering bitterness Leslie had worked hard to deny.

The words stayed with her throughout the day and continued to echo long into the evening. She turned them over and over in her mind and vainly searched her own heart for the type of peace that Sarah expressed. Instead, she found humiliation. Embarrassment. Defeat. And when she finally arrived back at her tiny garage apartment and crawled into bed, it was the missed deadline, and not the insightful words of a missionary, that caused Leslie to lie awake the entire night, staring at the same spot on the ceiling.

◁▷

It came two days before the motion to dismiss hearing. It arrived in a plain 8½-by-11 manila envelope bearing a Norfolk, Virginia, postmark. Ahmed read the contents of the package for the third time, still incredulous at his good fortune.

The envelope contained two documents. The first document was one page long, and the second was nearly twenty pages. The long document was titled "Preliminary Game Plan for *Reed v. Saudi Arabia*." It contained lists of potential witnesses, experts, exhibits, and relevant documents. It appeared to be some sort of analysis of the case by the plaintiff's lawyers.

The other document was a note composed of letters and numbers cut from magazines and pasted on a plain white sheet of computer paper. Ahmed would ask Barnes to analyze both documents for fingerprints and other trace evidence, although he really didn't expect to find anything. The note was simple and direct: *This first installment will cost you $50,000 U.S.D. More will follow if you obey my instructions and do not investigate. Make payment before the conclusion of the motion to dismiss hearing.*

The second paragraph contained wiring instructions for a Cayman Islands bank account that undoubtedly belonged to a shell corporation whose officers and shareholders would be untraceable. The note was, of course, unsigned.

Ahmed called Barnes and speculated about the note for the better part of an hour. It could come from any number of sources, they agreed. The most likely scenario, Ahmed offered, would be an employee of Carson & Associates. A truly disgruntled insider who was fed up and saw this case as a surefire way to make big money fast.

But Ahmed also recognized that there were many other less desirable possibilities. In fact, the meager amount of money demanded concerned Ahmed. Perhaps the source was not a member of the plaintiff's team. Such a person would have placed a higher value on the case. It could be a roommate or friend. It could be their clumsy Saudi lawyer, el Khamin. It could even be a friend of Sarah Reed. For that matter, it could be the janitor in Carson's building or just a good old-fashioned thief. The possibilities were endless, but the promise in the note of future installments certainly had Ahmed's attention. He had to know the source so he could verify the credibility of this information.

"Frederick, why do you think I pay you all this money? I must know who sent this, and I must know soon. Is that understood?"

"You will know, Ahmed. Just give me some time."

17

THE ALARM SEEMED LOUDER THAN NORMAL, partly because it was set an hour earlier and partly because Brad had never achieved deep sleep during the night. 5:30 a.m. He forced himself out of bed and stumbled downstairs to start the coffee. He would add two miles to his morning run today, an extra fifteen minutes, because he needed the additional time to clear his mind and prepare for the day's events.

His first mile was always a grind, and starting an hour early didn't help. The endorphins kicked in at mile two, freeing his mind for deep thinking. He hit his stride by 5:45 and started to sweat in the early morning heat and humidity of Tidewater.

By the end of mile three he was in the zone. He determined that the best way to combat a Rule 11 motion was to act the part of a reasonable and careful lawyer. He would save the dramatics for trial. Today he would argue the law in scholarly tones and be the very picture of an attorney who would never consider filing a lawsuit unsupported by the current state of the law. He would leave the name-calling and insult-hurling to Strobel. Brad promised himself he would behave.

He would have Leslie handle the motion to compel. She would fall on her sword, admit her mistake, and plead for mercy. She would undoubtedly generate sympathy. A judge would be more likely to feel sorry for a law student than a seasoned litigator.

On his fourth mile, he thought about how he would handle the motion to dismiss and adjust his style based on the judge assigned to the hearing. That was the one great wild card remaining to be dealt. Norfolk Federal Court was famous for concealing the judge's identity until the morning of the hearing. To keep the litigants guessing, the court would even change judges on a case from one hearing to the next, up until the morning of trial. The trial judge would remain a mystery until the morning of jury selection.

Brad dreaded the possibility that he might draw Ichabod. If she showed up today wearing the black robe, he might as well get out his checkbook to pay the sanctions and kiss the case good-bye. No adjustment to his style could overcome the ire of Ichabod.

If he could pick his judge, he would ask for Judge Samuel Johnson, the only African American on the Norfolk bench and the only judge whose career did not include a stint with a big firm defending cases for corporate clients. More than any other member of the bench, Brad suspected Judge Johnson would be open to his argument that outrageous violations of human rights, like those at issue here, must have a remedy in international law. Johnson would understand the basic parallels to civil rights laws in this country and would not be intimidated by being the first judge to do what was right.

Brad used the last three miles of his run to rehearse his arguments. By the time he finished at 6:15, he was relaxed and ready for the day's maelstrom.

◁▷

By 9 a.m., Norfolk Federal Court was a media madhouse. Though court rules prohibited cameras in the courtroom, the First Amendment kept the judges from extending their ban to the steps and sidewalks in front of the large brick building. Accordingly, the local media hordes transformed that area into a gauntlet of cameras and microphones poised to engulf the lawyers and their clients as they entered the sanctuary of the court.

Strobel and his entourage showed up first. They arrived simultaneously in several luxury cars, transporting no fewer than eight lawyers and paralegals. All were dressed in expensive dark blue or gray suits. While the rest of the team busied itself by unloading boxes of documents and notebooks, Strobel held forth for the reporters.

"What are your chances of having this case thrown out today?"

"We think they are excellent, or we would not have filed the motion."

"Do you expect to get sanctions against Mr. Carson?"

"Will you be calling any witnesses today?"

"Will you appeal if you lose?"

"One question at a time please. No testimony is heard when the court rules on a motion to dismiss. We do not believe we will lose this hearing, but if we do, we cannot appeal a motion to dismiss ruling until the entire case is over. As for the sanctions against Mr. Carson, that will be for the court to decide."

"Are you pleased with the selection of Judge Johnson to hear this motion?" Strobel hesitated. His eyes flashed; then his game face returned.

"I'm sure Judge Johnson will do a fine job. The judge assigned makes no difference to us. All of the jurists in this court are fair and impartial. Now, if you'll excuse me, we need to get ready."

◁▷

Brad caught himself smiling as Judge Johnson took the bench, fashionably late to his own hearing. Brad wiped the grin from his face as the spectators stood and fell into hushed silence.

"You may be seated," the judge said in a rich, slow Southern baritone. "Counselors, I've reserved two hours for your arguments, no more. The court has read every word of your briefs, so do not waste the court's time by simply repeating arguments you've already made. Is that understood?"

"Yes, Your Honor," Brad said simultaneously with Mack Strobel.

"Mr. Strobel, we are here on your motions, you may proceed."

Strobel strode confidently to the podium to address the court. He took a massive notebook with him and left another just out of reach at his counsel table.

"If it pleases the court, we are here today on a number of defense motions." His confident voice bellowed throughout the courtroom.

"I will address three motions: the motion to dismiss plaintiff's case because this court lacks jurisdiction, the corresponding Rule 11 motion we have made requesting sanctions against plaintiff's counsel for the filing of a frivolous lawsuit, and our motion to compel answers to the interrogatories that we filed based on the fact that counsel for plaintiff did not file any timely objections."

"Let's deal with the motion to compel first," Johnson suggested. "It seems like that issue is pretty straightforward, and we ought to be able to resolve it quickly before we get into the more complicated motion to dismiss."

A thin smile creased Strobel's face, and for the next several minutes he set forth his reasons for wanting every interrogatory answered, but particularly the one requesting names of every church member who ever worshiped with the Reeds. The names were relevant, he argued, so that he could take the depositions of these former church members and find out if the Reeds were really missionaries or just clever drug lords. Besides, he asserted, the plaintiff waived any objection when her attorneys missed the deadline for filing objections.

"Is that true, you missed the deadline?" Judge Johnson asked Brad.

So much for reading the briefs, Brad thought. *We only spent about ten pages on this issue.*

Though Johnson was looking at Brad, Leslie stood. "I'm afraid it is, Your Honor." She looked appropriately nervous, eyes darting around, voice slightly quivering. Brad was proud of her.

"And it's entirely my fault. I'm a rising third-year law student helping Mr. Carson on this case, and I missed the deadline for filing objections. I didn't know about the local fifteen-day rule, although I also recognize it is entirely my responsibility to be familiar with that rule. I bring the court no excuses, just a simple request that the court not hold my client responsible for my failure by making us produce the names. We are prepared to answer every other interrogatory, but if we have to produce these names, we sincerely believe that it is just a matter of time before they are tortured too."

Johnson thought about this for a second, indecision etched in the wrinkles on his forehead. Leslie gingerly sat down, never taking her eyes off the judge. He stared at the back wall, saying nothing.

Finally, he spoke. "I read in the briefs that your client will drop the case rather than produce any names. Is that true?"

Whoa! He has read the briefs. The earlier question was just a setup, a credibility check to see if we would fudge the issue. We passed.

Leslie was on her feet again. "That's correct," she said tentatively.

"And if I give you a simple order to produce to Mr. Strobel all the names of alleged church members who worshiped with Sarah Reed, you would rather drop the case than obey my order?"

Leslie shifted her weight from foot to foot, the pain of this answer registering in her eyes.

"I wouldn't phrase it that way, Judge. But with all due respect, my client has decided not to produce the names under any circumstances."

Johnson shifted his stare to Sarah. "Is that true?" he inquired.

Sarah stood. "Absolutely, Your Honor."

"That's what I thought," Johnson said. "And it's the only thing that makes my decision easier." He flashed a quick grin at Sarah. "You may sit back down, Mrs. Reed."

"Thanks," she said, embarrassed.

"This case reminds me of the biblical story of Solomon and the two women fighting over the baby. Solomon said he would split the baby and give half to each woman claiming to be the mother. He knew the real mother would never allow that to happen. And so he awarded the baby to the woman who begged the king not to kill the child."

Brad felt a small smile creep across his lips.

"In the same manner, I am impressed by the sincerity of Mrs. Reed. She is prepared to drop this case rather than reveal the names of alleged church members. She must sincerely believe they would be persecuted for their faith. I realize that her lawyers missed a deadline, but this court is not willing to make Mrs. Reed pay so dear a price for the mistake of her lawyers.

"Accordingly," he concluded, "we will take a page out of Solomon's book and see if we can split this baby. Mrs. Reed must answer each and every interrogatory except she will not be required to reveal the names of the alleged church members unknown to the defendants. In exchange, Mrs. Reed will not be permitted to mention or testify at trial about any alleged church members other than the Friday night group that the defendants already know about. I know it's not a perfect remedy, and whatever judge tries this case may decide to do something different, but it's the best I can do for now. After all, I'm no Solomon."

A collective sigh of relief registered at the plaintiff's counsel table. They had dodged at least one bullet today. This judge was Solomon incarnate, as far as Brad was concerned. Brad leaned over and whispered to Leslie.

"Nice job," he said. "You looked pathetic."

"Thanks," she whispered back. "It's my specialty."

Strobel appeared unfazed. He had undoubtedly seen his share of surprises through the years, and you could never tell from his demeanor if he had been dealt a serious blow. He remained stoic, thanked the judge for the ruling, and launched into his argument on the motion to dismiss with undiminished vigor.

"The courts of the United States have honored the immunity of other nations from lawsuits for more than 180 years," he asserted. "From the time Chief Justice John Marshall decided the case of *Schooner Exchange v. M'Faddon* in 1812, through this very day, courts have honored the bedrock principle of international law that each country has exclusive and absolute territorial jurisdiction over actions that occur within its territory. Therefore, countries grant each other immunity over lawsuits—"

"Skip the history lesson," Johnson cut in. "Let's bring it up to at least 1976, shall we? Would you agree that in 1976 Congress passed the Foreign Sovereign Immunities Act and that is the statute we need to interpret today?"

"Yes, Your Honor. And that statute makes it clear that the defendants are entitled to immunity from this lawsuit." Strobel looked the part of the big-firm defense lawyer. He stood erect, and his full and deep voice originated from deep down in his diaphragm, reverberating throughout the courtroom.

"Plaintiff claims there should be an exception to this statute for torture arising out of religious persecution," he continued. "She says that torture violates a fundamental norm of international law, also known as a *jus cogens* law, and therefore nations cannot claim the immunity of international law when they act in ways that violate the very essence of international law. But this claim has been considered and rejected by other courts. For example, the Ninth Circuit Court of Appeals, in the case of *Siderman v. Argentina*, rejected the claim of a Jewish citizen from Argentina who had been arrested and tortured because of his faith—"

"Speaking of the *Siderman* case," Judge Johnson said, waving the lawbook in his hand, "let me ask if you agree with some quotes from that case that I find very persuasive. Do you agree, sir, with the following quote: 'The right to be free from official torture is fundamental and universal, a right deserving of the highest status under international law, a norm of *jus cogens*. The crack of the whip, the clamp of the thumb screw, the crush of the iron maiden, and, in these more efficient modern times, the shock of the electric cattle prod are forms of torture that the international order will not tolerate. To subject a person to such horrors is to commit one of the most egregious violations of the personal security and dignity of a human being.' Do you agree with that, Mr. Strobel?"

Johnson glared down at Strobel, still holding the *Siderman* case in one hand as if it were an original copy of the Ten Commandments. For the first time all day, Brad slid back in his chair, crossed his legs, and relaxed.

"I agree that torture violates the personal security and dignity of human beings but—"

"Then don't you also agree, Mr. Strobel, that when a nation violates this fundamental rule of international behavior, the cloak of sovereign immunity that is provided by international law falls away, leaving the nation vulnerable to suit?"

"No, Your Honor," Strobel said with great confidence. Even when he spoke to a judge, he had a certain air of authority. "You quoted some select language from the *Siderman* case, but the ultimate decision in that case rejected the very argument you just raised—the court ultimately said that the act of torture did not strip away the right to sovereign immunity."

"Let me put it to you this way, Mr. Strobel: Suppose I agree with the language of the *Siderman* case but not the ultimate reasoning. I don't have to follow that court's reasoning. Are you aware of any U.S. Supreme Court case that says a foreign nation that tortures U.S. citizens cannot be sued in U.S. courts?"

"No, Your Honor, the Supreme Court has not squarely addressed this issue." Strobel's confidence took on a tone of frustration. "Based on other decisions regarding similar subjects, however—"

"If neither the Supreme Court nor the appeals court for this circuit have squarely addressed this issue, then it seems to me I've got to do what I believe is right. And it just doesn't seem right that foreign countries can torture American citizens and then scream sovereign immunity when they get sued in American courts. If all courts in the past had read the law as narrowly as you do, Mr. Strobel, we would still be in the Dark Ages when it comes to civil rights in this country. Justice and common sense require something more. Now that's just my initial inclination in this case. I'm willing to give you every opportunity to talk me out of it."

For the next hour, Strobel tried heroically to do just that. But Johnson's "initial inclination" proved to be a stubborn one indeed. The more Strobel talked, the bigger the hole he dug. And after exhausting every argument and citing nearly every case in his handy black notebook, Strobel reluctantly sat down, needing a miracle.

Brad practically floated to the podium. But before he could speak, Johnson put his upcoming argument into the proper perspective.

"Now, Mr. Carson, there's one thing I'd like you to keep in mind as you begin your argument." Brad listened intently to the soothing baritone drawl. He wanted to address every concern and allay every lingering doubt that Judge Johnson might express. "I've read all the briefs, and I've now heard Mr. Strobel's eloquent arguments. Despite those arguments, I'm leaning toward allowing the case to go forward. Of course, if I did that, I would also dismiss the Rule 11 motion, since you can hardly be fined for filing a frivolous case if I decide the case has enough merit to proceed. Now having said all that, Mr. Carson, I am certainly willing to give you all the time you need to help me rethink this matter and change my mind."

Brad glanced quickly down at his yellow legal pad and all the arguments he had worked so hard to refine. He thought about the press corps behind him waiting to be impressed with passionate oratory about the virtues of religious freedom and the vices of religious bigotry. He thought about his own reputation, about how few chances a lawyer had to mesmerize this type of gathering. But then he also thought about Sarah and the torture and her children being raised without a father.

Silence was, after all, a virtue.

"In that case, Your Honor, I believe I can be very quick. We would simply like to rest on the arguments previously submitted in our briefs."

"A wise choice," Johnson said, and Brad returned to his seat.

"The court will take a ten-minute recess," Johnson said, "and then I will announce my decision."

◁▷

Thirty minutes later, Brad was in the process of reassuring Leslie when Johnson reentered the courtroom. The chattering immediately stopped. "Remain seated," Johnson said to the crowd.

"Don't worry," Brad whispered. He could tell his words just bounced off Leslie's furrowed brow.

"Then why did he take so long?"

"What did I say?"

"Do I look worried?"

Brad scrunched his face and nodded. "Yep."

"I will be filing a lengthy written opinion in the weeks ahead," Johnson said, "but I thought it only fair to the parties that I state for the record my intentions with regard to the ruling so they can plan accordingly."

The judge surveyed the crowd, put on his reading glasses, and commenced with the opinion he had written just minutes earlier in his office.

"The United States, Saudi Arabia, and most other civilized countries are members of the United Nations and therefore signatories of the United Nations Universal Declaration of Human Rights," he began. "Article 18 of that document states that 'Everyone has the right to freedom of thought, conscience and religion; this right includes freedom to change his religion or belief, and freedom, either alone or in community with others and in public or private, to manifest his religion or belief in teaching, practice, worship and observance.'" He stopped reading for just a moment and glanced up at Sarah. He looked back down and continued.

"Moreover, both Saudi Arabia and the United States have signed the International Covenant on Civil and Political Rights. That document repeats this commitment to religious freedom and also states that 'Each state party to the present Covenant undertakes to ensure that any person whose rights or freedoms as recognized herein are violated shall have an effective remedy.' Furthermore, as the court noted earlier, it is a fundamental norm of international law that citizens of all countries should be free from torture at the hands of governmental officials.

"In order to give substance to the international rights contained in treaties and charters signed by our own government, this court must open its doors for serious and substantial human rights claims against foreign governments. It makes a mockery of these treaties, and of the human rights that undergird them, to suggest that nations can violate these rights at will and then hide behind the doctrine of sovereign immunity. Accordingly, I am denying defendant's motion to dismiss and dismissing defendant's Rule 11 motion."

A murmur drifted up from the spectators. Hushed and excited whispering could be heard. Strobel stared ahead, his face betraying no emotion.

"I am also mindful that justice delayed is justice denied. This case has already been pending for more than three months. Plaintiff is entitled to her day in court. Accordingly, I am setting a trial date for the third Monday in October, less than three months from today's date."

After reading this last sentence, Judge Johnson banged his gavel, rose from the bench, and walked regally out the back door of the courtroom. Brad thought that the crusty old judge looked remarkably like an angel.

◁▷

Later that night, after an impromptu celebration dinner died down, Brad walked Leslie to her car. He gently put his arm around her shoulder. She snuggled against him, and they walked slowly, completely in sync.

The adrenaline that had coursed so freely through her body earlier in the day was now completely gone. She was so totally relaxed, she felt like a limp dishrag. She wanted nothing more at this moment than the very thing now happening. The case was moving forward. And Brad Carson, the man she had thought about nonstop for two months in England, was walking with his arm around her and holding her close, like they would never be apart again.

"Leslie, I'm sorry about that night in Williamsburg . . ."

"You don't need to apologize."

"I do," he urged softly. "I'm sorry that I tried to push our relationship too far, too fast. I didn't know about Bill. I've been doing a lot of thinking since that time, and I've come to realize that you were right. It's not good to start a relationship in the middle of a pressure cooker like this case. Especially when you're still trying to recover from Bill's death. Let's wait till this case is over. That'll give us both more time to sort things out. If there's anything real between us, it'll survive. If there's not, then it wasn't meant to be."

They stopped walking, and Brad took her gingerly by both hands, the same way he had in Williamsburg. "Anyway," he said, "that's what I've been thinking."

It wasn't at all what Leslie had been thinking. And looking deep into Brad's penetrating gaze, those intense steel blue eyes, was not helping to clear things up. At this moment, she was more confused than ever.

Should she tell him how she felt? *Forget that night in Colonial Williamsburg, Brad Carson. Forget my hesitation and second-guessing, my "I need more time" protestations. I'm ready now. I've thought this through. Banished my demons of doubt. And I've decided that I need you more than you'll ever know. Not when the case is over, but now. Right now. Tonight.*

But when she opened her mouth, none of those words came out; none of those feelings found expression. "Thanks, Brad," was all she could bring herself to say.

He kissed her gently on the cheek, then turned and walked away. He didn't even notice the mist gathering in her eyes.

PART III
DISCOVERY

18

IT'S ONE THING TO ALLEGE TORTURE at the hands of a foreign government; it's another thing to prove it. This harsh reality dawned on Brad and his legal team the morning after the hearing, as the euphoria of surviving the motion to dismiss gave way to the reality of the task before them.

To get this next phase started on the right foot, Brad called an all-hands meeting for 8:30 a.m. Nikki arrived at 9:15, and Bella pried herself free from the phone and a cigarette a few minutes later. Leslie had already been in the conference room for two hours, refining her preliminary game plan and developing a list of potential witnesses for trial.

Brad was pacing, thinking out loud, and twirling his glasses.

"These cases are won or lost with expert witnesses. Experts can give opinions about anything. If we get the right ones on the stand, experts that the jurors like and understand, we can blow this case wide open. We've got to have guys who don't condescend to the jury—juries hate that, you know— and guys who will stand up to Strobel on cross-examination without being obnoxious.

"Our deadline for naming experts is a week from Friday. How're we coming, Nikki?"

Nikki's head jolted up. "Yep, I agree."

Bella rolled her eyes. After twelve years working together, Brad knew what she was thinking: *We're paying Nikki how much for this?*

"You agree with what?" Brad asked. "I'm asking you, how're we coming on our experts?"

"Okay, I guess," Nikki said. She looked a little sheepish. "You said you knew an economist who could testify about the economic impact of Dr. Reed's death—lost wages, loss of services, that type of thing. So I haven't done anything yet on the economist."

"There's a surprise," Bella muttered.

Brad ignored her, as did Nikki. Leslie ignored everybody as she continued to write.

"Bella, get Nikki the contact information for Dr. Calvin Drake," Brad said. "Have him sit down with Nikki and Leslie and draft an opinion before the deadline. The total economic loss needs to be about two million. Who else have we got?"

Nikki casually checked some notes. "We've got the toxicologist, Dr. Nancy Shelhorse. She'll testify about the blood tests and urine tests given at the two hospitals and the toxicological tests that were part of the autopsy. It's her opinion that Sarah and Charles Reed were injected with cocaine by the police at the time of the arrest."

Nikki glanced up from her notes, this time looking extraordinarily pleased with herself. She smiled at Bella.

"Sounds pretty strong," Brad said. "What else do you have?"

"Our star will be Alfred Lloyd Worthington, a Washington lobbyist who works with multinational corporations and serves as an adjunct professor of international law at George Mason University. Worthington is a former congressman who got caught up in the demographic shift from Democrat to Republican in northern Virginia. During his time in Congress he served on the House Foreign Relations Committee. He's got a great résumé, and he sees this case as his ticket back into the spotlight. He's qualified to give opinions on international treaties and the miserable track record of the Saudis when it comes to religious liberty. He'll prove that the Saudi government knew all about the activities of the religious police and sanctioned this type of conduct."

Brad tried not to look as surprised as he felt. Nikki had been busy. "Sounds great. Leslie, can you spend some time prepping Worthington as well?"

Leslie nodded and made some more notes.

"How much are all these wonderful wise men and women costing us?" Bella asked. "I don't want to be the killjoy, but isn't three experts a bit much?"

"Not when the defendants have twelve," Leslie said.

"Three experts should be plenty," Brad said. "Having more than one expert on the same subject only gets confusing."

"Confusing and expensive," Bella said. "How much are these guys charging us?"

"The usual," Nikki said. "A couple hundred an hour each."

"A few million here, a few million there. Pretty soon you're talking some real money," Bella griped.

"Isn't it time for you to go get another cigarette?" Nikki asked.

Brad shot a warning look toward both Nikki and Bella.

"Brad, I just don't see how we can possibly get everything done," Leslie piped in, studying her notes. "Kilgore & Strobel sent deposition notices this morning for Sarah, her kids, all her doctors and counselors, and a number of former church members living in Saudi Arabia. Strobel's boys have been calling all morning demanding to know who our experts are so they can schedule their depositions. We will want to depose, at a minimum, all of their experts and Aberijan. The way I see it, we've got at least thirty days of depositions waiting for us, and you're the only one who can do them."

"Can't you take some of the depositions under third-year practice rules?"

"Not unless you or some other lawyer is sitting there with me, which defeats the purpose."

"Brad, you can't even start these depositions for thirty days," Bella said, ever anxious to be the bearer of bad news. "You're booked solid on other cases through the end of August."

"Look," Brad said, "we're into this case, and we've got to figure out a way to get it done. Y'all have been great at identifying problems, now how about a little help with some proposed solutions?"

The entire team silently mulled that one over. After a few seconds of avoiding eye contact with Brad, Leslie swallowed hard and spoke. "I'll take a semester off from school and work full-time on this case. An opportunity like this only comes along once."

Brad caught himself staring at her and thought about how great it would be to have her around more. Still, he forced himself to give an appropriately sensitive response. "I wouldn't ask you to do that," he heard himself say.

"You didn't ask, but I'm going to do it anyway. You wanted solutions, that's my contribution."

Careful, big guy. Don't give her too many opportunities to rethink this, to wiggle away. Having Leslie around full-time would be great for you and equally great for the case.

"Then let's at least get you an apartment here in Tidewater for the next several months," Brad offered.

Bella's face registered her disapproval. Brad was glad to be pacing, or he would have been kicked.

"No thanks," Leslie said, taking the tension out of the room. "I can do a lot of my work at the law library and stay in Williamsburg."

"I'll clear the decks of my other cases," Brad offered, inspired by this turn of events. "I can pass some off to my buddies and get continuances on others. It'll take me thirty days, but I'll clear the decks and focus entirely on this one."

He caught Nikki's frown out of the corner of his eye. "Every case except Johnson, of course."

"And I'll continue to perform my stellar legal work in the same manner as I have, even though I'm grossly underpaid," Nikki said. Nobody laughed, but Brad sensed Nikki said it less to draw a laugh than to aggravate Bella.

"All of this is wonderful," Bella said gruffly. "Warm and fuzzy and all that. But it still doesn't solve the problem of covering the depositions. We need another licensed lawyer, a warm body to sit with Leslie."

Nikki sat straight up, her eyes suddenly sparkling. "Why didn't you say so?" she asked. "I know the perfect warm body, and he won't cost us a dime." She had Brad's attention. "We go to the Rock and ask him to sit in on a few depositions with Leslie. In exchange, we offer to make him co-counsel on the Johnson case, which Brad stole from him anyway, and we give him a small split on our fee. We also make him co-counsel on the *Reed* case and offer him no part of the fee. He's the one plaintiff's lawyer in Tidewater who will join us in the case and not charge us a dime just because it's megafree publicity. The Rock *lives* for free publicity."

Brad hated the idea. But no one offered a better plan.

By noon they had retained the Rock.

◁▷

Mack Strobel was at his best when bullying younger members of his firm. On the morning after the motion to dismiss hearing, Mack was in rare form.

The unsuccessful hearing was, of course, the fault of the brief writers. Their prose failed to persuade Judge Johnson, and even the brilliant oral arguments of Mack himself could not salvage the situation. He ripped into the inept associates and sent them back to the library to work on a new set of briefs for other important pretrial hearings. One young female associate actually left the room in tears. Mack made a mental note to veto her from future high-profile cases.

The honeymoon was over, Mack announced. They had made the mistake of underestimating this case once. It would not happen again. No more country-club environment and twelve-hour workdays. It was time to buckle down.

Mack also called another meeting of his brain trust. There had to be a way—there must be—to ensure he did not get stuck with Johnson as a trial judge.

◁▷

As Rasheed had requested, Hanif came a full hour early for the Friday night worship service. After affectionate greetings, Rasheed silently nodded his head toward the door, and Hanif followed him outside. The brothers walked several feet down the sidewalk before Rasheed started talking.

"The Muttawa know about us," Rasheed said. He waited a few seconds to allow the awful news to sink in.

Hanif did not break stride. "I am not surprised." He kept his eyes glued to the sidewalk.

"Our apartment is bugged."

No response.

"A few weeks ago, they came to visit."

The quiet padding of Hanif's shoes against the pavement stopped. "Why didn't you say something?"

"I wanted to so badly, but I needed time to sort it out, decide what to do." Rasheed's voice was cracking with emotion. He stared straight ahead and continued talking. "They made Mobara and me promise to disband the church. They made us promise to give videotaped testimony against Sarah Reed. They made us promise . . ." His bottom lip trembled, and his voice trailed off. Instead of continuing, he handed Hanif an envelope.

The letter inside was addressed to church members.

The letter said that the Berjeins' home had been bugged and that the members should not say anything out loud but simply read the letter. The letter explained that, for the sake of the recording devices, Rasheed would declare the church disbanded. The members should act appropriately dismayed but ultimately agree not to meet.

The letter also gave the location for the next week's meeting and told the members to never mention this location out loud. Each subsequent week, Rasheed wrote, he would provide a new letter specifying the meeting place for the following week. He instructed the members never to say a word about the chosen location and to destroy the letters after noting the next place of worship. They should not call or otherwise contact the Berjeins.

The second page of the letter had been the hardest for Rasheed to write. He watched as Hanif read it, disbelief slowly forming on his face.

"For reasons I cannot explain, I will only be able to meet with you for a few more weeks," Rasheed had written. "And it is obvious that I can no longer be the pastor of this fellowship. If you will allow me, I would like to pass that mantle of leadership to my brother, Hanif, whom the Holy Spirit will empower to lead this church through this most difficult hour. Please give him all the love and respect you gave me. Though I will only be with you a few more times, you will forever be in my prayers."

Hanif looked up from the letter and into the tear-filled eyes of Rasheed. "I can't . . . I just can't . . . ," Hanif stammered. "I don't know how . . ."

"You must," Rasheed responded emphatically, grabbing his younger brother by both shoulders. "I will teach you. Quietly. Secretly. We will study God's Word together. The Muttawa promised to leave the others in the church alone, including you, if Mobara and I give testimony in the case against Sarah Reed. That testimony will take place in a couple of weeks. Nobody else in the church must ever know about this." Rasheed again fell silent, struggling against his rising emotions, taking a few fitful breaths.

"You can't do that," Hanif protested. "It doesn't matter what they promise."

"Leave that to me, Hanif. And trust me completely. I will do what I have to do. God has given me a plan." Rasheed squeezed his brother's shoulders. "Your job is to build this church. Nobody else can do that but you."

Hanif exhaled deeply, the weight of the responsibility already showing on his face. "Okay," he said, looking his brother squarely in the eye. "I will try."

Then the two men embraced, their strength flowing into each other. Rasheed had never been more proud of his little brother.

◁▷

Worthington would be magnificent. Even during his prep session, Leslie could tell he would make a great witness. He had credentials, neatly groomed gray hair, and an extensive vocabulary befitting an international law guru. Leslie asked him the toughest questions she could fathom, and he handled them with ease.

"The Saudis have always given lip service to religious tolerance, but in point of fact their Islamic regime is one of the world's most oppressive governments," he explained. "They systematically violate the United Nations Universal Declaration of Human Rights. Their very own laws require that all Saudis be good Muslims, and the infamous Muttawa brutally enforce strict compliance with these laws. The crown prince of Saudi Arabia is fully apprised of the activities of the Muttawa, and the crown prince himself sanctions their use of the police power to keep the people in line."

"What is the basis for that opinion?" Leslie asked.

Worthington responded with a series of past examples, recalling precise dates, names, and places with an almost photographic memory. After three hours of probing for a chink in his armor, Leslie was satisfied none existed. He seemed too good to be true.

Unfortunately, he was.

Just before their time ended, Worthington hinted at the one skeleton in his closet.

"As I understand it, Leslie, the defense lawyers will be able to ask me only about past felonies and misdemeanors involving moral turpitude, but no others. And they can't ask about charges, only convictions. Is that right?"

"Sure," Leslie replied, her mental red flags suddenly flapping wildly. "Misdemeanors that go to the credibility of a witness, like lying, cheating, or stealing, are fair game. Other misdemeanors are not. Crimes charged are not relevant unless the charge results in a conviction. Why?"

Worthington's eyes darted around the room, as if there might be hidden cameras present. He lowered his voice. "Is our conversation covered by the attorney-client privilege?"

"Sure," Leslie said. *I think,* she said to herself. Technically, Worthington was an expert, not a client. But he had piqued her interest. She would tell him what he needed to hear in order to bare his soul.

"About two years ago, I was arrested and charged with disturbing the peace," he said in a whisper, staring down at folded hands. "My lawyer cut a deal, and we pleaded no contest. The judge took the case under advisement for six months, with the understanding that if I stayed clean, the charge would be dismissed. I didn't even jaywalk. At the end of that time, the judge entered a not-guilty finding. It's all in the court records."

"They shouldn't be able to ask about that incident," Leslie said, suddenly more curious than ever. "It's a misdemeanor, and you technically weren't convicted. We should have no trouble keeping it out. What was it for anyway?" She tried to sound casual, though her voice was noticeably higher.

"Is that really relevant?" His voice turned the question into a statement. He folded his arms.

"Just curious."

"If I told you, I'd have to kill you," Worthington said, forcing a chuckle.
Leslie smiled politely, determined to find out.

◁▷

Nikki seemed to know every police officer in Tidewater. Those officers had
friends in Alexandria, and friends of those friends included an officer who
was part of the misdemeanor investigation of Alfred Lloyd Worthington.

"The guy is a wife beater," Nikki reported. "The Mrs. finally had enough
and called the cops. But when the case went to court, she no longer wanted
to press charges. They're back together now, the perfect suburban couple."

◁▷

Never answer the phone after 5 p.m. This simple rule had spared Bella from a
multitude of crises designed to destroy relaxing evenings. Answer the phone
after 5 p.m., and you can kiss the evening good-bye.

Tonight, however, the logistical challenges of the *Reed* case and the
financial challenges of the entire office had so completely distracted her that
she did not notice the time until she held the receiver in her hand. 5:06.

"Carson & Associates, how can I help you?" Bella asked, not sounding
the least bit helpful.

"By dropping the *Reed* case," said the muffled voice on the other end. "You
tell your boss he's in over his head. If he doesn't, he'll wish he had never met
Sarah Reed. And we'll come after you first." The caller paused. "You got that?"

The phone shook in Bella's hand. She had received plenty of prank calls
in her time. This one was different.

"Are you threatening me?" she asked as bravely as she could.

"Drop the case and you'll have nothing to worry about. You've got one
week."

What scared Bella most was the monotone delivery, the lack of emotion.

Bella was so flustered she couldn't think of a thing to say. Not that it mattered. The phone went dead.

She returned the receiver to its cradle with shaking hands. She stared
straight ahead, alone in the office, suddenly feeling vulnerable. She would
mention the call to Brad first thing in the morning—one more reason to
drop this risky case—but she knew what his reaction would be. They had
been threatened on other cases. "We can't let those nuts scare us off," Brad

would say. But this one was different. She couldn't explain why. But she could *feel* it.

This guy meant business. And Bella would have to be prepared.

For the first time in weeks, she left work before six. Instead of heading to her small apartment in Chesapeake or to the nursing home to visit her mother, she took off in the direction of the strip malls on Military Highway. Shortly before seven, she walked sheepishly into the Military Highway Sports Shop. She headed directly to the sales counter, looked around at the few browsing customers to make sure she was unnoticed, then talked in hushed tones to the clerk.

"I need to buy a gun. Something small that I can carry in my purse."

In response, the clerk ushered Bella into a quagmire of hidden weapons permits and Second Amendment rights. He was more than happy to help her navigate these waters and collect both a consulting fee and a large commission on the fine piece he would eventually sell her.

Six days, one affidavit, two court hearings, one concealed weapons permit, and two store visits later, Bella was the proud owner of a Berretta 9-millimeter repeat-action handgun, and a new oversize purse that would be its home. She paid the clerk to take her to the shooting range and show her how to use her new equalizer. She was no expert markswoman, but she learned how to load, unload, and most important, unlock the safety.

If the coward on the phone ever came by the office to make good on his threat, he would first have to get by an armed and dangerous receptionist. For the rest of the *Reed* case, and maybe beyond, Bella Harper would be packing heat.

◁▷

It came in the same type of 8½-by-11 manila envelope as before. It was again addressed to Ahmed Aberijan. Like the prior package, the only hint of origin was the Norfolk, Virginia, postmark.

But this time the envelope contained only one page. The sender had again meticulously cut out letters and numbers from magazines and pasted them on the page to form a message.

> Plaintiff's expert Worthington has a crippling Achilles heel.
> Check Alexandria General District Court records and talk
> to Officer Beecher of the Alexandria police force. $100,000
> keeps more coming.

Wiring instructions to a different bank in the Caymans followed. Ahmed read the letter four times, thanked Allah, then got on the phone to Frederick Barnes.

"What have you learned about the first letter I received containing the preliminary game plan for Mr. Carson?"

"The *first* letter?"

"Answer my question."

"We have been unable to trace it so far. There were no prints or residue on the papers inside the envelope. The true owner of the bank account where we deposited the money is shrouded by a maze of offshore corporations that are not required to do public filings. We hit a dead end."

"Frederick, I must know who is sending these letters. I just received another about Carson's expert witness. We will pay for the information, but I must know who I am paying."

"We will need a little time—"

"We don't have time!" Ahmed screamed.

"It's got to be an inside job," Barnes said calmly. "Nobody else could know the information or appreciate the significance of it. We can at least narrow it down to the members of Carson's team. I'll have them all followed."

"And you should tell Strobel of this information, but do not tell him of the source."

"Understood," Barnes said.

19

"IF LITIGATION IS WAR, then depositions are hand-to-hand combat," Mack told one of his young associates as they drove to the offices of Carson & Associates for the second day of Worthington's deposition. "There is no judge and few rules, so the name of the game is intimidation and persistence. Get the witness talking long enough, and he's bound to make some mistakes. He'll either contradict something he's already said or forget some minor detail. Your job is to turn that minor detail into a federal offense."

The associate listened intently. He had watched the great man in action yesterday. He had now been given a rare invitation to ride with Strobel from their office in Norfolk to Carson's office in Virginia Beach. Strobel, the motion to dismiss now a part of the distant past, was in one of his mentoring moods.

"Take one of two approaches, depending on the witness. If it's a neutral witness, try to charm him. Get him relaxed and talking and keep him relaxed and talking. Find out everything you can about his testimony, and get some quotes you can use to trip him up at trial. That's easier to do if he's relaxed. If the witness is hostile, browbeat him into submission. Establish who's boss. Ask your questions with a sarcastic tone, stare him down, laugh at the lawyer if she makes objections. Drag out the deposition until you wear him down. Tired witnesses make mistakes."

"Will you finish with Worthington today, or are you going to stretch this out all week?" the young associate asked.

Mack just drove on in silence. A man of his stature did not have to acknowledge the question of a lowly associate. He would finish today. But he had a few fireworks planned first.

◁▷

The chore of defending the Worthington deposition fell to Leslie and the Rock. She had prepared the expert carefully and was in the best position to guard against his weaknesses.

On this second day of Worthington's deposition, the Rock showed up an hour late, and by then Strobel was in a foul mood. Strobel started hammering on Worthington right from the start, and Leslie couldn't provide Worthington much cover from Strobel's bullying tactics. The Rock might as well have stayed home.

By midafternoon, the stale air in the conference room was thick with tension. The unflappable Worthington held his own in the face of Strobel's relentlessness, which only seemed to frustrate Strobel and make him more obnoxious and cantankerous than ever.

"Mr. Worthington, have you discussed this case with Ms. Connors or the other lawyers for the plaintiff?"

"I object," Leslie said. "Those conversations are attorney work product."

"Don't mind her," Strobel said to Worthington, as if Leslie were an annoying child. "She doesn't know the rules for a deposition yet; she's just learning. Now answer the question please."

"Don't answer that question," Leslie said, seething at the arrogance of Strobel. "He's just being argumentative."

"That's a first," Strobel mocked. "Instructing your witness not to answer the question on the grounds that it is argumentative. Read the rules someday before you finish law school."

Strobel's associate smirked at Leslie.

"Mr. Worthington, as I said, don't bother answering that question."

"Grow up," Strobel said. It came from deep in his throat—a guttural threat. Then he looked at the Rock and smiled. "Mr. Davenport, you've taken a few depositions in your day. Tell your little protégé that she can't just instruct the witness not to answer if she thinks the question is argumentative. Otherwise, we'll call the judge, and I'll ask for sanctions. This is ridiculous."

The Rock was sweating profusely. He had a nervous twitch in his left eye that was acting up noticeably. "Go ahead and answer the question," he said to Worthington.

Leslie stared at the Rock and frowned. The Rock pretended not to notice.

"I don't remember the question," Worthington said.

"That's because your counsel insists on littering the record with frivolous objections," Strobel said. "And I want the record to reflect that in my more than thirty years of trial practice, I have never heard more unfounded objections interposed in bad faith than I have today."

The court reporter, who worked frequently for Strobel, smiled as if she could type that line from memory. Leslie suspected Mack used it in every case.

"And I want to say for the record," Leslie responded, "that I have never seen a lawyer be more obnoxious and rude than I have today." Her hands were shaking, partly from nerves and partly from anger.

"Okay," Strobel said, turning his attention back to Worthington, "tell me everything you and your lawyers talked about."

For the next ten minutes, Worthington recounted in detail numerous conversations he had with Leslie, giving a full account of all discussions they had regarding why the Saudi Arabian government should be found liable in this case. When Worthington was finished, Strobel just smiled and asked, "Aren't you leaving something out?"

"Like what?" Worthington asked defensively.

"Like whether you've ever been convicted of a felony or misdemeanor involving moral turpitude."

Leslie knew this was coming. She had prepared Worthington for this type of question. All he had to do was follow the script.

"No, I have not been."

"Have you ever been accused of a felony or misdemeanor involving moral turpitude and pleaded guilty to a lesser offense?"

"Objection. That is not relevant or admissible and not likely to lead to admissible evidence." Leslie scooted to the edge of her seat.

"Are you instructing him not to answer the question, Counsel?" Strobel asked with mock incredulity. "Does he have something to hide?"

"Of course not, but we both know the question is improper."

"Let me tell you what I know, Ms. Connors. And let's go off the record." Strobel turned to the court reporter he had hired for the deposition. She quit typing.

"I know that your wonderful expert witness is actually a wife beater with a real anger problem. I know that he likes to lecture juries about abuse of innocent victims overseas and then go home and inflict a little abuse himself on the missus. After this deposition, I'll add to my witness list the names of two police officers who will testify that Mrs. Worthington looked like a punching bag the night she finally summoned the courage to press charges. I know that our little choirboy here pleaded no contest to the charges and that a judge eventually let him off.

"I also happen to know that your Mr. Worthington has plans to run for political office again or at least get a plum political appointment. And finally, I know that if he takes the stand in this case, I will ask about these allegations, even if technically your objection will be sustained. The jury will hate this man, and his career will be over. Now, if you don't withdraw him as a witness, I'm willing to go back on the record today and ask these questions right now. If you are willing to withdraw him as a witness, we can let this deposition record be silent on the matter. And may I remind you that this deposition record must be made available to the press."

Leslie looked at the Rock, who stared at Worthington as if the man had some type of communicable disease. She looked at Worthington—the blood had drained from his face.

"I'll need a minute to confer with Mr. Worthington," she said.

"Request denied," Strobel responded, as if he were the judge. "This is an easy issue. Either you tell me today, right now, that you are withdrawing him as an expert, or I'll start interrogating him on the record about the fact that he beats his wife, and I'll release the transcript to the press."

"That's blackmail!" Leslie shot back, her voice rising. "And I will not be part of it. I'll move to seal the transcript and file an affidavit with the court explaining that you are trying to use inadmissible evidence to blackmail an expert witness. I'll also file a complaint with the state bar. You'll be lucky if they don't pull your ticket."

Leslie stood and prepared to march out of the conference room with Worthington in tow. She would show Strobel she could not be intimidated. "C'mon," she said to Worthington as confidently as possible. "This deposition is over."

But Worthington remained seated. "No, it's not," he said, without looking at Leslie. "I'm withdrawing myself as an expert."

"What?!" Now Leslie turned on her own witness. "You can't do that. We've retained you."

"You're a free man," Strobel said. "They can only force fact witnesses to testify. They can't force you to testify as an expert if you have no firsthand knowledge of the facts."

Worthington looked sheepishly at Leslie, then across the table at the expressionless Strobel.

"I've got to do what's right for me and my family," Worthington said. "Sorry, Leslie."

"Let's go back on the record," Strobel said.

"I don't want any part of this," Leslie said. "You two deserve each other." She threw her papers and legal pad into her briefcase and stalked out of the room. She slammed the door as she walked out, leaving behind her stunned co-counsel and her former star witness.

◁▷

"He did what?!" Nikki screamed into the phone. "Why didn't you threaten to reveal his secret to the press if he didn't testify for us? That would at least give him a little incentive to do the right thing."

"Really, Nikki," Leslie said, "what kind of expert will he make if I have to object every time Strobel asks him if he ever beat his wife?"

"The guy is scum. What now?"

"Pray for a lenient judge who will not require that we provide direct testimony on how the government of Saudi Arabia sanctions the techniques of the Muttawa. We have plenty of circumstantial evidence against the government even without Worthington. It's just that he's the one guy who could have pulled it all together."

When Nikki hung up, she immediately dialed a friend at the local paper. Worthington would pay for his cowardice with a headline tucked away in the next day's local section. It would read: "Attorneys fire expert witness over abuse allegations." The story, citing unnamed sources, would detail the charges against Worthington and praise the law firm of Carson & Associates for boldly dismissing their own expert witness in light of his checkered past.

◁▷

Rasheed knew his brother, Hanif, had a gift for teaching God's Word. He harbored no jealousy. The church would soon be led by Hanif, just as Rasheed had hoped. He sat back in the meetings and marveled at God's hand of anointing on his younger brother.

The crowd became so large on Friday night that Hanif told Rasheed he had decided to add another weekly service. With each new convert, though, the circle of danger broadened. Rasheed could not know whether each new member represented the blessing of another sinner saved by grace or the curse of a government informant. He always assumed the former.

Rasheed savored each night with the church, knowing his time was short. His deposition would take place in two weeks. He knew what he had to do, but he also knew it wouldn't be easy. No man should be put in a position of choosing between his God and his family.

◁ ▷

Friday night, after a string of sixteen-hour days, Brad and Leslie hit the town with a vengeance. They gorged themselves at an Italian place, enjoying each other's company and temporarily forgetting the case that had brought them together.

They tried to burn off a few calories with a long stroll down the boardwalk, taking time to admire the paintings of local artists and the trinkets of local artisans. Brad, ever observant, slyly took note of Leslie's admiration for a painting of the Cape Hatteras lighthouse. A little farther down the boardwalk, as Leslie stood watching another artist dab at his canvas, Brad doubled back to pay for the painting under the guise of going to the men's room. He ran with the painting to a hotel across the street and left it, along with a substantial tip, with the concierge. He returned in a few minutes to Leslie, still mesmerized by the amateur painter and entirely unfazed by Brad's insistence that the nearest bathroom was half a mile away.

They completed their evening with a late movie. Brad wanted a thriller, but Leslie talked him into a chick flick. Brad slept through the last hour and was newly energized when the movie finally let out at 11:45. Leslie, however, fell sound asleep in the car within five minutes of leaving the theater.

Brad silently vetoed the original plan of taking Leslie back to her car at the office and instead drove directly to his home in Virginia Beach. He pulled into the circular drive in front of his large house and turned off the motor. He reached over and gently touched Leslie on the shoulder. She started and jerked straight up in her seat.

"What the . . . where are we?" she demanded, as her eyes popped open.

"Calm down, girl. You're in good company. You were sleeping so soundly I decided to bring you to my place to crash."

Leslie relaxed and rubbed both eyes. "I'm sorry, Brad. I was just having these nightmares—"

"Hey. After a week like this week, you're entitled to a few nightmares."

Leslie's eyelids looked heavy. She shook her head to clear her senses and fought back a yawn. To Brad, this woman who couldn't get the sleep out of her eyes, whose hair was darting out in different directions from static electricity, had never looked more beautiful.

"I'm fine, really. Just get me a little caffeine, and I'll hit the road." She gave him a sleepy smile.

"Yeah, right. Let's go." Brad got out of the car and went around to open Leslie's door. She got out and stretched.

"No, really, Brad, I'm fine."

"Look, I've got a guest room suite upstairs that never gets any use. I'd feel better if you wouldn't try to head up to Williamsburg without getting some sleep."

Brad was already on his way to the front door. Leslie protested as she followed.

"I'll just crash on the couch for a few hours."

"Leslie—"

She held up her palm, her eyes half-closed. "It's the couch or nothing."

Brad shook his head. "All right, at least let me get some blankets, sheets, and a pillow."

After fixing a place for Leslie while she crashed in one of the chairs, Brad leaned down, gently brushed her thick auburn hair out of her beautiful face, and kissed her ever so softly. He was dizzy with emotion.

"I had a great time tonight," he whispered. His face was just inches from hers. He couldn't take his eyes from hers. He didn't dare blink.

"Thanks," she said and flashed a soft smile under heavy eyelids that lit up the room. "Me too."

"I put one of my T-shirts on the couch, if you want something comfortable to sleep in. There are towels and washcloths in the bathroom. And a spare toothbrush."

"A toothbrush?" Leslie smiled. "I won't even ask."

He kissed her again on the forehead, brushed his hand softly against her cheek, then turned and headed for the stairs.

"We make a pretty good team," he said as he walked away.

He meant it in a lot of different ways.

◁▷

Brad set the alarm for 6 a.m. and resisted the strong urge to go back downstairs before then. He slept fitfully, but he slept smiling. He woke up on his own a few minutes before the alarm and rose quickly to fix breakfast.

The couch was empty. Though the T-shirt was gone, Leslie left the sheets and blankets neatly folded on top of the pillow along with a note of thanks. Brad shook his head in disbelief. She must have called a cab. He would never understand that woman.

Later that morning, Brad drove a half hour from his house to the beach to pick up the painting and then another hour to Williamsburg to deliver it. He left the artwork carefully leaning against the outside door of the garage that housed Leslie's apartment.

◁ ▷

One of Barnes's men, increasingly bored with his uneventful surveillance of Brad, decided to have a little fun. As Brad drove away down the long dirt road that led from Leslie's home, the man slipped out of his car and placed the painting in the trunk. His wife would love it. One of the perks of an otherwise unrewarding job.

20

MACK STROBEL PERSONALLY COUNTED no fewer than eighteen empties scattered around Teddy Kilgore's private yacht by the time he joined the brain trust. Teddy had docked across the street from the office, in a reserved slip at the Waterside Marina, to pick up Mack so the brain trust could plot Carson's defeat. The heat and stickiness of the mid-September day clung to Mack like a leech. He'd been working on the case all day while his cohorts hit the links and floated the waterways, drinking, eating crab, and billing their time to the *Reed* file. And what had they accomplished?

"Where's Phillips?" he asked without bothering to greet anyone.

"Gone below." Mackenzie gestured below deck with a low chortle.

Strobel leaned over the stairway and bellowed. "Mel! Let's get on with it."

Mackenzie slapped a hand on Strobel's shoulder. "No, I mean he's *gone* below." Mackenzie tipped his hand like a bottle to his lips, indicating that Phillips had downed more than his share of brew and would not be participating in this evening's meeting. Mack cussed. Mackenzie laughed, nearly giddy.

After delivering a scathing piece of his mind, a tirade that had no discernible impact on his partners, Mack kicked back in a lounge chair himself and opened his first brew. If he couldn't beat them, he would join them, and at least salvage what remained of this miserable autumn day.

Elbow deep in crab legs and failing miserably in his attempt to pry some meat out of the pesky bones, Teddy Kilgore played his usual role of conciliator.

"Mack, my man. The way I see it, you're just working too hard. That's why we've got associates. Let them take all those depositions. Conserve your strength, that's what I say."

Kilgore took a break from his losing battle with the crabs, proud of his advice, and gloated in the manner of those who drink too much and say something simple that they find to be incredibly profound.

"Thanks," Strobel said sarcastically. He was tired of carrying this firm on his back.

Teddy smiled. "Don't mention it." He took another swallow of his Michelob and dove back into the crabs.

"The way I see it," Mackenzie said, "you've really only got one problem— Judge Johnson. You just pulled the wrong judge for that hearing. Otherwise you'd be home free."

"I never would have thought of that," Strobel said, even more sarcastically than before. "Unfortunately, the court doesn't consult with me when it assigns the cases."

"What judge do you want?" Win asked, tossing Mack another beer. "Here, Teddy, let me help you with that. I can't believe you've lived in Tidewater all these years and still don't know how to shell these things."

Teddy smiled as he let Win pick the good meat out of the crabs and put it on a plate for him. "I let the hired help take care of that," he said.

Strobel had witnessed this scene before. Teddy was probably the most skilled crab-picker of the bunch, but he was also the laziest. Teddy had learned a long time ago that the best way to get good crab meat without the hassle of picking the shell was to look helpless and wait for a volunteer. There was always a volunteer.

"Baker-Kline would be a home run for us," Strobel said. His mood was sweetened some as he saw Teddy sandbag Mackenzie. "She's usually pro-defense, and she hates Carson. Threw his sorry bones in jail for contempt last year."

"I know," Win replied. "That case was all over the tube."

As they talked, Melvin Phillips staggered up the steps, walked over to the cooler, and took out another beer. He belched loudly, then turned and looked at Mack.

"What do you think?" Mack asked sarcastically. "About the *Reed* case— the one you're billing your time to today."

"Mmm," Phillips said, as he carefully headed back toward the stairs, leaning on objects as he navigated his way. "Settle." Then he belched again and headed below.

"Any more beer in that cooler?" Teddy asked. He needed something to wash down the crab legs. "Who are the possibilities?"

"For what?"

"For the judge. What else are we talking about?"

"There are five slots for judges not on senior status," Strobel explained. "One of those slots is vacant, waiting for Congress to approve the president's chosen man. Judge Stonebreaker is about halfway through a major antitrust trial that has been dragging on for months, and the defense just started. Even if she finishes by mid-October, which I doubt, they would never send her right back into another long and complex case."

"Who does that leave?" Teddy asked. He threw an empty toward the cardboard box from the Waterside Wharf that they were using for trash. The can bounced harmlessly on the deck, several feet short.

"It leaves Johnson, Baker-Kline, and Lightfoot, who is too liberal for my liking."

"Then let's get rid of Lightfoot," Win said. "Let's do a little judge shopping."

"How?" Mack asked. "Call some of your Mafia buddies?"

"Don't need to with Lightfoot," Win said smugly. "Don't forget, before he was a judge, he was a career politician, and our family financed major portions of his reelection campaigns."

"That's probably why he lost," Mack mumbled.

Win ignored the comment. "Some of the money was dirty," he explained. "Dummy corporations set up to evade federal limits, that type of thing. I can tell Lightfoot our clients have been snooping around, that this guy Barnes got wind of those financing irregularities and is threatening to leak them to the press if Lightfoot comes near this case."

Mack was intrigued by the idea of knocking Lightfoot out of the running. "But even if we give Lightfoot an incentive not to hear the case, he can't take himself out because he doesn't make the assignments. That job falls to Baker-Kline, since she's the current chief judge of the Eastern District of Virginia."

"You're right, but a chief judge never messes with another judge's vacation. I'll explain the score to Lightfoot, then give him an out by inviting him to join our family at our vacation place in the Blue Ridge Mountains during the second week of October. It would be hard for him to try the case in Norfolk if he has plans to hunt with me in Charlottesville."

"The problem," Mack replied, " is that your plan leaves me with a toss-up between Johnson and Baker-Kline. Heads I win; tails I lose. I think I would rather keep Lightfoot in the running and at least lessen the odds of getting Johnson."

Win Mackenzie caught Mack's eye and nodded toward Teddy, whose head was tilted back so far it looked like his neck might snap off at any minute. His eyes were closed, but his mouth was wide open, sucking in the humid Tidewater air. As usual, this strategy session had boiled down to the two hard-core litigators.

"How important is this case?" Win asked, lowering his voice. "I want a serious answer, not sarcasm."

"It's one of the biggest I've ever tried." Mack ruminated as he gazed out at the sailboats meandering down the river. "The publicity for the firm will be huge. Win or lose, we'll be a household name."

"Then let's pull out all the stops," Mackenzie said. "I've got a deal for you. Name me as the lead lawyer for the case on appeal and the media spokesman during trial. I'll guarantee that you get Baker-Kline as your judge."

The prospect of getting Baker-Kline for the case struck Mack as too good to be true. But the price was high—letting Win have a piece of the glory. Mack leaned back in his chair, took a long pull on his beer, and chose his words carefully.

"How you gonna do that?" he asked. "And how could you be media spokesman if you're on vacation in the Blue Ridge Mountains?"

"I never guaranteed that an emergency would not arise and keep me from going."

"What about Johnson?"

Win's lips curled into a smug little smile. "Leave that to me. Some things you don't want to know." He paused and looked at Mack. "Deal?"

Strobel narrowed his eyes, pictured Ichabod seated on the bench—glaring down at Carson, slicing him down to size—then Strobel extended his light beer toward Mackenzie. They sealed the deal with a toast, set to the backdrop of a busy evening at the Waterside and the sound of Teddy's snoring.

◁▷

Unlike the lawyers he had hired, Ahmed was more concerned with the jury than the judge. Accordingly, when he received the list of more than one hundred prospective jurors from his lawyers about a month prior to trial, he took immediate action. As usual, he started with a phone call to Barnes.

"Did you get the list of prospective jurors?"

"Yes, it came this morning. We're on it. Give us two weeks, and we'll have a complete report."

"I can get a report from the lawyers. I need more from you. We need some of these jurors in our pocket. Can you make that happen?"

There was silence on the phone line. Ahmed waited Barnes out.

"I don't know," Barnes finally said. "That's serious stuff in the United States. You can pull time for messing with a jury."

"Humor me. How could you do it if you wanted to?"

Barnes waited a few more beats before answering. "Well, off the top of my head, I'd start with the first thirty or forty prospective jurors and ask Strobel who he'll strike with his preemptories. Then I would hire some local investigators to do some background work on the remaining jurors. Go through their garbage, check out their places of employment, talk to some of their friends, those types of things.

"We would pick the ten most vulnerable jurors and start laying the foundation for buying or blackmailin' 'em if they get selected. We prefer blackmail. It's cheaper and more effective. There's a good chance that 20 percent of these folks are cheatin' on their spouses, lookin' at pornography on the Internet, or stealin' from their bosses. We trade our silence for their vote.

"Any preliminary contacts with jurors would be done only by one of my top two men. We would be very discreet in our approach. You can usually find out if someone can be bought without ever asking the question. We only need one member to hang the jury in a civil case. But two can provide moral support for each other during deliberations."

"Make it happen," Ahmed said, "and you've increased your bonus by one million. Pay whatever it takes to buy the jurors."

There was a long silence. Ahmed sensed Barnes's reluctance and decided to wait him out again. Barnes was not used to refusing an order. And a million dollars was a lot of money, even to Barnes.

"No promises, Ahmed. I'm not willing to go to the big house over a civil case."

"Get it done."

Ahmed hung up the phone.

Justice in America was not cheap.

◁▷

Brad had a less ambitious plan for the list of prospective jurors.

"Bella," he said into the speakerphone. "Have you got a minute?"

"No," she snorted. "But I'll come in anyway."

A few seconds later she lowered herself into one of the client chairs across the desk from Brad.

"Would you take the list of prospective jurors and send it to these folks?" Without looking up from his paperwork, Brad handed her a list of fellow lawyers he could trust. "Draft a cover letter asking them to take a minute and look at the list to see if they know anyone on it. Give them your number to call if they have any information. Let's get those letters out today, if possible."

Bella didn't move. As usual, Brad had been taking the lady for granted. When there was no discernible response to his request, he looked up from his work for the first time and noticed that her eyes were watering. He couldn't recall the last time he saw that happen.

"What's wrong?" he asked as he put his other work aside. She had his full attention.

"Brad, we've got a serious cash-flow problem. It hasn't been this tight since the first year we started." She placed a stack of papers on his desk. "These are the invoices just for the *Reed* case." She placed a smaller stack next to them. "These are the other invoices we've received in the last thirty days. If I paid everything in both of these piles, we'd have only fifty-five thousand in the bank. Between the experts, Nikki's trip to Saudi Arabia, the deposition transcripts, and the usual salaries and overhead costs, we're burning through almost seventy-five thousand a week. Even if we max out our line of credit with Virginia National and drag out our creditors as long as we can, I figure we could get through an eight-week trial, but no more. If we lose, we're sunk. Even if we win, we don't have the cash flow to get us through an appeal."

She sighed, as if a huge weight had just been lifted from her shoulders. The bills remained on the corner of Brad's desk. Bella was the master of anxiety transfer.

Brad was used to Bella being the purveyor of bad financial news. What struck him this time was the intensity of her emotions. They had been through tougher times when they first started, and Bella had never been so despondent.

"We've just got to settle some of these other cases we have kicking around the office," Brad suggested. "We'll get through this. We're survivors."

"What other cases? We've already settled or farmed out just about any case of value except the Johnson case. I think it's time to settle Johnson."

"Bella, we've had this conversation before. The insurance company always lowballs the settlement offers until the eve of trial. It'll be months before we can get a trial date and scare them into a reasonable offer. I won't sell out one client for the good of another."

"Brad, I'm telling you, we don't have any choice. We either settle Johnson, or we bankrupt the firm."

They were both raising their voices, each retort louder than the last.

"Bella, it's not an option. End of discussion. We would file for bankruptcy and drop the *Reed* case before we would start selling out our clients." Brad took a breath and lowered the volume. "Now, what are our other options?"

"You can take out an equity line on your house . . ."

"Good. Work up the paperwork. How much will that net?"

"About another 150 if we're lucky. You've already got a serious first mortgage on that monster."

"Okay, what else?"

Much to Brad's surprise, the tears welled up again. But this time Bella didn't hold back as the tears tumbled quietly down her cheeks and onto her lap. Brad had never seen her this way and didn't quite know what to do. He slowly rose, grabbed some tissues, and went over to put a hand on Bella's shoulder. He crouched down in front of her.

"This isn't about the money, is it?"

Bella shook her head. Brad waited patiently with his hand on her shoulder. She finally began forcing the words out.

"We could . . . should . . . stop paying salaries . . . for a little while. But I can barely afford . . . Mom's home. I'm in huge debt. She's all I've got. I don't want to lose her." The words came tumbling out in a fit of emotion.

"Bella," Brad said softly, "it's gonna be all right. . . . You're not going to lose her. . . . It's gonna be all right."

◁▷

When Bella left, Brad closed his door and slumped into his chair. His head throbbed, and his chest felt tight. This was the price he paid for the freedom of being his own boss—the loneliness of leadership.

He leaned back in his chair, put his hands behind his head, and stared hard at the ceiling. He took inventory. In one month, he would be trying a case that many thought was unwinnable. His usually steady secretary was in a state of panic. He had fallen hard for a woman whom he could not figure out. The steady barrage of sixteen-hour days had set his nerves on end. He had just lost his main expert witness in a bizarre deposition that made him think his office might be bugged. He had decimated his practice to handle this case and now risked bankruptcy even if he won. And to add insult to injury, he would have to share the contingency fee on the only good case he had in the office—the Johnson case—with the most pitiful plaintiff's lawyer in Tidewater: the Rock.

There was only one solution. He would work harder. And he would streamline the case. He would cut expenses. He would take it one day at a time. If he won, other major cases would pour into the office. Even if he lost, it would be a glorious loss, and more cases would pour into his office.

Besides, his client was a missionary and presumably had a direct line to the Almighty. It was a good thing. He could use a little divine intervention or at least a little luck.

◁▷

Just down the hall, Leslie refined her preliminary game plan to reflect the recently completed depositions and other developments in the case. The fifty-page document outlined the witnesses and their expected testimony. It discussed various evidentiary issues and the law supporting the plaintiff's position on each issue. It outlined the exhibits and documents they intended to introduce at trial, together with any anticipated objections. Each page of the valued document was appropriately marked: *Confidential: Attorney/ Client Privilege and Trial Work Product.*

As she prepared to leave the office, Leslie made four copies. She hand-delivered two copies in confidential envelopes to the desks of Nikki and Bella and slid a copy under Brad's door. She tucked the fourth copy in her own briefcase and left the original on the corner of her desk.

◁▷

Nikki left the office a few minutes after Leslie at 6:30. Unlike Leslie, she had no intention of taking work home with her. Nikki did, however, return to the office just before midnight as she had for the last five nights in a row. The first night Leslie was still working at the office, so Nikki just threw a few things in her briefcase, said hello, and headed home. The other four nights, the office had been empty except for the occasional visit by the cleaning crew. Nikki worked each night for almost three hours, and tonight she would do so again. By her rough calculations, she figured that she should be able to mail the last letter out by 3 a.m. If not, she was determined to stay until she finished.

Nikki's advanced warning system consisted of a listening device of the type parents used to monitor their babies. She placed the receiver in the lobby in an out-of-the-way location. The monitor sat on her own desk as she worked. Each time that the cleaning crew came in the first few nights, the system had given Nikki the advanced warning that she needed to sweep the documents off her desk and into one of her empty desk drawers. Her office was at the end of the hall away from the reception area, a short walk that would take no more than fifteen seconds from the front door, just enough time to return her office to normal.

Nikki took the monitor with her as she headed to the kitchen to pour her first cup of coffee. As was her habit, she turned off the light to her own office and walked quickly down the hall. Just as she was about to walk through the reception area, she heard the distinct noise of a key being inserted, the door-knob turning, and the front door opening. She had no chance to get to the kitchen to turn off the coffee or to sneak back and clean up her own office in the dark. Instead, she slid into the nearest office, which happened to belong to Brad, and sat by the open door for a few seconds in the pitch dark.

She heard footsteps coming down the hallway toward the office. They were fast and determined, landing hard like a man's. She didn't hear the usual noise of the handcart or the clunking of cleaning supplies.

It must be Brad! It was Nikki's worst nightmare.

The hall light flipped on. Nikki froze in a moment of panic. How could she explain herself if he caught her in his office in the dark? She actually considered, just for a moment, hiding behind the door and slamming Brad in the back of the head to knock him unconscious. She would slip out, and the whole incident would be written off as a burglary gone awry.

Instead, she made a quick move for his massive oak desk and slid underneath it, in the hollow where Brad would put his legs if he sat in his desk chair. The man entered the room and flicked on the lights. She heard the deafening noise of her own heart pounding in her ears. She tried to control the sound of her breathing and found herself holding her breath to remain as quiet as possible. She covered her face with her hands, every muscle of her body tensed.

She fully expected Brad to sit at his desk and unavoidably kick her when he sat down. She would be discovered, fired, and perhaps arrested.

But the man in the room did not sit down or even move behind the desk. She heard him rummage around the papers on top of the desk, finally finding the object of his search. He seemed to hesitate, possibly reading the document, then turned and headed for the door. After what seemed like forever, the man turned off the lights and left the room.

Nikki sat shuddering under Brad's desk, doubled over in the fetal position, not able to move her limbs for several minutes. She eventually calmed her nerves, walked to the kitchen, and turned off the coffeepot. She went to her office and locked the door.

She left the offices of Carson & Associates and came back fifteen minutes later with a bottle of rum. She needed something stronger than caffeine to help get her through this night.

Three hours later, at precisely 3:30 a.m., she licked the last stamp and sealed the last envelope.

21

THE PANIC USUALLY SETS IN ABOUT a month prior to a big trial, when the lawyers realize how much still needs to be done and how little time there is to do it. For Brad, the pretrial panic arrived right on schedule. He had four lousy weeks left to prepare witnesses, review depositions, prepare an opening statement, and complete a million other detailed tasks that would mean the difference between a good case and a mediocre one. The fact that he would have to spend one of those weeks in Saudi Arabia taking depositions exacerbated his jitters.

Complicating things even further were some lingering questions that Brad could not answer or ignore: How did the defendants find out about Worthington's arrest? And why did the defendants seem to anticipate every legal argument that Brad and his team made in their briefs? It was as if someone were reading their mail. Or worse. And it was this lingering paranoia that drove Brad, one day before leaving for Saudi Arabia, to the office of Patrick O'Malley, private investigator.

Patrick was a step above the average PI who worked out of his home and spied on unfaithful spouses. Patrick had an office in a run-down strip shopping center on Military Highway in Virginia Beach. He specialized in electronic surveillance and in finding missing persons.

Brad arrived at the office after a long day of depositions. He opened the door and looked around the reception area's yellow walls and stained carpet. The magazines were about two months old, which appeared to be the same general time frame of the last office cleaning. If O'Malley was making money, he had certainly not squandered any of it on first impressions.

O'Malley appeared from the back, a tall, slim figure with a bushy Fu Manchu mustache from another era. He wore cowboy boots, faded jeans, and a denim shirt.

"Brad, my man," he said and gave Brad an enormous bear hug. "Why this sudden urge to slum it and meet in my office?"

"Just wanted to see what 'uptown' looks like."

"You are the personification of 'uptown,' Mr. Bradley Carson, attorney at law, proud owner of a Dodge Viper, and landlord of the estate on the river." O'Malley bowed deeply. "May I kiss the ring?"

"Give me a break."

"Just don't forget us little people."

"That's why I'm here. I want to hire one of the little people."

"This isn't about your ex, is it?"

"No." Brad laughed. "I wish it were that easy. Look, I don't have much time, and I don't have much information. But I'm working on this case, and the other side seems to know what I'm thinking even before I figure it out. I don't have any hard evidence, but I'm concerned the office might be bugged. Can you check it out?"

"Absolutely, man. Are you talking about the Reed case?"

Brad nodded.

"Saw your mug in the paper," O'Malley continued. "Want my advice?"

"No."

"Settle, baby. You're in the big leagues on that one. Take the money and run. You'll have a hard time winnin'. Just be happy with the publicity you've got and move on."

"Thanks for the encouragement," Brad said.

"You know how the song goes: 'Know when to hold 'em and know when to fold 'em.' Now, what do ya need?"

In five minutes the two men put together a plan to sweep the office for bugs every morning. Brad would have the locks changed on the doors and issue new keys to his team. He would hire a new cleaning crew for the next few months. He would have everybody change computer passwords, voice mail passwords, and phone numbers. Brad would have Bella send a list of the new passwords to O'Malley so he could check the computers and phones for outsiders tapping into the system.

Brad would tell each of his team members to be attentive for any suspicious signs.

Brad could not bring himself to believe that any member of his inner circle was involved. He may be paranoid, he told O'Malley, but he was still a good judge of character, and he knew he could trust Leslie, Nikki, and Bella. The Rock, on the other hand, would be totally cut out of the loop.

◁▷

Chesapeake Estates looked pleasant enough on the outside. Manicured lawns surrounded the dark brick building with the huge white pillars, giving the place a Southern colonial feel. It also featured a large front porch, on which the residents would sit and rock for hours while they discussed the weather and complained about the government. Unlike isolated nursing homes, the facility rested snugly on the outskirts of the exclusive Riverwalk development in the heart of Chesapeake. The nurses and staff seemed to genuinely care about the residents at Chesapeake Estates. The care didn't come cheap, but like so many other things in life, you got what you paid for. As far as Bella was concerned, there was no nursing home good enough for her mother—Gertrude Harper—but Chesapeake Estates came close.

The pristine appearance of the place stood in stark contrast to the turmoil going on in most of the residents' lives. Many struggled with Alzheimer's, dementia, Parkinson's, and other diseases that tormented an aging mind and body. Bella's mother suffered from advanced Parkinson's. She had her good days and her bad days. Lately, the good days were scarce.

It was a beautiful fall afternoon, and Bella intended to leave work early and take her mother for a walk. But nobody left Carson & Associates early these days. And so Bella did not arrive at Chesapeake Estates until nearly 7 p.m. She went straight to her mother's room.

Getting her mom out of that room had become more of a challenge as Gertrude's nervous system and muscle control deteriorated. Doctors told Bella the disease did not affect her mother's mind, only her physical ability to communicate her thoughts. Bella didn't believe it. Some days Gertrude didn't even recognize her and called out incessantly for Bella's father, who had divorced Gertrude more than twenty years earlier and been dead more than five.

Bella took Gertrude for a long walk and tried to convince her that her ex-husband was not coming back. Gertrude unloaded her many concerns about things that made no sense to Bella, undoubtedly driven by conversations she had overheard from the other residents. Bella found it nearly impossible to understand Gertrude, who shook uncontrollably as she talked. Her walking pace was incredibly slow, and she was stooped almost in half. Sometimes during these walks Bella would think about her mother in the vigor of her youth, how she would always have the answers for life's many challenges. Oh, how she wished she could turn back the clock and tap into some of that wisdom now.

At nearly 9 p.m., exhausted and hungry, Bella kissed her mom on the forehead—the same way that her mom used to kiss Bella when she was just a little girl—and told Gertrude she would be back soon. As Bella left Chesapeake Estates, she wondered if her mom would even remember the visit. Bella felt the tears welling up in her eyes as she turned to leave, desperately missing the only person in her life who had ever cared enough to wipe them away.

◁ ▷

Win Mackenzie picked up the phone and dialed the clerk's office for Judge Samuel Johnson. He asked to speak with Alex Pearson, one of Johnson's two law clerks.

"Alex, this is Winsted Mackenzie, a litigation partner at Kilgore & Strobel. How's it going?"

"Great," Alex said. "Working with Judge Johnson is excellent. I've learned more in my first few months on the job than I did in my entire third year of law school."

Mackenzie, himself a University of Virginia man, did not doubt that. Alex had attended Washington and Lee.

"Alex, let me cut right to the point, because I know Judge Johnson keeps you hoppin'. Every year, Kilgore & Strobel gets literally hundreds of résumés for the few litigation spots that open up for first-year associates. I have personally reviewed your résumé and heard about your work ethic in federal court. We've checked out your references and law school class ranking."

Win Mackenzie paused for a second to let the suspension build.

"Alex, you are this firm's number-one choice for next year. We'd like you to start full-time at Kilgore & Strobel next year as a litigation associate without the necessity of the interviews with firm partners we normally require. You'll be getting a letter confirming all this, but I wanted to personally call and tell you myself."

There was silence on the other end of the line. Win figured Alex was probably pinching himself to make sure it was true.

"That sounds great," Alex finally managed. "Will the letter give the details of the offer?"

"It will," Win said. "But let me also handle some of those myself."

For the next several minutes, Win Mackenzie, trained trial lawyer, put the hard sell on a flabbergasted Alex Pearson. The generosity of the firm and the flattery of Mackenzie just about rendered poor Alex speechless. When Win mentioned a special ten-thousand-dollar signing bonus, he could almost hear Alex panting on the other end of the line.

Oh, the innocence of the young, Mackenzie thought.

"Take your time making this decision, Alex. I know you'll ultimately make the right choice."

Win hung up the phone and dialed another number. This time it was not a law clerk but a federal appeals court judge who answered the phone. After exchanging pleasantries, Mackenzie got right down to business with his cousin.

"I hope this isn't improper, but I may need your help with something that just came to my attention. Can I talk to you confidentially—dead man's talk here—and get some advice about a potential conflict of interest?"

"You know you can, Win. What's up?"

"Our firm has made an employment offer to one of Judge Johnson's current law clerks, and I just found out we've got a small problem. I'm trying to look out for Judge Johnson, who I know is a personal friend of yours. He admires you greatly. Johnson is one of several judges who may have an opportunity to handle the Reed case, in which our firm is representing the defendants. Word has it that the plaintiff's lawyer would make a motion to disqualify Johnson based on a conflict of interest if he were selected. They would say that he can't be objective when one of his law clerks, who is helping him research the case, has an employment offer to work for the firm representing the defendants. Their point has some merit. Johnson doesn't need the bad publicity, and it puts him in a no-win situation. You know him well. Can you say something to the guy?"

"Sure, Win. Lots of other judges can hear that case. No sense in Samuel putting himself in that situation. I'll call back if there's any difficulty. Thanks for the heads up. And, Win . . ."

"Yeah."

"Good luck in the case. The nation will be watching."

◁▷

After waiting forty minutes in Baker-Kline's reception area—the price any lawyer pays for showing up unannounced—Win was eventually ushered into the presence of the Haughty One. He filled the air with ten minutes of small talk before Her Honor's impatience got the better of her.

"I know you didn't just come here to talk about community politics, Win, and I've got to be back on the bench in ten minutes."

Perfect, Win thought. He leaned forward and lowered his voice a notch. "What I'm about to say is just between us—stays right here?"

Ichabod nodded, her impatience replaced by curiosity. "Of course."

"It's about the spot on the Fourth Circuit Court of Appeals." He noticed Ichabod's eyes light up. That spot, one step below the Supremes, occupied every district judge's dreams. "As you know, my uncle sits on the Senate Judiciary Committee. The politics of these appointments is getting very interesting."

"I'm sure," Ichabod said, studying Win intently.

"Of course, the president makes the nominations, and you're not exactly—how do I say this discreetly?—his type of candidate." Win shifted in his seat, crossed his legs, and put on the most solemn, secretive face he could muster. "But we control the Senate Judiciary Committee. And right now, the president's candidates just can't seem to get out of committee."

This brought a knowing little smirk from Ichabod. Win was sure she had followed the proceedings carefully.

"As always in politics, talk of compromise has cropped up. My uncle and his buddies could let most of the president's nominees out of committee if he throws them a bone by nominating someone who cares about our agenda . . . like the rights of women."

Ichabod was nodding with her whole body now. She could obviously see where this was headed.

"Your name's been floated, and, well, my uncle is one of your strongest proponents. The problem is . . ." Win paused and pursed his lips, as if trying to figure out how best to say this without hurting the judge's feelings.

"Win," Ichabod said, "don't tiptoe around this. If there's a problem, I need to know."

Win still feigned hesitation. "Well, word is that the administration fears you might be anti–big business and adverse to the administration's foreign policy direction. I mean, they know they have to accept at least one pro-choice judge, just to get their own pro-life judges through, but they don't want it to be someone who's also going to create problems on other fronts."

Ichabod looked past Win, her brow furrowed, digesting this information. She had bought the whole thing. Now, for the delicate part.

"Judge, there's a high-profile case on the court's docket right now that could demonstrate just the opposite, that you are not inclined to counteract the administration on foreign policy. It's more or less a slam dunk, but our firm's involved, and I don't know if it'd be proper to discuss it with you . . ."

Ichabod looked at Win with narrow eyes. "Tell me about the case, Win." Then she tapped her finger on the desk. "But realize that I will not now, nor would I ever, commit to rule a certain way on the case until I've heard the evidence."

"I know that, Judge," Win responded quickly. "I just thought if you knew the facts of the case, you could decide if you even wanted to get involved. By a twist of fate, our firm has a conflict of interest with the one other judge who *could* hear it, so we could basically . . . well, we could increase the odds of you winding up with the case if that would be helpful."

"You understand," Ichabod warned, "that I'm making no promises."

"Yes, Your Honor."

"Then tell me about your case."

◁▷

Though Brad's door was closed for privacy, Nikki barged in without knocking. She slammed the door behind her, loud enough for Bella to hear in the reception area.

Brad's head jerked up. "Sure, come on in," he said.

Nikki slapped a pink phone slip down on Brad's desk.

"This time she's really done it," Nikki fumed. "Either she goes or I do."

Brad put down his pen and raised an eyebrow. He glanced down quickly at the phone slip. "Can't be that bad."

"It is. And don't even bother sticking up for her—she's way out of line this time."

"Okay . . ."

Nikki paced furiously in front of Brad's desk. "The Trader's Insurance Company offers $550,000 to settle the Johnson case—$550,000!" Nikki yelled. "Chump change . . . ridiculous . . . insulting! I wouldn't even dignify it by taking it to my client—"

"Our client," Brad interjected.

Nikki scoffed and kept pacing. "The case is worth more than a mil—easy.

Anything less is just a sellout so we can keep the doors open while we chase the *Reed* case. It's not right . . ."

"Settle down," Brad said wearily. "Nobody's telling you to take their offer—"

Nikki grabbed the phone slip and waved it under Brad's nose. "She already did! Bella found out about the offer and told my client—" Nikki paused and looked directly at Brad—"*my* client—about the offer. He jumps all over it, desperate for cash, says he needs money right away, and tells her—tells Bella, who he has never met before—to take it!"

Just retelling the story made her blood bubble all over again. Johnson was her case, her bonus, her call as to whether it should settle. She looked at Brad expecting a confirmation that the firm's matriarch had seriously overstepped her bounds this time. Instead, Brad just gave her a sympathetic look combined with a "What do you want me to do about it?" shrug.

"What?" Nikki snarled. "You aren't going to try to defend her on this, are you?" She paused, waiting for some type of outburst, a threat against Bella, a reprimand . . . anything to indicate Bella would get what she had coming.

"Did you inform your client about the settlement offer?" Brad asked patiently.

Nikki threw herself into a chair, as if the question itself had knocked the wind out of her and sucked every ounce of energy from her body. "I knew it."

"Look. Don't get defensive. Bella crossed the line, and I'll talk to her about it."

"Talk to her about it!" Nikki nearly screamed aloud. *That's it?! I could have "talked to her about it" myself. . . .*

"I'll make it clear she is not to speak with Mr. Johnson again," Brad continued, "except to take a phone message. But, Nikki, if the client wants to settle, we've got to settle."

Nikki stared at Brad in disbelief, her jaw hanging open. She should have known better than to approach Brad with this mess. As usual, she would have been better off taking matters into her own hands.

Without another word, Nikki shook her head, stood up, and headed for the door. *"Talk to her about it,"* she repeated to herself.

"Her or me," Nikki said over her shoulder. "As soon as we get past the *Reed* trial, take your pick."

"Nikki," Brad barked.

She stopped and turned.

"I *will* talk to her about it. And it *won't* happen again. But if the client says settle, you settle," he said firmly.

She gave Brad a smart salute, then marched out of the office, yanking the door closed behind her.

◁▷

By now Ahmed had begun looking for the 8½-by-11 manila envelopes. He gloated at his good fortune in having this unsolicited, unnamed inside source, then seethed at the thought that the incompetent Barnes could not determine the identity.

As usual, the latest envelope contained a cut-and-paste message. It also contained a thick report titled "Revised Preliminary Game Plan for *Reed v. Saudi Arabia*." This second document set forth the plaintiff's revised strategy for the case: who to call as witnesses, what to introduce as exhibits, what objections and legal arguments to make. He would make sure Strobel received this updated information.

Like the first game plan he received, the revised game plan would prove invaluable, but the message intrigued Ahmed more:

> Worthington worth every penny of $100K. The enclosed
> will cost you another. Same wiring. Shelhorse must come
> down too. More details to follow. Real-time surveillance info
> is now critical. We need to meet. Norfolk General District
> Court, Traffic Division Room #2, Monday fortnight, 9:30a.
> Bring three phone bugs. Come alone or deal is off.

Ahmed read the letter over and over. His elusive and mysterious ally was going to march out in plain sight! The audacity!

Ahmed agreed about Shelhorse. She was a powerful expert; her toxicology evidence was the most damaging in the case. How could Carson possibly win without an expert in toxicology?

On the other hand, Ahmed was not convinced that bugging the office, which he presumed the informant planned to do, was the right strategy. It was risky and probably would not reveal much more than his source could provide.

Ahmed understood immediately the purpose of holding the meeting in Norfolk General District Court. The place would be crawling with police officers. The metal detectors at the door would screen out all weapons. The court would be incredibly hectic, with masses of people milling around. The best place for their meeting to go unnoticed was the middle of a large crowd.

Ahmed thanked Allah and started making plans for the rendezvous. Once he learned the identity of this source, he would again be in control.

22

AS BRAD PREPARED TO BOARD the plane for Saudi Arabia to attend the depositions of former church members, he was unsure of how destructive to the case those depositions might turn out to be. Strobel had scheduled them. Sarah warned Brad that these particular church members, with the exception of Rasheed Berjein, had never really made all-out commitments to Christ or the church. They would probably say anything the Muttawa wanted. Unfortunately, because they lived outside the jurisdiction of the court, their videotaped depositions could be used in lieu of live testimony at trial.

Brad decided to take Nikki on the trip both because she knew her way around and because she knew Rasheed. Nikki's presence might give Rasheed some security and confidence. Besides, Brad would have fun seeing how Nikki handled the customs of this chauvinistic country. Bella had objected based on cost, but Brad overruled her and promised to pinch pennies while abroad.

Money would prove to be the least of their problems.

Weather delays caused Brad and Nikki to arrive late at Reagan National Airport and miss their connection to Riyadh. Hours later they boarded the next international flight, which promptly suffered a mechanical problem. After two hours of broken promises, the airline conceded defeat and announced that the next flight to Riyadh would not leave until the following morning.

While Nikki ranted, Brad contacted Sa'id el Khamin and told him they would be late for the depositions. They wouldn't arrive until late afternoon; get a one-day continuance, Brad instructed Sa'id.

The next morning Brad and Nikki slipped into their seats in coach, fulfilling their promise to Bella to avoid first class no matter what. Brad squeezed in between two heavyweights, one male and the other undecided. Nikki had the honor of sitting between a talkative and nervous older lady on one side and a six-year-old kid on the other. The flight seemed interminable.

◁▷

As Brad and Nikki suffered over the Atlantic, Mack Strobel surveyed the small army of lawyers gathered in a plush office in the heart of Riyadh and prepared to commence the depositions.

The defense side of the conference table was full of dignitaries and heavy hitters. Ahmed himself was there, sitting next to Mack, along with another partner from Kilgore & Strobel and three local lawyers. The local lawyers had retained an interpreter, reputed to be one of the best in Riyadh. His language skills were good, the lawyers said, and whenever a controversial issue of interpretation arose, he always remembered who paid his bill.

The court reporter and videographer were poised and ready, and the first witnesses waited in a conference room down the hall. Nearly every witness had rehearsed their testimony ad nauseam, with Mack himself practicing the direct examination and his partner performing Brad's role on cross-examination. They had done this for all the witnesses except Rasheed Berjein, who steadfastly refused to practice what he would say.

The plaintiff's side of the conference table was inhabited only by the lonely-looking Sa'id el Khamin, who would act as local lawyer and interpreter for Brad and Nikki. Sa'id had apologetically explained to Mack that Brad and Nikki were having flight problems and could not be there until the next day. Mack nevertheless insisted on proceeding with the depositions, and at 9 a.m. sharp, he marched the first witness into the conference room and had him sworn in.

"For the record," Sa'id said, his voice hoarse and shaky, "the plaintiff objects to beginning this deposition without Mr. Carson present. Mr. Carson called late last night and said that his flight had been canceled due to mechanical problems. We therefore respectfully request that the depositions be started one day later."

"For the record," Mack replied, his authoritative voice filling the conference room, "this deposition has been scheduled for more than three weeks. Mr. Carson is well aware of the vagaries of international travel and could certainly have scheduled himself a little lead time. Mr. el Khamin is a capable local lawyer retained by Mr. Carson and can handle the cross-examination of these witnesses. The depositions will go forward as scheduled. You can object if you want and take it up later with a judge, but the depositions will start on time."

Mack glared at el Khamin, practically daring the little man to provide any further argument. When none came, Mack turned to the court reporter, also hired by Mack, and told her, "Swear the witness in."

El Khamin quietly mumbled, "We still object," and the depositions were on.

Tariq Abdul took the oath first. He testified that he and his wife, Semar, had been members of the Reeds' church. He described the enterprise, through the translator, as an attempt by the Reeds to proselytize Muslims and recruit them for a drug ring. Tariq and Semar attended several meetings of the group but, according to Tariq, were never converted to Christianity. Therefore, Tariq said, he was never fully trusted and never given an opportunity to use or sell the drugs that were in such plentiful supply for those who did convert. He quickly added, without being asked, that he would never have participated in such an insidious enterprise even if he had been given the opportunity.

Although he never personally used or sold any drugs, Tariq did witness others doing so firsthand. He provided specific names and instances. While he was not there the night of the arrest, it did not surprise him to learn that Dr. Reed had resisted arrest. He had seen the normally mild-mannered Reed lose his temper on more than one occasion, especially if anyone challenged his authority. All in all, Tariq was sorry that Dr. Reed had died while apparently resisting arrest, was sorry that he, Tariq, had been an unwitting part of this criminal enterprise, and was sorry that he had not reported these activities to the police earlier.

The necessity of translation made the testimony stale and laborious. Tariq stayed on script but testified without emotion. His direct examination lasted nearly two hours and didn't pack much punch. Worse, the man's eyes darted all over the conference room whenever he talked about drug use by the Reeds or other church members. Mack had coached him to look only at the camera, but apparently that advice was too difficult for this frightened witness to follow in the heat of the moment.

By the rules of court, the video shown to the jury would consist of a static headshot of Tariq. Mack made a mental note not to show this tape after a big lunch or in a warm courtroom. No juror could be expected to stay awake for two straight hours while watching a talking head testify with no emotion. On the other hand, with those shifty eyes darting this way and that, maybe sleeping jurors would be a good thing.

After a short break, Sa'id began his cross-examination, which consisted of only three questions, all translated by Mack's paid translator.

"You were not there when the Reeds were arrested, right?"

"Yes, that's true."

"So you have no firsthand knowledge as to whether they were tortured or beaten by the police?"

"As I said before, I was not there, and I do not know."

"So it could have happened just the way Mrs. Reed described it?"

"I don't know how to answer your question because I don't know how Mrs. Reed described it. But if she said the police planted drugs, I don't believe it. There were already drugs in that apartment."

"Thank you, Mr. Abdul, that's all I have for now."

Mack could hardly conceal his excitement. Three questions! And none of them even remotely tough! El Khamin was weaker than Mack had imagined.

So weak, in fact, that Mack shot a sideways glance at Ahmed, just to judge the man's reaction. Ahmed did not seem at all surprised by this turn of events; his intimidating glare never changed. Could el Khamin be in Ahmed's back pocket too? It seemed that every other person Mack met in Saudi Arabia, including each of the witnesses now testifying, was more than anxious to cooperate in this case. It made him wonder how far Ahmed's influence reached and what means had been used to gain such far-reaching complicity.

After el Khamin's anemic performance, Mack changed his strategy. He dispatched a local lawyer to find out when Brad's flight would land. He called and questioned the next witness quickly. With any luck at all, Mack figured he could blitz through five of the six witnesses before the end of the day, leaving only Rasheed Berjein for tomorrow.

By the mandatory midday prayer break, Mack had dispensed with the first four witnesses. In addition to Tariq and Semar Abdul, another couple also confirmed the Reeds were selling drugs and then pressuring Muslims, particularly young children and their mothers, to convert to Christianity. The second couple went a step further than the Abduls by admitting their own use of drugs, ultimately resulting in a guilty plea and a suspended jail sentence. Again the cross-examination was short and sweet, establishing nothing more than the uncontroverted fact that this couple had not personally witnessed the arrest of Dr. and Mrs. Reed.

After the prayer break, Mack swore in his fifth and final witness of the day—Omar Khartoum. Mack was anxious to get Omar finished before Brad Carson arrived, and therefore decided to skip most of the preliminary questions.

◁▷

After wrestling his way through customs and surviving a frenzied taxi ride from the airport to the law firm, Brad Carson burst through the conference room door. Chairs and startled faces swiveled in his direction as if he were a junior-high teacher who had just entered class in the middle of a spitball war. He sported jeans and a T-shirt, disheveled hair, and he smelled like a man who had spent all night on a plane. A flustered receptionist speaking rapid and forceful Arabic followed on his heels, complaining because Brad had ignored her protests.

Brad stopped in the doorway and pointed at the witness. "What's going on here?" he demanded of Strobel. The receptionist bumped into his back. Brad ignored her.

On the other side of the conference table, Strobel stood. "Counsel, we are in the middle of our fifth deposition of the day. We started this morning at the agreed-upon time, and you were not present. Unfortunately for you, the world does not suspend all of its activities while it waits for the great Bradley Carson to stroll in."

After a long day and little sleep, Brad was in no mood for Strobel's condescension. "You arrogant jerk . . ." Brad lunged around the conference table toward Strobel, but the granite figure of Ahmed Aberijan blocked him. Brad was lucky to be restrained, as the older but more powerful Strobel had two inches and fifty pounds on him. The two lawyers traded insults while Ahmed acted as a human barrier between Brad and Strobel and slowly nudged Brad back to his side of the conference table.

Brad got no backup from Sa'id, who sat frozen in his chair, his mouth wide open and his eyes even wider.

After the yelling subsided, and Brad had placed every objection fathomable into the record, Strobel concluded his direct examination. The parties took a ten-minute break while Sa'id briefed Brad on the testimony. Sa'id made his own cross-examination of earlier witnesses seem impressive enough, and Brad calmed down a little. From the sounds of things described by Sa'id, the little man had done a good and thorough job of discrediting the others. Brad was thankful that they had retained this quirky little lawyer, even if he was costing them nearly three hundred bucks an hour.

◁ ▷

Forty-five minutes into the cross-examination, Nikki slipped into the conference room dressed no better than Brad and took a seat right next to him. She handed him two plastic bags under the table—one full of a substance that resembled marijuana, the other full of a white powder. She leaned over and whispered in Brad's ear.

"This better work, babe. It's not easy getting this stuff."

Brad squeezed her knee. "Thanks," he whispered.

He carefully placed both bags on the table in front of Omar Khartoum.

"I would like the court reporter to mark, for purposes of identification, plaintiff's Exhibits 1 and 2. And I would ask the witness to please identify these exhibits."

"I object," Strobel proclaimed loudly.

"There's a surprise," Brad said.

"This is obviously some kind of trick by Mr. Carson to bring in substances that look like marijuana and cocaine. Of course, if they were the real thing, Mr. Aberijan here is an officer of the law and would have to arrest Mr. Carson." Strobel said it calmly but forcefully, just the right tone for the video camera.

Khartoum heard the objection and seemed to take the hint. He looked at the materials in the bags. He reached in and touched the materials, then tasted a small portion from the tip of his finger.

"It is fake cocaine and fake marijuana," he announced proudly.

"How did you know it was fake from tasting it?" Brad asked. "How is this substance different from the real cocaine that you've tasted?"

After the translation, the witness pondered the question. "This substance is sweeter."

"Is that how you tell whether a substance is cocaine? You see how sweet it is?" Brad's toxicologist, Dr. Shelhorse, would testify that the telltale sign for cocaine was the numbness it caused on the tongue and mucus membranes.

"Yes," Khartoum replied; this time his tone of voice was a little less sure.

"But these exhibits at least look like the types of drugs you bought from Mr. and Mrs. Reed?"

"Yes."

"Did you buy these drugs by the gram?"

"Yes."

"How much did you pay for the marijuana, and how much did you pay for the cocaine?"

Khartoum was actually prepared on this point and answered quickly and confidently. "Two hundred riyals per gram for the marijuana. Fourteen hundred per gram for the cocaine."

"How many grams would you say are in this bag that we have marked as 'Exhibit 1'?" Brad asked, holding up a bag of oregano.

Khartoum stared at the bag for two full minutes. "I don't know," he said at last.

"Guess," Brad insisted.

"He doesn't have to guess," Strobel said. "If he doesn't know, he doesn't know."

"Humor me," Brad said. "He says he paid big money for these drugs. But he doesn't have the foggiest idea how much these substances weigh?"

"Thirty-five grams," Khartoum said. It sounded more like a question than an answer.

Nikki pulled out a small set of metric scales, and Brad put the bag on the scales.

"Would you read that please?" Brad said.

"Seventy-five grams," Khartoum said sheepishly. "But I could never tell. That's why we always weighed it."

"Did the Reeds always weigh these drugs?" Brad asked.

"Sure."

"Then why did the police not seize or inventory a scale when they searched the Reeds' apartment?"

"Objection," Strobel said. "He can't possibly know why the police did what they did."

"Nor can anyone else," Brad said. "Did you ever freebase the cocaine?"

"I do not understand," Khartoum replied.

"Let me ask it this way: What did you do with the marijuana and the cocaine?"

Khartoum looked puzzled, but he had apparently seen a few movies. "We would smoke the marijuana and sniff the cocaine up our noses."

"Show me how you would 'sniff' the cocaine," Brad said as he handed the witness plaintiff's Exhibit 2.

Khartoum looked at the substance like it might bite.

"I object," Strobel said. "This is totally improper."

"You've made your objection," Brad answered. "Now let the witness answer the question."

Khartoum dumped the powdered sugar onto the table in a long thin line and put one nostril down next to the pile, closing the other nostril with his finger. "We would do like that and breathe in," he said.

"All of it?" Brad asked. This was too good to be true.

The witness shrugged when he heard the translation.

"No, just a small part of the pile," Khartoum said.

"Show me how much," Brad demanded.

Using a piece of paper, Khartoum gingerly separated out a portion of the substance. To Brad's delight, it was a large amount.

"Now weigh it," Brad said.

"I object." Strobel's tone was no longer controlled for the camera. "This is nonsense."

"Just weigh it," Brad said.

"About twelve grams," came back the translated reply.

Brad smiled. Dr. Shelhorse would testify that a fatal dose of cocaine is generally considered to be only one gram, although there were stories of experienced users surviving more than twenty grams. Certainly, the amount separated by Khartoum was not an ordinary dose.

"Did you ever *smoke* crack cocaine, or did you ever see the Reeds smoke crack cocaine?"

By now, Khartoum had apparently determined that vagueness was his friend, so he resorted to an appropriately vague answer.

"Sometimes," he said.

"Sometimes what?" Brad pressed. "Sometimes you smoked crack, or sometimes the Reeds did, or both?"

"Sometimes the Reeds did. They tried to get me to do it, but I wouldn't."

"Explain the process of how they would prepare the crack and then smoke it."

After hearing the translated question, Khartoum sat thinking for quite a time. His eyes were blank, wandering over to Strobel for help that was not forthcoming. Then he gave a slow, calculated answer.

"Because I wouldn't join them in smoking crack, I never actually saw them do it. I know they did smoke crack because I saw them heating the cocaine and preparing the crack."

"How did they heat it? How hot?"

Another pause. More vagueness. "It is a complicated process that I cannot describe. I believe temperatures would be very hot—more than 250 degrees."

Brad knew, again from information provided by Dr. Shelhorse, that the cocaine powder would vaporize at temperatures over 200 degrees Celsius, destroying most of the active ingredients. Crack was made by vaporization and extraction of the hydrochloric salt in the cocaine at a much lower temperature. Brad would not make these points now and give Khartoum a chance to correct his testimony. He would wait until Strobel showed the jury the videotaped deposition at trial; then Brad would call Dr. Shelhorse to the stand on rebuttal and prove Khartoum a liar.

◁▷

As Khartoum fidgeted in his chair, dodging questions and glancing at Strobel for help, Nikki diverted her gaze to the stoic face of Ahmed Aberijan. She stared at him, though he refused to look back. She just wanted him to look over at her one time so she could despise him with her eyes.

But the man just sat there, across the table and two seats down from Nikki, glaring at the witness with a look that promised future pain. Nikki saw the fire smoldering in Ahmed's eyes, the all-too-familiar look of an abusive temper ready to explode. It was the same steeled look, the same glare, that Nikki had so feared in her own father's eyes. It was that point in time when the eyes go from fire to ice, from anger to a cold resolve to hurt somebody. It would be a signal to Nikki, even in grade school and then in junior high, to grab her sister and get out of the room. She would turn on her boom box and drown out the noise of another terrible argument, of her mother taking the abuse for all the girls in the family.

Nikki had always melted in terror at the same look that she saw now. And she had never forgiven herself for failing to stand up to the man.

But she was older now. And wiser. And stronger.

Look at me! she wanted to shout. *I will not turn away!*

But even as the thought flitted across her mind, she was not absolutely certain she could do it even now.

◁▷

"One final question," Brad announced. "When you snorted cocaine, how long did it take before you felt the rush, and how long did the rush last?"

This question, like the others, had been suggested by Shelhorse. She had explained to Brad that smoking crack gives an immediate euphoria that lasts only ten minutes or so and is followed by an intense downswing of mood, leaving the smoker irritable and wired. On the other hand, Shelhorse explained, those who snort the drug will not obtain the rush for several minutes, as the absorption process takes place, but the euphoria would last longer, sometimes as much as an hour.

But apparently nobody had explained these facts to Khartoum. "I would get a huge rush right away," he explained, "and I wouldn't come down for hours."

"That's exactly what I thought," Brad said. "No further questions."

23

RASHEED BERJEIN DID NOT MATCH the mental picture Brad had constructed months earlier after talking to Nikki. Subconsciously, Brad had stereotyped Rasheed as a Middle Eastern version of Charles Reed—a soft-bellied and soft-spoken Christian about Sarah's age. But Rasheed looked ten years younger and far more rugged than Brad imagined.

Rasheed's thobe could not entirely cloak his athletic build. Thick, short-cropped hair framed his clean-shaven face, which featured a prominent, broad nose. Large, dark semicircles underneath his deep-set eyes mirrored the enormous eyebrows above them. His skin was leathery and tanned. He looked more like a young man you would want on your side in a street brawl than he did Brad's preconception of a shy and retiring Christian.

Brad was trained to recognize signs of distress, and in Rasheed he saw them all. The man entered the room with his eyes downcast, darting around as he took his seat. He made no effort to shake hands with or even look at the lawyers. Brad noticed his hands trembled, and he blinked his eyes frequently. Brad stared at Rasheed, hoping for some eye contact, but Rasheed pinned his gaze on his hands.

Brad had no doubt that Rasheed was about to fabricate testimony against Sarah Reed.

"Please state your name for the record," Strobel instructed.

Rasheed looked up from his hands and locked his mournful eyes on Nikki.

"Rasheed Berjein," he said.

He continued to stare at Nikki for a long second. Brad thought he noticed a slight twinkle of the eyes and an almost imperceptible lifting of the cheeks, but the signs of recognition disappeared as quickly as they came.

◁ ▷

On the other side of town, Mobara Berjein sat quietly on a folding metal chair, her hands clasped in her lap, head bowed in prayer. The Muttawa stood by the door, staring impassively at Mobara, listening intently to the deposition being piped into the small room and silently daring her husband to deviate from the plan. Everyone in the room knew that Mobara's life depended on how well her husband followed the script.

◁ ▷

Sarah Reed's closest friends started arriving at her small house at 12:30 a.m. Sarah had started the coffee at midnight and had not even attempted to sleep. But Sarah's preteen children could sleep through anything, and so she began the impossible task of waking them up only a few hours after they had dozed off.

She went to Steven's room first and was struck again by how much the boy resembled his father. Even when he slept, the similarities were unmistakable. They both slept on their backs with their mouths open, hands flung up somewhere over their heads, sheets and blankets strewn everywhere, the result of a hundred thrashing movements that were prerequisites to falling asleep. Steven had his dad's eyes, his dad's mouth, and his dad's mannerisms.

Steven also inherited his dad's undying optimism and unfailing loyalty. He had taken seriously his new responsibilities as "man of the house" and had proclaimed on more than one occasion that he would live at home even as he attended college and afterward when he began his hoped-for career as a major league baseball player. He shouldered heavy responsibilities for an eleven-year-old, and the thought of it made tears well up in Sarah's eyes. It was not the first time she had stood in the dark by Steven's bed and cried.

By 1 a.m., the cul-de-sac where Sarah lived had been transformed into a parking lot. Chesapeake Community Church members filled the family room, spilling into the kitchen and down the hallway. An excited buzz of conversation filled the tiny house as the church members anticipated this most unusual meeting.

Chesapeake Community Church did not have the most inspired preaching or the most moving music, but it was a praying church, and the people in Sarah's home had been called to prayer. And so, at the precise moment that Rasheed started answering questions in Riyadh, the Reverend Jacob

Bailey quieted the conversation and pointed the group's prayers heavenward. They prayed for wisdom and courage for Rasheed; they prayed for safety for Rasheed and Mobara; they prayed for blinders on the eyes of Strobel and Ahmed and for slowness of understanding. They prayed for Brad and Nikki and even Leslie, who had declined Sarah's invitation to attend. They prayed for God's work to go forward and God's will to be done through His church in Riyadh. For two hours, they prayed and they prayed and they prayed.

Reverend Bailey and his church in Chesapeake were not the only ones petitioning the God of the universe for safety, courage, and wisdom. Rasheed's flamboyant brother, Hanif, led a similar prayer effort in Riyadh. The language was different, the style was different, and the intensity was very different. The raw emotion of the Riyadh meeting far exceeded that of the Chesapeake church. Many in Riyadh had been introduced to Christ by Rasheed, and all knew him personally. The meeting was characterized by a passion borne of persecution, the intensity heightened by the knowledge that this meeting could be their last. They shed tears unashamedly, and with loud voices they begged God to intervene.

◁▷

Brad took copious notes as the object of everyone's prayers relentlessly blasted Sarah Reed's case. Rasheed confirmed that Charles and Sarah Reed had in fact sold drugs and admitted using the drugs himself. He was more articulate than Khartoum and came across as infinitely more believable. He preemptively handled all the issues Brad had used so effectively on cross-examination the previous day by describing in great detail the way the drugs were used.

After ninety minutes of damaging testimony, Strobel passed the witness for a cross-examination that Brad knew would not be easy.

No sense beating around the bush.

"Are you or your wife being threatened by the nation of Saudi Arabia and forced to give untrue testimony in this case?"

"Objection," Strobel interjected. "That's outrageous! You have no foundation for that accusation."

Brad leaned forward and pointed directly at Ahmed. "Why don't you ask Mr. Aberijan if there's a foundation for my question?" Then he pointed at Rasheed. "Why don't you march this man's wife into the conference room so I can ask her?" He turned to Strobel, who was by now also leaning forward on the table. "How can you sleep at night representing people who torture and kill and then intimidate witnesses into lying about it?"

Strobel responded with a withering gaze. When he finally spoke, he did so loudly and slowly, emphasizing every word.

"You listen to me, Mr. Carson. Don't you ever again make accusations you can't back up. I'm tired of your nonsense. If you have one more outburst like that, I'll leave, and I'll take Mr. Berjein with me to file a criminal complaint against you with the Riyadh police." Strobel turned to the translator, "Don't translate that last question. I objected to it, and it's not worthy of being translated."

Brad and Mack stared hard at each other for a few seconds. Brad leaned back first.

"Did you meet with Nikki Moreno and Sa'id el Khamin several weeks ago?" he asked.

The question was translated. Brad knew Rasheed wouldn't deny this meeting. Both Sa'id and Nikki could be called to testify. They could also produce the affidavit Rasheed had signed.

"Yes."

"Isn't it true, sir, that you told Mr. el Khamin and Ms. Moreno that neither Charles nor Sarah Reed had ever used drugs?"

"Yes."

"Isn't it also true that you told Mr. el Khamin and Ms. Moreno that you were tortured by the Muttawa the same night that the Reeds were tortured and Mr. Reed was killed?"

"Objection," Strobel said, this time in a more businesslike voice. "The question assumes facts that have never been proven."

Rasheed's translated answer was really a question. "Should I answer it?"

"Yes," Brad said. "The judge will decide later whether to sustain the objection."

The translator passed on the message. "That's what I told them," Rasheed said.

"Were you lying when you talked to Mr. el Khamin and Ms. Moreno, or are you lying now?"

"Objection."

"Just answer the question," Brad demanded.

The question, objection, and comment were translated.

"I was lying to them," Rasheed admitted.

"Do you lie when it suits your purposes?" Brad asked.

"Objection."

"Sometimes," Rasheed said through the translator.

It was one of the more truthful answers Rasheed would give on cross-examination. He proved to be a slippery and skillful witness. And at the end of two frustrating hours, Brad had still been unable to undercut his testimony. He decided to try one final, desperate question, one final stab at the truth.

"Look me in the eye and tell me that you are not being intimidated or threatened by the Saudi Arabian authorities."

"Objection," Strobel said evenly, "but he may answer the question. I'll take this objection up with the judge later."

As he had done all afternoon, Rasheed looked at the translator as he interpreted the question. But this time, rather than look at Brad when answering, Rasheed looked down at the table and muttered his reply.

"No such thing has occurred," the translator said.

"Then I have no further questions," Brad said.

The final image for the jury would be the top of Rasheed's head.

◁▷

Bella cleared everything off her desk except the firm checkbook, the firm ledger, and the huge pile of bills causing her to lose sleep. Her new weekly ritual was to stare at the firm's checking-account balance and then prioritize the bills she could pay. The trial was still three weeks away, and the firm was burning through cash even quicker than Bella thought possible. The firm now operated off a three-hundred-thousand-dollar line of credit that had been drawn down to seventy-five thousand. All Brad's assets were pledged to secure the loan.

She wondered how long it would be until the Johnson settlement check came through. She certainly wasn't about to ask Nikki. Wrapping up these settlements could take weeks, even months, and Brad had admonished her to have no further contact with that file. Every other case with a potential for settlement had been put to bed.

Just in case, as a final contingency plan, Bella ordered twenty-five new credit cards for the firm, each from a different bank. The average credit limit for each card was a little over five thousand. If necessary, these cards could provide another $125,000 of operating income, but at a very steep price in terms of interest rate.

In the meantime, Bella would have to make do. Brad had stopped taking a salary several weeks ago, and that helped. Bella suggested that Nikki should also forego her salary, but Brad wouldn't hear of it.

As she always did, Bella put the bill from Worthington on the bottom of the pile. She couldn't believe he had the audacity to withdraw from the case and then send them a bill for expert services rendered. Bella wouldn't have paid Worthington if she had all the money in the world.

Bella unilaterally decided to cut several "discretionary" items from the firm's budget. Brad belonged to many legal associations but infrequently attended the meetings. Bella decided he wouldn't miss his memberships as long as she intercepted the letters asking him to reconsider his withdrawal. She also decided that legal periodicals Brad never read were a waste of money. No sense killing those trees for nothing. These were the easy calls.

Slightly more difficult was the weekly bill for the office cleaning crew. But even with the crew in full swing, the office looked like a hazardous-waste dump. Besides, Brad, Nikki, and Leslie were all grown-ups and could pick up after themselves. The cleaning crew would be suspended.

The three bills that almost made the final cut but didn't were the ones she would hear about. Carson & Associates not only paid Brad's salary and bonus; it also made his car and boat payments. Brad would be way too busy in the next few months to ever use his boat. As for the cars, she figured she could buy at least ninety days before the repo man paid a visit. With any luck, the trial would be over by then. Bella divided the bills into "pay" and "no pay" piles. She thought about all the money that had flown through the firm in the past twelve years. Until the *Reed* case became the sole focus of the firm, they always had enough cases in the pipeline so that the contingency fees would just keep rolling in, each seemingly bigger than the one before. But that was yesterday's money, and it had already been spent. Now Brad had decided to risk it all on one case, something they had never done before. A foolish gamble. And Bella was not feeling lucky.

As she had so often since Nikki claimed that whopping salary, Bella turned her attention from the firm's bills to her own financial obligations. Only one commitment really concerned her, but it was enormous. As much as she cared for Brad, she would not let his financial indiscretions rob her of her livelihood and her precious mother's care. If she kept at her plan diligently enough, with great care and caution not to misstep, that would never happen.

◁▷

On the flight home from Saudi Arabia, Brad's mind raced with thoughts of incomplete pretrial tasks, the impact of the depositions, and his worries about confidential information leaking to the other side.

His thoughts also turned to Leslie often. He had grown accustomed to seeing her every day and missed her greatly on this week-long trip. He gave up trying to fool himself into thinking that their relationship was just professional or that they were merely friends. You didn't think about a "friend" every second you were away from her. You didn't find yourself constantly wondering how a "friend" would react to the things you were doing or wondering what that "friend" was doing at that very instant. You didn't spend your time in a strange and exotic land desperately wishing that your "friend" could be there to share the memories.

Their kiss at The Trellis aside, he wasn't sure Leslie shared his feelings. Brad had dropped repeated hints about the lighthouse painting but never received a word of thanks. This woman was indeed a mystery. Was he the only one getting emotionally involved? Was it just the pressure and trauma of the case that sparked an occasional chemistry between them—and his thoughts now? He didn't know much for sure except that he missed her smile, her touch. He missed staring at her when she wasn't looking. He missed the way she made him feel.

He was now three weeks from the biggest trial of his life, wholly unprepared, and all he could think about was this strange and wonderful woman who dominated his thoughts. This wasn't friendship; it was love.

There. He had said it, if only to himself. He loved her. It made no sense, the timing was bad, and she might not love him. But none of that mattered. This was an issue of the heart, not the head. He loved Leslie Connors. And he would tell her that and let the chips fall where they might. As soon as he had a chance. As soon as he got the courage. Brad Carson, the intrepid trial lawyer, fearless in the courtroom, and a coward in the game of love. He would tell her.

As soon as the case was over.

◁▷

Back on American soil, as they waited for their connecting flight at Reagan National, Nikki slipped away and called her home answering machine. She

204 || DIRECTED VERDICT

had sixteen new messages, an average number for a socialite of her caliber. She skipped through the first twelve, then heard the voice she was hoping to hear. Rasheed Berjein. Sounds of vehicles punctuated the background. Rasheed was on a pay phone.

He softly but distinctly repeated a phrase in Arabic, then hung up. Nikki was not fluent in the language, but she had learned a few phrases during her trips to the Kingdom. She and Rasheed had agreed that they would use this one as the code.

"Everything is fine," he had said.

"Thanks be to Allah," Nikki mumbled sarcastically. She smiled and holstered the cell phone without finishing her messages.

24

AHMED ARRIVED AT Norfolk General District Court, Traffic Division, ahead of schedule, at precisely 8:30 a.m. He passed through the metal detectors without event, turned left down the hallway, and located Courtroom No. 2, one of two traffic courtrooms in the building. Ahmed sat in the second row and watched the parade of American reprobates arriving for their day in court.

Ahmed's instincts told him to be leery of a setup, but reason told him he had already gained too much advantageous information for this to be a sting. Still, he would feel better once he met the informant and gained some insight into motive.

Within a few minutes of one another, three of Barnes's best operatives took their spots in the courtroom. The first was a twenty-six-year-old in over-size baggy jeans, a ratty T-shirt, lots of jewelry, and at least two earrings. His keys and wallet were attached to his belt by a chain. He took a seat directly behind Ahmed. The second posed in the front of the courtroom as a washed-up attorney in a pair of frayed dress slacks, a stained red tie, matching suspenders, and an ill-fitting sports coat. A third man, a middle-aged investigator with no distinguishable features who could blend into any crowd, stood on the other side of the courtroom.

◁▷

The informant entered the doors of the General District Court at 9:50, fashionably late. She cleared the metal detectors and went straight into the women's rest room. She leaned forward over the sink and looked closely at her face in the mirror, giving herself a little pep talk, calming her nerves. She washed her hands in hot water, vigorously rubbing them together and drying them roughly on the paper towels. Still ice-cold. She determined not to shake hands with Ahmed.

She walked slowly into the courtroom, eyes darting around the gallery, taking in every look, every movement, evaluating every person for whether they belonged. She had spent enough time here recently to know the lawyers, the court personnel, and the rhythm of the General District Court—who belonged and who didn't. She clung to a small leather briefcase with both hands. She walked deliberately to the second row and sat down next to Ahmed.

He stared impassively ahead. "You?" he hissed.

She ignored the comment. "I told you to come alone," she whispered, her voice hoarse with emotion.

"I did," Ahmed said calmly.

This whole meeting was high risk, but she had to raise the stakes. Ahmed seemed so at ease, so in control. She had to do something to rattle him. These first few minutes were critical.

"Just behind the counsel table on the left." She nodded toward a lawyer seated there. "Partially bald. Red tie. Red suspenders." She had never seen him in this courtroom before even though the same lawyers seemed to show up every day. Plus, he had only a few manila folders in his hand, each representing a separate case, and no traffic court lawyer could survive on such meager volume. In General District Courtroom No. 2, the lawyers handled cases by the truckload. The other lawyers had manila folders everywhere.

She stood to leave. "He's one of yours," she whispered. "The meeting's off."

Ahmed grabbed her forearm with thick fingers and jerked her back into her seat. The uninhibited force of it, right there in the middle of General District Court, made her tremble.

"Impressive," he hissed. Then he released her arm. "I'll send my men out." Ahmed turned and nodded to the man sitting directly behind them.

"Leave. And take your friend with you." Ahmed nodded toward the man at the front table. The informant kept her gaze straight ahead, watching in silence as the men left.

She felt her heart pounding in her throat, each beat ringing in her ears. Goose bumps, clammy skin, her stomach in knots, the works. But still she willed herself to relax—deep breaths, stone-cold face, deliberate movements. Who would take control? Who would blink first? Who would flinch from the task before them?

"If you ever try that again," she whispered, her voice steady now, "the whole deal's off. I deal with you. No intermediaries. No extras."

Out of the corner of her eye, she could see Ahmed swallow hard. He'd better get used to taking orders from a woman.

"Did you bring the transmitters?" she asked.

Ahmed held them out in his unwavering right hand. She took them, taking care not to touch his skin. She placed them in her briefcase.

"These are magnetic, just attach them to any metal surface," he explained, his voice barely audible. "They operate off shortwave radio technology and send a coded signal to a receiver."

He turned to look directly at her. She froze, then inhaled evenly. "I don't actually believe these are necessary," Ahmed said. "Do you really think that we couldn't have done this ourselves if we wanted to?"

Though Ahmed looked straight at her, straight through her, she kept her eyes pinned on the front of the courtroom. "I will attach them to the three main telephones," she said through clenched teeth. "Carson sweeps for bugs at the same time every day. I'll attach them after those sweeps and take them off at night."

She was ready to bolt. This man, inches away, penetrating her with his eyes and sickening her with his putrid breath, was almost more than she could take. She had accomplished her purpose for this meeting. Why wait?

"How do you plan to take out Shelhorse?" he asked.

"It is enough that you know it will be done. I'll contact you with our next meeting time and place. If you try to follow me or in any way contact me, we're through."

With that parting instruction she stood, glanced down at him—stared at him—as she hovered there for a moment, then walked quickly from the courtroom. She rushed past the metal detector and out the doors, anxious to fill her lungs with some fresh air. She glanced around, consumed by the suspicious looks of dozens of strangers, each a potential accomplice to Ahmed. She resisted the urge to run or scream or dart into some crowd and slip into some back alley.

What good would it do? They knew who she was now. The game was on. Her only hope was to stay one step ahead.

◁ ▷

Later that day, Brad gathered his team in the main conference room, which Nikki had appropriately dubbed "the war room." It looked like Sherman had ransacked the place on his March to the Sea, leaving behind papers, deposition transcripts, folder files, empty cups, paper plates, and dirty napkins.

In the vortex of the mess, Nikki sat in one chair with her legs up on another, papers spread across her lap, the table, and the floor around her. Nikki's three Diet Coke cans, all partially full of flat soda, probably from yesterday, sat together on a paper sign that Bella had taped to the wall a week prior: "Your mother doesn't work here, so please clean up your own mess." Nikki had redeemed the stained sign from the floor, where it eventually fell, and now used it as a large coaster.

Leslie walked into the war room and cleaned off a portion of the table, stacking the clutter in a neat out-of-the-way pile. Next to her, Nikki spread out a stack of what looked like surveys. The corner of one drifted across an invisible boundary line. Leslie lifted an eyebrow, and without looking at Nikki, she pushed the page out of her way.

The clutter of the conference room was exacerbated on this evening, one week prior to trial, by large sheets of poster paper taped to the walls with the names of the first fifty jurors from the jury list scrawled across the top. As this was a civil case, the jury would ultimately consist of seven jurors, plus alternates. In Brad's experience, it could take up to fifty prospective jurors in a high-profile case like this one just to find the seven who would be qualified to serve. Brad stood next to a sheet titled "Model Juror Profile" and facilitated a discussion on desirable juror characteristics.

"Male or female?" he asked.

"Definitely female," Leslie said, making a neat notation on the legal pad in front of her. "Women will appreciate what it means to lose a husband and raise kids alone."

"I agree," Nikki said. "Plus they're smarter."

Bella grunted her approval, making it unanimous among the female team members. The Rock, of course, had not been invited to the meeting.

"White, African American, Hispanic, or Asian American?" Brad asked, rattling off the predominate ethnic groups he expected to see on the panel.

"Definitely black," Bella decided. She constantly had trouble remembering that Brad preferred she use the term *African American*. "They'll have a natural distrust of the police and authority figures. They'll hate Ahmed. Besides, look at the good rulings we've already gotten from Judge Johnson."

"Hispanics have attitude too," Nikki claimed. "We just need jurors with attitude."

Leslie furrowed her brow and stopped writing. "Can we even ask this question? Isn't discrimination while choosing jurors prohibited by the *Batson* case?"

"Technically, yes," Brad said. "But we're not discriminating here against minority groups, we're actually expressing a preference for them as jurors. Kind of like our own little affirmative action program."

Leslie frowned. "That's weak, Brad Carson, and you know it."

"Ex-cuuuse us," Nikki said. "Where did that attitude come from?"

Leslie ignored the question, and Brad decided he'd better move on. The chemistry among the women was fragile at best.

"All right, let's move off that point," Brad suggested. "How old is our model juror?"

"Young." It was Nikki again. "The old geezers will trust the police and not want to rock the boat."

Nobody else spoke. Brad took that as consent. He wrote it down.

"Religion?"

"Thought you would never ask—," Nikki began.

"Wait. We can't ask that either, can we?" Leslie's furrowed brow was back, this time combined with a disapproving twist of the head.

"Under *Batson*, we probably can't use our preemptory strikes on the basis of religion," Brad conceded. "But in this case, because it's so uniquely religious in nature, maybe we can get the judge to strike some jurors for cause based on their religion."

"Whatever," Nikki said, dismissing the legal niceties with a flip of her hand. "We've got to have fired-up, hard-core Christians on this jury. No Muslims. No atheists. No lukewarm fence sitters. We've got to have real Bible-thumpers. Hellfire-and-brimstone types."

They pooled opinions and justified their hunches for an hour. When they were done, Brad stood back and admired the profile of his dream juror: a young African American or Hispanic single mother with strong evangelical Christian beliefs, lower-income bracket preferred, and someone with at least one attempt at suing for personal injuries in the past. *Fat chance,* he thought.

Next they would rate the individual jurors on a scale of one to ten so the process would have at least the appearance of scientific exactitude. They all agreed that Brad would have the ability to change the ratings once they started questioning the jurors in court, but this would at least give him a starting point.

They came to a stalemate on the first juror, a single mother of two. Leslie gave her a five, Bella a two, Brad a seven, and Nikki a ten. Brad did the simple math, assigned juror number one a six, and then moved on to the second of the fifty jurors. It was getting late.

But Nikki was shaking her head. "Trust me on this one guys, she's a ten. If you get a chance, you've got to have her on your jury."

"C'mon Nikki," Brad groaned. "You had your vote. We'll be here all night if we all lobby for our favorite ones."

"Brad, I know what I'm talking about. Trust me."

"It's not a matter of trust," Leslie broke in. "It's a matter of fairness. We each get one vote, and then Brad can make whatever adjustments he wants at trial. We don't really have much to go on anyway. We don't even know what her race or religion is."

"What if I told you she faithfully attends an independent church named Grace Chapel and goes on at least one volunteer mission trip every year? What if I told you she seriously believes that everyone needs to hear about Jesus Christ? What if I could guarantee you she is a diehard supporter of all mission causes?"

"I'd change my score," Leslie admitted. "But how could you possibly know all that stuff?"

The looks on the faces of the others confirmed that they were all thinking the same thing. Brad was chewing on his glasses and raised an eyebrow at Nikki.

"Well?" he asked.

"Let's just say I have inside information on thirty-six of these fifty jurors," Nikki said, almost in a whisper. Brad started to say something, but Nikki lifted her hand to silence him. "I know the rules, Brad. No direct contact with prospective jurors. Don't ask how I got this information, but it's all legit. For most of these jurors, I can tell you more about their religious beliefs than their own mothers know."

Brad stared at Nikki in silence, searching her face for clues. They stood on thin ethical ice. He wanted this information—no, he needed this information. Desperately. But at what price?

"Are you sure you didn't contact any jurors?"

"No way."

"You sure it's all legal?"

"You bet."

He studied her for another moment, and she still didn't flinch.

"All right, then I change my vote to a ten," Brad said.

"Me too," Bella said.

"I'm staying with a five," Leslie said. "I don't trust any source that is unknown and cannot be tested."

Nikki rolled her eyes.

"Juror one gets a nine," Brad announced, crossing through the old score on the poster sheet.

And so it went, juror by juror, Nikki providing her mysterious insights and the group arriving at a judgment. At a quarter till one, the exhausted crew considered juror number fifty. They had abandoned extended discussion long before.

"You got any inside information on this one?" Brad asked.

"Yep," Nikki said. "I give him an eight."

"Me too, then," Brad said.

"Count me in," Bella said.

"Four," Leslie said.

"Juror fifty gets a seven," Brad said. "And I'm going home."

◁▷

The tired crew all filed out to the parking lot and dragged their weary bodies into their cars to head home. Nikki hadn't been driving five minutes when the phone rang.

"It's me," Bella said gruffly from the other end. "What's the deal with these jurors?"

Nikki was amazed Bella would even call. But tonight Bella had voted with Nikki, not against her. Maybe it was Bella's way of reaching out for some middle ground. Nikki knew she could never expect a full apology, but she was willing to meet Bella halfway. After all, Bella had called her; Willy had made the first step.

"Promise not to tell Brad?"

"Yeah."

"Okay. Well, the first thing I did was to send out a religious survey to each juror and all their neighbors. I didn't send the letter in my name, so I was telling Brad the truth when I said I didn't contact any jurors. The letter said it was on behalf of a new church that was going to start a service in Tidewater. It asked about the juror's religious beliefs in general, where they attended

212 || DIRECTED VERDICT

church, and whether they would want to join a church that was 100 percent committed to mission work and taking the gospel to the whole world. Most jurors didn't send the survey back, though some did. For those we didn't hear from, I had the Rock call them and ask those questions. There were still a few we just never reached, or they refused to answer the questions."

Nikki's explanation was followed by silence. Nikki knew that Bella was impressed but would try hard not to show it. She second-guessed herself for telling Bella and figured that Bella would say something to Brad first thing in the morning.

"I figured it was something like that," Bella said.

"Haven't you guys ever done this type of thing on your cases?" Nikki asked.

"Oh sure, we just don't like to talk about it."

Right.

"Gotta go," Bella said with her usual diplomacy. Before Nikki could respond, Bella hung up.

Nikki found herself wondering how Brad's firm ever won a case when he obviously invested no time in the investigation of jurors.

"He must be good on his feet," she mumbled to herself as she gunned the engine of her Sebring. She was just a few short days from finding out.

PART IV
THE TRIAL

25

THE SUN SMILED BRIGHTLY on the brisk October morning that greeted the first day of the trial. A cool northern breeze gently buffeted Norfolk and chased a few puffy white clouds quickly across the sky. A perfect day for protesting.

The demonstrators started arriving at 7:30 and arranged themselves neatly on the sidewalk in front of the massive stone federal building on Granby Street. On one side of the courthouse steps, and stretching down the sidewalk, were about one hundred fifty Christians from every walk of life led by the Reverend Jacob Bailey and a loyal band of prayer warriors.

While Reverend Bailey and his team prayed, others turned the vigil into a picnic, enjoying coffee and doughnuts and all sorts of other fast-food breakfast treats. They did have a few signs, mostly quoting Bible verses like John 3:16 or urging the court to "Stop the Torture." And at precisely 8 a.m., when the national morning news audiences peaked, they all stopped eating and joined Reverend Bailey in spontaneous prayer for persecuted Christians everywhere.

On the other side of the steps was a group of about eighty Muslims, there to support the freedom of the Saudi people to choose their own religion, free from Western interference. These protesters stayed entertained by a barrage of rhetoric from a small group of fiery leaders. Occasionally, they would break into chants, goading the more docile protesters on the other side of the steps. The press congregated with the Muslims, who tended to give more passionate interviews that lent themselves to better sound bites.

Not fitting into either group, but determined to exercise their First Amendment rights on such an important occasion, were a handful of miscellaneous protesters representing a half-dozen other causes. By far the most colorful of the bunch was the gentleman in a well-worn, bright yellow chicken suit carrying a sign that read "Jesus was a vegetarian." Most assumed he was with the People for the Ethical Treatment of Animals, and everyone gave him plenty of space as he roamed the sidewalks, goose-stepping so that he would not trip over his own large webbed feet.

As usual, the media seemed to outnumber the folks they were covering, and the reporters had the best seats in the house. Cameramen, talking heads, and a bevy of print reporters dominated the sidewalk directly in front of the courthouse. Local and national news trucks, with satellite dishes on top, jammed the streets.

At precisely 8:30, a black stretch limo arrived in front of the courthouse steps carrying Ahmed Aberijan and Frederick Barnes. Barnes parted the way for his infamous cohort, and Ahmed looked perplexed at all the English-speaking journalists who shoved microphones under his nose and shouted questions.

Mack Strobel, Winsted Mackenzie, and several of their partners arrived next, each carrying only one small briefcase. The associates from Kilgore & Strobel had already hauled neatly numbered boxes of documents and exhibits into the courtroom. Mackenzie stopped at the top of the steps for an impromptu press conference. Mack and the others stood and watched for a moment, unsmiling, then slipped into the courthouse.

"Will the defense claim that Dr. and Mrs. Reed were drug dealers?"

"We won't just claim it, we'll prove it."

"Will anyone from the Saudi Arabian government testify, such as the crown prince?"

"Mr. Aberijan will testify. There will be no need for others."

And on it went, endless questions and answers. Mackenzie willingly obliged the media with regard to any question, regardless of how trivial, as long as the cameras were rolling.

◁▷

At 8:45, Win lost his audience when Sarah Reed's team made its appearance. Unlike the chauffeured defense team, they parked two blocks from the courthouse and carted large briefcases and boxed documents up the street with them. Bella cleared the way and took no prisoners. Sarah walked between Leslie and Nikki.

As the only male in the group, Brad felt obligated to bring up the rear and pull the heavy dolly containing three large boxes of documents that would not fit into the briefcases. He struggled mightily as he yanked the dolly up the courthouse steps, feeling like a clumsy errand boy and not at all like a top-rate legal eagle prepared to handle a major case.

True to Murphy's Law, as he reached the second to last step, the top box wiggled out from under the bungee cord holding it in place and fell hard on the steps, regurgitating pleadings, exhibits, and deposition transcripts at the feet of the startled press corps.

What a way to make an impression on the morning news!

Brad smiled sheepishly and muttered the first thing that came into his mind: "Better not quit my day job." It sounded stupid, and he immediately wished he could take it back.

And then, to Brad's astonishment, he watched as reporters, cameramen, and protesters all leaned down to scoop up the documents and place them back into the miscreant box. Brad thanked them with a brief press conference, then carefully, ever so carefully, wheeled his documents into the courthouse and passed them through the metal detector.

He caught up with the rest of the team in the elevator and immediately noticed that the color was gone from Leslie's face.

"What's the matter?" he asked, out of breath from his work as the team's pack mule.

"We're in Courtroom No. 1," Leslie whispered, "the Honorable Cynthia Baker-Kline presiding."

◁▷

A hush fell over the spacious courtroom on the second floor of the court building as everyone rose to their feet. Judge Cynthia Baker-Kline entered through a large oak door several feet behind her bench, her long black robe flowing behind her. Her fury was evident in the speed of her stride, the pursing of her lips, and the slits of her eyes. She arrived at the bench, glowered at Brad, then turned her stare to those standing across the back of the crowded courtroom. The nostrils on her long nose moved quickly in and out, like a bull preparing for the charge.

Ichabod was firmly in control.

"Oyez, oyez, oyez. Silence is now commanded while this honorable court is in session. All those with pleas to enter and matters to be argued step forward, and you shall be heard. May God save the United States of America and this honorable court."

"May God save us all," Brad muttered quietly to himself.

"May God grant us wisdom and allow us to glorify Him," Brad heard Sarah whisper.

"You may be seated," Ichabod snarled.

She leaned forward and glared down at counsel.

"Gentlemen," she barked, "I am about to bring in the jury panel so that we can begin the selection process. This is an important case, and the world is watching." She turned directly to Brad, narrowing her eyes. "I'll expect you both to comport yourselves like officers of the court."

A warning shot across the bow.

Brad nodded with all the solemnity he could muster.

◁▷

"I do have a few questions for Mr. Robertson, Your Honor." Strobel rose confidently and approached the jury box to question juror number three, the first Baptist to be interviewed. Strobel straightened to his full height, buttoned the top button on his blue pin-striped suit, and began by graciously introducing himself and his client. Even Brad had to admit that Strobel cut an imposing figure, authority oozing from every pore.

He stood directly in front of juror number three, just a few feet from the jury box, thereby blocking Brad's view of the nervous juror. Brad assumed the block was intentional and slouched to his left in his chair so he could watch the juror's face.

"Are you a regular churchgoin' man?" Strobel asked in his best common man's vernacular. He undoubtedly knew the answer. So did Brad. According to Nikki, juror number three was a faithful member of Sandbridge Baptist Church. He had scored an eight on Brad's scale.

"Yes, sir, I try to be," Robertson admitted, looking sheepish.

"Where do you attend?"

"Sandbridge Baptist Church on Shore Drive."

"That church is pretty committed to mission work, isn't it?" Strobel said it like he'd heard of the church before.

"Yes, sir, it is."

"And, as a Baptist church, your congregation contributes to the Cooperative Program, which in turn helps support Baptist missionaries all over the world. Isn't that the way it works?"

Robertson appeared perplexed, his face flushed. He probably didn't have a clue how his church did its mission work. But how could he admit that to some pagan big-city lawyer?

"I . . . s-suppose that's pretty much the way it works," Robertson stammered.

"So, in a very real way, you and your church help to financially support every Baptist missionary who's sent out, correct?"

"I . . . I guess so."

"Well, do you give money to the church?"

"Oh yes, sir. Baptists are taught to tithe."

"And does some of that money go to the Cooperative Program?"

"That's my understanding."

"And missionary salaries are paid in part from the Cooperative Program?"

"I believe that's correct."

"And by the way, you also pray for these Baptist missionaries almost every day, don't you?"

A pained expression jumped on Mr. Robertson's face before he could suppress it. Brad could tell the poor guy probably didn't know the name of a single Baptist missionary and certainly hadn't thought to pray for them in quite some time.

"Probably not as much as I should, but I try."

Brad decided it was time to make some friends on the jury panel.

"I object, Your Honor," Brad said loudly. "Mr. Robertson isn't on trial here."

Strobel turned on his heels and gave Brad one of his steel-melting stares.

"You can't object to a question about the juror's background," Ichabod said. "Overruled."

Brad looked past Strobel and into the eyes of Robertson, sensing he had made a friend.

Strobel turned back to the juror. "Thank you, Mr. Robertson, for your honesty in answering these questions." Strobel then turned to the judge. "May we approach the bench, Your Honor?"

Ichabod nodded.

Strobel and three lawyers from his firm huddled in front of Ichabod's bench, as did Brad and Leslie.

"I move to strike juror three for cause," Strobel whispered. "The man has a financial and emotional stake in missionaries all over the world. How could he possibly be unbiased?"

"I could see that coming from a mile away," Ichabod replied. "Any objections, Mr. Carson?"

"Of course I object, Judge. Striking this juror for a religious reason violates the principles set forth by the U.S. Supreme Court in *Batson*."

"I'm not asking the court to strike him because he's Baptist," Strobel whispered. "Sarah Reed's not Baptist. But through his church, this juror gives his hard-earned dollars to missionaries all over the world who are similar to Sarah Reed. Asking him to ignore that would be impossible."

"Can't I at least ask him some questions to prove he can be fair?" Brad raised his voice so the jury could hear. He wanted the panel to know he trusted their ability to be fair and that his opponent was secretly trying to get them dismissed.

"Keep your voice down," Ichabod insisted in a loud whisper. She gave Brad a chastising look, then lowered her own voice. "Now, we have several well-qualified jurors on this panel. Some are probably Christian, some are probably Muslim, and some probably put their faith in their morning coffee. That makes no difference to me. But I'm not going to allow someone to poison the panel when I see a potential bias, no matter how tenuous, in favor of one of the parties in this case."

Brad opened his mouth to argue the point, but he was stopped by the judge's outstretched hand. "I've ruled, Mr. Carson. If you don't like my ruling, you can take it up with the appeals court when this case is over. Now, counsel may return to their seats."

The other lawyers turned and walked away. Brad lingered and stared at the judge momentarily. Then he shook his head and slowly sulked back to his seat.

"Mr. Robertson, you are excused from service," Ichabod announced. "Thank you for your time and forthright answers. You are free to go."

◁▷

At the end of the second day, Judge Baker-Kline swore in the jury charged with deciding the case of *Reed v. Ahmed Aberijan and Eight John Does*. Because of the procedural peculiarities of the Foreign Sovereign Immunities Act, Judge Baker-Kline herself would simultaneously render a verdict in the case of *Reed v. Saudi Arabia*.

Brad surveyed his jury—the jury that would decide the most important case of his career—with a growing sense of despondency. His model juror was nowhere to be found. One by one, Strobel had knocked out all the self-confessed mission supporters for cause. Then, with his preemptory challenges, Strobel eliminated three more jurors who had scored high on Brad's rating scale, including two churchgoing ethnics who had each earned a nine.

Of the seven jurors who would actually decide the case, there were only two minorities. One was an African American male who had not seen the inside of a church in years. The other was a female Hispanic who claimed to be Catholic but had trouble remembering the name of her church.

One Muslim left on the panel would serve as the first alternate. Despite Nikki's urgings to the contrary, Brad had refused to strike him. Any grounds for appeal based on Strobel's religiously discriminatory strikes would be worthless if Brad engaged in the same type of conduct.

As he prepared to leave the courtroom after the second day of jury selection, Brad studied the jury and alternates one last time, then glanced sideways at his client. Sarah the single mom, Sarah the missionary, Sarah the on-fire evangelical Christian was about to have her case judged by a jury of her "peers" that contained six men and three women, and only one person who looked even remotely like her. And that juror sat at the end of the last row, where she would view the trial as the second alternate.

◁ ▷

Strobel regarded this jury as a coup. He had eliminated almost all of the Holy Rollers and outspoken minorities. He had a bad feeling about juror number four, but Ahmed had been adamant that juror four be left on the jury. In the huddle around the counsel table, Ahmed, through a translator, said he had inside information about the juror that could not be shared with the legal team. Whatever else Strobel did, it was imperative that he leave juror number four securely in place.

◁ ▷

The protesters were out with a passion at the end of day two. Despite the steady drizzle, the ranks of the Christians had swelled to several hundred. News that the defendants were striking evangelicals right and left had ignited the sidewalks. Now outspoken pastors matched the fiery speeches given by Muslim leaders. As the crowd noise and fervency grew, the Reverend Bailey and his band of prayer warriors moved a half block away so that they could petition God in relative solitude.

Unlike the calm that greeted the participants as they exited the courthouse after the first day, the respective crowds erupted in cheers as their favorites emerged on day two. Even Bella had to smile as the Christian demonstrators assured Sarah she was in their prayers.

The escalating tensions delighted the man in the chicken suit, a veteran of many high-profile trials. He predicted that soon T-shirt vendors and other hawkers would start selling paraphernalia for both sides. A fight or two would likely break out, especially if the right-wing Christian militia groups could be enticed to enter the fray. It promised to be an exciting month on the sidewalks of Granby Street.

26

"**SARAH, YOU'RE READY,**" Leslie pronounced. "The main thing now is to get some sleep."

They had been at it four straight hours, from 6:30 to 10:30, using a clean end of the conference table as a makeshift witness stand. Leslie popped questions; Sarah responded; then Leslie critiqued Sarah's responses. Sarah's willingness to accept the criticism and carefully respond with another variation of the same basic answer amazed Leslie.

"Are you sure?" Sarah still sounded unconvinced. "Can't we go through the events on the night of Charles's death one more time?"

"Sarah, we've been through it three times already. If we do it again, it will sound like you've memorized it."

"If you say so."

"I do."

Leslie stifled a yawn and started packing her notes. The adrenaline from another day in court had long since seeped out of her body, taking every ounce of her energy with it.

"Leslie, I want you to level with me, okay?" Sarah looked up and waited for a promise.

"Sure."

"How bad are the judge and jury we ended up with?"

The frankness of Sarah's question caused Leslie to stop packing and look straight at her. Sarah's eyes, her most prominent and becoming feature, were bloodshot, the lids heavy, the wrinkles underneath more pronounced than when Leslie first met her. In fact, Sarah's whole face was drawn and gaunt; her clothes now seemed to hang on her frail frame. She looked so very fragile. Her husband's death, the post-traumatic stress, the strain of being a single mom, and the pressure of the case had all taken a considerable toll.

Through it all, Sarah had remained stoic and determined. And Leslie had never sensed that she wavered in her optimistic faith. Until this moment.

"The jury's pretty bad," Leslie said. "The judge is worse." She wondered how much more Sarah could endure.

"I thought so," Sarah said softly.

They looked at each other in silence.

"Go home!" Brad shouted as he burst through the door.

Leslie jumped and grabbed at her heart. To her surprise, it was still beating.

Brad laughed. "This is a marathon, not a sprint. My star witness and my star co-counsel better get some sleep."

Brad's exuberance instantly lifted Leslie's spirits. But she couldn't let him know he had the power to alter her mood so easily.

"What are you so happy about, cowboy?" she deadpanned. "Did you go to the same trial we did today?"

"Yes, and we sandbagged 'em beautifully." Brad strutted around the room. "Strobel is probably out getting drunk and celebrating, and here we are working our tails off. They're overconfident. It's working."

"Yeah, and you've got the judge wrapped around your little finger," Leslie mocked.

"Mr. Strobel," she continued, taking on the tone and air of Ichabod, "do you have any other jurors you would like to get rid of so that I can watch your opposing counsel squirm and squeal like a boiled lobster?"

Brad twisted his face and contorted his body, doing a pitiful imitation of a boiling lobster. They all laughed.

He stopped suddenly. "Sarah, I thought I told you to keep her out of the sauce," he said. "Go home, that's an order. You're both getting a little punchy."

"Us?!" the women said in unison. But Brad was already halfway out the door, in full retreat. Leslie looked at Sarah and shook her head.

"What got into him?" Leslie wondered.

"Whatever it is, I want some of it," Sarah said. "I love that guy." She said it without the least bit of embarrassment and apparently without even thinking about anything more than a fraternal attraction. "I'm so glad he's on my side."

"Mmm," Leslie muttered. She didn't understand the way Sarah spoke so casually of loving somebody. Leslie's own feelings for Brad went way beyond the "he's a great guy" attitude of Sarah, but she didn't dare call it love.

Then what was it, exactly? She had this longing to be with him. All the time. She came alive when he walked into the room, especially when he touched her. She studied his every move, loved the sound of his voice, every word. If this wasn't love . . .

Whatever it was, it scared her.

Her emotions had begun to decimate every detail of her life's plan that she had so carefully, so logically, constructed during the past two years. She needed advice.

"Sarah, do you think you'll ever remarry?" she asked before she realized she had verbalized the question.

Sarah's countenance fell. She sank back into her chair as if she couldn't will herself to remain standing. She had just answered dozens of questions about Charles and how much she missed him. But this unscripted query seemed to hit her so much harder.

"There will never be another Charles," Sarah said simply. "People tell me God has someone special for me—maybe not the same as Charles, but just as right for me. I smile and I nod, but I don't believe it. They didn't know Charles the way I did. Otherwise, they wouldn't say such things."

"Do you think it would be wrong to remarry? I mean, in the sense that it would somehow cheapen Charles's memory?"

"Heavens, no," Sarah exclaimed. "In fact, I believe Charles would want me to remarry. He's probably up in heaven right now saying, 'Sarah, have you thought about Richard?' or 'Sarah, Joe would make a great father for our kids; he's such a nice guy.'" Sarah smiled knowingly and sighed a beleaguered sigh. "It's just that I can't imagine ever loving someone as much as I loved Charles. But, Leslie, it's only been a year. If I do meet the right man, I'll know. And if my heart says go for it, I'll go for it."

Leslie knew Sarah discerned the real reason for the question. "That sounded more like a pep talk than an answer."

Sarah reached over and put her hand on Leslie's. "I'd have to be blind not to see the chemistry between you and Brad," she said softly. "Trust your heart, Leslie. Bill would tell you the same thing if he could."

◁▷

After chasing the women from the office, Brad polished up his opening statement and headed home. He arrived after midnight.

He had a good feeling about this opening. And a good feeling about

Sarah as his first witness. Tomorrow, the momentum would shift. Tomorrow would be a good day for the good guys.

Brad kicked off his shoes and threw the morning paper and unopened mail onto the kitchen counter, where it joined a pile of other unread papers and unopened mail. He slung his coat over a chair, loosened his tie, and went straight for the refrigerator. He chugged some 2 percent milk from a half-gallon jug. It had that tart taste of milk one day short of being sour, or maybe one day past. He made a face at the aftertaste, then twisted the top back on the jug and placed it back in the refrigerator. As he headed for the stairs, he noticed the red blinking light on his answering machine and punched in the code.

Four new messages.

"Brad, Jimmy Hartley here. Look, I know you're in the middle of a trial, but I've got to see at least some interest payments on the car loans and home equity line. I tried to call at work but—"

Brad hit star seven, and the message was gone. Bella would handle this. He made a mental note to remind her.

The next three messages were from Leslie. Strange that she would call the house instead of his cell phone. Leslie's first message came at 10:45 p.m. From the background noise, she was calling from her car.

"Brad, Sarah is ready. I mean, really ready. Direct exam will take about four hours. I'd like to talk about a couple of tricky areas at lunch tomorrow, or if it's not too late when you get this message, just give me a call. I didn't want to talk strategy in front of Sarah. She's nervous enough as it is."

The second message came five minutes later.

"By the way, Brad, I'm still concerned about the possibility of our office being bugged. I know we aren't using the office phones for anything confidential, but we are preparing witnesses in the war room. Is there any way we could get O'Malley to check for bugs at different times during the day? He always checks first thing in the morning, and if someone is taking the time and effort to bug our offices, they'd surely notice the pattern. Call me paranoid, but I'd feel better if he would check both in the morning and at some unpredictable time in the afternoon. Thanks."

There was a brief pause, and Leslie concluded, her voice uncertain. "And call me if it's not too late."

The third message, logged in nearly an hour after the first two, proved that Leslie was ignoring Brad's admonition to sleep.

"Brad, sorry to leave this on your answering machine, but it seems like we never get a chance to talk together . . . alone." Leslie's voice was tentative and so quiet that Brad pressed the phone harder against his ear. "And when we do . . . well, I've tried to say this a hundred times but never got it out. Brad, I know what you said about waiting until the case was over to, um, see where we stand. But that seems like such a long time from now and, well, I was just . . . um—" after a noticeable pause the words rushed out in a torrent— "wondering if we could try to maybe start over again this weekend. Like maybe Friday night. Well, if that works for you, just let me know. If not, you don't need to say anything . . . and I'll understand. If you'd rather just wait until the case is over . . . um, that's okay too."

A short beep signaled that Leslie was almost out of time for her message. Her voice continued at an even more rapid clip.

"Anyway, I didn't mean to ramble on. Just thought you might want a distraction this weekend after staring at the lovely Ichabod all week."

Brad checked his watch. It was 12:45, probably too late to call. The first two days of trial had been tough and unproductive. But his instincts were right. The third day would be a charm. And it had just gotten off to a rip-roaring start.

27

"MAY IT PLEASE THE COURT." Brad nodded toward Ichabod as he began his opening. He stood and moved with measured steps around the podium toward the jury box, buttoning his suit coat, and starting the timer on his wristwatch along the way. He half expected Ichabod to make him retreat to the podium. But he also knew she wouldn't want to jump on his case right away, for fear of alienating the jury.

He carried no notes or other distractions to occupy his hands. He wanted to have a little family chat, lawyer-to-jury, common allies in the search for truth. He moved as close to the jury box as possible without encroaching on the jurors' space. He stopped and made eye contact with each. He knew this first sentence was key. He had worked so hard to capture the essence of the whole case in the first few phrases that came out of his mouth.

"Ladies and gentlemen," he began in soft, confident tones, "this is the case of the lions and the saints. The persecution, torture, and abuse that is this very moment being inflicted on Christians around the world is both frightening and appalling. It is every bit as vicious and grotesque as when the first-century Romans marched the first-century saints into the Coliseum, cut them to watch them bleed, and cheered as the bodies of the Christians were shredded by starving lions. Many of the twenty-first-century victims, like Sarah Reed, have suffered similar fates. Many of the twenty-first-century victims, like Sarah Reed, have seen loved ones tortured and killed. And many of the twenty-first-century victims, like Sarah Reed, are U.S. citizens and deserve the protection of U.S. courts."

Brad delivered these words in a near whisper, and the entire courtroom seemed to grow even quieter as he spoke. He knew those in the back of the courtroom probably couldn't hear, and he didn't care. It was the jury, and only the jury, that formed his audience. This was their case now, and they listened intently, nearly holding their collective breath. Brad paused, surveyed every face again, and started pacing to put them more at ease.

He raised his voice a notch and empowered them.

"You now have the collective power to end the madness. Like no jury before you, you can send a message that will be heard by every dictator and abusive ruler around the globe. You, and you alone, can strike a blow for religious freedom everywhere and for everyone. What you decide in this case can protect the Buddhist and the Baptist, the Muslim and the Methodist. It can protect those in Africa and America, in Sudan, and yes, in Saudi Arabia. You, and you alone, can shut down this modern-day Coliseum."

Strobel was on his feet. "I *object!*" he bellowed. "Your Honor, I'm sorry. I hate to object during opening statements, but openings are supposed to be a preview of the evidence, not a sermon about human rights and worldwide—"

"Agreed," Ichabod said.

Brad checked his watch. A minute and thirty-five seconds. Strobel had disappointed him. Brad put five bucks on Strobel's objecting within thirty seconds. Nikki said less than a minute. Bella said ninety seconds based on tactical reasons, and Brad noticed Bella's "I told you so" grin out of the corner of his eye.

"Mr. Carson, please confine your opening to a preview of the evidence, not a stump speech. I will not have you turn this courtroom into a circus. And furthermore, please continue your opening statement from behind the podium."

"Yes, Your Honor."

Brad hid a smile and retreated to the podium. He not only anticipated the objection; he had instigated it. He wanted the jury to see him as a champion for justice, as the advocate for not just Sarah Reed but for persecuted persons everywhere. He wanted the jury to hear Strobel object, to see Strobel try to avoid the broader issues on everyone's mind, to sense that Strobel was trying to keep something from them.

Brad grabbed both sides of the podium and switched gears. The family chat through, he transformed into an evangelist for justice. The folks in the back row would have no trouble hearing this next bit.

"We will prove that this man—" and here he pointed directly at Ahmed Aberijan—"is the ruthless and repressive leader of Saudi Arabia's religious police, a group called the Muttawa. We will prove that he learned about Charles and Sarah Reed and their young children, missionaries to Saudi

Arabia, who were reaching out to the people of Saudi Arabia with the love of Jesus Christ.

"We will prove that this man, Ahmed Aberijan, masterminded a raid on the Reeds' small apartment for the sole purpose of torturing and humiliating the Reeds and learning the name of every church member, as well as leaders of other churches, so that he could terrorize and torture them as well. When Charles and Sarah Reed refused to give in to his demands, Aberijan and his men beat Charles Reed, breaking his wrist in the process, and repeatedly shocked him with a stun gun, sending electrical volts surging through his body."

Brad was in his rhythm now, his voice rising and falling with emotion. "You will hear testimony from Dr. Jeffrey Rydell, a physician who tried desperately to save Charles Reed's life. He will talk about the burn marks at the base of Charles Reed's skull inflicted by repeated use of a stun gun, even though Charles Reed could have posed no threat to the arresting officers.

"In fact, the evidence of that fateful night will support only one scenario. Based on the firsthand testimony of Sarah Reed, the marks on Charles Reed's neck, the broken wrist, and the autopsy finding that Charles Reed's stomach was essentially empty of all contents, it is clear that Aberijan first beat Dr. Reed and broke his wrist, then stood over Dr. Reed, screaming at him and torturing him repeatedly with the stun gun, while Dr. Reed lay helplessly on the floor in his own vomit, gasping for breath and begging for his life. With no mercy, Aberijan shocked Reed again and again, sending the electricity surging through Reed's body, frying nerve endings and singeing flesh, smiling in his arrogance while Reed writhed in pain. And all the while this man—Aberijan—was demanding names of other church members so that he could hunt them down like animals and torture them as well."

Brad shouted now as he glared and pointed at Aberijan. Aberijan glared back, smugly, as if he didn't understand the language. It was precisely the reaction Brad hoped he would elicit. Brad stopped to catch his breath. He had been carried away with his own passion and found himself exhausted by the intensity of his emotions. And he was just beginning.

The jurors were sitting forward, processing the accusations, waiting breathlessly for more. All except juror four, who sat back with his arms crossed, trying mightily to send the signal that he was not impressed.

"Sarah Reed will testify about the events of that horrible night that changed her life forever. Judge for yourself her credibility. She will tell you how Aberijan gave the order for his men to 'have their way with her,' an order that his men understood as permission to rape her. She will tell you how these animals began ripping her clothes off, how she tried to resist them, how they threw her to the ground, bouncing her head off the floor and rendering her unconscious.

"And then this man, Mr. Aberijan—" Brad sneered at the scum sitting at the defense table—"not satisfied with torturing Charles Reed and ordering the rape of his wife, thinking of nothing but his own reputation, committed another atrocity that night. With Charles Reed unconscious from the torture, and Sarah Reed unconscious from the blow to her head, Aberijan ordered that they both be injected with cocaine in order to set them up as common criminals deserving of such horrible mistreatment."

For one full hour Brad ticked off points of evidence and painted his client and her children as saints. He ran the gamut of emotions. Harsh and intense words for Aberijan and the government of Saudi Arabia. Words of compassion for the Reed family, for the children who lost a loving father, for the wife who lost her lover and best friend. He choked back tears; he shook his fist in anger. He mesmerized the jury. And he knew all the while that the reporters would eat it up; they loved this stuff.

At one hour, Ichabod began inquiring, in a studied monotone, as to whether Brad was almost done. Five minutes later she asked again. Ten minutes later she told him to wrap it up or she would cut him off. Brad decided it was story time. He knew it would be unorthodox . . . a calculated gamble, but he was banking on Strobel's reluctance to object during the opening statement and Ichabod's attempt to look like she wasn't paying attention.

"At the height of the degrading games and bloodshed of the Roman Coliseum, a monk named Telemachus lived in a monastery far outside the city of Rome. One day he heard God calling him to take a pilgrimage to the city of Rome, though he didn't know why. Small and stooped, he gathered all his belongings in a backpack and started on his long trip.

"When Telemachus arrived at Rome, he was swept up by the crowds and carried into the gore and violence of the Coliseum. There, to his horror, he saw the gladiators killing one another for sport. He could not stomach the shedding of innocent blood, and he knew he had to do something."

Brad noticed Ichabod shoot her eyes toward Strobel, trying to get Mack's attention, undoubtedly trying to prompt the man to object. *Speaking of doing something,* she seemed to be saying, *how about an objection here?* But Strobel seemed content to ride it out.

"So Telemachus jumped to the floor of the Coliseum, ran between two gladiators, held out his hands, and said, 'In the name of Christ, forbear.'" Brad stooped over and flung his arms wide—the very picture of Telemachus.

"At first, the crowd cheered, thinking Telemachus was a clown running around for their entertainment. But eventually, they began to boo and hiss as Telemachus continued to insert himself between combatants, trying to stem the flow of blood."

Brad sensed that this story had revived the jurors' interest. None fidgeted; none looked away.

"I object," Strobel finally announced. "This is supposed to be an opening statement, not story time."

Brad was sure story time was now over, but the mercurial Ichabod surprised him.

"I agree, Mr. Strobel," she said harshly. "But you should have made that objection a long time ago. By now, you've waived your objection. Mr. Carson, you may finish."

Brad figured Ichabod just wanted to know how the story ended. She could always gut its usefulness with a few well-placed words later.

"Thank you, Judge." Then Brad turned back to the jury, slipping out from behind the podium, wielding an imaginary sword. "Anyway, one of the gladiators got frustrated with this awkward little monk and ran him through with a sword. But even as Telemachus lay on the floor of the Coliseum in a pool of his own blood, he thought not of himself but only of those gladiators and of his mission that had now become so clear. And as life left his little body, with his dying breath, he lifted up his hands and begged one last time—" Brad lowered his voice, closed his eyes, and lifted weary arms ever so slightly—"'In the name of Christ, forbear.'

"A funny thing happened that day in the Coliseum. Disgusted by the bloody slaughter of an innocent monk, a spectator got up from his seat and left the Coliseum, never to return. He was followed by another and another and another. One by one, the spectators all rose silently in protest and left the bloody place. And history records, that from that day forward, the bloodletting in the Coliseum ceased forever."

Brad stopped speaking and stood perfectly still, letting the solemnity settle over the courtroom. The enormity of their task descended heavily on the jurors, as Brad stood before them with imploring eyes.

"In a real sense, you have been called, like Telemachus, as one man or one woman to make a difference. History will judge your verdict—"

"I must object," Strobel said forcefully, rising to his feet. "This is totally improper."

"Will you have the courage to end the bloodshed and violence?"

"Sustained!" Ichabod said. She slammed her gavel. "Mr. Carson, that is quite enough!"

"Are you willing to look at this animal, Mr. Aberijan—"

"I object," Strobel yelled. "The court has ruled. This is insane!"

"Mr. Carson, not one more word!"

". . . and say, 'In the name of justice—forbear!'?"

"That does it," Ichabod screamed. "In my chambers. Now!" She bolted from the bench, her black robe flying behind her. She left a chaotic courtroom erupting in her wake, excited murmuring, reporters writing furiously, jurors sitting wide-eyed, and Strobel shooting daggers at Brad with his eyes.

In the swirling madness, Brad walked quickly but calmly to his counsel table. He stopped next to Leslie, placed an arm on the back of her chair, then bent over and whispered in her ear.

"I'd love to take you up on your offer for Friday night," he whispered, "as long as I'm not in jail."

28

ICHABOD TOOK sixteen and a half minutes to restore the integrity of the court. She needed ten minutes to deliver a vicious tongue-lashing to Brad. Another minute and a half for Brad to write his check for ten thousand dollars, payable to the U.S. District Court, for his contempt citation. Then five minutes for Ichabod to lecture the jury and ensure that Brad's shenanigans had not improperly influenced them.

"What the lawyers say in opening statements is not evidence," she explained. "And that is especially true if they resort to extraneous matters like telling stories about unrelated events. On the other hand," she warned, "you should not punish lawyers with an adverse decision just because they ignore the orders of the court and wreak havoc in the courtroom."

Ichabod assured the jury that she would take care of such offenders, as she had in this case. It was their job to focus on the evidence in the case and nothing else. After setting the jury straight, Ichabod called for another short recess.

◁ ▷

When court resumed, Strobel walked confidently to the podium, knowing precisely what he had to do. Years of experience had taught him that when you represent an unpopular defendant, you appeal to logic, not emotion. Take the heat out of the case. Become the master teacher. Reason with your friends on the jury.

"Ladies and gentlemen of the jury—" Strobel's baritone voice filled the courtroom—"there are two sides to every case. That's why you took an oath to keep an open mind until you hear all the evidence." Strobel stood erect behind the podium, a model of decorum. "One of your greatest tools in your search for truth will be your own common sense. Don't allow Mr. Carson's emotional appeals to alter what your common sense tells you is true." He paused and searched the jurors' faces, looking for an implicit promise that they would indeed follow their common sense wherever it took them.

"Don't be afraid to ask the hard questions as you evaluate the evidence. Why would Ahmed Aberijan and his officers inject Charles and Sarah Reed with cocaine? The Reeds lied to get into Saudi Arabia and broke the law in their attempts to convert Muslims. What the Reeds did was blatantly illegal under Saudi Arabian law, and everyone knew it. Mr. Aberijan had every right to arrest them and deport them. He certainly didn't need to fabricate a drug charge to do that.

"And why would he allegedly torture them and then take them to a hospital for treatment? If he wanted to kill them, as Mrs. Reed claims, why would he take them to a hospital so they could get treated and survive?

"And why, if Mrs. Reed and her husband were just innocent victims, did the arresting officers have abrasions and contusions, including scratches inflicted by Mrs. Reed's fingernails and a large gash on the face of an officer from a punch thrown by Charles Reed?

"And where is the corroboration? Where are the witnesses? There are none to back up Mrs. Reed's fabrications. Yet numerous members of her alleged church have testified against her. They have confirmed that the so-called church was only a front for a powerful drug ring."

Strobel rolled highlights from the deposition videotapes. The jury soaked in the words of the first witnesses they would hear testify.

He took an hour and a half to methodically walk through the evidence he intended to introduce during the trial. It was show-and-tell time. He did his best to juice it up with multicolored charts and enlargements of documents, but as the minutes ticked by, several of the jurors checked their watches and began to fidget. Strobel noticed them stirring and decided to wind it down.

"I will close with a story too," Strobel said. "But mine is a true story. It is the story of a twenty-first-century Muslim who has served his country well for many years. It is a story of how that man did his job, broke up a drug ring in his country, and had to endure vicious lies and accusations by a greedy plaintiff's lawyer in another country. It is the story of how that devoted Muslim and faithful civil servant put his faith in the American system of justice and in a jury that has promised to look at the evidence with an open mind and render an unbiased verdict.

"You will write the last chapter of that story, and you will determine whether our system can survive the test of being fair to those who think and believe differently than we do. You can write a chapter for religious freedom by honoring the freedom of the people of Saudi Arabia to chose their own religion and worship their own God, free from Western imperialism."

Strobel paused, looked the jurors directly in the eye, then strode confidently to his seat. Juror number four nodded his head in support as he rocked back and forth. The others cast thoughtful but suspicious looks toward Sarah Reed.

◁▷

The rules of elevator etiquette had established themselves during the two days of jury selection. The lawyers and contending parties would let the jurors and spectators take the first few elevators down. Sarah Reed and her team took the next, reserving the last elevator for Ahmed Aberijan, Mack Strobel, and the rest of the defense team. As the participants headed to lunch after the opening statements, they followed the same unwritten protocol.

As a critical part of the plaintiff's team, Aberijan's informant joined Brad and the others on the elevator, all facing front, all carrying their briefcases, all waiting for the doors to close. Nobody said a word, but she could sense that the team would erupt in high fives and backslapping as soon as they got some privacy. Brad's opening fell nothing short of masterful.

But as the doors began to shut, a hand reached in and pushed against the rubber safety strip on the inside of the doors. The doors sprang back to reveal a beefy, middle-aged man who had been sitting in court behind the defense table. Ahmed Aberijan stood at his shoulder. Amid quizzical looks from Brad's team, the two men boarded the elevator.

Ahmed moved to the back wall, stood next to his informant, and silently watched the lit floor signs as they descended.

What's going on here? Is he trying to intimidate me?

She wanted to lash out at him, give him a piece of her mind. Such a bold move would enhance her cover, make her a hero to the others. But nobody said a word; they all just stared straight ahead. And as the doors opened at the ground floor, Ahmed and his ridiculous little sidekick stepped off first.

"What was that all about?" she said just loud enough for Ahmed and his partner to hear.

"Who knows?" Brad said.

She found out right after she had ordered lunch.

When she reached for her briefcase to retrieve some documents, she discovered a legal-size manila envelope wedged in the outside pocket.

Suddenly the conversation around her faded in the background, like she was operating out of some deep well. She had to know what was in that envelope. Nothing else mattered. With a catch in her voice, she excused herself. She retreated to the rest room and opened the envelope carefully in a small stall. The note was short and to the point. Ahmed apparently thought he was back in control.

> The bugs are useless and create a grave risk. Remove them
> immediately and return them to us. We need details on the plan
> for Shelhorse. Meet at the same location, Friday at 8:30 a.m.

She read the letter twice. And she trembled. She was clearly in over her head, but she could not turn back now. She didn't like Ahmed's boldness in contacting her. She didn't like his giving the orders. This was not her plan. Things were happening too fast. She needed to think straight. She needed to act fast. She needed to get back in control.

◁▷

Sarah told her story beautifully. She and Leslie started with the events of the night on which Charles died, and Sarah recounted those events with precise memory of what she had seen and heard. She told of the Muttawa raid, the beatings, the attempted rape, and the events at the hospital later that night. Her unconsciousness, of course, left a huge gap in the story surrounding Charles's actual torture.

Sarah hardly looked or acted like a drug pusher. She seemed on the verge of tears throughout the emotional part of her testimony but broke down only once, as she recounted learning about the death of her husband. Sarah was blessed with a slender build and looked absolutely diminutive as the large witness stand and the massive grandeur of the courtroom dwarfed her. Leslie thought she could sense an almost palpable empathy flowing from the jury box.

After the emotional testimony about the Muttawa raid, Leslie took Sarah through an hour of background information about her life with Charles and their mission work in Saudi Arabia. This part of the testimony gave Sarah emotional downtime and allowed the jury to gear up for the emotional dam that would burst when Sarah talked about her children.

"I loved the Saudi people," Sarah testified, "and I believed my calling was to share the greatest thing that had ever happened to me with them. Charles and I were called to take the gospel to the land of Saudi Arabia."

"Did you have much success at first?" Leslie asked.

"It depends on how you define success," Sarah explained. "If you mean did we have a huge church right away—no. But if you mean were we able to reach out and help some folks who were walking through some tough times—yes. Our first convert was an elderly lady who had no family and no way to take care of herself. Meredith—that's my daughter—and I would go sit with her for hours, listen to her stories, and while we were there, we would clean her house and cook some meals. We tried to take care of her without hurting her pride. At her own time, and in her own way, she came to Christ."

Throughout most of the afternoon, Sarah described the life of a missionary. The heartaches and challenges, the love for the people, the fear of the government. Strobel made a concerted effort to look bored. At 4:30, Leslie decided to end with the impact on the family.

"How has Steven handled the death of his father?" she asked.

Sarah's top lip quivered. She dabbed at her eyes with a tattered Kleenex she had wadded up in her right hand and toyed with for the past few hours.

"Steven misses his dad so much, but he tries hard not to show it. He's had to grow up so fast. He sees himself as the man of the house. Every Saturday morning, when his buddies are off swimming or playing ball, he's mowing the lawn and helping around the house. I try to be both mom and dad, but it's not easy."

The tears rolled quietly down her cheeks.

"With my schedule, I've told him he can play one sport in city league. He loves soccer. Last Saturday, his team lost a game on penalty kicks, and Steven missed his. I tried my best to console him, but he didn't respond. As we drove off, I saw him looking out the passenger window at the field. He was watching one of the other kids who had missed his penalty kick too. The boy was out there practicing penalty kicks while his dad played goalie."

Sarah stopped for a second to wipe back some tears. Leslie found her own eyes burning.

"I knew he was crying and missing his dad," Sarah continued in a whisper, "because his shoulders were shaking. He kept his face to the window all the way home."

No one in the jury looked at Sarah now; her pain made them visibly uncomfortable. Leslie needed to move on, but she sensed Sarah was not yet done. She waited an extra beat.

"It's not easy raising a young man coming into adolescence without a father, even though I know God is the Father to the fatherless."

"Do you need a moment?" Leslie asked. Sarah was crying harder now.

"No, I'd rather keep going," Sarah answered through the sobs.

"Tell us how Meredith is handling this," Leslie asked gently.

"Not as well as Steven," Sarah confessed. "Meredith blames God. She asks questions I can't answer. Like, 'Why would God allow Dad to die if he was doing God's work?' She's becoming rebellious and hard to control. She doesn't want anything to do with church." Sarah paused, searching for the right words. "Charles was always much better at handling her than I am. There's something special between a father and his daughter. I don't know what to do. . . . I feel like a complete failure as a mom. I've tried so hard—"

Sarah couldn't finish. As the tears flowed freely down her cheeks, the Kleenex no longer of any use, she simply repeated the words "I'm sorry" over and over.

"May we take a short recess, Your Honor?" Leslie asked, fighting back tears of her own.

"Yes." Even the granite heart of Ichabod seemed to have been touched. "Court now stands in recess."

As the judge and jury filed quietly out, Leslie approached the witness stand and embraced Sarah. The two women hugged, mourning husbands they had loved and lost. For Leslie it was the first time in nearly a year she had allowed herself to cry over Bill. In an odd sort of way, she felt a release from her own guilt and a forgiveness that flowed as freely as the tears.

◁▷

As he rose to cross-examine Sarah Reed, Mack Strobel knew the jury would despise him. But he also knew that Ichabod would call it a day in only thirty minutes, making it imperative for him to draw blood quickly.

"Good afternoon, Mrs. Reed." He stood comfortably behind the podium, smiling at Sarah.

"Good afternoon." She did not return the smile.

"I'd like to show you what has been marked for identification as Defense Exhibit 1. Do you recognize it?" Mack's smile was now gone.

"Yes."

"Well, what is it?"

"It's the application I filled out to get a visa to live in Saudi Arabia."

"Your Honor, I would like to move this into evidence as Defense Exhibit 1. I also have an enlargement I would like to show the jury."

"No objection," Leslie said nonchalantly.

"Is that your signature at the bottom of the document?" Mack asked.

"Yes."

"All right, then. Looking at the third-to-last answer on the first page. Tell me what this document says you will be doing while in Saudi Arabia?"

"It says 'school administrator.'"

"And isn't it a fact, Mrs. Reed, that your primary reason for going to Saudi Arabia was to be a missionary and as a missionary to try to convert Muslims to Christianity?" Mack's voice was loud and staccato, accusatory in its tone.

Sarah's answer was soft. "Yes, I went to be a missionary, but I did not intend to limit my work to Muslims; I wanted to share with anyone and everyone about how to be a Christian."

"You knew it was illegal in Saudi Arabia for someone to convert from the Muslim faith to Christianity, didn't you, Mrs. Reed?"

Sarah looked down at her folded hands. "Yes."

"And you also knew that if you put the word *missionary* on this visa application, you wouldn't be allowed into the country. Isn't that right?"

"I suppose so."

"Then is it fair to say you lied on a visa application to gain admittance into a country so that you could then teach others how to break the law and convert to Christianity?" Mack stared hard at Sarah, waving the visa application with his right hand.

Sarah bit her lip.

"I wouldn't phrase it that way," she said at last.

"Then how would you phrase it?" Mack loved it when witnesses fought with him. It only served to highlight his points.

"I don't know," Sarah admitted. "I guess I would say that we didn't reveal certain things on the visa application because we knew it would disqualify us from entering the country."

"I see," Mack said. "It's okay to withhold information from the authorities if you deem it to be appropriate . . . information like using marijuana and cocaine, Mrs. Reed?"

"No, we never used marijuana or cocaine," Sarah answered emphatically.

Mack would come back to that point later. But he only had a few more minutes on this day. He wanted to make them count.

"Do you remember testifying on direct examination about the night the Muttawa came to your apartment?"

"Yes, sir."

"To your knowledge, had Mr. Aberijan or anyone else from the Muttawa ever been inside your apartment prior to that night?"

"No, sir."

"And yet you watched them with your own eyes as they found small plastic bags of cocaine in places like the cushions of your couch. Correct?"

"Yes, it all happened very fast. But yes, that's true."

"And isn't it also true that they had to cut those cushions open to get at the bags of cocaine?" Mack continued.

"Yes."

"So it's not like they could have just dropped them in there the same night and pretended they found them a few seconds later."

"I guess that would have been hard."

"Mrs. Reed, are you telling the jury today that you have no idea how those plastic bags of cocaine came to be, among other places, sewn into the lining of the cushions of your own couch?" Mack sounded incredulous.

Juror four raised his eyebrows.

"Objection, argumentative," Leslie called out.

"Overruled," Ichabod snapped.

"That's what I'm saying," Sarah answered.

She might be speaking the truth. Mack didn't know. He was more interested in the fire forming in Sarah's eyes. She was growing weary of being misinterpreted, misquoted, and misled. He could tell that she was ready to take the bait and do what Leslie and Brad had undoubtedly warned her against.

She was ready to pick a fight with Mack Strobel.

"Why would I leave plastic bags of cocaine just sitting around the house when I knew the Muttawa were coming?" she asked. "Why do you think we called off the worship service that night? We knew they were coming. How dumb do you think I am?" Her face was flushed, her voice rising in frustration.

He fought back a smile. "Mrs. Reed," Mack responded evenly, "you may very well have thought that hiding the cocaine in the couch cushions would

242 || DIRECTED VERDICT

keep the religious police from ever finding it. But it's not for me to testify. I ask the questions."

"I object and ask that Mr. Strobel's speculation be struck from the record." Leslie was on her feet again.

"Sit down," Ichabod barked.

"Does that mean my objection was sustained or overruled?" Leslie was still standing.

"It means you sit down and I'll tell you."

With a huff, Leslie sat.

"Overruled," Ichabod said.

"May I proceed, Your Honor?" Mack asked politely. He was amused by this turn of events and ready to turn the hostility of the witness to even greater advantage.

"Yes."

"Mrs. Reed, did you just testify that you knew the Muttawa were coming?"

"Yes."

"How did you know?"

"We had a source."

The answer was just what Mack wanted, just what he would have scripted. He turned and looked at Bard Carson and Leslie Connors, as if accusing them of hiding some critical piece of evidence.

Brad's head was in his hands. Leslie dropped her pen and stared at the witness like she didn't recognize the woman who had just spoken.

Mack turned back to the witness, twisting every muscle on his face to register surprise. "You had a source?" he asked.

The witness had opened the door. The name of the source was now relevant. There could be no more argument against it.

"Who was your source? Who told you the Muttawa were coming?" Mack pressed.

"I can't answer that question," Sarah said softly.

"Can't or won't?" Mack bellowed.

"Won't," Sarah confirmed.

"You will in my courtroom," Ichabod said, hunkering forward as she glared down at the witness. "You have testified that you knew the Muttawa were coming because you had a source. You testified that it would be ridiculous for you to knowingly have cocaine in your apartment since you knew the Muttawa were coming. The issue of a source is therefore relevant. For that reason, I am ordering you to answer the question."

"I won't," Sarah whispered, looking at the floor. "It might endanger his life."

"Mrs. Reed, this court is not asking you to think about whether you will tell me the name of the person, apparently a male, that you yourself made relevant. This court is *ordering* you to do it. You should have thought about these issues of confidentiality before you filed suit and certainly before you made his name relevant. You cannot use him to bolster your credibility and then hide him behind this cloak of anonymity"

Sarah simply sat on the stand, her lip trembling, slowly shaking her head from side to side.

"Bailiff, please dismiss the jury," Ichabod ordered.

The jury shuffled out in silence. Several jury members glanced over their shoulder at Sarah on the way out. Their sympathetic looks worried Mack.

"Mr. Carson," Ichabod said, "this has been a long and emotional day for everyone." Ichabod appeared to be working hard to maintain her composure. "I know your client is exhausted and not thinking clearly. We will reconvene tomorrow morning, and Mr. Strobel will again ask his question. You will have Mrs. Reed prepared to answer, or I will entertain a motion to dismiss her case."

Brad silently nodded his head.

Mack returned to his seat and found a note waiting from Ahmed's translator.

Good work, it said. *Whatever it takes, get me that name.*

29

SHE HAD TO GET TO THE OFFICE ahead of the others. Ahmed's note radically changed her plans. The first order of business was to retrieve the listening devices from the phones. The small magnetic radio transmitters, no larger than a quarter, were attached to the bottom of each office phone. It would take only a few minutes to retrieve all three, but to do so she had to arrive at the office first. Alone.

She left federal court slightly ahead of the others, hustled to her car, and drove like a wild woman down the interstate. She hit the inevitable backup a few miles outside Norfolk on Interstate 44 and was actually grateful. By weaving in and out of traffic, even using the HOV lane, she gained valuable time on the others.

She parked in the handicapped spot immediately in front of the building and took the elevator to the fifth floor. She took a hard right off the elevator and got out her key as she approached the suite. She slipped into the reception area. The lights were on, just as the team had left them that morning. She walked across the reception area and took a left toward Brad's office.

She turned the corner into the semidark hallway and gasped, stopping short. She was inches away from and face-to-face with Patrick O'Malley.

"Sorry," he said. "Didn't mean to scare ya, but we got trouble here."

He held out his palm. In it were the three transmitters.

"I know," she said, still out of breath. "That's why Brad sent me ahead of the others. There's a few things he wanted me to talk to you about. Step in here for a second." She pointed to the war room, and the two of them stepped inside and closed the door.

◁▷

Sarah stared out the window of Brad's car as though he were taking her for a date with the firing squad. She thought of Saudi Arabia and the struggling church she was trying to protect.

"We're dead in the water," she finally said.

"Ichabod won't dismiss the case," Brad said confidently. "We'd have her reversed in a heartbeat on appeal. And she knows it. She could possibly fine you. She could have the jury assume there is no snitch. She could even jail you. But she can't just dismiss the case."

"Oh, that's better!" Sarah groaned. "Jail."

"She's bluffing," Brad promised. "That's why she said she would *consider* dismissing the case. Don't let her distract us with a bluff. We need to prepare like the case is going forward tomorrow . . . because it is."

Sarah felt little consolation from Brad's assurances. The prospect of facing hours of cross-examination from Strobel tomorrow was nerve-racking enough. But now she also had to face an irate judge who had the power to throw her in jail for something Sarah couldn't control. She had a splitting headache. She closed her eyes and tilted her head back against the headrest, unwilling to go back to the office and into the war room to endure more hours of preparation. After all, it hadn't done much good today.

"What do I say when Strobel asks again?" She tried to rub the tension out of her neck. How did she get herself into this mess?

"The same thing you did today," Brad responded. "Just tell the court that you respectfully refuse to answer on the grounds that it will endanger the life of an innocent man. The jury will love you for it. Leslie and I'll take over from there."

"Yeah," Sarah said, eyes still closed. "And the judge will chew me up and spit me out."

◁▷

"That's a no-brainer," Win said, slouched in a chair in front of Teddy's massive oak desk. "We start off tomorrow by asking Sarah Reed again for the name of her informant. She refuses. Ichabod dismisses the case. Carson appeals. If we're lucky, he wins the appeal and gets a new trial. We bill a couple more million and win it fair and square next time around. Everybody's happy—except Carson, and he doesn't deserve to be happy."

Teddy sat straighter in his high-back leather chair. "I hope you're not serious," he said sternly. "Our obligation is to do what's right for the client, not to figure out a way to bill this file until we all retire."

Mack knew Win was serious. But he also knew Win wouldn't argue. Poor naive Teddy. The times had passed him by.

But this time, Mack was thankful for Teddy's outdated ethical standards.

"That's part of my problem," Mack explained. "As ironic as it sounds, what's best for the client in this situation is probably not a dismissal this early in the case on a technicality. Carson would appeal, and our research guys tell me he would probably win. I think it serves the client better if we let Ichabod hear the whole case, then recall Reed and ask her this question at the end of the case. That way Ichabod can say she's dismissing the case both because the case has no merit and because the plaintiff refused to answer a relevant question.

"We'll have a much better chance of sustaining the ruling on appeal. And frankly, Win, I don't want to have to try this case again, even for all the billable hours in the world. Reed makes a good witness, and Carson's a tough advocate. At my age, you don't retry cases like this one."

"But you've already asked Reed the question," Win protested. "The cat's out of the bag. How do you get Ichabod to wait?"

"It's my question. I'll just withdraw it and ask the judge for permission to recall the witness at the end of trial."

"I like it," Teddy affirmed.

"I still say take the win and hope for the best on appeal," Mackenzie said stubbornly. He was probably counting on a controversial victory to land him an appearance on *Larry King Live*.

"There's another problem." Mack turned and looked hard into Teddy's eyes. "I think Sarah Reed is right to withhold the name. I hate to even say it, but I think my client would order the informant killed in a second."

"Since when did you start having fits of conscience?" Win asked. "You can't start thinking that way, Mack. You owe your client zealous representation. You start believing the other side, and you might as well throw in the towel."

Mack walked over to where Winsted Aaron Mackenzie IV was sitting and towered over him.

"Listen, you little prima donna," Mack said slowly, each word crawling across his lips. "I don't need you telling me how to try this case. I'll chew Reed up tomorrow and spit her out without that ridiculous question. Aberijan and Saudi Arabia are getting zealous representation like they would get nowhere else. But that doesn't mean you put an innocent man's head on the guillotine."

Win's eyes widened as he looked up at his irate partner. He spread his palms and shrugged his shoulders.

"Gentlemen," Teddy said loudly. Strobel stepped away from Mackenzie. "I agree with Mack. Our firm will not be used as a stool pigeon so some autocrat from Saudi Arabia can get the name of an informant and wipe him out. On the other hand, I think Mack is worrying about nothing. Mrs. Reed has already shown her stubborn unwillingness to give up any names."

Teddy leaned forward with his elbows on the desk, lost in thought. He made a small humming noise from deep in his throat. Mack knew it was the noise Teddy made when he was racking his brain. He also knew that what followed this little humming display was usually pretty profound. After more than a minute, Teddy looked up.

"If Mack withdraws the question tomorrow and then calls Mrs. Reed back to the stand at the end of the case and asks her the same question, two things will happen. Both of them good. First, we'll have a better chance to defend this case on appeal. Second, if the informant ever was in danger, and his name is not revealed until the end of the trial, then he will have between now and the end of the trial to find a way to dodge the Muttawa. Mack, I am asking you, in my capacity as senior partner of this firm, to withdraw the question tomorrow."

"That's what I plan on doing," Mack agreed. "I just want you to be ready for an onslaught of bellyaching from our client."

"Let him complain," Teddy said. "Just make sure he pays the bills."

"What are your chances with the jury?" Win asked. The question signaled he would not challenge Teddy's decision.

"I'd say about fifty-fifty," Mack responded. He leaned back against the window. "It's still too early to tell. But one thing I do know. Sarah Reed makes quite a witness, and she wowed some jurors. It won't be easy."

"Then get a mistrial," Win advised. "Have your snoops follow the jurors for the next few days. They'll find enough for seven mistrials. I guarantee you that several of those jurors have been watching news of the trial or talking to each other about what the outcome should be."

Mack gazed across the room as if he were only half-listening. But he was thinking that Win might have a point.

"If Ichabod dismisses the jury, then she'll declare a mistrial on the case against Ahmed only, since that's the only count on which the plaintiff gets a jury trial," Win explained in his annoyingly patronizing tone. "Ichabod will then decide the case involving Saudi Arabia, presumably in our favor, and grant a mistrial on the case against Ahmed because of jury misconduct."

He's right, Mack thought. *The prima donna is onto something.*

"Plaintiff will not even ask for another trial against Ahmed since there's no real money in suing Ahmed," Win continued. "Ahmed is just window dressing. Get a mistrial based on jury misconduct, and your problems will disappear."

Mack snorted, as if dismissing the plan without saying a word. Then he turned and strode purposefully out of the office and straight down the hall. He would make a call to Barnes. Win was right; the jury was undoubtedly cheating. They always did in big cases, and Barnes was just the man to catch them at it.

"You're welcome," Winsted Aaron Mackenzie III muttered to himself a few seconds after Mack left the room. The comment struck Teddy as funny, and he let out a rumble of laughter that Mackenzie had not heard in years.

◁▷

"I can't believe you're doing this for me," Bella gushed, driving like a mad-woman down 464 on her way to Chesapeake Estates.

Riding in the passenger seat, Sarah put her considerable faith to the test, as she watched Bella take up the better part of two lanes. Hailing from Brooklyn, Bella couldn't talk without using her hands, even while she drove. Nor could she really connect with someone while talking unless she looked them straight in the eyes. Hailing from the South, Sarah believed it would be rude to tell Bella to keep her eyes on the road.

"Thanks for stopping for pizza with me," Bella continued. "I couldn't take another night of Chinese at the firm. I know you weren't hungry, but, girl, you've got to start eating something. Winning this case won't mean much if our client dies of starvation." She swerved into the exit lane at the last possible second.

"To be honest, Bella, I just want to get through tomorrow, you know what I mean?" Sarah referred as much to Bella's driving as she did to her second day of testimony.

"Yeah," Bella grunted. "That's the way I've been living since I put my mom into this home a year and a half ago—one day to the next. I just want to get through tomorrow too."

"Have you ever talked to your mom about spiritual things?" Sarah asked gently.

"Not really. At least not for a long time. When I was a little girl, she used to take me to church and stuff. But she always kept religious things to herself. After my dad left, she quit goin'. Divorce was pretty rare back then, and you know how church folks can make you feel uncomfortable. I don't really remember goin' to church after dad left, except for funerals and weddings."

Bella paused for a second, as if she regretted criticizing her mother. "She was a wonderful mother and a good person; she just didn't have time for organized religion."

Bella turned abruptly into the parking lot of Chesapeake Estates, and Sarah said a quick and silent prayer of thanks. She saw no reason to speak. Bella didn't seem to be looking for advice.

"Mom never did anything for herself," Bella explained. "She worked her fingers to the bone to provide for us. Dad's checks would show up some months; other months they wouldn't. He never did. Mom, on the other hand, never missed any of my school events. The older I got, the closer I got to my mom. She would drive me crazy sometimes because she was so protective and always worrying. But I realized a few years ago that she was not only my best friend; she was really my only friend. Now she's in this godforsaken home, and I can't do a thing to make things better."

Bella turned off the car and continued to unburden herself to Sarah.

"I don't think Mom has much time left. It's time for her to get things right with her Maker. I thought maybe you could help."

"What about you, Bella?" Sarah asked patiently as she climbed out of the car. The fresh air brought her relief from the stale cigarette smoke that saturated the car.

Bella opened the door and hoisted her considerable frame out of the driver's seat.

"Let's deal with Mom first," she quipped. "For some of us there's no hope."

"You might be surprised," Sarah said. But Bella was already hoofing across the parking lot, breathing heavily and burping up pizza.

◁▷

They found Gertrude in her small sterile room, sitting in her favorite rocking chair. The television was blaring, but Gertrude was not looking at it.

Bella turned down the television and plunked herself down at the foot of her mom's bed, next to the rocker. Sarah sat gingerly in the only chair in the room other than the rocker.

"Mom, this is Sarah Reed," Bella said loudly. Gertrude slowly turned toward Sarah and reached out her trembling hand. Sarah immediately got up, took the hand, and held it warmly in both of hers.

"She's a Baptist missionary," Bella said proudly. "Kinda like the Protestant version of Mother Theresa. Mom, does that make sense?"

Gertrude nodded her head, and Sarah felt the feeble woman softly squeeze her hand.

"I asked Sarah to come and talk to us about God and heaven, Mom. Is that all right?" Bella was shouting. Gertrude's door was open, and Sarah was sure that everyone in the building now knew who she was and why she was here.

Gertrude swallowed hard and struggled to talk. The words came out forced and breathy. "Okay. . . . I always . . . liked missionaries." And then her eyes smiled. Bella looked at Sarah and nodded. This was evidently her cue.

"Bella has told me all about you," Sarah started. She talked softer than Bella. And as she talked, she moved her chair right next to the rocker so they could talk face-to-face. Gertrude reached out and took her hand again. "About how you took care of Bella. I can tell that Bella loves you very much. You must be very proud of her."

Gertrude squeezed Sarah's hand again.

"The way you love your daughter, Gertrude, that's the way our heavenly Father loves us. And the way you took care of Bella, that's the way our heavenly Father takes care of us. Have you ever heard of John 3:16?"

Gertrude furrowed her brow. She stopped rocking for a brief moment.

"'For God so loved the world,'" Sarah quoted the verse, "'that He gave His only begotten Son, that whoever believes in Him should not perish but have everlasting life.'"

A flicker of recognition crossed Gertrude's face.

"Have you heard that Bible verse before?" Sarah asked.

Gertrude got ready to respond, but Bella beat her to the punch.

"Sure you have, Mom," Bella blurted out. "You used to say it to me all the time when I was little."

"But it's not enough just to know the verse," Sarah continued. "You've got to do what the verse says. You've got to believe on God's Son, Jesus Christ, for your salvation."

Bella's mom closed her eyes and continued rocking. Sarah looked back at Bella, who motioned with her hand to keep going.

"There's another verse of Scripture I'd like to share with you," Sarah said. "It's Romans 3:23. And it says: 'For all have sinned and fall short of the glory of God.' That means no matter how good of a mother you were, no matter how much you loved Bella and took care of her, you still did some things wrong that the Bible calls 'sin.' And this sin separates us from God, because God is perfect and holy and cannot tolerate sin. And the Scripture says that the wages of sin is death. Does that make sense, Gertrude? Do you understand that you and I and every person who ever lived are sinners and deserve to be punished by God?"

Gertrude betrayed no visible reaction. She just continued to rock in her slow, smooth, rhythmic way. Her eyes remained closed, and her lips stayed in a tightly pursed line.

"Think of the worst thing you've ever done, your greatest failure as a mom or a wife or just a woman. Then think for a minute about the price of that sin. John 3:16 says that God gave His only begotten Son. For you to be reconciled to God and forgiven of your sins, God had to send His own Son to this earth. And Jesus Christ, the only begotten Son of God, lived a perfect life and died a horrible and violent death on the cross. Our sins were placed on Him so that by His death He took our place."

Though Gertrude gave no visible response, Sarah was talking faster and getting excited. It always happened this way when she shared the good news.

"But the grave couldn't hold Him, and on the third day He rose from the grave, conquering death once and for all. And because of everything He did—living a perfect life, dying in our place, and then conquering death—we can have forgiveness for our sins through the blood of Jesus Christ. And if we're just willing to repent of our sins and ask Jesus into our hearts to be our Lord and Savior, then Scripture promises that we'll be saved. We'll have a personal relationship with Jesus Christ and live eternally with Him."

As Sarah spoke, the significance of the day's events fell away. Strobel's tough examination. Judge Baker-Kline's unsympathetic rulings. Leslie's valiant but futile efforts. None of that mattered any more. Life wasn't about federal court and all its trappings. At least not eternal life.

Sarah believed that her real accuser was Satan, that God was her Judge, and that Jesus Christ Himself was her Advocate. In the only courtroom that really mattered, her Advocate had taken her place as the defendant and endured her punishment. As a result, the Judge of the universe had declared her not guilty. And now, more than anything in the world, Sarah wanted Gertrude to experience that same liberation.

"The Word says that if you confess with your mouth that Jesus is Lord and believe in your heart that God raised Him from the dead, you will be saved. Gertrude, Christ died for you. And for me. We are the ones who should have been on the cross, but He took our place so that we might have eternal life when we die and abundant life while we live."

Sarah stopped and took a deep breath. She was a little embarrassed that she had been talking so fast and with such animation. But she was not embarrassed about the message. Just talking about Christ, sensing that a soul was hanging in the balance, invigorated her.

"Does that make sense, Gertrude?"

The rocking stopped, but Gertrude didn't speak. She sat in the chair in complete silence and stillness. The sound of Bella's labored breathing filled the room.

Sarah noticed it then. A small tear fell silently out of the corner of Gertrude's closed eye. Then another. And another. She started rocking again, and after a moment she opened her eyes, exposing their redness and the ragged emotion of a woman coming to terms with her eternal destiny.

"Yes," she said.

Sarah got out of her seat and knelt beside Gertrude. The elderly woman bowed her head, reached out, and gently placed a shaking hand on Sarah's shoulder. With her other hand, she clutched Sarah's.

"I'm going to ask you to pray with me now," Sarah said. "If you want, I'll say the words, and you can squeeze my hand if this is your prayer. Is that okay?"

A squeeze told Sarah to continue.

"Dear God. I know I'm a sinner. And I know I don't deserve Your mercy and Your grace. But I also know You sent Your only Son to die for my sins and make forgiveness available to me. I repent of my sins and receive Jesus as my personal Lord and Savior and ask Him to come into my heart and be Lord of my life. Thank You, God, for giving me eternal life. In the name of Jesus, amen."

Gertrude clutched Sarah's hand during the prayer and forced out an *amen* as Sarah concluded. Sarah looked at Gertrude and recognized the countenance. She had seen it before. A look of relief. A look of freedom. A look of acceptance. Gertrude could not smile with her mouth, but her reddened eyes were dancing. She almost fell from the chair as she reached out convulsively and gave Sarah an awkward hug.

◁▷

Sarah and Gertrude had not been the only ones praying.

Unnoticed, Bella had slipped off the bed and knelt beside it while Sarah prayed. To Bella, it seemed a fitting posture. It was how her mother had taught her to pray. But it also seemed appropriate to be on her knees, to actually humble herself, as she prepared to ask the God of the universe to forgive and forget a whole truckload of sin.

Bella mouthed the words silently as Sarah prayed. Like her mother, she followed Sarah's *amen* with one of her own.

When she stood, she felt a sudden need to sit again. She felt the unconditional love and acceptance that had eluded her throughout her life. The scenes of her past ran together in a swirling collage of misery—a neglectful father, an overprotective mother, teasing classmates, failed attempts at relationships, the hardening of her heart, the cynicism and hopelessness that resulted. But in this moment, it all seemed to be washed away in a flood of forgiveness and acceptance. An uncaring earthly father replaced by a loving heavenly one. So while Sarah and Gertrude hugged, Bella simply sat on the bed and basked in a wave of love and forgiveness that was unlike anything she had ever experienced.

30

"I **WITHDRAW THE PENDING QUESTION,** Your Honor," Mack Strobel announced as he stepped behind the podium Thursday morning.

"You what?" the judge exclaimed. She furrowed her brow in disapproval.

"I'd like to withdraw the pending question at this time," Strobel repeated confidently. "I would also like to reserve the right to recall Mrs. Reed at the conclusion of my case, if necessary."

Baker-Kline looked at Strobel like he had lost his mind. "It's your question," she said at last.

"Thank you, Your Honor."

Sarah couldn't fathom the reason for this surprising turn of events. From the witness stand she looked at Brad and registered her surprise. *What does this mean?* Brad could only shrug and smile. As Judge Baker-Kline permitted Strobel to proceed, Sarah realized she had been holding her breath and slowly exhaled. *Thank You, Lord.*

Her relief did not last, however, as Strobel spent the entire morning and most of the afternoon grilling her with misleading questions and innuendos. She hesitated and stumbled in several answers, fearful of misstepping again, and said a few things inconsistent with her deposition testimony. By the time the judge dismissed her from the stand, Sarah's credibility had been badly tarnished.

After Sarah stepped down, Brad called Dr. Patrick Rydell to the stand and questioned him for the rest of the afternoon. When court adjourned, Brad assured Sarah that she had done just fine and promised her that things would take a turn for the better on Friday.

◁▷

At 8:15 a.m. on Friday morning, she pulled up behind Patrick O'Malley's van parked on a side street about a block from Norfolk General District Court.

The timing would be tight. She was to meet Ahmed at 8:30. Brad expected her in Federal Court on the other side of town by the start of testimony at 9:00.

A nasty wind battered the streets of Norfolk, and it began to drizzle. She hopped inside Patrick's van. He handed her a manila envelope containing a note and the three transmitters from the office. The radio blared in the background as she unfolded the paper and read.

"I'll be listening on a frequency that picks up these transmitters. If anything goes wrong, I'll be there. These things don't have great range, so keep them close to Ahmed."

She nodded, glad to be operating with a partner now, and closed the envelope, leaving the note with Patrick. "Good luck," he mouthed as she climbed out into the cold.

◁▷

Ahmed stared ahead and did not acknowledge her presence.

"I thought I told you to come alone," she hissed.

"You're wired," Ahmed snarled back. He grabbed her left arm at the bicep and squeezed with powerful fingers, drawing her closer to him. She gasped. "And you're not in charge here anymore. The men stay."

"Of course I'm wired. I've got your bugs."

"Show them to me," he demanded.

"Then let go." She said it firmly. Could he sense her fear, smell her fright? Ahmed waited for an instant, then released her arm.

She pulled the envelope out of her purse and handed it to him. He turned to face her, staring right through her with those cold, gray eyes. His lips curled into a vicious little half smile. "You seem to be shaking, my friend." He had noticed; he knew he was in charge! He looked at the transmitters. "What's the plan for Shelhorse?"

Pull yourself together. Deep breaths. This guy is scum—treat him like it.

"As I told you before," she said evenly, "the plan is to prevent Shelhorse from testifying. When I do, you will deposit one hundred thousand dollars into the Cayman Island bank account referenced on this sheet." She handed him a slip of paper that contained the wire instructions. This time her hand was steadier.

She lowered her voice another notch and spoke slowly, deliberately.

"There is something else. I know a juror that we can buy. He's a leader. You buy him, you'll have your verdict."

Ahmed's eyes lit up. "Which one?" he demanded.

"None of your business." Her fear began to dissipate.

Ahmed turned to her and spread his hot breath across her face. "I'm making it my business right now. We already own one juror. I must know whether this is the same person."

He watched closely, unblinking. She could not hesitate on this, even for a fraction of a second. He was testing her. Her heart slammed against her chest.

"Juror number six," she said calmly. "Which one do you own?"

"That truly is none of your business," Ahmed said. He paused, staring. "But it is not juror number six."

The co-conspirators exchanged a look. She thought she could see a slight relaxation in his jaw muscles.

"What's the cost?"

"Two million," she said without flinching. "Here are the wiring instructions." She handed him a second sheet of paper, this time for a Swiss bank account. "If our juror doesn't deliver the rest of the panel, you owe us nothing."

"'Us'?" Ahmed asked.

"I'm no fool. And I don't trust you. What would stop you, once you get your defense verdict, from eliminating me?"

"You'll have my word," Ahmed said lamely.

"Worthless when I'm dead."

"What are you proposing?" Ahmed asked. His words had a sharp edge. His muscles were again tensed.

She waited just long enough to let him know she could not be intimidated. "The nation of Saudi Arabia deposits one hundred million dollars in trust in a Swiss bank account. I get a copy of this trust document—" she thrust it at him but held it tight—"signed by a Saudi official. *Not* you. That money serves as my life insurance. As long as I'm alive, the money stays in the bank. If I die, under the terms of the trust document, the person I appoint as the executor of my estate must perform an investigation of the circumstances of my death. If he, or she, concludes I was murdered or that there were suspicious circumstances surrounding my death, the hundred million goes to Sarah Reed and her children. If my executor determines that I died from natural causes, then the money goes back to Saudi Arabia."

She could sense Ahmed's rising frustration; the death stare was back. She kept her voice low and even. She leaned forward as she spoke, her mouth a mere foot away from the transmitters.

"By next Friday, I want the money on deposit, and I want this document signed by an authorized representative of the Saudi government and delivered to the Swiss bank. Questions?"

Ahmed took the trust document. He made a great show of studying it, turning the pages slowly and methodically.

He placed the document in his own briefcase, placed the transmitters next to it, then whispered in her ear, his words dripping with vitriol.

"You don't set deadlines; I do. I will have the document signed, but not until after you have delivered on your promise for Shelhorse. And I'll have the money in the account when I'm ready—sometime before the jury begins deliberations. Your arbitrary deadlines mean nothing to me. I'll call the next meeting, not you. . . . And one more thing, which I'm sure you've figured out. If you don't get rid of Shelhorse, or for some strange and tragic reason, we don't get a defense verdict, then you will die. And no escrow account will stop us."

She hardened her features, narrowed her eyes, and stared back.

"By the way," Ahmed said brusquely, "two million is too much. I'll set that price later." He stood, grabbed his coat, and headed out.

She watched him leave and clenched her jaw. She was at once frightened and angry. Her head throbbed as adrenaline coursed through her entire body. She had been threatened by a cold-blooded killer.

But she had looked him in the eye, backed him down, and demanded her two million. She willed herself to rise, thrust her jaw in the air, and walk fearlessly from the courtroom.

◁ ▷

As the chauffeur maneuvered against the morning rush-hour traffic, Ahmed had time to call Barnes and fill him in.

"Find out if she's got a will, and if so, who her executor is," Ahmed demanded. "She must have let the executor in on this little blackmail scheme. Wait until we get our defense verdict. Then, within twenty-four hours, I want both her and the executor dead."

◁ ▷

Patrick O'Malley picked up the conversation from a few blocks away on his digital recorder. He was now the executor, and he would have to be careful. But as far as he could tell, they would have at least until the jury returned its verdict to execute the plan.

He smiled as he thought about Ahmed arguing over the two-million-dollar price tag for the verdict. O'Malley had predicted that the Saudi would try to get by for half. And all the while, Aberijan had his eye on the wrong ball. Two million, one million, what difference did it make? A hundred million—that was real money. And that price was nonnegotiable.

O'Malley punched in the numbers on his cell phone and was not surprised to hear it answered after only one ring.

"It's me," an anxious voice said. "How'd it go?"

"Just like we planned," O'Malley crowed. "Hook, line, and sinker. He even tried to negotiate the cost of the verdict—"

His phone beeped with an incoming call. "Hang on a second," he said. He checked the caller ID.

O'Malley put the first call on hold and answered the second. "You were great," he said reassuringly. "The money's as good as in the bank. The Saudis will never miss it."

31

AT 9:05 A.M., with all the players in their respective seats, Dr. Jeffrey Rydell took the stand for a second day. Brad noticed one female juror nudge the one next to her and wiggle her eyebrows. Rydell had boyish good looks, a full head of blond hair, and bright blue eyes. He was the all-American boy next door, except that he also happened to be a board-certified internist and seemed to know everything about emergency room medicine.

Brad had spent the first day of Rydell's testimony rehashing his qualifications and his treatment of Charles and Sarah Reed. Today Brad planned to hone in on the critical medical issues of his case.

"Dr. Rydell, do you have an opinion, to a reasonable degree of medical certainty, as to whether cocaine was a contributing factor in the death of Charles Reed?"

"I do," Rydell replied. One of the things Brad loved about this witness was that he always answered only the question asked and did not prattle on just to show his intelligence.

"What is that opinion, sir?"

"Objection," Strobel said. Brad rolled his eyes. "Dr. Rydell is not a toxi-cologist and therefore should not be allowed to give opinion testimony on this subject."

"I tend to agree with Mr. Strobel," Ichabod said, to nobody's surprise.

"Your Honor," Brad pleaded, "he was the physician at the base hospital who personally treated Dr. Reed just prior to his death. Certainly he can give opinions as to the cause of that death based on what he observed."

"May we approach?" Strobel asked. Without waiting for an answer, he moved toward Ichabod's bench. Brad joined him.

"I don't object if he talks about his treatment of Dr. Reed and what he observed," Mack whispered. "But from his deposition testimony, it's obvious that he also intends to talk about the toxicological tests performed both at King Faisal Specialist Hospital and the base hospital and then discuss the differences in levels of cocaine detected. He was not there for the King Faisal tests and is not an expert on absorption rates and other factors that would affect the significance of those levels—"

"Judge, he relied on those tests from the King Faisal Specialist Hospital when he treated Dr. Reed at the base hospital." Brad's interruption drew a glare from Strobel, which Brad ignored. "The reason Mr. Strobel does not want those tests admitted is because the tests at the base hospital showed a higher, not lower, level of cocaine. This could only mean someone injected Dr. Reed with cocaine very close to the time of his admittance to the first hospital, so that as the injected cocaine became absorbed into the blood and processed in the urine, it registered progressively higher levels between the time of his first admittance to the King Faisal Specialist Hospital and the time of his later admission to the base hospital." Brad was speaking quickly, trying desperately to get Ichabod to appreciate the significance of this ruling.

She interrupted him with her outstretched palm.

"That's quite an elaborate theory, Mr. Carson, and based on no small amount of speculation. It does, as Mr. Strobel suggests, depend on such things as absorption rates for cocaine into the bloodstream. Mr. Carson, do you have a toxicologist you plan on calling as an expert?"

"Yes, Judge, Dr. Shelhorse, but—"

"Mr. Carson," Ichabod interrupted, "that was a yes or no question. Since you have a toxicologist, I'm ruling that the prior tests from the King Faisal Specialist Hospital are not admissible through this witness. We can deal with them when your toxicologist takes the stand."

Brad looked at the judge and registered a silent protest.

"Thank you, gentlemen," she said.

Brad huffed and stalked back to the podium.

"Dr. Rydell, please state your opinion as to whether cocaine contributed to the death of Dr. Reed, but in doing so, please do not discuss the prior drug tests from the King Faisal Specialist Hospital. Does that make sense?"

"No," the doctor said, "but I'll try.

"In my eleven years of experience in the management of critical-care patients, I have treated many who presented with various complications associated with cocaine usage. Cocaine is a powerful central nervous system stimulant that heightens alertness, inhibits appetite and the need for sleep, and provides intense feelings of pleasure. It is either snorted as a hydrochloric salt or boiled with sodium bicarbonate to produce a substance referred to on the street as 'crack,' which is then smoked and absorbed through the lungs. In rare instances, cocaine can be diluted with water and injected straight into the bloodstream."

Rydell talked straight to the jurors, and Brad noticed that they all appeared to be listening—with the exception, of course, of juror number four, who seemed to be much more interested in the tops of his own shoes.

"Regardless of how it is absorbed, cocaine causes a number of potentially fatal complications, including some that directly affect the heart. Even in relatively small doses, cocaine increases blood pressure and constricts blood vessels. It also stimulates the formation of blood clots, disrupts normal heart rhythm, and can bind directly to heart-muscle cells, thereby weakening the heart's ability to pump blood. A variety of cardiovascular conditions and diseases have been associated with cocaine use, including hypertension, arrhythmias, cardiomyopathy, strokes, aneurysms, myocarditis, and heart attacks. Many first-time users have experienced heart attacks that have proven to be fatal.

"In the case of Dr. Reed, the effect of an enormous dosage of cocaine, as revealed in toxicological tests taken at both hospitals—"

"Objection!" Strobel shouted.

"Sustained!" Ichabod snorted. "The jury will disregard that last statement. Dr. Rydell, you are in no way allowed to refer to the toxicological tests from the King Faisal Specialist Hospital. Is that clear?"

"It is now, Judge," Rydell said, unfazed. "I thought before that you were just saying I couldn't tell the jury about the precise levels."

As Ichabod shook her head in disapproval, Rydell turned back to the jury with a level gaze and continued his lecture.

"Charles Reed already had a bad heart. He had fairly advanced coronary artery disease, which means that the flow of oxygen-rich blood to his heart was severely restricted. In my opinion, a combination of the stress from being arrested, the effects of the cocaine injected into his bloodstream, and the pre-existing coronary artery disease all led to the death of Dr. Reed. The cocaine stimulated the formation of a blood clot that may not have been fatal in the arteries of a normal man, but it led to a total restriction of the flow of blood to the heart of Dr. Reed. In medical terms, we call it an acute myocardial infarction, but it simply means that the heart fails to receive any oxygen and is severely damaged as a result. In Dr. Reed's case, it was fatal."

Rydell looked back at Brad, apparently satisfied with his answer. So was Brad.

"You said Dr. Reed died from complications associated with an injection of cocaine; is that your testimony?" Brad wanted to make sure that no juror missed this crucial point.

"Yes, it was definitely an injection of cocaine."

"Well, Doctor, how can you tell that the cocaine was injected into Dr. Reed as opposed to absorbed in some other way . . . like snorting or smoking?"

"My conclusion is based on the level of cocaine found in the urine of Dr. Reed at the base hospital," Dr. Rydell explained. He looked again at the jurors. "This is not a level typically associated with snorting cocaine. When the drug is snorted, it actually narrows the blood vessels in the nose, reducing the flow of blood in that area and creating a slower absorption rate through the blood vessels into the bloodstream.

"On the other hand, the types of elevated readings we see in this case generally come from either injecting cocaine directly into a vein or smoking crack cocaine. Smoking crack, as it is called, delivers a concentrated amount of the drug to the lungs, brain, and bloodstream in mere seconds. That is why injecting cocaine or smoking crack gives users an immediate rush, whereas snorting cocaine can take several minutes to deliver a high. It all has to do with absorption rate. In my view, it would be nearly impossible to obtain the level of cocaine found in Dr. Reed from snorting cocaine several hours before the lab tests were run."

"Dr. Rydell, that would seem to explain your conclusion that Dr. Reed did not snort the cocaine that led to his death. But how could you conclude that he did not smoke crack cocaine?" Brad asked. He was following the script that he and the doctor had carefully crafted the night before.

"Judge, I object." Strobel was out of his seat again, sounding annoyed that he would have to bother to make another objection. "Same basis as before. Dr. Rydell is not a toxicologist, and he is very far afield with this line of testimony."

This time Ichabod hesitated. "I'm going to overrule your objection, Mr. Strobel. If he strays outside his area of expertise while answering the question, I'll strike the answer and instruct the jury to disregard the testimony."

"May I answer?" Dr. Rydell asked politely, looking at the judge.

Brad turned and smiled at Leslie.

"Yes, just stay within your area of expertise," Ichabod instructed.

Rydell nodded his head. "In my line of work it is customary to consult with specialists while treating patients. That is essentially what I did in the case of Dr. Reed. In this instance, I continued to consult with other special- ists even after Dr. Reed's death in order to piece together what happened.

"Do you have a copy of the lab reports from the hospital?" Dr. Rydell asked. This request looked spontaneous, but it was, of course, scripted.

Brad pulled out a thick black notebook and fumbled around until he found the right tab. "Let the record reflect that the lab reports from the base hospital have been previously admitted into evidence and marked as Plaintiff's 37."

Brad handed the report to Rydell.

"Here it is," Rydell explained, pointing to a certain page. "This really didn't mean anything to me the first time I looked at it because it wasn't essential to Dr. Reed's treatment, but this urine test has no positive finding for methylecgonidine."

"And what is the significance of that, Dr. Rydell?"

"Well, you don't really smoke cocaine, you smoke a form of freebase of the drug that we have been calling 'crack.'" Rydell resumed his role as pro- fessor. "That freebase is made by boiling powdered cocaine with sodium bicarbonate, a process that frees the cocaine base from the cocaine hydro- chloride. The base separates in chunks of crack cocaine. Then, when this product is smoked and absorbed into the bloodstream, it is processed by the body and produces a metabolite that will show up in a user's urine. That metabolite is called 'methylecgonidine.' The presence or absence of certain quantities of this substance is how you tell a snorter from a smoker.

"In the case of Dr. Reed, after finding a positive screening for cocaine using an immunoassay test, the lab performed a more sophisticated analysis that tested for both cocaine and its metabolite. This more sophisticated test is called a gas chromatography with mass spectrum detection, which basi- cally creates a drug fingerprint and quantifies the drug. The cocaine was confirmed, but its metabolite, this compound called methylecgonidine, was not present in quantities that exceeded a standardized cutoff level. Thus it was not reported as positive."

"So if the user smoked crack cocaine, you would expect to find this sub- stance. But you did not find it here?" Brad asked innocently. He wanted to make sure that every juror heard this at least twice.

"I object," Strobel bellowed again. "That last question is a leading question and should be struck. But more important, Judge, this whole line of testimony is way outside this doctor's area of expertise. May I voir dire the witness to show the court what I mean?"

"You've got to be kidding," Brad responded. "He's not allowed to voir dire my witness in the middle of his testimony. He can deal with this issue on cross."

"I'll allow a short voir dire," Ichabod ruled, sitting back and crossing her arms.

Brad held up both palms in silent protest, then turned and took his seat. Strobel rose quickly to begin his examination, his look of disdain showing the jury he was not the least bit impressed with Rydell. Strobel started peppering the witness with questions even before he got to the podium.

"Dr. Rydell, you're not a board-certified toxicologist, are you?"

"No."

"In fact, if you had a patient who presented with an unusual toxicological symptom, you would get a consult from a specialist more skilled than you in this area. Correct?"

"That's correct," Rydell said, "but I wouldn't call a cocaine overdose an unusual toxicological problem."

"Your Honor," Strobel pleaded, "please instruct the witness to just answer the question."

"Dr. Rydell," the judge chided, "please do not volunteer extraneous information."

Before Rydell could answer, Strobel was on the attack again.

"These lab reports, including the urine test, were in Dr. Reed's medical chart all the time, is that correct?"

"Yes, to my knowledge, they were," Rydell responded.

"And as the treating physician, you would have presumably reviewed them. Correct?"

"That's also true."

"But the absence of methylecgonidine meant nothing to you at the time because you knew nothing about that substance. Correct?"

"The absence of the compound did not mean anything to me at the time. That doesn't mean I knew nothing about the substance."

"Well, Dr. Rydell, isn't it fair to say that even when your deposition was taken in this case, some three months ago, you still hadn't attached any significance to the absence of this substance?"

"Yes. At the time of my deposition, I had not realized the significance of this laboratory finding. Dr. Reed tested positive for a very high level of cocaine. The absence of significant amounts of its metabolite did not impress me at the time as being that important."

"Dr. Rydell, you stated that these drug tests were confirmed with something called a gas chromatography with mass spectrum detection method, what you called a 'fingerprint' of the drug. Is that right?"

"Yes, I think that's what I said."

"Your Honor, may I approach the witness?" Strobel asked.

"Yes," Ichabod said without looking up.

Strobel began making his way toward Dr. Rydell, waving two papers, one in each hand.

"I have here two actual gas chromatographs, one that is of this compound you mentioned, methylecgonidine, and one that represents an entirely different compound. I'd like to show them to you and see if you can even tell me which is which."

Brad jumped to his feet to object, but before he could talk, the witness was answering.

"Don't bother," Rydell said. "I wouldn't have the foggiest idea. I would rely on the toxicologist to interpret those for me."

Although he conceded the point, he did it in such a nonassuming manner that it appeared he had not conceded a thing. This aggravated Strobel, who was not about to let the point die a quiet death. He stood just a few feet from the witness box and jabbed the air with the gas chromatographs.

"In fact, everything you have testified about today you gained from talking to others or reading research papers, because you are not a trained toxicologist. Until you talked to someone else, you had no idea what this substance even was, did you?"

"It's correct that everything I know about methylecgonidine I learned from others in the last few months. But the reason I researched the issue was because I watched the videotaped depositions of those witnesses that you took in Saudi Arabia. You know, the former members of the church— the ones who claim that the Reeds used cocaine. As you know, Sarah Reed claims that her husband must have been injected with the drug, but your witnesses claim—"

"Just answer the question that you've been asked, Doctor, and save the speeches," Strobel demanded. His face was red, and he emphasized each word in a staccato style: "Did you or did you not learn everything you know about methylecgonidine from talking with others or from reading research papers in the last few months?"

"Yes, I did."

"Then isn't it true, Doctor, that you would defer to those with specialized training and experience as toxicologists?" Strobel's voice was gaining volume.

"Yes, I would defer," Rydell said matter-of-factly.

"And if they had different opinions about the absence of this compound in the urine, then you would defer to the opinions of those specialists. Correct?"

"I suppose that would depend on the reasons, but generally, yes." Rydell obviously saw no harm in conceding the obvious.

Strobel then turned to Ichabod to make his case. "Then, Your Honor, in light of the witness's own admissions, I would ask that all testimony from this witness, with regard to whether the cocaine in Dr. Reed's system was snorted, smoked, or injected, should be struck as outside the realm of his expertise."

"I agree," Ichabod said as Brad was opening his mouth to respond. Ichabod turned to the jury. She left Brad standing speechless at counsel table, his face showing his disgust.

"You will disregard any and all testimony by Dr. Rydell about whether Dr. Reed had been injected with cocaine. In that regard, you should also ignore all testimony about this compound . . . uh, what's it called, Doctor?"

"Methylecgonidine, Your Honor," Rydell pronounced the name of the metabolite slowly and distinctly so that the jury could remember.

"Yes. You will disregard all testimony about that substance. You may not base any aspects of your deliberations on such testimony. For all practical purposes, you must simply eliminate that testimony from your mind and give it no credibility in this case. Now, is that understood?"

The jurors nodded and assured Ichabod they would wipe their thoughts clean of this enticing information. But the genie was out of the bottle and could not be put back. Most all of the jurors appeared to like Rydell. It was obvious. And Brad suspected the questions on the jurors' minds were no longer about whether Dr. Reed had been injected with cocaine, but how and why. And by whom?

Brad continued to look disgusted as he walked behind the podium to resume his examination of Rydell. He pouted through the next few questions, just to emphasize to the jury how unfair Ichabod had actually been.

Inside, he was smiling.

◁ ▷

Rydell's testimony would have been the perfect way to end the first week of trial if Ichabod had not decided to weigh in with some preliminary opinions after she dismissed the jury for the day.

"Don't forget, Mr. Carson, that the jury only decides the case against Mr. Aberijan, but I must decide the case against the nation of Saudi Arabia. And I must say that I'm very disappointed that we've completed our first week of testimony and I have yet to hear any evidence that would implicate the nation of Saudi Arabia."

She paused, sighed, and glanced around the courtroom, as if searching for some shred of evidence that might impress her. She turned back to Brad.

"Even if I had not struck the testimony of Dr. Rydell, the most you would have is a client whose husband had been injected with cocaine. Now let's assume, although you have put no evidence into the record showing this to be true, that Mr. Aberijan himself injected Dr. Reed with cocaine. Does that mean that the nation of Saudi Arabia has to answer for everything Mr. Aberijan did? I think not."

The words, the tone, the matter-of-fact dismissal of some of his strongest evidence chiseled away at Brad's confidence and enthusiasm. Though he knew the rest of his team, including Sarah, would take their cues from him at this critical moment, he still couldn't help but lower his eyes and sag a little deeper in his chair.

"It seems clear to me that if Mr. Aberijan did any of these terrible things you have accused him of doing, he would have been exceeding his authority as an agent of the nation of Saudi Arabia, and therefore Saudi Arabia would no longer be responsible for his actions. I am therefore assuming you have some direct evidence that the nation of Saudi Arabia, through its official representatives, either authorized beforehand or ratified after the fact the alleged actions of Mr. Aberijan." She raised her eyebrows to emphasize her point. "Without that evidence, you cannot win this case."

Brad vehemently disagreed with the court's reading of the legal standard required to sustain a verdict against Saudi Arabia, but he also knew that five o'clock on a Friday afternoon was no time to start that argument. The eyes of Ichabod, his own team, and the rest of the courtroom were now on him.

He rose from his seat and stood straight, meeting the judge's steady gaze, and buttoning his top suit-coat buttons.

"We have clear and convincing evidence on just that point, Your Honor," Brad promised.

And at that very moment, he and everyone else in the courtroom wondered what in the world it could possibly be.

32

BRAD HAD BEEN WAITING for this night for a long time and was determined to make it special. He raced home after court to get out of his navy blue, pin-striped suit and yellow power tie and throw on a comfortable pair of jeans and a golf shirt. He was tired of dressing up and being on display. Tonight would be laid-back and casual. He would relax with a vengeance. He also threw on a pair of penny loafers with no socks. It was the Virginia Beach way.

He had offered Leslie a chance to change at his house, but she had declined. Instead, he would pick her up at the office. She wanted to cram in a few more minutes of work before taking the night off. Brad had never seen anyone obsess over a case like she did.

The rain had stopped, but it was still brisk. Brad grabbed a Windbreaker and the keys to the Viper he kept nestled in the garage. His Cherokee would have to sit this one out. The Jeep was his workhorse, and it was littered with transcripts, trial notes, soda cans, and coffee cups. It was in no shape for a date.

But the Viper was another story. He'd bought it three years ago as his reward for a surprisingly big verdict in a notoriously tough case. Now it was in danger of becoming a collector's item. It had not been out of his garage for months, because he saved it for those leisurely drives that he never found time to take or those special occasions that somehow never came. But tonight qualified. This night would be special. And Prince Charming intended to show up in his jet-black, albeit dusty, Dodge Viper. Cinderella would love it.

The drive from his house to the office generally took twenty minutes without traffic, with an additional twenty minutes in rush hour. Tonight, anxious to see Leslie and driving the Viper opposite the homeward-bound traffic, he made the trip, portal to portal, in just over fifteen.

Brad parked in the fire lane outside his office building, bounced into the lobby, and waited impatiently for the elevators. Just for good measure, he punched the Up button several times before the elevator finally arrived, an action that only seemed to slow things down. An interminable two minutes later, he stepped off at the fifth floor and entered the office of Carson & Associates.

He found her sitting in the war room, hunched over a deposition transcript, chewing on the top of her pen. She looked up when he entered and broke into a bright smile that accentuated her beautiful white teeth, high cheekbones, and sparkling blue eyes. Leslie was gorgeous. Her auburn hair was pulled back and clipped and fell softly against her white cotton blouse. She had caught the spirit of the night and wore blue jeans and white docksiders sans socks to honor the culture of the beach. Brad stared—awestruck for a moment at her natural beauty, the graceful lines of her face—then caught himself feeling embarrassed to be gawking like a teenager.

"You look great," he managed when all his glib trial skills failed him. "It's nice to see you looking so relaxed."

"Thanks, boss," she replied with a bounce in her voice. "I've been looking forward to tonight."

"Me too," Brad said, cursing himself for not being able to think of anything more clever and for not being able to take his eyes off her. "You ready?"

"I've been ready." She came over, took his hand, and gave him a quick kiss on the cheek. "And I'm starving. Where're we headed?"

Her soft touch electrified him, an invigorating surge that brought every nerve alive. Just holding her hand energized his body and paralyzed his brain. He couldn't speak, couldn't force himself to let go, couldn't alter the intensity of his gaze into her eyes.

She must have felt it too. Her eyes conveyed a depth of emotion that had never been spoken.

How can someone I've been spending so much time with suddenly make me so tongue-tied? Brad wondered. He didn't want to leave the office; he would just hold her and kiss her on the spot. He wanted to draw her to him and tell her eloquently and passionately everything he felt. She made him complete. She made him alive. She made him dizzy with emotion. Weak-kneed.

But in this defining moment, his greatest asset failed him. The tongue wouldn't work. He could think of no words to express the depths of his emotions. He was mute. Incapacitated. He would tell her later. For now he would chicken out.

"It's a surprise," he said gamely. "You'll have to trust me."

He took her hand, led her down to the Viper, and started another tour of his favorite spots in Tidewater.

"Rule number one," Brad insisted, "is that we do not discuss work tonight."

Leslie looked at the list of questions she had jotted down on an index card, pursed her lips, then stuffed it into her pocket. "Okay," she said grudgingly, "but I'll bet Strobel's not taking the night off."

"You're incorrigible," Brad complained.

"And you love it," Leslie teased, reaching over and rubbing the back of his neck.

Indeed he did!

This was not a night to discuss the case. It was a night for wisecracks and laughing, for deep conversations, for building on the explosive chemistry between them. It was a night for holding hands and acting crazy. It was a night to become soul mates.

The couple began with a relaxed dinner at the Boulevard Café, an out-of-the-way place featuring exotic food and indoor-outdoor dining. They chose to sit under the stars and enjoy the cool evening breeze of the perfect autumn night. Much to Brad's delight, the breeze and nighttime air combined to chill Leslie, causing her to move closer to him after the main course. He wrapped his arm around her and kept her warm while they nursed some hot chocolate.

For dessert Brad took her to a Tidewater icon—Doumar's Drive-In. This quaint Norfolk restaurant claimed to be the original home of the ice-cream cone and remained the undisputed ice-cream champ in the Tidewater area. Here the couple shared a banana split the old-fashioned way, as waitresses on roller skates delivered dessert to the Viper, though Brad insisted they not hook a tray on the driver's window. For tonight, and tonight only, Brad would violate one of his hard and fast rules that strictly forbade any eating in his beloved automobile. After all, rules were made to be broken.

From Doumar's, they went to MacArthur Mall for a movie. Not just any movie, but a romantic chick flick that would require no thinking, only feeling. But as the plot dragged on and the adrenaline wore off, the exhausting week in court caught up with the two of them. Leslie dozed first, then Brad succumbed, and together they slept through the second half of the film.

They laughed as they exited the mall into the parking garage and were greeted again by the cool night air. Brad told himself that he had stalled long enough. It was time to tell Leslie the depth of his feelings toward her, how much she really meant to him. The night had been perfect, and soon it would be time for a perfect ending.

"Do you remember what level we parked on?" he asked. The little things in life had never commanded much of his attention. He clicked the remote lock button on his key chain, listening for the telltale beep from his faithful Viper.

"I could have sworn we were in 3A," Leslie said, tucked under Brad's arm.

"Oh well, it's a beautiful night for a walk," he muttered.

And walk they did. They scoured all levels of the parking garage, middle to top and back again, before they reached the only reasonable conclusion.

"It's stolen," Leslie surmised. "I know we parked on level three. We should call the police."

"I can't believe this," Brad fumed. It would be hard to pour out his feelings without the Viper. The back of a cab just didn't have the same ambiance. "It's the only mall in America that charges you to park, and they don't even patrol the garage? These rent-a-cop guards at the mall are a joke. With all the money they're making off parking fees, you'd think they could afford—"

It hit him in midsentence. A scenario worse than a stolen car. This couldn't be happening. *Couldn't be.* Not tonight.

Only one person would know. He needed to call her, but he had left his cell phone in the Viper. "Can I borrow your phone?" Brad asked.

A few minutes later he was on the phone with a groggy Bella.

"I'm sure they repossessed it, Brad. I've been stalling your banker all week. I made a few payments on the Jeep, but I knew you never used the Viper. Frankly, your banker said he had to do something to make it look like he's being aggressive. I told him not to touch the Jeep or the house. I guess he took that as a green light to go after the Viper. I'm sorry, Brad. I figured it wouldn't see the light of day until the case was over."

"Don't worry about it, Bella. You're doing the best you can. We'll just catch a taxi."

"No you won't, Brad Carson. I wouldn't hear of it. You just sit tight."

Shrugging off Brad's protests, Bella showed up at the parking garage ten minutes later. She was wearing her bathrobe.

"Hop in," Bella said cheerily—and entirely out of character. "I'll chauffeur you guys to your destinations."

Brad opened the back door of the Honda Accord and choked slightly on the smell of cigarette smoke. He moved a few empty fast-food bags and their matching cups. Carefully avoiding the stale fries on the floor, he slid over next to the dry cleaning, and Leslie gingerly joined him.

For the next twenty minutes, they listened politely, and sometimes even responded, to Bella's endless banter about the case and Ichabod. Bella insisted on using the rearview mirror to maintain eye contact as she talked, a habit that only exacerbated her horrid driving skills. After a few minutes of foolishly trying to survive Bella's chauffeuring without seat belts, Brad and Leslie pulled the begrimed belts from between the seat cushions, dusted off the crumbs, and put them to good use.

They were greatly relieved when Bella pulled next to Leslie's car in the parking lot at the office.

"Thanks so much, Bella," Brad said as he and Leslie climbed out of the car. "Leslie can give me a ride home from here."

"Nonsense," Bella replied. "She's got to drive all the way to Williamsburg. I'll take you home. I've got nothing else to do. And, Leslie, you can stay at my place tonight if you want to."

"Thanks, Bella," Leslie said without a moment's hesitation. "But I really do need to get home tonight. I've got lots of errands to run first thing in the morning."

"Suit yourself." Bella shrugged her shoulders and took out a cigarette. "Brad, this will give us a chance to talk about the financial picture and any personal items you had in that Viper. Besides, I've got some news on my mother you'll love to hear."

"Okay," Brad said, looking at Bella and winking. "Just give me a minute."

He was determined not to let this opportunity pass. He walked Leslie to her car and helped her in. She rolled down her window, and he leaned down to talk out of Bella's hearing.

"Sorry about the way this ended," he said. "It wasn't exactly how I planned it."

"But it was still perfect," she said. "Because I got to spend time with you."

Leslie placed her hand behind Brad's head and gently pulled him toward her. They closed their eyes and savored the moment, lost in the gentle passion of the kiss, the warm rush of emotion, oblivious to the missing Viper, Bella, or anyone else in the world.

It was, Brad thought, the perfect ending to the perfect night.

◁ ▷

Hanif completed his sermon with a flourish and closed his Bible. He lowered his voice a few notches and stopped his pacing. Now was not the time for motivation but for a straightforward family chat.

He looked into the eyes of the upturned faces of the church members. They occupied every inch of the living room and spilled into the kitchen.

"Two things can bring this church down," he began in an earnest tone, "and both have to do with controlling the tongue. Remember the words of James, 'The tongue is a little member and boasts great things. See how great a forest a little fire kindles!'

"There are some among us who cannot keep the secrets and confidences of this church. I have reason to believe that in the days ahead the persecution of the church will intensify, and the efforts of the Muttawa to hunt us down and destroy us will increase. If you are not ready to endure for the cause of Christ, then you should leave now."

Hanif paused and surveyed the room. He saw little fear. His tone remained calm and reassuring. "If you leave, this church will understand, and you will not be held in contempt. We will not speak or think badly of you. The narrow path is not for everyone."

He waited again. Nobody moved. Most scarcely breathed.

"If you stay, we must demand utmost secrecy in the days ahead and your complete allegiance. Remember, 'God has not given us a spirit of fear, but of power and of love and of a sound mind.'"

The *amens* floated upward.

"There is one other matter of the tongue," Hanif continued. "It has to do with spreading rumors about one another."

He again paused and looked around, intentionally catching the eyes of the most likely offenders. "One rumor in particular has to do with one of the founders of this church, my brother, Rasheed, and his wife, Mobara. I have heard it rumored that Rasheed sold out this church, gave testimony in the American legal system against the matriarch of the church, Madame Sarah Reed, and then turned his back on the faith."

He had their attention. The rumors had indeed been flying. And it didn't help matters that Rasheed and Mobara had been absent for months from the meetings of the very church they had helped establish.

"I know personally that these rumors are not true. I know things I cannot tell you. On this, you must trust me. But I can tell you that my brother and his wife have never turned their backs on this precious faith. They no longer attend this church because they are being watched closely and followed by the authorities. They love this church too much to thrust it into danger. They have banished themselves from meeting with you. But they asked me to express their love and prayers."

Hanif paused, and silence engulfed the small room. "It is true that Rasheed gave testimony in the American case involving Madame Sarah Reed. Again, there are things I cannot tell you about that testimony. But this I can say: Mr. Ahmed Aberijan has not heard the last from Rasheed Berjein."

Hanif looked around the room. Heads were nodding. Those who knew Rasheed seemed glad to see the rumors put to rest.

"I wish I could tell you more, but I may have already said too much. At the right time, not so long from now, you will understand completely. 'Now we see in a mirror, dimly, but then face to face.' Until then, hold all these things in strictest confidence. Now let us pray."

As Hanif closed his eyes to lead in prayer, he wondered if he had done the right thing. "Tell the truth and trust the people," Rasheed once told him. But maybe there were some things better left unsaid.

◁▷

Nikki's peaceful Sunday morning faded a bit more with each click of the remote. Coverage of the trial was everywhere. Judge Cynthia Baker-Kline's intemperate remarks at the close of court on Friday sent a shock wave of urgency into the public relations war. The Christian Right sensed another betrayal coming from the leftist and elitist judiciary. Conservative talk-show hosts and firebrand preachers took up the cause and filled the airwaves with dire predictions and sky-is-falling rhetoric.

In the other corner, the radical Muslim groups used Baker-Kline's comments to paint the picture of a case built on evidence so flimsy that not even a judge biased against their cause would buy it. What a travesty, they suggested, if such a spurious case went to this prejudiced jury, who would then find against them based solely on Arab and Muslim stereotypes.

Nikki poured herself another Diet Coke, energized by the caffeine and the controversy.

The renewed intensity of the debate sparked threats of protests and civil disobedience from various antiestablishment groups. The leftist fringe groups, from hard-core environmentalists to libertarians, took the opportunity to rail against a corrupt American judicial system and to promise all sorts of trouble for the overworked police. The right-wing militias could not sit idly by as their counterparts on the left took up arms. The militias railed against the corrupt American judicial system and threatened to take matters into their own hands if the police couldn't handle the nuts on the left.

National networks and cable news channels, loving the hailstorm of controversy, spent their time interviewing the most colorful and outspoken proponents of the various causes and reminding the public of upcoming special coverage. Even the president got into the act. He called for cool heads and peaceful protests and, together with the governor of the Commonwealth, ordered the Virginia National Guard to be on standby with full riot gear when the courtroom opened on Monday morning.

"I can hardly wait," Nikki muttered and turned to MTV.

◁▷

"I don't know why you're so stubborn about when Shelhorse is going to testify," Leslie huffed, her arms folded in exasperation. Friday night seemed distant. The happy couple had morphed into two strong-willed, disagreeing attorneys by Sunday afternoon.

"I told you, we've got to finish strong," Brad insisted. "We already have one dynamite rebuttal witness. If we save Shelhorse for rebuttal as well, then we'll finish with a very strong one-two punch before the case goes to the jury."

"We may not even get it to the jury if we don't put on our best witnesses when we have the chance," Nikki argued. "Shelhorse is strong. She may help turn Ichabod before it's too late."

Brad had cleared a path for pacing around his side of the large conference room table. He gnawed on his glasses.

"But if we put her on before Strobel's case, before Strobel shows the videotaped testimony from those former church members, her testimony will lose its impact. If we wait, she'll make it plain that Khartoum is a liar. Putting her on first will just cause Strobel to withdraw the testimony of Khartoum and not show the videotape."

"He can't do that," Leslie said. "He's already showed portions of those videotapes in his opening statement."

"And you think that will stop him?" Brad asked, his voice rising.

They had debated this for thirty minutes, and Leslie sensed that any further argument would fall on deaf ears. She instead tried to convince Brad with stony silence, pursing her lips and pinning her eyes to the table. When all else failed—especially with a guy who's nuts for you—pout.

Nikki joined her in this quiet conspiracy.

"Look," Brad said finally, "I know you don't agree with this strategy, and if Bella were here it would probably be three against one, but my gut tells me this is the way to go. We put Aberijan on the stand as a hostile witness for cross-examination on Monday. Then we put our police-brutality expert and our other docs and nurses on the stand Tuesday and Wednesday. We end our case with the kids on Thursday.

"Then we hunker down for Strobel's case. He'll play the videotapes and put about ten experts on the stand to contradict everything we've said. That will take two weeks. Then we call our rebuttal witnesses—including Shelhorse—and leave their compelling testimony ringing in the ears of the jury just before closing arguments. Do you really think that's such a bad plan?"

"Yeah." Nikki shrugged.

Leslie still had her arms folded and lips pursed. "Does it matter?" she asked sarcastically.

"Not really," Brad said. "Let's get busy."

"You're such a chauvinist." Leslie could not let it go.

"Don't give me that," Brad said. "This has nothing to do with what sex you are; it has everything to do with who's financing the case and who has twenty years of experience, and who's ultimately responsible for calling the shots. I highly respect you and Nikki and your opinions. But on this one, I've got to go with my gut."

"That's what I'm saying," Leslie retorted. "This 'go with your gut' thing, this 'make the tough call on your own' mentality even if everybody else thinks it's a bad idea—it's all such a macho deal to you."

To Brad's credit he stood his ground in silence for a full minute as the women stared at him.

"I've got to make this call, and my gut tells me this is the way to go," he said finally, almost to himself.

Leslie and Nikki looked at each other and shook their heads. "He's a chauvinist," they said in unison.

◁▷

Bella had dreaded it all weekend. But she absolutely knew she needed to speak to Nikki. She had tried on Friday night, but the timing wasn't right. Saturday and Sunday had been major workdays, and now it was already Sunday night.

Bella decided to have one more cigarette first, just to calm her nerves. She shuffled down to the kitchen, feeling more guilty than ever about her cigarette breaks. One more nail in her coffin, as Nikki would say. She was definitely going to quit. She was dead serious about it. Since becoming a Christian, she had started praying that God would take this habit away. If He didn't do it by the end of the *Reed* case, then she would take matters into her own hands.

One way or the other, she was going to quit. Definitely.

She lit the cigarette and inhaled deeply, the very rhythm of it calming her down. She craved her smokes more than ever these days. Just knowing that she would soon quit had her thinking about it all the time. She sucked on the thin white stick again, a long and smooth breath, and sent smoke rings toward the ceiling.

How would Nikki react? Would she scream and cuss? faint? just stand there stunned?

Another drag, this time not as hard. She wanted to make this one last. Afterward, with no excuses, she would march straight into Nikki's office and confront the matter. No sense rushing that moment.

Quicker than she would have liked, her cigarette was gone. She snuffed it out, thought about another, and talked herself out of it. She would come back after her talk with Nikki. She would certainly be entitled by then.

She walked slowly down the hallway, her head down. Against all of her rationalizations, she walked straight to Nikki's office, defeating one by one each of the excuses her brain was throwing at her. The door was open, and she walked in.

To her great surprise, and even greater relief, the place was empty. Nikki had already left.

It must not be God's will to do this, Bella thought. *At least not tonight.*

She had tried. God knew she had tried.

She sighed and headed back toward the kitchen. She covered the same ground more quickly this time, and her lighter was in her hand before she made it through the kitchen door.

33

MONDAY MORNING, after a few hours of last-minute cramming, the trial team from Carson & Associates piled into Brad's Jeep for the morning commute. Bella stayed behind to call witnesses and tend to other office matters. Leslie drove so that Brad could spend a few more minutes going over the planned cross-examination of Aberijan.

"You ready?" she asked.

"I don't really know. You tell me at lunch whether I was ready. I ought to be done by then."

"I expect him to break down on the stand and start crying, Perry Mason style," Nikki said from the backseat. Brad immediately thought about Sarah's performance as a witness, and an awkward silence followed.

The point appeared to be lost on Nikki. "Hey, can you turn that up?" she asked. The radio station was playing one of her favorites.

"Actually, could you turn that off for a few minutes?" Brad asked. "I need to go over this one more time, and it's hard to concentrate."

"Tomorrow, I drive my own car," Nikki declared. "You can't get ready for trial without tunes."

Leslie killed the radio, and the crew drove on in relative silence. While Nikki hummed, Brad looked through the contents of his briefcase one more time, reviewing the tools of his cross-examination.

He glanced over the marked and indexed deposition transcript of Aberijan. If the man tried to deviate from the deposition in the slightest way, Brad was prepared to beat him up with the prior testimony. He double-checked the exhibits he would be using as well: medical records for Charles and Sarah Reed, the police report from that fateful night, and the court records of the former church members who testified against Sarah.

Brad's briefcase nearly overflowed with weapons for cross-examination.

Aberijan didn't know it was coming. He would never guess Brad would call him to the stand as an adverse witness in the middle of the plaintiff's case. Brad couldn't wait to see the look on his face.

There was nothing Brad liked better than trial by ambush.

◁▷

As Brad and his team walked around the corner and onto Granby Street, they got an up-close look at the chaos outside the federal courthouse. The huge block-and-mortar special, built during the public works projects of the Depression years, spanned the entire block. The sidewalk in front was cordoned off by police tape and a human wall of law enforcement officers and National Guardsmen, working valiantly to keep the sidewalk open for court personnel and others with official business.

Demonstrators pressed against the line of officers and spilled out into Granby Street, blocking traffic. As usual, the camps squared off against each other in the roadway.

As Brad walked toward the volcanic mass of humanity, he had a feeling that something didn't seem quite right; something other than the magnitude of the crowd was different today. In the next instant, he realized what it was. For some reason, possibly having to do with who arrived first at the courthouse that morning, the demonstrators had switched sides. Today, the people who were sympathetic to Saudi Arabia and the various leftist causes stood between Brad's team and the courthouse.

There would be no high fives this morning. Instead, Brad and the team would have to run the gauntlet of a hostile crowd.

Brad instinctively picked up the pace and moved in front of the women on the sidewalk. He pulled Sarah close to his right side. Nikki fell in step behind Brad, Leslie behind Sarah. Brad missed Bella.

"It's Carson and Reed," a cameraman yelled.

As if on cue, a wave of demonstrators pivoted in the team's direction and hurled themselves forward in fits and surges. The police line held, their shields and arms forming a barrier for Brad and his team. Brad stared ahead and set a faster pace, concerned about the uncontrollable sea of wild-haired radicals, some with signs and others with that possessed look in their eyes, pressing in on the police officers. The crowd lunged again, and the officers hoisted riot shields and started pushing against the crowd, holding them back.

Who started what, Brad had no idea, but screams and the sound of breaking bottles filled the air. The mob panicked.

"Run!" Brad yelled.

He and the women sprinted for the courthouse steps. He reached out to grab Sarah's arm and glanced over his shoulder just in time to see a protester with a leather vest and orange hair break through the police lines and grab Nikki. Brad turned and swung his briefcase with all his might, catching the demonstrator on the shoulder and neck, knocking him to the ground. Nikki's blouse ripped, but she pulled free, kicked off her heels, and raced toward the steps.

The police instantly subdued the demonstrator, but by breaking ranks they allowed another wave onto the sidewalk. Bent on revenge, the angry group grabbed Brad and mauled him.

He landed on the ground with what seemed like two tons of humanity on top of him. Pain shot through his right knee and hip. He tried to catch himself, but his arm buckled and his elbow bounced on the hard surface. He tried swinging his arms and kicking his legs against this suffocating mass. A fist caught him in the right eye. He tried desperately to get up, but his arms and legs were pinned beneath the mass of bodies, the piles of beefy flesh on top of him.

He heard somebody yell "tear gas," and he closed his eyes and held his breath. In the next moment, he felt the bodies rising off of him. He struggled free, squinting to see. A huge mountain of a man helped him to his feet. The man propped Brad up, wrapped a thick arm around his slender shoulders, and shielded the attorney as they walked toward the courthouse. Brad coughed and hacked, his eyes watering. He saw at least two bottles bounce off the man's shoulder as they advanced together toward the steps.

The man opened the door and nearly threw Brad inside; then he followed and pulled the door shut behind him. Leslie and Sarah, who had each somehow avoided the clutches of the mob, embraced Brad. Nikki sat in the hallway in her stocking feet. She looked stunned. Brad's benefactor and new friend helped her to her feet. He wore a federal marshal's uniform. The man's massive back muscles heaved as he caught his breath.

"You okay?" he asked.

"Yeah, I'm great," Nikki answered. She had apparently conquered her initial fear and now looked thirsty for revenge. Fire blazed in her eyes. "Let me borrow your piece, and I'll go out there and calm things down."

The man laughed deep and loud, then turned to look at Brad. "You okay?" he asked.

"I guess," Brad said, letting out a huge sigh as he let go of Sarah and Leslie. He extended his sore right arm to shake the man's hand.

"Clarence!" Brad suddenly exclaimed. He threw his arms open and gave Clarence a huge hug. "Where would I be without you, man?"

"I reckon you'd still be a human punching bag outside," Clarence drawled. "Where's that beefy secretary of yours when you really need her?"

Brad laughed—it felt good to laugh—and then he began taking stock. He had lost his briefcase in the struggle, and his arm ached where his elbow had hit the pavement. His ribs hurt, his right eye throbbed, and both eyes stung from the tear gas. He wondered if the right eye would bruise and make him look like a raccoon. His knee and hip, however, hurt the most. He noticed a small tear on the knee of his pants and a slight trickle of blood. He was beaten and bruised, but worse, he couldn't remember landing a single good punch.

As the adrenaline began to wear off and pain surfaced in its place, the voices in the hallway became distant. Clarence and the others swirled around him. Nausea. Vertigo. Brad looked down at his trembling hands, tried to steady himself, and decided to find the men's room. He staggered down the hallway, refusing assistance, one hand steadying him along the wall. He made it into one of the stalls, bent over the toilet, and hurled his breakfast.

A few minutes later, he heard the door open and the sound of heavy steps on the tile floor.

"The ladies sent me in to check on ya. How're ya doin'?" Clarence asked.

"Never better," Brad gasped between heaves.

◁▷

Judge Cynthia Baker-Kline stared impassively at Brad Carson in her chambers as he recounted his ordeal.

"I need a one-day continuance, Your Honor. After what happened this morning, I just need a little time. Look," he said as he showed the judge his ripped pants. "Plus they took my briefcase, which has my notes for my examination of the next witness."

Baker-Kline removed her glasses and rubbed her eyes. She was suddenly weary. *This can't be happening. What is it with this guy? Always the martyr.* She would have to tread carefully here.

"I'm sorry you were assaulted," she began. Her face betrayed no emotion. "If you need medical help, let's get you to the hospital." She paused for a beat and sucked in a huge breath. "But if not, I'm not inclined to delay the trial. They'll just be back in greater force tomorrow if they know they can disrupt these proceedings, and we've already got the jury here. We can't let the protesters run our trial schedule."

Brad Carson stared at his feet and shook his head.

She could feel the sympathy in the room. Even Strobel didn't look happy. Silence descended on her chambers.

Leslie finally broke the quiet. "You've got to be kidding," she said incredulously. "This man almost got killed outside, the police had to use tear gas to control the mob, and you're not going to give us one lousy day to get his notes back together?"

Just what I need. Brad Carson in a skirt.

"Don't take this out on me, young lady," Baker-Kline scolded, now standing behind her desk. "I'm sorry you went through a gauntlet out there, but maybe if the lawyers in this room would keep their mouths shut—" she realized her voice had crescendoed, and she stopped to catch her breath and soften her tone—"if they would not be so vitriolic when the media start asking questions, we wouldn't have such a circus out there."

"This is ridiculous," Leslie muttered under her breath.

"Do you have something to say?" Baker-Kline shot back.

"Not to you."

"Then you'd better keep your mouth shut, or you'll be reading about this case from jail." Judge Baker-Kline stared Leslie down for a moment as the words echoed in her chambers. Leslie stared back, refusing to divert her eyes and give Baker-Kline a psychological victory. Finally, the judge looked at Brad, released a huge sigh, and sat back down in her chair. She took a few deep breaths, and some of the tension seeped from the room.

"Look, I know this is not easy for anyone," she said at last. "So here's what I'm going to do. I'll give you the morning off to get checked out and to get a change of clothes. We'll reconvene at 1 p.m. I'll keep the jury waiting in the jury room until then. I don't want to send them out past that mob." She paused and took a reading of the lawyers in the room. "Is that acceptable, Mr. Carson?"

"If we can't get a full day's continuance, then I'd rather start this morning," Brad said stubbornly.

284 || DIRECTED VERDICT

Baker-Kline snorted. *Whatever!* "All right then. Have it your way. Court will reconvene in fifteen minutes. Let the record reflect that I offered Mr. Carson a continuance until this afternoon and he refused."

"And let the record reflect that I object," Brad added.

The judge bolted up out of her chair and surveyed the room. "You are dismissed," she said. She leaned forward, unsmiling and impassive, on her desk as Brad, Leslie, the court reporter, and Strobel filed out of her chambers.

It was not easy being a federal court judge. But even in chaotic times like this morning, some principles were intransigent, unchanging, and sure.

Justice delayed is justice denied, she reminded herself as she slipped on her black robe and prepared to enter her fiefdom. Things in the street might border on anarchy, but in Courtroom No. 1, Judge Cynthia Baker-Kline maintained order with an iron fist.

◁▷

If he was surprised, he didn't show it. When he heard his name called as the next witness, Ahmed Aberijan stood up tall and straight and absolutely sauntered to the witness stand. He proudly took his seat and glared at Brad with cold, dark eyes. A translator stood next to him.

"Raise your right hand and repeat after me," the court clerk said. The translator spoke. Ahmed did not move his hand. He spoke back to the translator in Arabic.

"He cannot take the oath," the translator said, "for religious reasons."

Ichabod seemed irritated, but she had undoubtedly confronted this before. "Just ask him if he promises to tell the truth," she instructed the translator. "Tell him it's not an oath. But also tell him that if he does not tell the truth, he will be guilty of perjury and face a possible fine or jail time."

After speaking to Ahmed, the translator turned back to Ichabod. "He understands," he assured the judge. "And he wishes me to thank this court for not forcing an oath."

Brad rolled his eyes and took his place behind the podium, shielding the small tear in his slacks. Nikki had told him there was a dark shadow forming around his right eye and suggested he turn a little more to the left so the jury would notice it. Brad ignored her advice and stood squarely facing Ahmed. He had no notes or papers at the podium with him. He felt vulnerable and exposed, nearly naked, the weapons of his cross-examination lost somewhere on Granby Street.

He began his questions more confidently than he felt. "We can dispense with the pretense that you don't understand English, can't we, Mr. Aberijan? Isn't it true that you speak English very well?" Brad asked sharply.

The translator did his work and issued his reply. "This is not true. I do not understand more than a few words of your language."

"Do you remember when you were personally served with this lawsuit by my paralegal, Ms. Moreno, at the law firm of Kilgore & Strobel?"

"Yes, I remember very well," came back the translated reply.

"And isn't it a fact, Mr. Aberijan, that you threatened her in English? that you said to her, after she served you with the suit papers: 'You will pay'?"

After the translator finished, Ahmed looked perplexed. He gave a lengthy reply that the translator interpreted in segments.

"No, this is not a fact. Your paralegal, this Miss Moreno, she comes running at me at the law firm like she will attack me. Mr. Strobel is running behind her because she has entered his offices illegally. I think maybe she carries a gun. She throws the papers at me and is arrested for her unlawful conduct. I speak to her in Arabic saying, 'What is the meaning of this?' I do not give her any threats or say anything in English."

As Ahmed answered, Brad kicked himself. *Never ask a question that allows the witness to give a narrative response. Never ask a question you don't know the answer to. Establish rhythm. Keep him off-balance. C'mon, Carson. It's Lawyering 101.* He took a deep breath.

"I noticed you refused to take an oath because of religious reasons. True?"

"This is true," the translator said after an exchange with Ahmed.

"And you believe this court should not require you to take an oath. Correct?"

"This is also true," the translator affirmed.

"In fact, if the court had tried to make you take an oath on the Christian Bible, you would have refused to do that because of religious reasons. Correct?"

"Objection," Strobel said, standing. "This is irrelevant."

"I will link it up if the court allows me a few more questions," Brad promised.

"You're on a short leash, Counselor," Ichabod warned. "Go ahead."

The translator spoke to Ahmed. "Yes, that is right."

"And the basis on which a person like you can refuse to take an oath in an American court, if the oath violates your religious beliefs, is because we have freedom of religion based on the U.S. Constitution and the UN Declaration of Human Rights. Correct?"

"How can he possibly know that?" Strobel jumped up and asked. "He's not a lawyer."

"Is that an objection?" Ichabod asked.

"Yes."

"Sustained."

Though the words had not been translated, the smug look on Aberijan's face deepened. Brad's goal in this examination was to wipe it off.

"Well, Mr. Aberijan," Brad continued, "you are an officer of the law and of the courts in Saudi Arabia. Correct?"

"Yes, that is true," the translator answered.

"And in Saudi Arabia, the court procedures and laws are based on Islamic law, and no one can refuse to follow them even if they have different religious beliefs. Is that true?"

The question and answer were translated.

"Yes, Mr. Carson. Our people are an Islamic people. Our laws and our procedures follow the Koran and honor Allah. When foreign citizens like Mrs. Reed come to our country, they know that they must follow our customs and our laws to live in our country."

"Is your country a member of the United Nations?" Brad asked. It was hard to get a rhythm with this guy. The translator interpreted the questions and answers slowly, giving Ahmed plenty of time to phrase his answers.

"Yes."

"And your country has signed the UN Charter and the UN Universal Declaration of Human Rights. Correct?"

"Yes, we have."

"Are you aware that Article 18 of the Declaration states as follows—" Brad reached down and took a copy of the exhibit from Leslie. Fortunately, Leslie had kept a copy of this one critical document in her briefcase—"'Everyone has freedom of thought, conscience and religion; this right includes freedom to change his religion or belief, and freedom, either alone or in community with others and in public or private, to manifest his religion or belief in teaching, practice, worship and observance'?"

The article was translated in bits and pieces to Ahmed. He thought for a moment, recognizing the precariousness of his position, and apparently decided that ignorance would be bliss.

"I am not aware of the exact language, no."

Brad looked incredulous. He hoped the jury was watching.

"You mean to tell me that you are the head of the Muttawa, the religious police in Saudi Arabia responsible for enforcing laws that govern religious activities and worship in your country, and you are not familiar with the language from the UN Charter that your country signed?"

The heads on the jury swung from Brad to Ahmed during the translation. Their faces were skeptical.

"This Charter is not what governs my work in our country. Our laws require our citizens to follow Islamic law and practice. The United Nations is not sovereign in my country; the government of the Kingdom of Saudi Arabia is sovereign."

"In Saudi Arabia, does a Muslim have the freedom mentioned in Article 18 to change his religious beliefs and become a Christian?"

"No," was the translated reply.

"Does a Christian in Saudi Arabia have the freedom mentioned in Article 18 to practice his religious beliefs, if that practice includes seeking converts?"

"No."

"And isn't it true that if someone tries to convert from Islam to Christianity in your country, they can be punished with death?" Brad picked up the volume, the pace, and the intensity of his words.

"Objection," Strobel inserted. Brad knew the old warrior was just trying to disrupt his rhythm.

"Based on what?" Ichabod asked.

"Relevancy," Strobel explained. A typical answer when lawyers don't know what else to say.

Ichabod smirked. "Nonsense. Overruled. Mr. Carson is asking about the very law Mr. Aberijan enforces."

Brad was surprised and energized by her ruling. Could it be that Ichabod was finally starting to support his cause? He would push it and find out, but first he waited for Aberijan's reply.

"Yes," Aberijan admitted through his translator. "We are an Islamic country founded on Islamic laws. Conversion to another religion is blasphemous of Allah and punishable with death."

"And you yourself, Mr. Aberijan, have presided over numerous public beheadings of those whose only crime was to follow another religion. True?" Brad rocked forward as he spoke, his tone and face registering his total condemnation, his disgust for the man sitting before him. The man with the smug little smile.

"Objection," Strobel said. "This is ridiculous. Prior actions of this man are not relevant. We are here today only with regard to what happened between Mr. Aberijan and the Reeds, not with regard to the alleged punishment of others who violated Saudi law in the past."

"I agree," Ichabod snarled. "Mr. Carson, that question is improper. Ladies and gentlemen of the jury, you will ignore the question and any implications associated with it. You must completely erase it from your mind. Whatever Mr. Aberijan did or did not do in the past is not relevant here. You are to judge only his conduct on the night in question."

So much for Ichabod's changing her mind.

The jurors nodded their agreement with Ichabod's instructions, but their eyes betrayed a growing distrust for Ahmed. Brad decided to drive the point home.

"And it's the job of your agency, the Muttawa, to enforce these laws that require death for any Muslim converting to Judaism or Christianity or Buddhism or—"

"Objection!"

"Mr. Carson," Ichabod interrupted, almost simultaneously with Strobel's objection, "move away from this line of questioning and get to the facts of this case *now*." Her telltale vein became noticeable.

"Judge, I believe we have a right to show that the laws of this man's country permit executions for religious reasons, and that this man has himself executed offenders in the past and would not hesitate to do so with regard to Dr. Reed, even without the formality of a trial and conviction."

Brad had lit the fuse, and the Ichabod bomb responded. "Dismiss the jury," she ordered.

The jury stood and filed out. Some members quietly glanced over their shoulders at Brad, offering support with their eyes. It was all the encouragement Brad needed to face the fuming Ichabod.

For the next five minutes, Brad endured a tongue-lashing that made him wish someone would throw him back to the demonstrators. Ichabod's adjectives for his conduct included everything from *unethical* to *childish*. Her threats ranged from contempt to reporting his conduct to the state bar to ensuring that he would never practice law in federal court again. Her speech was punctuated with "yes, ma'ams" from Brad and an occasional "sorry, Your

Honor." He sounded contrite and fell all over himself to apologize. He took his licks, content in the knowledge that while Ichabod screamed, the jury sat in the conference room and contemplated the likelihood that, as part of his job, Ahmed had killed previously in the name of religion and would probably do so again.

The Ichabod storm eventually fizzled out with no major damage to Brad's wallet and no jail sentence. Brad considered himself a lucky man. Ichabod called the jury back into the courtroom.

◁▷

The drama created by Ichabod's wrath and the showdown between Brad and Ahmed caused all eyes to focus on these actors at center stage of the theater of the courtroom. For that reason, no one but Leslie seemed to notice when two well-dressed, middle-aged men with thin briefcases entered through the back door and squeezed into the seats on the first row just behind the barefooted Nikki.

Nikki whispered something to the men, but Leslie could not hear her words. One shook his head. "Not yet," Leslie saw him mouth to Nikki, who turned back with a frown. Leslie could not catch her eye.

The men turned their attention to Brad's cross-examination. Leslie pretended to be equally focused, but she kept watch on the men—and Nikki.

◁▷

Brad shifted his weight, wincing at the pain that stabbed his knee, and reached for his reading glasses from his suit-coat pocket. Gone. Lost in the ruckus that morning. With or without his glasses to gnaw on, he decided to attack the issue of whether Ahmed had been acting as an agent of the government of Saudi Arabia when he visited the Reeds' apartment.

"Who was paying your salary on the night in question?"

"The government of Saudi Arabia." Brad could see the wheels turning in Ahmed's head as he tried to anticipate where Brad was going.

"And who paid the salary of the other members of the Muttawa?"

"The government of Saudi Arabia."

"And who owned the squad cars that transported you to the scene?"

"The government of Saudi Arabia." A light of recognition dawned in Ahmed's eyes. That smug, tight-lipped smile, however, never changed.

"You do admit, do you not, that a stun gun was used that night on Dr. Reed?"

"Yes, a stun gun was necessary to subdue him. He was violent and out of control, probably because of the drugs he had taken."

"Who owned the stun gun?"

"One of my officers."

"No. I mean, who provided all the equipment—the handcuffs, the stun guns—all the things you used as an officer of the law."

Ahmed hesitated after the translation. "They are provided by the government of Saudi Arabia."

"You, sir, were there to enforce a law of the Kingdom of Saudi Arabia in your capacity as head of the Muttawa, the religious police of Saudi Arabia. You were paid by Saudi Arabia, equipped by Saudi Arabia, and authorized by Saudi Arabia. Isn't it true you were acting as an agent of Saudi Arabia at the time of this arrest?"

For Brad and, he hoped, for the jurors, the answer was obvious. He didn't really care what Ahmed said in response. The power was in asking the question.

Still Ahmed appeared unfazed.

"I was acting as an agent of Saudi Arabia to enforce its laws," the translator explained. "And as long as I and the other officers acted lawfully, we were within our authority. And we did nothing wrong. But if any officers had done what your client suggests, if any officers had tortured the Reeds or planted drugs or killed Dr. Reed or Mrs. Reed, those officers would have been outside their authority and no longer acting lawfully on behalf of the Kingdom. Our highest-ranking officials have made it clear that they will not tolerate any kind of police misconduct."

"Did anyone from Saudi Arabia ever investigate your conduct on the night in question?"

"Of course," was the reply. "We were investigated by many."

"Did any government official ever discipline you, reprimand you, or in any way tell you that they disapproved of your conduct?"

"No, because we did nothing wrong."

"Charles Reed died!" Brad blurted out. "And you have the audacity to say you did nothing wrong?" Brad was livid at Ahmed's cool and calculating manner on the stand. The smug little act of this unflappable sadist was getting under his skin.

The translator gave Brad a puzzled look. "Could you use a different word than 'audacity'?" he asked innocently. "I do not think I can translate that word."

Juror number four snickered.

"Withdraw the question," Brad snapped. "Why did you raid the Reed's apartment on a Friday evening?"

"We were informed they would be having a meeting of their church and drug operation at that time."

"Were they?"

"No, the other members of the drug ring were not present. We believe someone inside the church found out about our plans."

"And therefore when you arrived on Friday night, the only persons home were the Reeds. Correct?"

"Yes."

"Then answer me this," Brad said. "If someone informed the Reeds that you were coming, and they canceled a meeting of the church, why would the Reeds inject cocaine before you came, knowing that they would just be arrested and thrown into jail?"

"Objection," Strobel announced. "He can't possibly answer that question without being a mind reader."

"That's precisely the problem," Brad answered before Ichabod could rule. "Nobody could possibly answer that question, because no logical answer exists. I'll withdraw the question at this time."

It was one of many unanswered questions from Brad's seven-hour cross-examination of Ahmed Aberijan that would later haunt the jury.

At 5 p.m., Ahmed dodged his last question, and Ichabod dismissed court for the day. The two well-dressed gentlemen and Nikki exchanged some notes and a handshake. Clarence reappeared at Brad's elbow and escorted all the lawyers and litigants out a well-concealed side exit, away from the volatile demonstrators on Granby Street.

◁▷

Brad had been practicing law for twelve years and had never endured a day remotely like this. He had been roughed up by demonstrators, chewed out by the judge, and forced to conduct the biggest cross-examination of his life while wearing torn clothes and without the benefit of his notes or his beloved reading glasses. As Leslie drove back to the office and the sun inched lower in the sky, Brad felt the adrenaline and energy leave his body. The boisterous voices of the women, who were making fun of Ahmed's evasive answers, faded into the background and morphed into Brad's dreams. By the time they reached the parking lot, he was fast asleep.

They didn't move him or wake him as they softly closed the car doors and cracked the windows. Leslie would handle the medical doctors and nurses who would testify tomorrow. The least they could do was allow Brad a few hours of well-earned sleep. So, while the rest of the team prepared for court on Tuesday, and while commentators around the world critiqued the day's events, the man who had been at the vortex snored soundly, sprawled out in the front seat of his Jeep in a Virginia Beach parking lot. For an hour and a half, he enjoyed dreams of captivated jurors and endured nightmares of outraged judges. And for an hour and a half, the world turned without the help of Brad Carson.

34

TUESDAY PROVIDED a much-needed respite in the trial's intensity level. The demonstrators discovered that the National Guard and Norfolk's finest were serious about arresting anyone who disturbed the peace again, a fact that had a calming effect on all but the most radical elements. Ichabod had no more to say about the paucity of Brad's evidence, giving the demonstrators one less reason to get their blood in a boil. All in all, Tuesday was just another day in court.

Leslie handled the witnesses while Brad sat at the counsel table and nursed his shiner. The doctors at the base hospital who treated Charles Reed marched to the stand and swore under oath that the stress, the cocaine, and a weak heart combined to take the missionary's life. They testified that Reed exhibited none of the classic signs of habitual cocaine use. On cross-examination, they endured attacks on their integrity, consistency, and credibility. They left the stand bowed but unbroken, tarnished by Strobel's subtle implication that the doctors sought someone else to blame for their own failed medical treatment.

◁▷

That evening, Barnes chewed on the stub of a fine Cuban cigar while he waited for Strobel to invite him into the firm's luxurious conference room. He decided not to light the cigar at this particular moment. He had other ways of knocking the socks off these prissy big-firm lawyers without destroying the uneasy peace he now shared with Strobel.

"This is Mr. Frederick Barnes," Strobel explained, introducing Barnes to the three men sprawled around the conference room table. "He is an eminently qualified private investigator and consultant hired by Mr. Aberijan. At our last meeting, Win suggested we engage someone to tail each juror.

I hired Mr. Barnes to conduct the surveillance, and well, I'll let him tell you what he found."

Barnes took a seat, tucked the cigar stub into a corner of his mouth, and cleared his throat. He looked into the expectant faces around him and savored his moment in the spotlight.

"We found some of the usual stuff you might expect on a case of this magnitude. Jurors reading the newspaper when they think no one else sees them, that type of thing. One juror even went to a Barnes & Noble and bought a book on Saudi Arabia. But none of this provided much to hang our hat on until we got a break with juror number four, Zeke Stein."

The faces around the table remained blank, but Barnes knew he had them. Lawyers liked nothing better than a little intrigue on the jury.

"Mr. Stein met with an unidentified man on three separate occasions in three different public places during the first few weeks of trial. At the third meeting, Stein accepted an envelope from this guy. We had a hunch that maybe Stein was getting paid off, so my men conducted a thorough search of his house the next day. We found the envelope in the bottom of a sock drawer. There was ten thousand in cash stuffed in it. If we check his bank account, we're liable to find a lot more."

Barnes could read the worry and delight that mingled on the faces. An illegal search! A corrupt juror! Bribery! Blackmail! These men were silk-stocking lawyers, not used to playing at this level of corruption.

Barnes reached into his pocket and threw a series of photos on the table. Zeke Stein sat on a park bench shoulder-to-shoulder with a man. Barnes's favorite shot showed Stein accepting an envelope, clearly visible, from the other man.

"So what's our next step?" Strobel asked his partners. "How do we play this out?"

"We go straight to the court," Teddy answered without delay. "You get your mistrial, and this juror serves time. I don't see anything to discuss."

From the looks on the other faces, it was clear that they thought there were several matters to discuss. But nobody wanted to be the first to tell Teddy.

Finally, when it was obvious the others would just sit there, Barnes spoke up. "What do you plan to tell the judge?" he asked Teddy. "That you hired a PI who saw two men meet and then broke into the house of a juror and found a bunch of money stashed in an envelope? Assuming my guys would be willing to say that and risk going to jail, which they wouldn't, there's still one small problem. We don't have the money, and it would be our word against Stein's."

"How do you explain the fact that you're surveilling the jurors?" Melvin Phillips queried.

"And how do you know Ichabod won't just dismiss Stein and replace him with one of the alternates?" Win asked.

Barnes kept an eye on Strobel as the questions flew.

"Wait a minute," Mack said, with the kind of authority that demanded everyone's attention. "Juror number four is the one juror who's giving us all kinds of positive body language. If there's one guy on the panel who we've got, it's him. How do we know that one of Ahmed's own men is not paying him?"

The carefully phrased question shielded a more pointed question that Mack had decided not to ask his partners. Barnes and Mack were the only ones in the room who had been part of the jury selection process in the courtroom, the only ones who knew juror four was only on the panel because Ahmed had insisted they select him.

Mack's eyes narrowed and caught Barnes's as he waited for the answer. They were accusatory eyes, and they were telling Barnes that Mack wanted no part of this sinister plot.

"We don't know who's paying Stein," Barnes said with a straight face, "but I think the court will assume that if you're the ones bringing this to the court's attention, then you must not be the ones doing the bribing."

"What are you suggesting?" Strobel asked.

"I say we wait until deliberations begin," Barnes schemed. "That way the judge will have to declare a mistrial because a tainted juror has participated in the deliberative process."

Strobel looked at Mackenzie and raised an eyebrow.

"In a few more days, I'll provide you with an anonymous tip, complete with photographs, alleging that Stein is getting paid off," Barnes continued. "That will give me time to check his bank accounts." He noticed surprised looks. "Don't ask how. You take the photos to the court and ask her to authorize a search of Stein's house and a subpoena for his bank records. You'll have your mistrial, and this guy will be on his way to the pen."

Strobel was shaking his head. "I don't like sitting on this information. This ought to be brought to the court's attention immediately."

"We can't prove anything yet," Barnes insisted. "We don't have any legally permissible evidence to show this guy accepted any money. We've got to have a little time to build the case, and coincidentally, I'll deliver my evidence to you a few hours after the deliberations begin."

Teddy had been making faces that grew more contorted as the conversation progressed. Finally, he said, "I don't like it, but I really don't see that we've got any choice. Mack, you know my style; I would never advocate hiding anything from the court. But we've got to have something more solid before we go to Judge Baker-Kline."

"I don't like it either," Strobel grumbled. "It's one thing to follow the jurors around and obtain evidence to justify a mistrial. It's another thing altogether to engineer a mistrial ourselves."

"Relax," Barnes snorted. "You aren't engineering anything. We'll just follow our boy Stein around and see what we come up with. Look, we're not the ones giving or receiving bribes. We're just trying to catch this man in a way that benefits our case." He chewed on his cigar and spat a small piece on the conference room floor. "What're you guys feeling so guilty about?"

Barnes had presented them with a storybook ending. He was sure they would accept it, even if it meant they had to get their hands a little dirty.

"All right," Strobel said as he broke the long silence. "But as soon as you get solid evidence you bring it to me—whether the jury has begun deliberating or not. Now, let's get back to work."

Barnes allowed himself a cocky grin, cigar and all. He was buoyed not by what Strobel said, but by what Strobel didn't say. For whatever reason, Strobel had apparently decided to keep to himself the fact that Ahmed had demanded juror number four stay on the jury. This implicit pact of silence was all that Barnes could ask for.

"Why do I always feel like I need to shower after I meet with you?" Mack asked in a whisper as he showed Barnes to the door.

◁ ▷

In less than a week, Hanif's promise that his brother would have the last word with Ahmed had evolved into a widespread rumor that Rasheed himself was plotting an assassination attempt. The news reached Ahmed on Tuesday night.

"Increase surveillance on Berjein," the director of the Muttawa ordered. "Wire his phones and follow him day and night. If he makes any attempts to contact Carson or any of his associates, including Sa'id el Khamin, let me know immediately. I will personally fly back to Riyadh and deal with him. If he makes any attempt to leave the country, terminate him."

◁▷

On Wednesday, Brad ended his case with a whimper. Dr. Calvin Drake, an economist, testified about the value of Charles Reed's life. He talked about the lost income and the lost services to Sarah and the kids. He tried to put a dollar value on the emotional suffering, but Ichabod wouldn't let him. The jury was as well qualified to decide that issue as the distinguished economist, Ichabod said, and therefore did not need his expert help. Brad kept Drake on the stand for less than an hour as he talked about the loss of earnings potential, present value calculations, and inflationary factors.

Although the eyes of most jurors glazed over after only a few minutes, Brad felt they would generally believe Drake because he sounded like he knew so much about the Byzantine world of economics and because he had an elaborate graph to support every one of his opinions. The bottom line, according to Drake, was that the missionary pastor could have earned a nice round one million dollars over the rest of his working years if his life had not been cut short by the events of this case.

Strobel's associate performed a nifty cross-examination of Drake, poking holes in both his math and underlying assumptions. None of the jurors appeared interested. The situation was helped neither by the economist's monotone and soothing voice nor by the fact that the courtroom seemed noticeably warmer than usual. Brad managed to stay awake by analyzing the body language of the jurors with Leslie. Nikki stayed alert by sending e-mails via her PDA, which she had managed to sneak into the courtroom. Bella made lists of things she should be doing at the office, although she had insisted on coming to court this morning so she could be there when Brad concluded the case.

By the end of Drake's testimony, three of the jurors had fallen asleep, their heads bobbing erratically on rubberized necks. This sideshow was sufficiently interesting to keep the other jurors awake and snickering at their compatriots. The end result was that Drake's cross-examination was heard in its entirety by only four of seven jurors and by both alternates, although Brad doubted any could have passed a pop quiz on a single thing that Drake had said.

After Drake stepped down, Brad stayed true to his earlier determination to save his expert toxicologist, Nancy Shelhorse, for a rebuttal witness. When Dr. Drake's uninspiring testimony was complete, Brad shocked the world and awakened the three slumbering jurors by proudly announcing, "Plaintiff rests, Your Honor."

"You what?" Ichabod asked, making no effort to hide her surprise.

"The plaintiff rests," he repeated.

Strobel stood immediately. "Then I have a motion to make, Your Honor," he announced, loud enough for everyone in the courtroom to hear it, "and it may take a fair amount of time to argue it."

Brad knew Strobel was referring to a motion for a directed verdict. He would ask the court to throw out the case based on insufficient evidence. It was a routine motion, typically made by a defendant whenever the plaintiff rested her case. In most cases, it would be routinely denied.

But Ichabod sat up straight, apparently energized by the thought.

Out of the corner of his eye, Brad caught Leslie's "I told you so" look.

"I believe Mr. Strobel's motion merits serious consideration," Judge Baker-Kline said. "Accordingly, we will take a ten-minute recess and then use the rest of the morning to argue the motion. The jury will be reconvened, if necessary, after lunch."

With that short speech, Ichabod turned the dull events of the morning into high drama. As soon as she left the bench, the courtroom erupted. Reporters used their cell phones, spectators chattered, and the lawyers headed to the hallway to plot strategy.

◁▷

As she walked down the aisle with the rest of Brad's team, she noticed that Ahmed Aberijan lingered behind at his own counsel table, engrossed in writing a note. She had been looking for this type of opportunity all morning, so she headed back to her own counsel table and wrote a quick note of her own, anxious to deliver the message before the chance passed. She would have to hurry before the team missed her.

She finished the short message, folded the paper, and placed it under a deposition transcript. As she turned to walk out of the courtroom, she dropped the folded paper onto the table directly in front of Ahmed. Before he could unfold it, she was halfway down the aisle heading out the back door.

◁ ▷

Ahmed looked around to see if anyone had seen the subtle exchange. He opened the paper and quickly read it.

> *Our case is finished, and Shelhorse did not testify. It's time to pay. I'll expect the money and the signed trust agreement by the end of the day tomorrow. The price for the verdict is still two million.*

Ahmed jammed the note into his pocket and stroked his beard. He thought for a few minutes, then took out a fresh sheet of paper and scribbled his reply. He needed to make the words vague so they would not be incriminatory if they ended up in the wrong hands, but the message must be clear. He settled on two simple sentences: *I choose to wait until the pending motion is resolved and rebuttal witnesses are called. If necessary, we will proceed at that time.*

◁ ▷

Ten minutes later she followed the rest of Brad's team back down the aisle and toward the counsel table. Her mind raced with thoughts of the upcoming argument, her note to Ahmed, the implied threat from Ichabod to dismiss the case. Where would her little scheme be then?

For his part, Ahmed was already seated at the defense counsel table, looking away from her and talking to the interpreter. He acted like he didn't have a care in the world.

Halfway down the aisle, she felt a tug at her elbow. She turned and encountered the squat face of a man who had been with Ahmed every day of the trial, either a bodyguard or some type of private investigator.

"You dropped this," he said, stooping to retrieve an envelope from the floor.

As he handed it to her, she was too stunned to think or talk or do anything except take the envelope, fire off a reproving look, and hustle to her seat.

They had contacted her in the middle of the courtroom! In broad daylight! Within spitting distance of Brad Carson and within plain sight of her colleagues.

She slumped in her chair and stared at Ahmed's back, willing him to look so she could scold him with her eyes. When he didn't, she sat up and hunched over a document, slipping the envelope open in front of her. Ahmed's cryptic note was not the answer she expected. Things were spinning out of control.

Until she had the escrow agreement with a hundred million tucked away in a Swiss bank account, the only thing keeping her alive was the promise that she could keep Shelhorse from testifying and sway juror number six in the deliberations. These were no small matters, but she was also smart enough to realize that if Ichabod granted the motion for a directed verdict, Ahmed would no longer need her services. She would be expendable. A liability. She reviewed again the plans she had made for such a contingency and waited for Ichabod to return to the bench.

She took one last look at Ahmed, who suddenly turned and stared back. Narrow eyes. Lasers drilling through her. The smirk was gone.

Ahmed was all business.

◁▷

When court resumed, Strobel was ready. Before starting his argument, he handed the judge and Brad a copy of a forty-five-page brief setting forth the reasons why Ichabod should dismiss the jury and enter a directed verdict for the defendant.

For nearly an hour he argued his case, referring the court to the appropriate passages in his brief and supplementing his written submission with a passionate oral plea.

Ichabod listened intently and asked no questions.

Brad sank in his seat. He had not expected the motion to be taken so seriously. The blow could be fatal. So much for his chauvinistic gut. He could not look either Leslie or Nikki in the eye.

Brad and Leslie took turns responding to Strobel's undeniably strong submission. Unlike Strobel, they had no written brief to give the court. Unlike Strobel, they did not experience Ichabod's silence. She peppered them with questions, interruptions, and sneers. She thought out loud about every reason that would justify dismissing the case and sending everyone home.

But at the end of their argument, Ichabod simply postponed her decision.

"Counsel," she announced, "this motion has strong merit, and the cases cited in Mr. Strobel's brief appear to be on point. Nevertheless, I want to act cautiously as I make my decision. Accordingly, we will recess for the rest of the day so that I can do my own research. Mr. Carson, I would have been better prepared for this motion, but I didn't realize your case would end quite so abruptly. I will be prepared to announce my decision tomorrow morning."

Ichabod stood to leave the courtroom.

"All rise," the court clerk demanded.

◁ ▷

Before leaving, Judge Baker-Kline stole a quick glance at a worried Brad Carson, who looked pale, tired, and beaten. *This will teach him,* she said to herself.

35

JUDGE BAKER-KLINE ENJOYED THE THEATER of the courtroom, particularly when she took center stage. On Thursday, she entered her packed court with her robe flowing behind her and a legal pad tucked under her arm. All eyes followed her as she took her seat and prepared to announce her ruling. She paused to look over the top of her glasses at Brad Carson and his team. His eyes were sad and bloodshot, deep wrinkles creasing his forehead. She had made him sweat it out; now she would do what she had intended to do all along.

"I have before me a defense motion for a directed verdict. By his motion, Mr. Strobel is requesting that I dismiss the jury and direct a verdict in favor of both the individual defendant, Mr. Aberijan, and the codefendant, the nation of Saudi Arabia. In considering this motion, the standard is clear. To grant the motion I must find that no reasonable jury could find in favor of the plaintiff on this evidence."

She hesitated for effect. And she looked down at the lawyers, who held their collective breath. She locked on to Win Mackenzie, seated directly behind Ahmed. He was ready for the payoff. She could see it in his eyes.

"I am *not* prepared to say that a reasonable jury could not find in favor of Sarah Reed against Mr. Aberijan. On the contrary, a jury could easily find the testimony of Sarah Reed, Dr. Rydell, and other plaintiff's witnesses to be credible testimony in providing evidence that Mr. Aberijan at the very least injected both Sarah Reed and her husband with cocaine in order to justify an arrest. A reasonable jury could very well conclude that an overdose of cocaine was a contributing factor in the death of Charles Reed. A reasonable jury could believe Sarah Reed when she testified that Mr. Aberijan, in essence, ordered his men to rape her. And a reasonable jury could believe that the only reason the rape did not happen is because Sarah Reed resisted so violently that she was knocked unconscious before this heinous act could occur. In short, Counsel, I am denying the motion insofar as it pertains to Mr. Aberijan."

Sarah, Brad, Leslie, and Nikki let out a collective sigh of relief. The sad, long face of Brad broke into a small smile.

Baker-Kline, however, was not finished. "With regard to the codefendant, the nation of Saudi Arabia, I find this to be a much more difficult call. Frankly, I have listened to day after day of testimony and have yet to hear anything that convinces me that the nation of Saudi Arabia authorized Mr. Aberijan's conduct either before or after the night in question. I still have some doubts as to whether Mr. Aberijan even did the awful things he is accused of doing. But I have no doubt that if higher-ups in the Saudi government were aware of such conduct, they would have ended it immediately."

She glanced up from her papers again, catching a hopeful look from Mackenzie.

"Nevertheless, the appellate courts caution us against granting directed-verdict motions without hearing the entire case. I am not sure if anything would change my mind on this matter, but I will reserve my judgment until I hear all the evidence from both sides. I am therefore denying Mr. Strobel's motion at this time, but I am also issuing a very strong warning to plaintiff's counsel that I am not yet convinced that the plaintiff should recover even one dollar from Saudi Arabia.

"You may bring the jury into the courtroom, and we will hear Mr. Strobel's case."

◁▷

Carson and his associates had dodged a bullet. He and Leslie smiled broadly. He took her hand under the table and squeezed it.

Nikki, who was sitting at the far end of the table, couldn't resist responding more verbally. "Yes!" she whispered loud enough for everyone in the first three rows to hear. Sarah looked toward the ceiling and mouthed a silent thank-you.

The celebration was short-lived. Within minutes, Strobel called his first witness, and it was time for Sarah and her lawyers to face the best defense that money could buy.

◁▷

For the first two days of his case, Strobel trotted out character witnesses who vouched for Ahmed Aberijan's credibility. These witnesses seemed to come out of the woodwork, and all swore that Ahmed was a devout Muslim who would rather die than lie. Each was prepared to give specific examples of his fairness and truthfulness, but each was prohibited by the federal rules and Judge Baker-Kline from doing so. Although the process was cumbersome and the testimony became bogged down in translation, the cumulative effect was still strong.

Friday afternoon, just before court adjourned for the weekend, Strobel dimmed the lights and played the videotaped testimony of the former church members.

The jury leaned forward and listened raptly as Tariq Abdul testified that he and his wife had been members of the Reed's drug operation. They heard Tariq describe the volatile temper of Charles Reed and the strong-arm tactics the Reeds used to get Muslim children to convert to Christianity. They heard Tariq describe the drug use by the Reeds and other members of the church. And they saw the token cross-examination conducted by the timid Sa'id el Khamin.

All afternoon the jurors kept their eyes glued to the portable television screen. And during the fifth videotaped deposition, the jury seemed especially intrigued by the cross-examination conducted by Brad Carson. Some jurors even wrote down the final few questions and answers.

"Did you ever smoke crack cocaine, or did you ever see the Reeds smoke crack cocaine?"

"Sometimes."

"Sometimes what? Sometimes you smoked crack, or sometimes the Reeds did, or both?"

"Sometimes the Reeds did. They tried to get me to do it, but I wouldn't."

"Explain the process of how they would prepare the crack and then smoke it."

There was a long pause and a slow, calculated answer. "Because I wouldn't join them in smoking crack, I never actually saw them do it. I know they did smoke crack because I saw them heating the cocaine and preparing the crack."

"How did they heat it? How hot?"

Another pause was followed by another evasive answer. "It is a complicated process that I cannot describe. I believe temperatures would be very hot—more than 250 degrees."

"One final question. When you snorted cocaine, how long did it take before you felt the rush, and how long did it last?"

"I would get a huge rush right away, and I wouldn't come down for hours."

"That's exactly what I thought. No further questions," Brad said as the tape faded to black.

Strobel was apparently not content to let the jury think about the cross-examination of Omar Khartoum all weekend. He asked if they could at least begin the videotape of Rasheed Berjein.

"How long is his testimony?" the judge asked.

"Less than two hours," Strobel promised.

Baker-Kline deliberated for a moment. Her reputation as a no-nonsense, workaholic judge was on the line. In a high-profile case like this one, her work habits could reach legendary status if she played her cards right.

"Mr. Strobel, I will not only let you start his videotaped testimony tonight, but I will also require that you play that testimony in its entirety. This type of firsthand testimony is too important to break up."

Several jurors crossed their arms and scowled. Before long, however, the testimony of Rasheed transfixed them.

The jury watched unblinking as Rasheed handled every question Brad threw at him. You could almost feel the momentum in the case shifting ever so slightly with every condemning word Rasheed spoke. After a fast-paced ninety minutes, the screen again faded to black.

Judge Baker-Kline decided to punish the jurors for their sulking about the late working hours and at the same time impress the world with the speed of the "rocket docket." And so, at 6:30 on Friday night, she announced that court would begin Monday promptly at 8 a.m. and conclude no earlier than 6 p.m. In fact, the judge said, the entire week would proceed in that fashion, and she expected Strobel to rest his case by the next weekend. She saw no reason why they could not have closing arguments a week from Monday, thus allowing the jury to begin deliberations later that same day.

It was not a matter open for debate, and it was a good thing. Many of the jurors looked like they were ready to revolt at the first opportunity. By judicial fiat, Baker-Kline had kept everyone late and thrown day care arrangements and other weekend plans into chaos, thus imposing a great burden on the only people in the courtroom who were not being well paid for showing up.

36

THE WEEKEND FLEW BY, leaving Brad and Leslie no time to focus on each other. Instead, they worked with Nikki and Bella around the clock to prepare for a full week of Strobel's hired guns—the expert witnesses. They knew that Strobel would not disappoint.

Mack Strobel started bright and early Monday morning with the medical experts. His first witness, who was sworn in promptly at 8 a.m., was a world-class toxicologist. For two hours he wowed the jury with charts and videos, educated them about the effects of cocaine use, and described the toxicological testing for the drug. In a polite way, the witness said that Dr. Jeffrey Rydell was either lying or misinformed about his toxicological analysis. There was no way, according to this expert witness, to tell from the lab data whether the cocaine in the blood had been injected, snorted, or smoked.

Brad and Leslie had already decided on the theme for their cross-examination, and Leslie wasted no time in getting to the point.

"Doctor, what is your hourly rate for this testimony?"

"I am not charging for my testimony. But I do bill my services as an expert at $350 per hour."

Leslie looked at the jury and saw eyes popping out. They each received twenty dollars a day in jury pay.

"And you also charge a premium when you testify, don't you, Doctor? Tell the jury what that number is."

"Four hundred per hour."

Leslie thought she heard one of the jurors let out a soft whistle.

"And you also have a minimum charge per day, don't you? In other words, whether you work five hours a day or not, if you pick up the file and travel on a case, your client pays you two thousand dollars for that day. Correct?"

"Yes, that's right."

Leslie shook her head almost imperceptibly, emitted a nearly silent "wow," then started in on the rest of the expert's testimony. For the next hour or so, she chipped away at his foundation, bit by bit, piece by piece. She concluded by asking for an estimate of the total amount he had billed Kilgore & Strobel to date.

"About twenty-three thousand dollars," the expert replied.

"And one last thing, Doctor," Leslie said as she returned to her counsel table and turned around. It was a move she had seen Brad do many times. "You never actually treated either Charles or Sarah Reed, like Dr. Jeffrey Rydell did. Correct? I mean, your opinions are based on a cold and impersonal review of the records."

"That's right," the expert responded.

Leslie harrumphed and sat down. She stared impassively ahead as the expert stepped down. Under the table she softly slapped Brad's palm.

Strobel followed his toxicologist with a well-paid and well-known cardio-vascular surgeon. This expert testified in detail about all the weaknesses of Charles Reed's heart caused by advanced hardening of the arteries. He told the jury that other issues probably impacted Charles Reed's poor health, including extended use of cocaine. He further opined that Charles Reed would have died on the night in question from a heart attack, with or without the cocaine in his body. In laymen's terms, it was a bad heart, not cocaine, that killed Charles Reed.

To nobody's surprise, the cardiologist hauled down more for his testimony than the toxicologist. And to nobody's surprise, Brad Carson explored all the details of his compensation on cross-examination. This expert actually charged five hundred dollars per hour for his time, and he reminded Brad that he could make more if he stayed in surgery and didn't mess with the lawyers. Brad got the man to admit that he had billed Strobel a total of forty-five thousand dollars to date and, like the toxicologist, charged a minimum per-day fee. Brad acted surprised to discover that the cardiologist did not bill a premium for time spent in court. Just before returning to his seat, Brad suggested that the witness might want to add that little trick for his next case. The jury laughed, and from the looks on their faces, they did not appreciate Ichabod's prompt and stern lecture on courtroom decorum.

The parade of highly paid experts continued for two days. An expert in international human rights praised the Saudis' continuing improvement in the area of religious freedom. He charged only $250 per hour and clearly had a thing or two to learn from the doctors.

An expert in police tactics testified that Ahmed and his gang did everything by the book in dealing with the drug-crazed conduct of Charles and Sarah Reed. He was Strobel's best bargain, charging only $150 per hour, but he made up in volume what he lacked in price. Even Leslie was stunned to learn that he had managed to bill Strobel more than fifty thousand dollars for services to date.

Experts in intergovernmental relationships testified that the Saudis had already been held accountable for their conduct as a result of the scathing report issued by the Senate Foreign Affairs Committee. These experts were in the middle range, billing around $250 per hour. By the time their cross-examinations were completed, however, it was clear that if Strobel gave them a dime, he gave them too much.

◁▷

While Brad and Leslie grilled the expert witnesses, Nikki was en route to Saudi Arabia. If successful, she would help Rasheed and Mobara gain political asylum through the U.S. Embassy, and she would have Rasheed prepared to take the stand as a rebuttal witness the following Monday. Brad believed Strobel might finish his case on Friday morning. Brad's own toxicologist, Dr. Nancy Shelhorse, would be called as a rebuttal witness and take the remainder of the day on Friday. It was critical, Brad told Nikki, that Rasheed and Mobara not arrive in the United States any earlier than necessary in order to maximize the element of surprise and thwart any attempts by Ahmed to intimidate or coerce the Berjeins.

Brad and Nikki carefully prepared the documents requesting political asylum, explaining the circumstances of the *Reed* case and documenting the threats against Rasheed and Mobara if they testified truthfully. Upon her arrival in Saudi Arabia, Nikki would also obtain, from Sa'id el Khamin, a videotape through which Sa'id outlined the circumstances of the case and the reasons why political asylum would be appropriate for the young couple.

Nikki flew out of Washington late Wednesday evening. She would meet Sa'id Thursday to prepare the final details of the application and take Rasheed and Mobara to the embassy late on Friday afternoon. If all went according to plan, Nikki and the Berjeins would leave Riyadh together late Friday night and be on American soil by early Saturday morning.

◁ ▷

The Moreno girl has left the country.

Ahmed read Barnes's note during the experts' testimony. Within twelve hours, he was headed for Saudi Arabia in his private jet. Something was afoot with the Berjeins. If they attempted to help the plaintiffs, Ahmed would personally preside over their executions, even if it meant he had to miss two days of expert witness testimony to do it.

◁ ▷

Nikki's first meeting with Sa'id transpired right on schedule. By late Thursday morning, Riyadh time, they had finalized the asylum petition. Rasheed and Mobara would join them at Sa'id's office the next day at five o'clock, and they would all head to the Embassy together. Sa'id was confident the petition would be granted.

Late Thursday night, Nikki went to a pay phone in the hotel lobby and phoned Bella to inquire about the trial.

"Brad told you not to use the phones," Bella chided her. "O'Malley says they might be tapped."

"Don't worry about it."

"Well, use your BlackBerry next time. O'Malley tells me those doohickeys are as good as a phone, even over there. They're safer anyway."

"Takes too long," Nikki said. "And besides, I can't get reception here."

"Is everything all right with Rasheed and Mobara?" Nikki heard concern in Bella's voice. An unauthorized phone call usually didn't portend good news.

"Everything's on schedule," Nikki assured her. "How's the trial going?"

"I ate lunch with Brad and Sarah, but I've been at the office since. They said it was more of the same. One high-paid expert after another. Strobel apparently told Ichabod that he would finish tomorrow morning. We'll put Shelhorse on as a rebuttal witness tomorrow afternoon and then Rasheed on Monday."

"Any chance that Ichabod will hold court on Saturday?"

"She hasn't mentioned it, and I think she would make a lot of jurors upset if she did. We're safe betting on Monday."

"With Ichabod you never know. Is Brad sure he can stretch Shelhorse out through the entire afternoon on Friday? I mean, if he gets done early, we would have to rest our case without putting on Rasheed."

"Don't worry, Nikki. Brad said he's got six hours of questions for Shelhorse if he needs 'em." Bella was starting to sound defensive.

Nikki had what she needed. "Give my best to Brad and Leslie," she said.

"Okay. Be careful, Nikki."

"Right. Careful's my middle name."

Nikki hung up and looked at her watch. It was now 10:30 on Thursday night in Riyadh. She was eight hours ahead of Norfolk time. She checked her notes and phone numbers. The timing would be critical. And the timing would be tight. Everything would have to work just as she had planned.

◁▷

O'Malley had planted his own bugs in the phones at Carson & Associates on Wednesday night while he supposedly swept the office for bugs. He monitored the calls all day Thursday. He took his cue from the phone call between Nikki and Bella.

He stopped by Carson & Associates a few minutes later. He greeted Bella and began his rounds, letting her know he would be checking each phone. When he was finished, he declared the office clean and told Bella that he had a few hours to kill. He talked her into going to court with him to watch some of the afternoon testimony. Anything she had to do at the office, he assured her, could wait.

They rode to court together, and for a few minutes they enjoyed watching Brad get after another one of Strobel's expert witnesses. But suddenly O'Malley remembered that he was running late for an appointment. Bella assured him she could get a ride back to the office with the trial team at the end of the day.

◁▷

Dr. Nancy Shelhorse enjoyed her work as an expert witness. Toxicology, her daily work, could be dry stuff. The same could not be said of serving as an expert in a high-profile case. And the pay wasn't bad, either.

Shelhorse had once heard a lawyer describe a perfect expert witness as a glib person with a résumé and a suitcase. She qualified on all three counts. Shelhorse was a natural teacher, serving as an adjunct at the University of Richmond Medical School and teaching clinical courses to residents. She also had the credentials. She was experienced and board certified, and she had published enough peer-reviewed articles to bring down several trees. And in this case, like so many others, she was testifying outside the Richmond area, where she lived and practiced medicine. For some strange reason, lawyers and juries seemed to believe that nobody could be an expert unless they traveled great distances to testify or at the very least were not one of the "locals."

She was not just qualified; she was also prepared. The prior night she had driven two hours to Norfolk so she could spend another night rehearsing her testimony with Brad and Leslie. They had run through several mock cross-examinations, but the lawyers couldn't put a dent in her testimony. Brad finally declared her bulletproof and sent her back to Richmond. She planned to return again tomorrow—Friday morning—and wait in the hallway outside the courtroom until she was called to testify. She was looking forward to it; she had so much to say.

For that reason, the message she received at the hospital at 3:30 on Thursday afternoon was both a disappointment and a surprise. Her assistant said someone from Brad Carson's office had called and indicated they might not need her to testify after all. According to the caller, she should check her e-mail as soon as possible, where she would find a full explanation.

Anxious to know what was happening, and knowing it would take thirty minutes to get from the hospital to her office, Shelhorse asked her assistant to log on and retrieve any messages from Carson & Associates.

"Here's what it says, Doctor: 'We are truly sorry for the short notice and the change in plans, but the trial has taken some interesting twists this afternoon. As a result, we will not need your testimony. In fact, we believe the defendants will try to contact you and somehow subpoena you and force you to testify. This would be very damaging to our case.

"'You have done nothing wrong. But this is a complicated and unexpected occurrence that could greatly work to our advantage so long as you cannot be found or forced to take the stand. Accordingly, we will pay for your full day tomorrow at your customary hourly rate, but we would ask that you find a secluded place for all of tomorrow and Saturday, do not tell ANYONE where you are going, and do not communicate with anyone until Saturday night.

"'We can assure you that there is no subpoena for you to testify as a witness at this time. But please do not attempt to contact us after you receive this message. If Mr. Strobel is granted a court subpoena for your appearance, and you call us, we would be forced to disclose your whereabouts. I know that this is an extraordinary request, and we would not make it if it were not absolutely necessary. Thanks for your understanding. We will be in a position to explain fully our strategic reason for doing this when we call you on Sunday.'

"And then at the bottom, there's a note that says 'From the Handheld BlackBerry Device of Nikki Moreno, Legal Assistant, Carson & Associates.'"

Shelhorse was shocked. It took her a minute to gather her thoughts.

"Are you still there?" her assistant asked.

"Does this make sense to you?" Shelhorse responded.

"Not really. But I don't understand how trials work very well, either."

"When was the message received?"

"The header says 2:47 this afternoon."

Shelhorse thought about the implications. She was insulted to think that the defendants somehow thought they could now turn her testimony to their own advantage. She saw her moment in the spotlight slipping away, her escape from monotony closing off, her expected career boost imploding.

"I can't believe Strobel would have issued a subpoena for my appearance already. I'm calling Carson."

Shelhorse pushed the End Call button on her cell phone and dialed the number for Carson & Associates. She heard the recorded and dreary voice of Bella give her the extensions of the various staff members. Shelhorse pushed the numbers for Brad Carson. His voice mail told her how important her call was to him and asked if she would leave a message.

"Brad, this is Nancy Shelhorse. What in the world is going on with regard to my testimony tomorrow? Call me back on my cell as soon as you get a chance. If I don't hear from you, I'll just assume Strobel has issued a subpoena for my appearance, and I'll lie low as you suggested on Friday and Saturday."

Shelhorse hung up the phone and shook her head in disgust. "Lawyers," she mumbled with heartfelt disdain.

◁▷

O'Malley's appointment took him straight back to the offices of Carson & Associates. He parked himself at the receptionist's desk and patiently monitored the phone numbers that registered on the switchboard every time an outside call came in. He also periodically checked everyone's e-mail and voice mail.

At 3:38 the phone rang. The receptionist's screen reflected a Richmond originating number. O'Malley listened intently as he heard Brad Carson's phone ring on an internal line. The call had been transferred.

He waited a few minutes, then logged on to Brad's voice mail using the passwords Bella had provided him weeks ago. He listened to the message from Shelhorse, deleted it, and left the offices of Carson & Associates, locking the door behind him.

37

NIKKI MORENO'S WAKE-UP CALL came bright and early, just a few minutes before noon. She mumbled her thanks to the operator without enthusiasm and slid lower under the sheets. Slowly, room 703 came into focus, and she began to review the challenges of the next twelve hours. She forced herself out of bed, one leg at a time, and shuffled over to the sliding glass door that led to her balcony.

Her head throbbed, and her stomach was in knots. Her mouth was dry as cotton, her nose stuffed up—she basically felt like scum. She looked down at the dresser and cursed last night's bottle of scotch that was the source of this morning's pain. She had been lonely and wired last night, unable to sleep. To comfort and calm herself, she had allowed herself a few too many shots from the bottle that had made the transatlantic trip in her garment bag. If her first trip to Saudi Arabia had taught her anything, it was that she would have to bring her own booze to this parched country or go without.

This morning—or was it this afternoon already?—she wished she had gone without.

Nikki took her time showering and primping, as if slow movements would calm her stomach and stop the pounding in her head. Today she would be as inconspicuous as a tattooed Latino could be in Saudi Arabia. She wore no makeup and threw on the hated abayya that Sa'id had given her on the first trip. She could not possibly wear the head covering in the heat, but she would try her best not to be noticed. She would not carry a briefcase. She would not look men in the eye when she talked. In fact, she would avoid talking whenever possible. She would focus on her plan and nothing else.

◁▷

At 9 a.m. in Norfolk, Bella hit the panic button.

Shelhorse was nowhere to be found.

She was supposed to meet them in the hallway outside the courtroom at 7:30. But she was late. Experts were always late. That part irritated Bella but did not panic her. But now Shelhorse was beyond late. Something serious was wrong. And Bella was frantic.

Brad had been at it for more than an hour and was running out of cross-examination questions for Strobel's last witness. While pretending to listen to an answer, he scribbled a note and handed it to Bella. *I can make this last till ten, no more. Go find Shelhorse.*

Bella hustled into the hallway and repeated her earlier series of phone calls. She called Shelhorse's office and left her third urgent message of the morning. She called Shelhorse's cell phone. Another recording. Another message. No answer at the home phone. No response to the page. Bella was going crazy.

It was now 9:15. Bella stared at the pay phone. Another minute ticked by. *The firm's voice mail.* Maybe Shelhorse had an accident or some other unexpected occurrence and had left a message. Bella turned in her Day-Timer to the page containing the passwords she had given O'Malley.

She started with her own phone, then Brad's, and then Leslie's. She heard plenty of messages, including a sweet one from Leslie to Brad, but nothing pertaining to Shelhorse.

Nikki's messages, of which there were many, proved far more interesting. Bella listened with sordid amusement to the personal calls from the various men who didn't seem to know that each other existed. But it was a business call that riveted her attention. She played it back several times and wrote it down word for word.

"Ms. Moreno, this is Chad Hamilton again. We've been playing some serious telephone tag lately. And rather than continuing to trade calls, let me just give you the bottom line. One point five million. Take it or leave it."

Bella raced back into the courtroom. Brad was still methodically questioning the witness and taking increased heat from Ichabod to move his cross-examination along. When Brad saw Bella plop back down in her seat at counsel table, he gave her an expectant look. Bella frowned and shook her head no. Brad returned to his questioning, rehashing some turf he had already covered.

"No message from Dr. Shelhorse anyplace, and she doesn't answer any of her phones," Bella whispered to Leslie. "It's like the woman just dropped off the face of the earth. So I called our office to check voice mail messages. Look at this note. It was a message left on Nikki's voice mail."

"Did you go into my voice mail too?" Leslie whispered before looking at the note.

"Just read the note," Bella said, louder than she intended. Ichabod glared at her. Bella mouthed a silent sorry.

"Don't you ever go into my voice mail," Leslie warned.

"Just read the note."

As Leslie read it, she furrowed her brow. "What do you make of this?" she whispered.

"I thought you might know."

Leslie didn't. She gave Bella a blank shrug, then retreated to her thoughts while the witness droned on.

"Here's what I want you to do," Leslie whispered at last. "Go back to the office. On the way, call O'Malley and have him meet you there. Keep calling Shelhorse. If you find out anything, buzz my BlackBerry. When you get to the office, you and O'Malley go through everyone's e-mail and see if that helps. I'm not accusing Nikki of anything, but we've got a missing witness and a strange phone message."

"Okay," Bella said, frowning. "I knew we couldn't trust her."

◁▷

Nikki arrived late because she couldn't communicate with the cab driver and he didn't have the foggiest idea where he was going. Sa'id's office was not exactly center city with the top-tier firms. Nor was it in an industrial or office park where the second-tier firms were located. Instead, the one-story law office was on an out-of-the-way side street flanked on one side by a small Laundromat and on the other side by a cramped restaurant that also sold groceries in bulk—the Riyadh equivalent of a deli.

Narrow alleys separated the three bland, stucco commercial buildings. All needed repair, Sa'id's especially. The numbers on his building had long since disappeared, exacerbating the problem for the already confused cab driver.

When Nikki finally arrived at 5:20, Sa'id greeted her warmly at the front door.

◁▷

He pulled the nondescript black sedan over and parked a block away from the building. He immediately radioed the others.

"She just entered the lawyer's office," he reported. "Can't tell if she's armed."

"You may be getting some more company soon," came the reply. "Wait there."

◁ ▷

Once Nikki was inside, Sa'id introduced her to Hanif. Immediately, Nikki noticed his striking resemblance to Rasheed. Sa'id explained that Hanif wanted to ride to the embassy with them to see his brother off. Hanif, all smiles, shook Nikki's hand with unbridled enthusiasm.

Sa'id shared his building with three other tenants, all with small offices adjoined by a common hallway. Sa'id took Nikki and Hanif to his cramped office to view the videotape Sa'id had made. His prior shoddy work aside, the man had done a good job with this. Hanif split his attention between the tape and the front window of the office, where he separated the blinds with his fingers at eye level to watch for his brother.

On camera Sa'id was passionate and earnest, clearly presenting the case against his own government. Nikki was impressed that a devout Muslim would put his reputation on the line to gain religious and political freedom for a Christian couple he did not even know. Sure, so it wasn't much of a reputation. But still . . .

Despite Sa'id's roly-poly build, unkempt and gnarly beard, annoying habits, and awkward attempts at flirtation, Nikki liked the little guy. He seemed to have no God-given talents or graces, that is, aside from a sunny disposition and a huge heart. Even those traits probably weren't worth the sixteen hundred Saudi riyals per hour he was hauling down. But in the grand scheme of things, he had exceeded her expectations.

Nikki thanked Sa'id for the excellent work on the tape and watched him beam. She then tucked it inside her loathsome abayya and joined Hanif as he kept watch at the window.

◁ ▷

The Berjeins did not arrive until nearly six.

"How could you be so late?" Nikki fumed. "We're supposed to be at the embassy in ten minutes."

Sa'id tried to translate Nikki's tone as well as her words. The Berjeins looked crestfallen.

"We were being followed," Rasheed said. "We tried to lose them but couldn't. We think they are still outside."

This chilling news caused Hanif to dart back to the window for another look. Nikki leaned over his shoulder. A black sedan contained two men, who were both looking at the building. The one nearest the building was slender and evil-looking, with beady, dark eyes and a signature scar that graced his left cheek and disappeared into his beard. The other agent towered over the first and barely fit in the passenger car seat.

The Berjeins had indeed been followed. And the men out front didn't seem to care if the Berjeins knew.

They stepped away from the window, and everyone but Nikki began speaking in Arabic at once. She tried desperately to think despite the noise and confusion. She could finally stand it no more and simultaneously stamped her foot hard on the floor and screamed.

"Stop! Just shut up for a minute!" All gave her their undivided attention.

"I'll call the embassy and get the meeting postponed for a half hour," she said. She waited for Sa'id to translate.

Then she looked at Sa'id. "How far away is your house and in what direction?"

"North of the city. Forty minutes by car."

"That'll never work," she said, then paused. "Okay, here's what we're going to do."

She looked from one brother to the other and smiled at her good fortune. Rasheed, the older brother, was taller by about two inches, and about ten pounds heavier. But their similarities swallowed their differences. Same athletic builds, same prominent noses, same huge deep-set eyes underlined by large circles. The male genes in the Berjein stock were strong and distinctive.

Nikki tried to imagine Hanif with a haircut and no beard.

She looked at Rasheed, then back to Hanif one more time. "It's time to use a little misdirection," she said, "which happens to be my specialty. Sa'id, do you have a pair of scissors and a razor?"

"I have scissors, of course. We could buy a razor next door."

"Good. Hanif will shave his beard and cut his hair to look as much like Rasheed as possible. They will also change clothes. I am about the same size as Mobara. We will change clothes, and I will wear her abayya and face shawl. Hanif and I will leave the building first, disguised as Rasheed and Mobara, and drive to my hotel. Sa'id, you will leave next, taking a different route, then meet us at the hotel."

She paused again. More translation. More skeptical looks. She decided to sound more animated, act more enthusiastic. Maybe they would buy it. After all, it was the only plan she had.

"We will both watch our mirrors. Hopefully these men will follow Hanif, Sa'id, and me to the hotel. If my plan doesn't work and they don't follow us, then Rasheed and Mobara should stay put until we come back here. Sa'id, is there a rear exit in this place?"

Sa'id nodded.

"Call a cab to pick up Rasheed and Mobara back there. Tell them they should watch and see if the men out front follow us. If they do, tell Rasheed and Mobara to take the back exit and grab the cab to the embassy. Give them the videotape. Have them wait for us there."

Sa'id translated Nikki's impromptu plan for the sake of the others. They argued briefly in Arabic.

"They said it will never work," Sa'id reported.

Nikki threw her hands in the air. "Then tell them to come up with something better," she snapped.

Two minutes later, Sa'id headed next door to buy a razor.

◁▷

Nikki, dressed in Mobara's abayya, stood and admired the new clean-cut Hanif. She had him stand next to his brother. She looked from one to the other and back again. A smug smile graced her face.

"You're the spittin' image of your brother," she said to Hanif.

He gave her a puzzled look.

"Never mind," she said and turned to Sa'id.

The little guy looked more excited than ever, his eyes practically glowing with the enthusiasm of the moment. At once, Nikki felt a wave of gratitude for the man and a wave of guilt for putting his life in such danger. "You don't have to do this, you know," she found herself saying.

"I know," he replied, looking more determined than ever. "But I've never been a part of something like this before . . . something this important—" he waved his hand in an arch—"people this committed."

Nikki nodded her thanks and patted him on the side of his arm. "Give Hanif directions to the hotel and ask if he's ready."

320 || DIRECTED VERDICT

Sa'id explained the route to Hanif and told Nikki that he was indeed ready. Hanif turned and faced his brother. They blinked back the tears. They both seemed at a loss for words.

After a few beats of respectful silence, the brothers exchanged some solemn sentences in Arabic while the others looked on. Then Hanif gave his older brother a bear hug, and tears welled up in both men's eyes. They ended their embrace, and Rasheed patted Hanif on the shoulder, nodding his head with pride and looking steadfast into his brother's glistening eyes.

Without a word, Hanif turned toward Nikki, grabbed her hand, and headed out the front door.

Sa'id followed a step behind.

38

THE TWO MEN IN THE BLACK SEDAN took notice as the couple left the building and hustled into their automobile. The lawyer followed on their heels and went to his car. "Follow him," the slender man instructed his partner. "I'll call for backup to come keep an eye on Moreno." The mountain man climbed out of the sedan and raced to another car, bent over to avoid attention, keeping one eye on Sa'id.

The other man followed Hanif and Nikki and called in the situation. "Moreno is still inside. She came in a cab and should be alone now. If she leaves, call me."

Then he put a call in to Ahmed, who had been on his way to Sa'id's office. The strike would take place elsewhere now, and the best they could do was follow the prime suspects and figure out where.

◁▷

Nikki slouched low in the seat, resisting the urge to look at herself in the visor mirror. She wanted to tell Hanif he was doing great, but he wouldn't understand. She congratulated herself on the fine job she had done in cutting his hair, given the time constraints. In fact, Hanif looked handsome, in a rugged kind of way. She liked his style.

"You look good with your new do," she said.

Hanif glanced sideways at her, nodded his head in acknowledgment, and smiled.

"You don't speak English, do you?"

Hanif nodded his head again and gave her the same smile. Nikki breathed a sigh of relief.

She could see the black sedan in the sideview mirror. The driver appeared to be alone, and she hoped the other man followed Sa'id. By now, Rasheed and

Mobara should have left unnoticed out the back door, followed the alley to a side street, and hopped in a cab to the embassy. She hoped they had escaped safely. She didn't allow herself to dwell on the alternatives. Instead, she turned her thoughts toward what she and Hanif must do when they reached the hotel.

At present, she had no clue.

◁▷

By 10:05, Brad had exhausted his delay tactics and put Ichabod in a foul mood.

After the witness stepped down, Strobel proudly stood to his feet and announced: "The defense rests." He renewed his motion for a directed verdict, and the court again took it under advisement.

"Mr. Carson, do you have any rebuttal witnesses?" Ichabod asked without looking up from her writing. "And as I mentioned before, keep it brief."

Brad stood and glanced around the courtroom one more time, hoping that maybe Nancy Shelhorse had slipped in unnoticed. "Your Honor, we have two brief rebuttal witness. One is an expert witness, our toxicologist, and the other is a fact witness. Unfortunately, with Mr. Strobel's case concluding so unexpectedly, our witnesses are not yet here. Would it be possible for us to break now for the weekend and then briefly put those witnesses on the stand first thing Monday morning?"

You could tell from the looks on their faces that the jurors thought it would be a good idea. It was the first time they had had any life in their eyes all morning.

"Mr. Carson, you know the rules of this court. If your next witness is not ready, you rest your case. Madame Reporter," Ichabod said, turning to the court reporter, "let the record reflect that Mr. Carson will be calling no rebuttal witnesses."

"Wait, Your Honor," Brad blurted out. "That's not true. We do have rebuttal witnesses."

"Then where are they?" Judge Baker-Kline demanded.

"They're on their way," Brad insisted.

"And the check's in the mail," Ichabod said sarcastically. "Here's what we'll do, Counsel, and let me warn you that this is more than I usually do. It goes against my better judgment here, but I'll do it anyway. We'll take a fifteen-minute break, and if your witnesses show up, fine. If not, we'll proceed to closing statements."

"All rise," the court clerk announced. "This court stands in recess for fifteen minutes."

◁▷

"I'll kill her, Leslie. I swear. If I get my hands on her, I'll kill her."

"Bella, calm down." Leslie lifted the pay phone receiver a few inches away from her ear. "What did you find?"

"Nikki sent a message from her handheld last night telling Shelhorse not to come! Can you believe this!"

"How can you even know this, Bella, if she sent it from the handheld?"

"Because these newfangled BlackBerries automatically transmit a copy via satellite to your desk unit whenever your desk unit is hooked up to the Internet. It's there plain as day on Nikki's desk."

"There's got to be an explanation—"

"Why does everyone insist on defending this woman? First the voice mail. Some guy no one knows offers to pay her a million five. Now the e-mail deep-sixing our main expert witness. I think we've got enough to go to the cops."

"Bella, think for a minute. What if it's a setup?"

"Leslie!" Bella was screaming so loud that the reporters on the other pay phones could hear. "How can you get any more proof than a recorded voice mail and an e-mail? C'mon . . ."

"All right. But the first thing we have to do is find Shelhorse. She can confirm whether Nikki really sent her the e-mail. We've got fifteen minutes, Bella." Leslie's mind raced. She had to keep Bella calm. She had to break the news to Brad. She had to keep this fragile case from spinning out of control. "In the meantime, we can't let Nikki know we're onto her."

Leslie forced herself to speak slowly and calmly. She covered the phone and her mouth with a cupped hand so as not to be overheard. "I'll tell Brad about Nikki. And I'll call Saudi Arabia and warn both Sa'id and Rasheed not to trust her. If we're right about this, she'll just deliver them into the hands of Aberijan."

"Okay. And I'll keep trying to reach Shelhorse. But tell Brad that if I'm the first to see Nikki when she gets back into this country, he's gonna have a murder case to defend."

"Let's leave that stuff to Ahmed." Leslie forced a laugh, trying to lighten things up a little.

She received only a dial tone in response.

◁▷

Sarah watched and listened as Leslie rushed back to the courtroom to inform Brad.

"Why is Ichabod so insistent on starting closing arguments *today*?" Leslie sputtered. "You aren't ready, are you? I mean, is her beloved rocket docket so important that justice just gets steamrolled in the process?"

Brad listened without comment. "We just can't get a break," he said in resignation.

"This is so ridiculous," Leslie continued. "When the icewoman comes back on the bench, let me argue for a continuance. She can't make us start closing arguments today! She's at least got to give us the weekend to get Rasheed here . . . doesn't she?"

If Leslie's looking for encouragement from Brad right now, she's looking in the wrong place, Sarah thought.

"She's the judge. She can do whatever she wants," Brad said.

For the first time in the case, Sarah noticed a sagging of Brad's shoulders and a hanging of his head that told her the fight had gone out of him. He sat heavy in his chair, leaned back, and rubbed his face. It was the posture of confusion and defeat.

"You guys have been great," Sarah said with a soft tone of encouragement. "This will work out. You'll think of something."

"Thanks," Brad said. But his downcast face never changed expression.

"I'll get on the phones," Leslie said. She glanced down at Brad as she was leaving. "You okay?"

He nodded and slumped lower in his chair as she left the courtroom again.

Not knowing what else to do, Sarah sat beside him in his silence. He had been a great encourager throughout the case, had done more than any other lawyer could have done. He had fought the good fight. Now, if he needed someone to just sit beside him silently and watch the precious minutes tick away, that was the least she could do. She sensed that this was not a time for words.

The minutes passed, and the courtroom started filling back up. Brad sat up straighter in his chair and folded his hands on the table in front of him. He stared straight ahead, not breaking his silence. Ten minutes were gone. In five more, the judge would be back on the bench, demanding that they put up or shut up.

It was Clarence who finally got Brad to speak. The big marshal sauntered over to Brad and sat part of his haunches on the table. The oak squealed in protest.

"You don't need no rebuttal witnesses, Brad Carson. You've already opened a can of whuppin' on 'em just as it is. I'd jest dazzle 'em with one of yer fired-up closin' arguments and wait fer the money. Brad, I'm tellin' ya, them jurors is eatin' out of yer hand. Now git yer chin up before they file back in."

The simple and complete optimism of the man seemed to make an impact. After Clarence had finished, Brad looked up at the mountain sitting in front of him, forced a grin, and finally spoke.

"Thanks, Clarence. I might just do that."

Clarence gave Brad a playful punch on the arm, and Sarah noticed Brad wince. It would probably bruise. Sarah was glad the big man was on their side.

As the marshal walked away, a look of epiphany swept Brad's face. His eyes lit up, and his lips curled into an unforced smile.

"Wait a second, big guy," Brad called. "You got any big-time cocaine dealers in that jail of yours?"

◁ ▷

Ichabod glowered at him from her high bench. Brad needed another five minutes or so before Clarence would return with an inmate in tow. Getting those minutes would not be easy with the impatient Ichabod.

"Call your next witness," she demanded.

"Let me handle this," Brad whispered to Leslie. Her phone calls had been futile.

He rose and walked slowly to the podium. Very slowly. "Your Honor, may I explain the situation with my two rebuttal witnesses?" he inquired politely and deferentially.

Ichabod seemed pleased with his attitude but still emanated a "show-me" look. She leaned back in her chair, folded her arms, and sighted Brad over the end of her nose. "You may explain, Mr. Carson, so long as you don't hold out any hope that this court will entertain any excuses for witnesses being late. But if you just want to put your explanation in the record, feel free."

"Yes, ma'am," Brad replied. "I know the court wants to begin closing arguments on Monday. I would like to propose we have a brief session tomorrow, on Saturday, like we did last weekend, in order to accommodate some unavoidable problems with these two witnesses."

"I'm not inclined to make everyone in this courtroom come in on

Saturday just because you couldn't get your witnesses here on time, Mr. Carson." Ichabod paused and shook her head, as if she couldn't believe she was actually going to ask this. "Who are these witnesses, and what are their problems?"

Brad had his opening.

"The first is Dr. Nancy Shelhorse, an expert in toxicology from the University of Richmond Medical School. She will offer testimony about the toxicology results for Charles Reed and will also rebut the testimony of the former church members regarding the issues of cocaine usage. She was supposed to meet us this morning. We've been trying to contact her through cell phones, office numbers, beepers, and who knows what else. We are afraid that something serious must have happened to her on the way to court, and we request a day to investigate."

Brad didn't like the idea of announcing in open court his next rebuttal witness. But at this point he didn't have much choice.

"Our second witness is Rasheed Berjein, the same man who earlier testified in Mr. Strobel's case by videotaped deposition. Mr. Berjein is prepared to renounce his earlier testimony and state under oath that the only reason he gave such testimony is because he had been threatened by Mr. Aberijan. Mr. Berjein will further testify that there is no truth whatsoever to the allegations that Charles or Sarah Reed, or anyone else in their church, sold or used drugs."

"And why isn't he here?" Ichabod asked. Her eyes were still narrow, her arms still folded. The queen of cynicism.

"My paralegal is at this minute in Saudi Arabia helping him to obtain political asylum. We thought Dr. Shelhorse would be testifying this afternoon and Mr. Berjein would not be needed until Monday."

"Well, apparently you thought wrong," Ichabod said. "Mr. Carson, neither of these excuses is sufficient. Dr. Shelhorse should have come into town last night, and Mr. Berjein should have been brought to this country earlier. But I'm going to bend over backward to be fair to you without jeopardizing our trial schedule."

Ichabod thought for a moment, and Brad held his breath.

"I really don't have much sympathy with regard to Dr. Shelhorse," Ichabod continued. "She is a local witness and should have been managed properly. But with respect to Mr. Berjein, I can understand that political asylum can be an unpredictable process, and I'm willing to give you one more day to get him here. We will reconvene tomorrow morning at 8 a.m. If Mr. Berjein is not here by then, he will not testify. Closing arguments will commence as scheduled on Monday morning."

"Thank you, Your Honor," Brad said.

"Note my objection, Your Honor," Strobel said.

"Very well," Ichabod said. "Anything else for today?"

Leslie handed Brad a note. His eyes lit up, and he turned to see Clarence at the back door of the courtroom, squeezing the arm of a ratty-looking man in an orange jumpsuit.

"Yes, Your Honor," Brad said. "In light of the fact that Dr. Shelhorse will not be testifying, I do have one brief rebuttal witness to take her place today."

"And who is that?" Ichabod asked.

Brad turned and pointed to Clarence and his prisoner. "That man standing back there in the orange jumpsuit," Brad announced.

◁▷

Nikki barely had time to change out of the smelly abayya when she heard the knock on her hotel room door and went to the peephole. She kept the chain lock in place just in case. While she checked, Hanif hid inside a closet, ready to pounce on any intruder that might barge into the room.

She exhaled deeply when she saw the distorted and balding head of Sa'id. She unhooked the chain lock, cracked the door open, and yanked him inside.

Hanif slid back the closet door and jumped out. Sa'id grabbed his heart. His mouth was open, but no words came out. He finally managed to stammer out something in Arabic that made Hanif laugh. Still clutching his heart, Sa'id stumbled over to the king-size bed and flopped down, lying on his back.

"Were you followed?" Nikki asked, as she slid the chain lock back in place.

"Yes, but I lost him," Sa'id said. "They don't know the back streets in this city like I do."

"Good," Nikki said, encouraged by this rare piece of good news. "By now Rasheed and Mobara ought to be at the embassy. I'm going to pack my stuff up and join them." She looked around the room; her clothes and makeup were scattered everywhere.

Sa'id glanced around curiously at the mess in the room.

Nikki shrugged. "I thought I'd have some time to come back after we processed Rasheed and Mobara," she said. "Sa'id, can you give me a ride to the embassy and let Hanif know that he can go now? Tell him thanks for everything."

As Sa'id opened his mouth to reply, a blast in the hallway blew the door partway open. Only the chain lock kept it from opening completely.

"I thought you weren't followed!" Nikki yelled.

"I didn't think I was," Sa'id retorted, staring at the door in disbelief.

While Sa'id stared, Hanif reacted. He grabbed Nikki by the arm and lunged for the sliding glass door that led to the balcony on the opposite side of the room. He yanked it open and flung her out onto the concrete balcony. Another blast hit the hotel room door. This time the chain lock broke, and the door banged open against the wall.

A large concrete pillar on each side of the balcony separated it from those belonging to the adjoining rooms. A waist-high, cast-iron railing kept anyone from falling seven floors to the hard pavement of the parking lot below. In the split second available to decide, Hanif apparently decided to take an escape route that headed down.

He grabbed Nikki under both her arms and swung her over the railing. She was petrified and didn't dare move. Hanif let his strong hands slide up her arms as he lowered her quickly toward the deck of the balcony below. His hands gripped tightly around her forearms; then he swung her body slightly out away from the building and let the momentum carry her back toward the deck of the balcony. At the last second, he released her and Nikki landed shaken but unhurt on the balcony below. Hanif then swung over the railing himself, hung down as far as possible while grabbing the lowest part of the railing, and swung and jumped onto the deck next to Nikki.

After regaining his balance, he reared back and kicked with all his might, landing the heel of his shoe squarely against the sliding glass door of room 603. The door shattered, and in a heartbeat he unlocked the door and pulled Nikki inside the room. She heard a thud behind them, signaling the arrival of one of Ahmed's men on the balcony just a few steps away.

Hanif and Nikki sprinted into the hallway, slamming the door behind them. To their left, just a few short feet away, a large metal doorway led to a stairwell. To the right a long hallway led to elevators and another stairwell. Hanif pushed Nikki to the left and yelled, "I pick you up out back," as he sprinted down the hallway. Nikki stared for a split-second after him, wondering if she would ever see him again.

Stunned, she turned and ran through the door directly in front of her and into the stairwell. The metal door slammed, and she immediately felt claustrophobic, surrounded by masonry walls with no windows, trapped in a narrow stairwell with only one way out. She instinctively grabbed the handrail and took a few steps down. Then she heard it. The sound of heavy breathing in the stairwell below her, accompanied by hurried footsteps coming in her direction. The footsteps of a man, huffing as he climbed. Probably the mountain man she had seen outside Sa'id's office.

She could not go back through the steel door and into the hallway, because she might encounter the man on the sixth floor. She couldn't go down, or she would run smack into the arms of the mountain man. And so she started climbing as fast as her legs would carry her.

She went up six flights and started slowing, her legs heavy, her chest tight and heaving. The relentless sounds of the footsteps below were still coming, but they were farther away. Those hours on the StairMaster had paid off. The prey gained a few seconds on the predator.

She closed her eyes, took her chance, and ducked into the hallway of the twelfth floor. She ran halfway down the carpeted corridor, glancing over her shoulder and noticing that most of the doors on her right were open. She looked into one room as she was sprinting by and saw a maid with a cart of cleaning supplies. Nikki ran a few steps past the room, turned quickly around, and darted back into the room where the startled maid was making the bed.

"Do you speak English?" Nikki asked breathlessly, bent over with her hands on her knees, sucking wind.

The maid just lifted her hands, palms turned upward.

Nikki put her fingers to her lips, signaling the maid should be quiet. She then pulled a wad of riyals from her pocket and put them in the maid's hand. Without saying another word, Nikki climbed into the large cloth bag on the maid's cleaning cart, curled up in the bottom of the bag, and covered herself with used room linens. The maid apparently understood. Nikki could hear her humming and tucking in the sheets on the bed.

Nikki had never been so scared in her life. She lay perfectly still. The maid's humming was drowned out by the sound of Nikki's own ragged breathing and the pounding of her heart. She felt hot beads of sweat dripping down her back. She was helpless, totally at the mercy of a woman she didn't know, banking on that woman's willingness to help a stranger escape detection.

330 || DIRECTED VERDICT

Ahmed's men could enter the room at any time, and the maid needed only to nod toward the laundry bag. It would be over before Nikki even knew what had happened.

She thought about her life, all the things left undone. Her back to the wall now, all her cleverness, confidence, and guile were of no use. She didn't know what else to do as she lay there, curled up and trembling.

So she prayed.

Dear God, if You're out there, if You are as real as Sarah says You are, please help me! I know I don't deserve it, but I'm desperate, and Sarah needs me alive. Please blind these men looking for me.

Nikki thought for a moment about this next line. She had heard Sarah pray this way before, but it seemed to limit the type of God she was praying to. If the Hindus or Muslims were right, she was about to make a big mistake. But then again, if the Muslims were right, why would God rescue her anyway? After all, she was trying to help a Christian missionary.

In the name of Jesus, amen.

A few seconds later, Nikki heard a breathless male address the maid in Arabic. The woman responded, and a short discussion followed. Nikki braced herself for the sound of a gunshot, the feel of bullets ripping into her flesh.

But only silence ensued—no talking, no humming, no noise at all. Nikki thought about coming out from under the laundry. But just before she could make her move, she felt a strong hand reach through the sheets and pull her up by her arm.

Busted.

It was the smiling maid.

She was chattering in Arabic and pointing wildly in the direction she had just sent the Muttawa officer. Nikki climbed out of the laundry bag, but before she headed off in the opposite direction, she gave the maid a spontaneous hug. The maid seemed entirely unimpressed, and when Nikki released her, the maid held out her open hand for a more tangible reward. Nikki gave her another fistful of riyals, thanked her again, then headed out of the room and away from the stairwell—toward the elevators.

Nikki wondered how many members of the Muttawa still roamed the Hyatt. With any luck, only a few.

Where would I look if I were in their shoes? They last saw me climbing the stairs, heading up. They would be looking for me to escape using the stairs or climbing from balcony to balcony. No person in her right mind, fleeing for her life, would ever allow herself to be trapped in the elevators . . . so, that's exactly what I'll do. Take the elevator down to the second floor. Get below them. Then sprint down a flight of steps and into the parking lot.

Nikki's recklessness surprised even herself. She waited at the elevator door, glancing left and right, left and right, for an interminable two minutes. The car going down was empty. She jumped in and prayed some more. Amazingly, the elevator didn't stop until the second floor. When the elevator door opened, Nikki stuck her head out and quickly looked both ways. Then she ran down the hall and sprinted down the stairs, surprised not to see any of the Muttawa along the way. She slipped out the side door and into the parking lot.

As soon as she exited the building, she heard an engine turn over and, seconds later, saw a car swerving toward her. Hanif! She jumped in, glancing behind her. He gunned the engine and squealed the tires as he exited the parking lot.

"Thanks," Nikki gasped as they sped away.

"Any time. You still like my do?" he asked in stilted English.

"I thought you didn't speak English," she said sheepishly. "But the answer is yes."

She leaned her throbbing head back against the headrest and counted her blessings. They would soon be at the embassy, hopefully without further incident. "Thanks, God," she said under her breath.

She wondered what happened to Sa'id.

◁▷

Sa'id looked pathetic as Ahmed and the mountain man rejoined a dark-eyed Muttawa officer who kept watch in room 703. The trembling Saudi lawyer lay on the floor next to the king-size bed, his hands cuffed behind his back. The officer kicked Sa'id and commanded him to stand when Ahmed entered the room. He obeyed immediately but kept his gaze downward, not daring to look Ahmed in the eye.

"Take the handcuffs off," Ahmed demanded.

The man with the dark eyes and scar removed the slender manacles.

Ahmed walked over to Sa'id, towering over him. Sa'id, only five-nine when he stood straight, hunched forward in humility. Ahmed, nearly six inches taller to begin with, grabbed Sa'id's right hand and pushed the hand down toward the right forearm, nearly bending Sa'id's pudgy wrist in half.

Sa'id whimpered at first, then let out a bloodcurdling scream. "What do you want?" he cried in Arabic as Ahmed increased the pressure.

"Where did Rasheed and Mobara go? What happened to the American?" Ahmed hissed. He pushed harder on the wrist, forcing Sa'id to kneel in pain.

This was his moment of truth, left at the mercy of a man who showed no mercy. Whether he lied or told the truth, Sa'id sensed he was drawing his last few breaths. Rasheed, Mobara, and Nikki would need all the time possible to make the embassy, gain asylum, and leave the country. Every minute could be the difference between their survival or their capture. The truth might cost them dearly. But a lie would betray his country and his god. He had but a moment to think.

Like Nikki had done a few minutes earlier, Sa'id prayed quickly and silently. Another desperate prayer, but this one asked Allah for forgiveness.

"They are driving to Dhahran," Sa'id gasped, struggling for breath in spite of the pain. "Rasheed and Mobara . . . just left." His voice quickened, sharp words through the pain as the pressure on his wrist increased. "They are heading back to my office to pick up Moreno and will drive to Dhahran. They knew you would go to the Riyadh airport. . . . They will leave through Dhahran. . . . They already have visas."

◁▷

Ahmed squeezed on the wrist with all his might until he heard the pleasing sound of breaking bone. He released it, and the wrist hung limp. Sa'id whelped and collapsed on the floor, holding his broken wrist gingerly with his other hand. As Sa'id moaned, Ahmed withdrew his gun and pointed it at the attorney's forehead.

"Beg, you dog," he ordered. Sa'id was of no further use.

"In the name of Allah, please! I will help you catch them! Please, sir! Spare my life!" Sa'id struggled to his knees, holding his wrist in his left palm, begging for mercy and looking desperately at Ahmed.

"I said beg!" Ahmed yelled.

Sa'id fell on his face at Ahmed's feet, groveling and pleading for his life. When he had heard enough, Ahmed reached down and grabbed Sa'id under his chin. He pulled the man's head upward so he could enjoy the terror in Sa'id's eyes. With his free hand, Ahmed calmly placed his gun against the small man's forehead, smiled, and pulled the trigger.

"Clean this place up and write a report. Make it self-defense," Ahmed said to the man with the scar and the dark eyes. "I want the Dhahran airport crawling with officers. And send a few to Riyadh just in case, though I don't think this worm had the guts to lie."

Ahmed turned to leave the hotel room but first stopped in the bathroom to wash the blood from his hands.

39

THE PRISONER IN THE ORANGE JUMPSUIT took his time getting to the stand. He moved slowly because his ankles were chained together, and he clanged when he walked. Though manacled, the young man still managed to swagger. He strutted his youth, his dreadlocks, his multiple tattoos, and a five-day growth of curly stubble.

When he finally took the stand, he slouched in his seat, put his chin in his hand, and scowled.

"State your name for the record," Brad said as he took his place behind the podium, giving the convict a wary look. He was beginning to wonder if this was such a good idea.

"Othello Biggs," came the muffled reply. "They call me Shakespeare."

Brad couldn't tell whether the man was kidding, so he played it straight.

"Mr. Biggs, do you know why you're here?"

"Huh-uh."

"Mr. Biggs, this is a civil case. My client is Sarah Reed, this lady seated at counsel table to my right." Brad motioned toward Sarah, but Shakespeare didn't bother to look.

"So what?" he glowered.

"We have sued the defendants because we say the police in Saudi Arabia wrongfully arrested Mrs. Reed and her husband. We say they tortured the Reeds and ultimately killed Mr. Reed. So basically, this is a case where we are trying to prove police misconduct."

Shakespeare scowled at the defense lawyers. He had probably been the victim of police misconduct a few times himself. Brad could sense a little softening as Shakespeare turned back to him.

"The police say the Reeds were actually running a drug ring and selling cocaine and marijuana," Brad continued. "We say the Reeds were missionaries, just having a little church."

Shakespeare laughed out loud at that one.

"Very creative," he scoffed.

Strobel rose. "Does Mr. Carson have any *questions* for this witness, or does he plan to tell him about this case for the rest of the day?"

"I'm providing some context, Your Honor," Brad explained. "It won't take much longer."

"It better not," Ichabod warned. Brad took that as a cue to continue.

"We've heard testimony about the use of cocaine, a subject that I understand you might know something about. I want to show you some of that testimony and see if what they said is true."

As Brad spoke, Leslie prepared to cue the tape of Omar Khartoum's testimony.

"But first, I've got to establish your experience in this area. Mr. Biggs, how many times have you been arrested for drug use?"

"State or federal?" he asked proudly.

"Both," Brad clarified.

"I been arrested 'bout ten, twenty times. I only done time three times, 'cludin' this one."

"Mr. Biggs, you'll have to sit up straight and speak into the microphone," Ichabod scolded.

Biggs didn't move.

"How many of those were cocaine arrests?" Brad asked.

"Most of 'em."

"Have you ever been convicted of selling cocaine?"

"I said I did time. Somethin' 'bout that you don't understand?" Biggs's scowl told Brad they had spent enough time on his arrest record.

"Just a few more questions about experience," Brad said, treading lightly. "For how many years have you been involved with cocaine use?"

"Since I was thirteen," he said.

"And how old are you now?"

"Twenty-two."

"Do you have experience with smoking crack cocaine as well as snorting cocaine?"

Shakespeare snorted as if that were the dumbest question he'd ever heard. "'Course."

Brad signaled Leslie to begin the tape, and everyone watched a few minutes of the cross-examination. Khartoum was shown tasting the cocaine. Then Brad asked Khartoum, "How did you know it was fake from tasting it? How is this substance different from the real cocaine you've tasted?"

"The substance is sweeter," was the translated reply on the tape.

"Is that how you tell whether a substance is cocaine? You see how sweet it is?" Brad asked on the tape.

"Yes," was Khartoum's reply.

Brad hit the Pause button. "Is he right about the way cocaine tastes?" asked Brad.

"That fool's lyin'," Shakespeare said disdainfully, apparently happy to catch another witness in a lie. "He ain't never tasted rock, man. You know it's real 'cause it bites. Man, it numbs yo' whole tongue and the whole inside yo' mouth if it's pure stuff. Ain't nothin' 'bout it that's sweet." He furrowed his eyes at Brad, daring the attorney to question his judgment on this matter.

Brad rolled some more tape. Khartoum demonstrated how he would snort a large pile of cocaine.

"What do you think of that?" Brad asked.

"I said he's a fool," Shakespeare said, "or he's trippin'. You use a rolled-up bill, man. You don't jus' dump it on the table and snort." Shakespeare chuckled derisively. "And, man, if you snorted that much snow, you'd be dead like that." He snapped his fingers for emphasis.

Brad rolled some more tape. Khartoum described how they would cook the cocaine to make crack, at temperatures in excess of 250 degrees. This time, when Brad shut off the tape, he didn't have time to ask a question.

"If that boy heated coke at two-fifty, he's an even bigger fool than I thought."

Strobel shot to his feet again. "Your Honor, I object to the way this witness characterizes Mr. Khartoum. This is not testifying to facts. It's character assassination."

"I agree," Ichabod said. "Sir, please limit your testimony to your own factual knowledge. Do not evaluate the testimony of Mr. Khartoum."

Shakespeare just shook his head. "He still don't know what he's talking about," he said defiantly. "I know for a fact you don't make crack by cookin' it at like two-fifty. You get it that hot, you destroy the cocaine, it turns into vapor. I done it before, man. I know."

"One more question," Brad said. "Let me show you one more segment of this tape and ask if the testimony is accurate based on your own personal experience."

Brad rolled the testimony of Khartoum as he described the rush he got from snorting cocaine. "I would get a huge rush right away," Khartoum asserted, "and I wouldn't come down for hours."

"That fool's so full of it," Shakespeare interrupted.

"Objection," Strobel shouted.

"Sit down and shut up, baldy," Shakespeare snapped.

"You close your mouth, Mr. Biggs, or I'll hold you in contempt," Ichabod shouted.

"And what?" Shakespeare asked, in a mocking tone. "Throw me in jail? Now I'm *scared*."

Ichabod chose to ignore this last comment. She could no doubt tell he was not the least bit intimidated by her judicial powers.

"Objection sustained," she ruled. "And if the witness makes one more remark like the last one, I will dismiss him from the stand and strike his testimony."

Brad worked hard to keep from smiling. The marshals were probably loving this guy. Shakespeare might get a private cell tonight.

"Is it true," Brad asked quickly, "that you get a sudden rush from snorting cocaine and that the rush lasts for several hours?"

"No way," Shakespeare said, with the authority of a man who had been there a few times. "That's why you smoke crack. Snortin' don't give you no rush for a long time, and the high don't last that long once it comes. Maybe a half hour, maybe an hour . . . max. But smoking crack, man, that's a different game. It's like—" and now Shakespeare leaned back and brushed both arms up over his body—"this incredible rush hits you right away, man." He smiled, as if reliving a high right there on the stand. Then he turned serious. "But you don't get nothin' like that jus' from snorting cocaine. Nope. I don't care what this judge and baldy are saying, that man on the tape don't know what he's talking about."

◁▷

On mile four of his run Friday evening, Brad still couldn't make sense of anything. He couldn't believe that Nikki had sold him out. The e-mail from her computer to Shelhorse bothered him most. Why would someone as savvy as Nikki leave such obvious evidence of being a traitor? It only made sense if she had already cut her deal and decided to stay outside the country. If that were the case, Brad knew he would never see Rasheed take the witness stand the next day. In fact, the man was probably already dead.

But if Nikki had already cut her deal, then why was this man named Hamilton calling and offering her one and a half million? Was Nikki somehow double-crossing Ahmed and getting paid off by some third party? But why would this Hamilton leave such an incriminating message in such a nonchalant manner on Nikki's voice mail?

Every question yielded ten more. Where was Ahmed? Could someone have broken into Nikki's office and sent a message to Shelhorse over her computer? But how would you explain the other leaks, such as the inside information about Worthington that knocked him out of the case? Could there be another traitor on the inside, a person who saw an opportunity to set up Nikki while she was out of the country? And who could that possibly be? Bella? Leslie? Sarah? O'Malley? Brad could not make himself believe, even for a passing moment, that any of these would betray him.

Time would sort out the mystery. If Nikki returned on schedule early Saturday morning, it would be hard for him to believe that she was involved. If she did not, he would know she was rich and Rasheed was dead. But who was Chad Hamilton? And why would Nikki betray Brad and Sarah?

He ran farther and faster, but he could not clear his mind this evening. He could not exorcise the demons of doubt.

40

"THIS IS STUPID," Bella whispered to nobody in particular. "She isn't coming. Let's just face it."

Brad ignored her. He could do without her negative thoughts right now.

The jury gathered in the jury room, and the lawyers sat at their respective counsel tables. Few protesters met in front of the courthouse this morning; a few seats stood empty in the gallery for the first time in days. The early morning newscasts had speculated that today Brad would announce he was resting his case. Brad noticed that Ahmed was back in the courtroom, bearing his normal scowl. 8 a.m.

Nikki and Rasheed *could* show. It was still possible. If they had gotten out of Saudi Arabia late Friday evening, they would have just enough time to make it to Norfolk by early Saturday morning. But Brad had still not heard from them, and even the eternal optimist in him had to admit that he was out of options.

"All rise!" the court clerk commanded, hushing the crowd. "Silence is now commanded while court is in session. The Honorable Judge Cynthia Baker-Kline presiding. God save this honorable court."

God save me, Brad thought.

"Please, take your seats," Ichabod said in businesslike fashion. Brad remained standing in order to address the court and request additional time. He was not relishing the task.

"Call your next witness, Mr. Carson," the judge ordered.

"Your Honor," Brad began, "our next witness was to be Rasheed Berjein. As you know, as recently as yesterday, we were trying to gain political asylum for Mr. Berjein so that he could leave Saudi Arabia and testify in this trial. He's a critical rebuttal witness. Absolutely critical. He has already testified by videotape, but he is now prepared to correct that testimony in person. We have tried unsuccessfully in the last twenty-four hours to reach either Mr. Berjein or my paralegal who went to help him in this process. Accordingly, we would respectfully ask that his testimony be postponed until Monday."

"Request denied," Ichabod said firmly. Brad slumped his shoulders and pursed his lips. The fabricated testimony of Rasheed on videotape would stand.

"But I will grant a half-hour recess, Mr. Carson. A few minutes ago, in my chambers, I received a telephone call from your paralegal. She said she had been trying to reach you by phone but could not reach you, presumably because you could not bring your cell phone into court. She said that she had just received a number of e-mail messages on some kind of handheld computer device, now that she's back in the country and within range of the cells where it works, informing her about court this morning. Ms. Moreno said she would be at the courthouse in about ten minutes. I decided to be generous and give you half an hour."

The thought crossed Brad's mind that if Ichabod truly wanted to be generous, she would have told him about this development when she first took the bench, but he was not about to complain. Nikki *was* coming. And she *was* bringing Rasheed.

"Court stands in recess for half an hour," the clerk announced. Ichabod left the bench, and all eyes turned to the doors at the back of the courtroom.

None watched more intently than Ahmed.

◁▷

Twenty minutes later Nikki burst through the doors with Rasheed in tow. Neither had slept for nearly forty-eight hours, except for a few fitful hours on the plane. Cognizant that all eyes were on her, Nikki self-consciously took inventory of her haggard appearance. She wore a pair of skintight faded jeans, an untucked blouse, and no makeup. Her normally pampered hair was oily and unkempt. She couldn't remember when she'd last brushed it. At least her Oakleys hid her bloodshot eyes—assuming Ichabod didn't make her take them off. But when she saw Brad, she forgot all about that.

Nikki ran down the aisle and threw her arms around her boss. "I love this country," she whispered. "Hope I'm not too late."

"You're right on time," he assured her.

She turned to see Rasheed and Sarah embrace. Then Sarah tilted her head back, looked Rasheed over, said a few words of Arabic, and the two embraced again. Rasheed smiled widely with a kind of stupefied grin.

Bella stood a few feet away, left out of the original round of hugs. Nikki felt so good to be back on American soil, even if it was Ichabod's courtroom, that she took a step toward Bella to embrace.

But Bella's sour expression never changed. As Nikki stepped forward, Bella brought her two arms up like pistons, landed them hard against Nikki's shoulders, and jarred Nikki backward. "You traitor," Bella sneered. "How dare you come waltzing—"

Stunned by the reaction, Nikki stood frozen for a split second. But she wasn't about to take a blow from the whale woman without retaliating. She regained her balance and lunged at Bella, fingernails searching for skin, insults flying from her lips. Brad jumped between them, grabbing Nikki before she could land any blows. Facing her, he held her back as she hurled invectives at Bella.

He eventually talked Nikki into taking a seat at the end of the counsel table farthest from Bella. She did so only after promising she would rip Bella's lungs out, one at a time, as soon as court was over.

"This is the thanks I get?" Nikki asked. "For risking my life?" She stared at Bella, as if calling her out with her gaze.

Bella, now seated, stared stoically ahead and ignored her nemesis. Leslie sat next to Nikki, strategically placing herself in the way of Nikki's challenging stare. Sarah sat next to Bella.

Brad turned and addressed the curious reporters. "Just a little family feud," he said nonchalantly.

She's history, Nikki thought, plotting her revenge. *It's just a matter of time.* Bella didn't know who she was messing with. She didn't know the half of it.

"All rise," the court clerk commanded, and everyone scampered to their seats. In the next moment Ichabod dashed into the courtroom, looking furious as ever. She stared at Nikki, who stared back from behind her shades. They were not coming off without a fight.

Ichabod apparently decided not to push the point. "Is Mr. Berjein prepared to testify?" she asked.

"Yes, Your Honor," Brad announced wearily.

And at long last, Rasheed Berjein walked proudly to the front of this American courtroom, raised his hand, took the oath, and climbed into the witness box to testify against his tormentor—Ahmed Aberijan—in the U.S. District Court for the Eastern District of Virginia.

◁▷

Sarah listened intently to Rasheed's testimony, affirming him with her eyes. Even with the necessity of translation, his testimony was spellbinding. He spoke from his heart about the history of the small Riyadh church. He testified that, on the same night that Charles Reed died, Rasheed and his wife were arrested by the Muttawa on trumped-up drug charges as well. The Muttawa threatened them and beat them, made them recant their Christian conversion, then released them.

Rasheed described the sleepless nights after denying his Christian faith, his search for forgiveness, and the rebirth of the church. Without divulging the names of any church members, he detailed the tumultuous growth of the small church and the persecution it suffered. Sarah swelled with pride at the way the church had reestablished itself and carried on. She marveled at how the Lord had preserved some seeds from the church that was persecuted and nurtured them into a whole new church reaching the lost and preaching the gospel.

The thriving church was nothing short of a miracle, and it was marvelous in her eyes.

She glanced at Bella out of the corner of her eye. Rasheed's testimony had obviously not captivated the still-seething legal secretary. Sarah picked up her pen and carefully wrote on the yellow legal pad in front of her. She slid it in front of Bella.

I don't think Nikki did it, the note read. *Why would she have come back with Rasheed if she was a mole for the Muttawa? This testimony is too damaging.*

Bella read the note and scribbled something in response. She slid it back to Sarah. *Then how do you explain the e-mail from Nikki to Shelhorse and the voice mail offering Nikki $1.5 mil?*

Sarah thought for a moment, looking at Rasheed but not really listening. A lot of things didn't make sense. She wrote a response and slid the note back to her right, even as she looked at the witness. She felt like a schoolgirl passing notes in class.

Why would Nikki write the e-mail to Shelhorse from her own computer? the note asked. *Nikki knew we would eventually speak to Shelhorse and that Shelhorse would tell us where the message came from. Why would Nikki set herself up like that?*

Out of the corner of her eye, Sarah watched Bella read the note and shrug. She didn't pick up her pen to draft a response.

Sarah sensed that Bella was softening. She grabbed the paper again and decided to appeal to Bella's new spiritual side.

The Bible tells us not to judge one another, Sarah wrote. *Especially motivations. I think you owe Nikki an apology. How will Nikki ever be drawn to Christ if she doesn't notice a change in you?*

She said a quick little prayer and slid the paper down the table again. Bella read it and hung her head. A certain sadness crept into her eyes. She stared down at the table and eventually wrote a one-word response.

Okay.

Sarah gave her a small smile and a quick squeeze of the hand. Bella didn't squeeze back, and Sarah decided not to push her luck.

◁▷

"Did there come a time," Brad asked, "when you were approached by Ms. Moreno from my firm about the possibility of testifying in this case?"

"Yes, I remember the day well," the translator replied.

"Tell me about it," Brad said.

"Ms. Moreno and a Saudi Arabian attorney, a man named Sa'id el Khamin, told me what happened to Pastor Reed and Sarah." As he talked, Rasheed frequently looked over at Sarah, seemingly drawing strength from the brave missionary.

"I talked with your Ms. Moreno and agreed to give testimony in this case," the translator continued as Rasheed spoke. "We met in their car because Ms. Moreno believed my apartment was—how to say—others were listening to my phones. Your Ms. Moreno said I should be ready for a visit from the Muttawa as soon as Ms. Moreno and Mr. el Khamin leave. So we agree on a plan."

"What was that plan?"

"That day, I give your Ms. Moreno a written statement—how do you say it?—I swear is true . . ."

"An affidavit?" Brad offered.

"Yes, that is it," came back the translated reply. "Then Ms. Moreno says I will be asked to give my story before the trial in something called . . ." Rasheed could not find the word; the translator waited.

"A deposition?" Brad volunteered.

"Yes. So Ms. Moreno and myself agreed that I would say whatever the Muttawa wanted me to say in the deposition. They had my wife—"

The translator waited on the visibly shaken Rasheed. The memory of his wife's life hanging on his every word seemed to unnerve him anew. He shook on the stand, his lip quivering, staring at his hands, unable to speak.

The silence became uncomfortable, and Ichabod intervened. "Would the witness like to take a break?" she asked the translator.

The offer was translated, but Rasheed shook his head. "He just wants to get it over," the translator said.

After another awkward pause and a glance at Sarah for reassurance, Rasheed continued.

"They, the Muttawa, were listening to the deposition in another room with my wife—"

"Objection," Strobel called out, causing the witness to start and lean back in his chair, wide-eyed. "This is classic hearsay."

"Sustained," Ichabod said without enthusiasm. "Tell him to state only what happened and not what he heard from others," she instructed the translator.

Seeing the look of confusion on the translator's face, Brad intervened. "Did you tell the truth in your deposition?" Brad asked through the interpreter.

"No."

"Why not?"

"Because I had been threatened—"

"Objection . . . hearsay," an exasperated Strobel said.

"It's not offered for the truth of the matter asserted, Your Honor," Brad explained. "It's offered only to show motivation."

This bit of verbal hocus-pocus seemed to satisfy Ichabod. "I'll allow it," she ruled. "But, ladies and gentlemen of the jury, the alleged threats made against Rasheed should be considered only for the purpose of deciding whether he had a motivation to lie in his deposition. You should not concern yourself as to whether the threats were in fact true. Do you understand?"

Of course they didn't. But the jurors nodded their heads as if they understood perfectly, anxious to hear all about these threats.

"I was told that if I did not testify and say that Pastor and Sarah Reed, and even myself, used drugs, I would never again see my wife alive. But Ms. Moreno and myself, even in our first meeting, had already thought about this possibility and agreed on two signals. The first signal was for this jury." Rasheed turned and faced the members of the jury. "We agreed that Mr. Carson would ask a question a certain way and I would answer a certain way in order to show you, as the jury, that I was lying just to survive."

The slightest smile creased Rasheed's face, a smile of pride as he explained his clever little plot. Strobel rose to object but could apparently think of nothing to say. Without uttering a word, he sat back down.

"What was the question and answer?" Brad asked.

"You asked me to look you in the eye and tell you that I had not been threatened by the Muttawa. I was to answer but stare down at the table, to show the jury that I could not look you in the eye and say my testimony was true. This is universal language, Mr. Carson. Can you look someone in the eyes and tell them it is the truth? If not, it is a lie. This was my signal to this jury. I was telling them, by that signal, my deposition testimony was a lie."

Brad was sure the jurors had not forgotten the last question of Rasheed's deposition. The camera had focused on the top of his head as the picture faded to black.

"And what was the second signal?" Brad asked.

"The next day after the deposition, I was to go to a pay telephone and call Ms. Moreno. If I was still ready to give up my homeland, my church, my family, and my friends, if I was still ready to seek political safety in the United States and testify in this trial, then I was to tell Ms. Moreno 'everything is fine' in Arabic. I taught her that phrase during her first visit because we knew we would have no interpreter. If I was not willing to be involved any further, I was to tell her 'I must stay' in Arabic."

"Did you call Ms. Moreno, and, if so, what did you say?"

"I am here," Rasheed replied, "and it has not been easy. I called her and told her 'everything is fine.'"

41

LESLIE LISTENED TO Rasheed's testimony and, out of the corner of her eye, watched Nikki. Nikki was leaning forward, hanging on every word that came out of the witness's mouth, looking every inch a supporter of the witness. She did not bear the posture of a woman who had tried to sell out her own trial team.

Leslie leaned to her left, put an arm around the back of Nikki's chair, and whispered in her ear.

"Who is Chad Hamilton?" she whispered.

"Who wants to know?" Nikki whispered, shaded eyes still on the witness.

"I do," Leslie said, her mouth close to Nikki's ear. "Bella found a voice mail message on your office phone where this guy Chad Hamilton offered you one point five million."

"Bella's a pig," Nikki said with conviction, louder than a whisper, still looking straight ahead.

"Nikki, there's the voice mail message from Chad Hamilton, and there's also an e-mail message sent from your BlackBerry telling Dr. Shelhorse not to come and testify. And Shelhorse didn't show." Nikki took off her sunglasses and gave Leslie a dumbfounded look. "Who is Chad Hamilton?" Leslie asked again.

"Is that why Bella attacked me?" Nikki whispered through gritted teeth. "Does Bella think I'm some kind of spy for Aberijan?"

Leslie nodded her head.

"I barely escaped from Aberijan with my life." The color was rising on the back of Nikki's neck, and she shot a wicked glance at Bella.

"So who is Chad Hamilton?" Leslie whispered. It still made no sense.

"He's the insurance adjuster for the Johnson case," Nikki said. "Brad doesn't know it, but I'm negotiating an awesome settlement for Mr. Johnson.

Brad and Bella—heck, even the client—told me to settle for $550,000. I ignored 'em. And now it sounds like I'm going to get almost three times that. We'll make half a million in legal fees."

This bit of news rocked Leslie back in her chair. "Then who wrote the e-mail message on your computer to Dr. Shelhorse?" Leslie asked.

"Probably Bella," Nikki said, making no effort to whisper.

"Shhh," Leslie whispered.

"Probably Bella. Who else is in our office during the day while you and Brad are in court?"

Leslie did not respond. There was so much to process. Most of what Nikki said made perfect sense, except for one small item.

How did Nikki know the e-mail to Shelhorse had been sent while court was in session?

◁▷

While the ladies whispered and wondered, Rasheed concluded his testimony. "Please answer any questions Mr. Strobel might have," Brad said as he returned to his seat.

Strobel shot out of his seat and started firing questions even before he made it to the podium. Everything about his demeanor and tone of voice conveyed one message: he was on the attack.

"So let me get this straight," he boomed. "Your sworn videotaped testimony was just a bunch of lies. Is that right?"

"Yes," Rasheed admitted through his translator.

"And not only did you lie in that sworn testimony, but you and Ms. Moreno planned ahead of time that you would lie to this court and this jury. Right?" Strobel was livid, his face dark with anger.

"Yes," both Rasheed and the translator said meekly.

"And you say that you lied because you were afraid that Mr. Aberijan would harm your wife?"

"Yes, his men were with my wife during my deposition and would have harmed her if I told the truth."

"But today you're telling the truth because you have gained political asylum and are no longer afraid of Mr. Aberijan?"

"Yes, this is true."

"Then why didn't you seek political asylum before you ever gave your deposition so that you would not have to mislead this judge and jury?"

"I do not know, except that was not the plan."

"Who came up with this wonderful plan?"

"It was Ms. Moreno's plan."

"And did Ms. Moreno tell you that you could get political asylum and get a chance to live in the United States if you were willing to testify for Mrs. Reed?"

"Yes and no. She told me we could get, as you call it . . . political asylum, if I agreed to tell the truth."

"And did she promise to help you find work in America?"

"Ms. Moreno says she and Mr. Carson will try to help me."

"Are you glad you gained political asylum and now have a chance to live in America?"

"I look forward with hope to life in this country."

"In America you get a clean start, but in Saudi Arabia, Mr. Berjein, you were a convicted drug dealer, right?"

"I was forced to plead guilty, but I did not use drugs."

"Isn't it true that you did in fact use drugs, that your earlier testimony was true, but that you saw a chance to get a new start in the wealthiest nation on earth—the United States—and all you had to do was give a little false testimony to make it happen?"

"I object," Brad said. "That's argumentative and improper."

"I'll withdraw the question," Strobel said before Ichabod could rule.

For a full hour, Strobel attacked the witness. He painted Rasheed as an opportunist, ready to jump at a chance to come to the United States. He reviewed all of Rasheed's videotaped admissions about his drug use and pointed out that Rasheed knew a lot of details about cocaine for someone who now claimed he had never tried the stuff. It was a crafty cross-examination and a reminder that Strobel was well worth the four hundred dollars per hour that he charged his clients to dismantle witnesses like Rasheed.

But Rasheed survived the onslaught and nearly sprinted from the stand when Ichabod told him he could step down.

"This court will take a ten-minute recess," Ichabod declared and left the bench.

◁▷

Brad and his team breathed a collective sigh of relief as Rasheed rejoined them. Brad shook the man's hand, patted him on the back, then watched with satisfaction as Rasheed gently embraced Sarah, kissing her on both cheeks.

The others gathered around as well, slapping Rasheed's back or putting an encouraging hand on his shoulder.

As the team gathered around the table, Brad noticed Bella take a tentative step toward Nikki. He tensed, ready to spring between the two women who were now locking eyes.

"I'm sorry," Bella said, extending her hand. "What I did was stupid."

Nikki looked at Bella's hand, hesitated long enough to teach her a lesson, then accepted. "Don't worry about it," Nikki replied. Her voice was still sullen.

Brad felt some of the tension in the air dissipate.

"The voice mail from Chad Hamilton was about the Johnson case," Leslie said helpfully. "He's an insurance adjuster."

Brad looked straight at Nikki, who shot Leslie a "button it up" glance. "I thought we settled that case weeks ago," he said.

Bella, now standing with her arms folded across her chest, looked at Brad and nodded. *I told you so,* she said with her eyes.

Nikki twisted her lips into a sheepish grin and watched Brad for a hint of a reprieve. "It's a long story . . ."

"Make it short."

"Okay . . . I settled for almost three times the amount you told me to accept several weeks ago."

"You mean you ignored my instructions—the client's instructions."

"Look, if you don't want the extra money, I'll keep it." Nikki sighed and slumped her shoulders, playing the role of the persecuted. "I just knew I could get more money—a lot more money—if they could see us in action." She looked at Brad, whose expression had not softened. "So I invited Hamilton and his boss to the trial. I arranged it so they were here during the cross-examination of Ahmed Aberijan. They saw all the fireworks: Brad threatened with contempt, the works. They knew we'd do whatever it takes to win a case. I told them our bottom line was one-point-seven million, take it or leave it, by the end of this case. They've now offered one-point-five."

"Talk to the client," Brad said, but his voice contained no enthusiasm. "If he agrees, take the money." He looked down, searching for just the right words. "But, Nikki . . ."

"I know."

"You pull a stunt like this again and deliberately disregard my instructions—you're fired."

Nikki snorted. "You're welcome," she muttered, just loud enough for the others to hear.

"What about the e-mail to Shelhorse?" Bella asked. It was time to pile on.

Nikki shrugged. "The only thing I know about that is what Leslie told me while Rasheed was testifying. I couldn't have sent that e-mail from Saudi Arabia even if I wanted to—I couldn't get any reception for my BlackBerry."

Bella gave her a raised eyebrow.

"Check it out," Nikki said, holding the device in her hand. "I didn't send anything until I hit American soil. Somebody who had access to the office computers—" she looked straight at Bella—"sent the e-mail and made it look like it came from my BlackBerry."

This spawned a round of furious speculation about the e-mail to Shelhorse. Bella recalled that O'Malley had come by the office about an hour before the e-mail was sent and accompanied Bella to court for a few hours to watch the trial. Someone, she surmised, must have seen Bella and Patrick leave the office, then broken in and sent the e-mail. It was an outside job, no doubt about it.

Everyone but Brad nodded in agreement.

◁ ▷

"All rise," the bailiff cried. "This court is now in session, the Honorable Judge Cynthia Baker-Kline presiding."

In a few minutes everyone had scrambled to their seats, the courtroom was quiet, and the jury was seated in their box.

"I assume that the plaintiff now rests. Is that correct, Mr. Carson?" Ichabod asked.

"Yes, Your Honor."

Strobel was up. "We'd like to call one surrebuttal witness, Your Honor—Mrs. Sarah Reed."

Brad bolted from his chair and jerked his head toward Strobel. In the commotion of the last few days, he had forgotten all about Strobel's plans to recall Sarah and force a mistrial by asking her to disclose the name of her informant.

"If Mr. Strobel is recalling Mrs. Reed solely to ask the name of her informant, we would like to renew our objection," Brad said, addressing the court. "Not only does such a question unfairly require Mrs. Reed to jeopardize the life of this person, which she is not willing to do, but it also serves no useful purpose at this stage of the proceedings. It's not like Mr. Strobel now has time to subpoena this person and put him on the stand in this case. By waiting until the very last minute of the trial, Mr. Strobel has shown that the only reason he asks this question is to harass my client and force a mistrial."

"Your Honor," Strobel drawled, "we waited because we thought the information might come out by some other means and we could spare Mrs. Reed this question. But it did not, and so we are back where we started. The court ruled before that we were entitled to have this question answered. We are simply following through on that ruling now."

Judge Baker-Kline shook her head. Brad's heart raced. It was the first time in the trial Ichabod had shown any hint of being swayed by Sarah's case.

"You had your chance, Mr. Strobel. I would have made Mrs. Reed answer this same question earlier in the trial. But now, having just heard the testimony of Mr. Berjein, I am concerned about the safety of the informant. And I am also concerned about your timing, sir. If you really wanted this question answered, you should not have withdrawn it earlier. The objection is sustained. Mrs. Reed will not take the stand for surrebuttal."

As usual, Strobel's poker face did not show a hint of disappointment. "Then the defense rests," he announced to the jury, standing ramrod straight and looking them directly in the eye.

Brad had never felt better about his case.

"Thank you, Mr. Strobel," Ichabod said. "We will start closing arguments Monday promptly at 9 a.m. And, Mr. Carson?"

"Yes, Your Honor."

"I have yet to hear any evidence, not even one shred, that leads me to believe the nation of Saudi Arabia ratified this alleged misconduct. Keep that in mind as you prepare your closing. You may be able to change my mind. But right now, I just don't see it."

"Yes, Your Honor," Brad mumbled reflexively, as Ichabod burst the bubble formed by her own prior ruling.

What in the world does she want, Brad wondered, *an engraved letter from the crown prince?*

The irreverent sound of juror number four's snickering broke the courtroom's silence.

◁ ▷

It's amazing what you can do with a telephoto lens, Frederick Barnes thought. He'd caught the juror dead in the act on his Kodak digital camera.

Incontrovertible proof. Earlier today, he'd slipped the photos into a small white envelope with gloved hands.

His gloved hands placed two-sided tape on the outside of the envelope, and he now waited patiently for his chance to make a clean pass of the photos. Barnes was a careful man. He would wait for the perfect opportunity, or he would not do it at all.

The moment came right after the judge dismissed the jury, the moment that juror number four snickered.

Brad Carson had left a copy of Rasheed's deposition on the podium. One hundred pages of transcribed testimony bound with a soft plastic cover on the front and back. It was better than jumping on the elevator with them and trying to drop the photos in a briefcase. It was so natural. It was perfect.

Barnes slid out of his seat in the first row and walked nonchalantly to the podium. He glanced around, then picked up the deposition and taped the photos inside the back cover. He discreetly removed the latex gloves and stuffed them in his pocket.

He turned toward plaintiff's counsel table and tapped her on the shoulder.

When she turned, he caught the flash of anger in her eyes. A "how dare you come over here, to our side, and talk to me in open court" look. She seemed to catch herself, and wariness replaced the anger in the beautiful dark eyes.

"Mr. Carson left this deposition and these two exhibits on the podium," Barnes explained. "I didn't want them to get mixed up with our stuff as we packed."

She took the deposition, but her dark eyes never left his.

"Thanks," Nikki Moreno said.

42

BARNES RESPONDED IMMEDIATELY to the summons on his cell phone. Within minutes he joined Ahmed in his hotel suite. "She wants to meet tonight at nine," Ahmed said. "She wants to meet in the bar downstairs, corner table, on the pool room level. She gave me the usual nonsense about coming alone."

"I'll personally cover you," Barnes said. He walked over to the floor-to-ceiling windows that overlooked the harbor and stared at the driving rain pelting the glass. A ragged bolt of lightning electrified the sky, and the rumbling from the thunder rattled the two-inch-thick pane. "What's the plan?" he asked, turning to face Ahmed.

Ahmed sat down on the sofa, grabbed the remote, and clicked off the television. Barnes hated it when Ahmed did this—took his sweet time answering—just to show who was in control. "Do we need juror six, or can we get a mistrial without him?" he finally asked.

"I don't know yet. The plan's in place to bump Stein. But if the timing's not right, if Strobel has him dismissed before the jury begins deliberating, then the judge might say that the jury pool was not contaminated. She might just dismiss Stein and still not declare a mistrial. If she does that, then we'll need the vote of this other juror. Juror six is our insurance policy."

The Saudi looked up and stared at Barnes, looked right through him, and the silence became almost intolerable. But Barnes never considered breaking it or even moving until he had Ahmed's implicit permission to do so.

"How sure are we that our friend can deliver juror six?" Ahmed asked.

"She's delivered everything else."

Ahmed sneered at the thought. "We have come too far to take any chances now. We may need juror six. You talk to Strobel and make sure he waits until the jury begins deliberations to ask for a mistrial. I'll meet our friend tonight. When I do, I want you to wire her car . . . and her cell phone if she leaves it behind. I'll give her the trust agreement she's demanding, carrying the signature of the minister of public safety. We'll monitor her after our meeting. If she checks out, she'll find a hundred million in her little trust account on Monday morning."

The Muttawa leader slammed the jury consultant's notebook down on the glass coffee table. He stood and stretched his massive pecs and broad shoulders. He rotated his thick neck and rubbed vigorously at the base of his skull. This was not a man used to having things out of his control.

"We will play this game," he snarled, "and buy our verdict." He paused and looked at Barnes through cold gray eyes. "As soon as the jury returns its verdict, she dies."

"And let a hundred mil pass to Sarah Reed and her family?" Barnes asked incredulously.

Ahmed scoffed. "I said the trust agreement had the signature of the minister of public safety. I did not say the signature was genuine."

"What good does a forgery do? The money's still held in trust."

"If the signature is a forgery, then the terms of the trust agreement fail, and the money in the account reverts back to its original owner—Saudi Arabia." Ahmed paused. "Our friend is not as clever as she thinks."

He walked over to the small wet bar in his room, poured himself another soda, and took a long swig. "Nobody blackmails Ahmed Aberijan and lives."

"What's your plan for taking her out?" There was a slight tremor in Barnes's voice. He was trying to act tough, like this was all in a day's work, but he had never been an accomplice to murder before.

"Not *my* plan," Ahmed laughed. It was a hollow and mirthless laugh. "I'm leaving the country as soon as the jury starts deliberating. How she dies, that's up to you. It's why you get paid so handsomely."

Ahmed pretended to ignore the stunned look of silent protest on the face of Barnes. In truth, he had no intention of leaving such an important and rewarding matter in the hands of a hired henchman. But the look on Barnes's face told him everything he needed to know. When push came to shove, the investigator could not be trusted. He simply didn't have the guts to kill, or worse, he had determined that it was not in his best interest to do so.

Either way, Ahmed would be forced to take matters into his own hands. And with that issue settled, Ahmed receded back into his own little world, deep in thought. He stared out the window for several minutes, soaking in the storm, and did not blink as Barnes left the room, softly shutting the door behind him.

◁ ▷

Barnes arrived fifteen minutes late for his meeting with the brain trust, an unlit stogie tucked firmly in the corner of his mouth. The greetings were cool and guarded, and Barnes got right down to business. He stood at the end of the conference table, his large girth nearly resting on the table itself. The group's mood matched the weather, and they frowned disapprovingly at this man whom fate had chosen to be their ally.

"Here are some more photographs," he said, slapping a folder down on the table. "I'll have the man who took the photos ready to testify in court tomorrow."

Strobel grabbed the folder and ripped it open. The photos showed the face of juror number four and the back of another man. There were two sets of photos from two different restaurants.

"They have met at least three times in the last few weeks," Barnes said. "In one of the restaurants, my man was seated close enough to overhear some of their conversation. Stein has promised his vote for one hundred thousand cash, fifty now, fifty later. If you check his bank account at the Bank of Tidewater, you'll see that fifty has already been deposited. He's definitely working for Brad Carson."

"How do you know that?" Teddy asked.

"I can't say," Barnes answered smugly. "But I'll stake my reputation on it." He paused for a moment and eyed the lawyers, daring any of them to challenge this information.

"Why would a juror take this incredible chance for a mere hundred thousand?" Win asked. "It almost destroys your faith in the system."

"A hundred thousand is still a lot of money to some people," Barnes replied. His voice reproached these big-firm lawyers. He looked from one to the next with disdain. He took a small bite of the cigar, spitting the piece to the side. "But that's beside the point," he continued. "Our old buddy Zeke Stein happens to be cheating on his wife. So the deal is not just his vote for a hundred thou; it's his vote for a hundred thou and the silence of the plaintiff's investigator.

"Here are the pictures to confirm the affair, if you're interested," Barnes said, tossing another folder onto the table. Unlike the other folder, nobody snatched this one up. All four men stared at the folder, resisting the urge to grab it, tear it open, and gawk at the contents. Their dignity and status in life required no less . . . at least for now.

"How did you find out about the affair?" Win asked.

"You mean juror four's affair?" Barnes asked, as he tossed an accusatory look toward Win.

"Of course."

Barnes smirked. "My man will testify that he heard juror four and Carson's lackey, the man whose back you see in the pictures, talking about it at the restaurant. That man confronted juror four with pictures of the affair.

"And after the conversation in the restaurant, my man followed Mr. Stein around for a while and—*voilà*—we've got our own photo gallery of him and his little mistress. It seems our man just can't stand to be away from his Internet sweetheart. He's probably with her right now."

Win couldn't seem to take his eyes off the folder, obviously riveted by the thought of what it might contain.

"I'm assuming that you're planning to take this information to the judge first thing tomorrow morning?" Teddy said to Mack.

It was not so much a question as a command. But Barnes harbored no respect for the old guy and did not realize that Teddy's suggestions should be treated like they came down from the mount.

"I would still recommend holding it until the jury actually starts deliberating," Barnes suggested before Mack could reply. "That way you've got a surefire mistrial because, by then, this juror will have poisoned the deliberations. If you unveil this stuff first thing Monday morning, the judge could just dismiss juror four and allow the other jurors and substitute alternate to begin deliberations." Barnes paused, chomping down hard on his cigar. "And, fellas, I don't want to be the one to break it to you, but you don't have the most appealing jury case."

Teddy Kilgore clenched his jaw and stood slowly, using the table to help himself up. He extended a long, bony, trembling finger toward Barnes. "Listen here, sir, you will not come waltzing into these offices and tell us how to try this case. Your suggestions are both unwise and offensive." His voice was rising, nearly cracking with anger.

"You suggest that this firm should lie to the court for strategic reasons? sacrifice the integrity of this firm and the trust of the bench, which has taken decades to build, just to get a mistrial? If we wait until after the jury begins deliberations to put your man on the stand, the judge will rightfully ask why we didn't bring this to her earlier. And either your man lies, and he says we just found out about it, or we look like complete fools. Am I right?"

Barnes knew better than to answer the question.

"Then what you are actually suggesting is that your man perjure himself on the stand and that Mr. Strobel should knowingly present perjured testimony to the court," Teddy continued, the long knobby finger pointing at Barnes's stubby nose.

It was exactly what Barnes was suggesting, although he may have phrased it somewhat more delicately.

"You obviously do not know this firm very well," Teddy huffed. He sat down, but his gaze did not leave Barnes. "You'll have your man in the courtroom, ready to testify, first thing tomorrow morning. Mr. Strobel will keep the photos of the meeting between juror four and Carson's gopher for evidence. You may take your other sleazy photographs and get out!" With this, Teddy waved his hand in a long arch, dismissing Barnes, the photos, and a guaranteed plan for a mistrial.

Out of the corner of his eye, Barnes saw Win, ever so subtly, cock his head to the side and look at Mack. *Do something,* the look screamed.

But Mack ignored him. Teddy still had a towering presence and great influence in this firm. And it was obvious that he had just levied a non-negotiable edict.

Even Barnes knew better than to take on the man in this setting. Instead, he stuffed the folder back into his briefcase and stalked out of the conference room, cursing Teddy Kilgore under his breath.

His plans for a mistrial had been dealt an unexpected blow. But for something this important, Barnes believed in redundancy planning. Exploiting juror number four was now a bit more challenging, but Barnes still had a way. And securing the vote of juror six was no longer a luxury. The informant would have to deliver.

He flicked some ashes on the Persian rug as he headed for the elevator.

◁▷

She drove like lightning through the downpour. At ten minutes until nine, she was still twenty minutes from downtown Norfolk. Brad had kept everyone late while he reviewed his closing argument. They had videotaped him, then spent several hours critiquing his closing. Listening and critiquing. Listening and critiquing. Afterward, he still wanted to practice it several more times.

As far as she knew, Brad was still pacing around the conference table, cajoling the empty chairs, choreographing every inflection and gesture. And here she was, about to meet with Ahmed Aberijan one last time and render that closing argument moot.

The rain continued to fall in sheets against the windshield, the lines on the interstate becoming a blur. At least the thunder and lightning had stopped. Her wipers beat furiously, but they were no match for this flood from heaven. She hit a pool of standing water, and the car pulled hard to the right, almost ending in a spin. Her heart pumped harder as she realized she had almost lost it. She strained her eyes for more dark pools of water. Her speedometer said eighty-five.

The cell phone rang, and she jumped. She slowed slightly and took one hand off the wheel.

"Hello," she said tentatively.

"Man, girl, you are bookin'. Slow down a little. Ahmed ain't goin' nowhere." It was O'Malley. She had lost his headlights in her rearview mirror a few minutes earlier.

"Are you sure this'll work?"

"Look, baby, you're totally wired. First sign of trouble, I'll be there," he promised.

"What if he pulls a gun?"

"I'll be right outside. Ten seconds, max. You've got to relax, hon. Aberijan can smell fear."

"Easy for you to say." She hydroplaned on another pool of standing water. "I've got to go. . . . Thanks for being here, Patrick."

"Don't mention it."

She made it safely to the hotel but was ten minutes late. She pulled up under the overhang in the front of the building and gave the valet her keys. She walked through the large revolving doors and into the luxurious lobby. She took a deep breath and turned left down the hallway toward the combination deli restaurant and bar. A waiter greeted her with a smile.

"May I help you?" he asked.

"No thanks. I'm just looking for someone."

She walked a few feet into the restaurant and took stock. Immediately in front of her, a few patrons enjoyed a late dinner and watched a large television. To her right, a few corporate road warriors sat in the sunken bar and talked to the bartender. A flight of stairs to her right led to a dimly lit area with a pool table and a few private dining tables. It overlooked the remainder of the restaurant and was bounded by a black iron railing. Two patrons played pool, but otherwise the upstairs room looked empty.

She headed up and wondered why she had chosen this place. The *Reed* case had received so much publicity that she could no longer meet with Ahmed in public. *But why here?* She had eaten here before—many times. But tonight it felt different. Darker. Musty. She could *feel* the evil.

She walked past the pool players and nodded at them. Then she saw him. Sitting in a booth in the far corner, not even visible from the main floor of the restaurant. He saw her too, and he locked on to her. She could not meet the gaze of his emotionless gray eyes.

She sat down at the booth without a word of greeting. She knew he could sense her fear, but there was nothing she could do about it.

"Did you come alone?" she asked.

"No," he said firmly. He was obviously done playing games.

She nodded in question toward the men at the pool table.

"No." He did not take his shrouded eyes off her; it seemed he did not even blink. She began glancing around the room.

"Give me the wire," Ahmed demanded.

"I don't know what you're talking about," she lied.

"You're wearing a wire. Either give it to me or this meeting is over."

Slowly, she reached under the table, under her fleece and sweater, and pulled out the small microphone, wire, and transmitter. She laid it on the table.

Ahmed picked it up carefully and studied the equipment. "The lady is signing off now," he said into the mike. Then he placed the equipment gently on the floor and stomped hard, crushing the pieces with his heel.

"Now we can talk," he said.

◁▷

Barnes watched the valet park the car in the first floor of the parking garage, then jog out of the garage to fetch the next one. He had been watching the young man for nearly twenty minutes and calculated it would take several minutes for the valet to return. Plenty of time to get the job done.

He pulled out a small black bag of high-tech gadgets and strolled toward her car. He popped the lock with a slim-jim and was inside in seconds. With a small screwdriver, a sharp knife, and practiced fingers, he unhooked the dome light, stripped the hot wire, and connected a small microphone to this energy source. No batteries necessary. It would record indefinitely.

He hid the mike inside the plastic covering of the dome light, clipped the cover back in place, and went straight for the cell phone. Nokia—perfect. Quickly, efficiently, he removed the plastic cover, planted the bug, then wired the bug to the cell phone's internal antenna. As he snapped the cover back on, he heard the muffled sound of a car engine. He softly closed the driver's-side door, slid down in the seat, and watched through the side mirror as the valet drove by. Barnes listened as the car engine shut off and the door closed. He sat still for another two minutes—enough time for the valet to be out of the garage.

Barnes slowly lifted his head, checked every direction, then opened the door and got out of her car. His task complete, he strolled calmly out of the garage and headed around the corner to the front door of the Marriott.

◁▷

"I came through on Shelhorse."

"And I came through on the money," Ahmed hissed.

She was very much alone. Terrified. Though her voice would probably tremble, she needed to stay on the offensive. "The Shelhorse money was nothing. I want the rest on deposit by tomorrow morning, 9 a.m., or we pull back our friend on the jury."

Ahmed laughed. It was a bitter, forced laugh. A mocking laugh. "Someone as smart as you proposes a plan like this? Let's see, I wire a million into one account—let's call it the 'verdict account.' And then a hundred million into another account—let's call it the 'trust account.' And then you say, 'Thank you very much,' leave the country, and are never seen or heard from again. You double-cross me, the jury returns a huge verdict against me, and I . . . do what? Go to the police? 'Officer,' I say, 'this lady did not uphold her end of a jury bribery scheme.'"

"The hundred million will be protected by the trust agreement."

"I'm not worried about the trust account," Ahmed snapped. "That money will be there before the jury begins its deliberation. But the verdict account—that million dollars is protected by what? Your *promise* that I'll get a verdict?"

"First, the price is two million, not one." She swallowed hard. "And second—"

At the edge of her peripheral vision, she saw a man just behind her shoulder. She flinched, ducking to the side and turning.

"Can I get you anything to drink?" the waiter asked.

It was impossible to respond immediately, her heart was in her throat. Ahmed flashed the same smug smile he had worn when he testified. She took a deep breath and ordered a Diet Coke so the waiter would be forced to return soon.

Ahmed ordered nothing. He did not even look at the waiter. His eyes remained glued on her, and she subconsciously slid to the end of the booth.

"Do you have the signed trust agreement?" she asked after the waiter left. She wanted to make this as quick as possible, to get out of a trap that she sensed would spring soon.

Ahmed took an envelope from the seat beside him and placed it on the table. He did not let go with his hand, and she did not try to take it.

"How do I know you will deliver juror six?" he asked.

"So you need him now?"

"How do I know . . . you will deliver?"

It was time to feign indignation. She scowled and spoke in an intense whisper, meeting Ahmed's fixed gaze with an unblinking stare of her own. "You don't trust me? I'm shocked."

"I love it when you talk tough," Ahmed mocked. "But I need something more than your word to justify this rather substantial investment. Tell you what. You deliver the verdict first; then I'll pay. You have *my* word for that."

That smirk was driving her nuts. *What does he know? What's about to happen?*

She withdrew a two-page document from her pocket and unfolded it, trying hard to control the trembling of her hands. "Here are the wire *and investment* instructions for the Swiss bank account where you wire the two million dollars. You can check this one out too. As soon as the money hits the account, it gets invested in put options on U.S. oil companies. There's also a caveat that these investment instructions cannot be changed for two weeks."

Ahmed gave her a puzzled look, and her confidence grew. "These put options are basically a bet that the stock prices of these companies will go down. If the stock prices stay the same, the put options will lose a little value, though not much. But we both know that a verdict against Saudi Arabia would destabilize relationships with the United States," she continued, "and cast a cloud over foreign oil supplies. If that happens, the stock prices for U.S. oil companies will go through the roof."

She slid her paper next to the envelope Ahmed was holding. "If the stock prices of U.S. oil companies go up, the put options that will be purchased with this account become essentially worthless. In other words, if there's a verdict against Saudi Arabia, the money in this account will disappear."

She looked dead into his eyes. "In addition to that, you have my word," she said sarcastically.

"Clever," Ahmed said. The detestable smirk was back. He took her paper and slid his envelope toward her. She carefully peeled it open. It appeared to be the same trust agreement that she had drafted, but she still read every word—forced herself to concentrate in spite of her fears—to ensure he hadn't changed the language. She saw the verified signature at the bottom of the last page, a signature belonging to the minister of the department of public safety. Two others had signed as witnesses. One of them was Ahmed. The signatures had been notarized.

She placed the agreement back in the envelope. "I'll have someone checking the accounts tomorrow morning," she promised. "If the money's in the trust account, and they confirm it's being held subject to this trust agreement . . . *and* if the verdict account contains two million dollars—" she paused— "you can start celebrating your verdict."

"Let's talk about the price of that verdict," Ahmed said. "I don't think we ever agreed."

She sensed that Ahmed was trying to keep her there for some reason, and she wasn't about to find out why. Out of the corner of her eye, she saw the waiter coming with her drink. It would be a good time to make her move. Perhaps her only time. She rose as the waiter approached the table. "My friend here will be getting the bill," she said crisply. She looked straight at Ahmed. "Two bucks," she said.

The waiter gave her a curious look.

"I've only got a buck fifty," Ahmed replied.

"Okay," she replied, slapping a dollar down on the table. "You pay a buck fifty, I'll cover the rest."

Then she turned and hurried down the steps.

She rushed outside the hotel and stood under the overhang, waiting for the valet to bring her car. The rain was still coming in sheets, blown sideways by the wind, and spraying her despite the protection of the overhang. She was thinking about Ahmed, wondering what was taking so long, when she felt a hand on her shoulder. She jumped and turned, her heart pounding madly against her chest. She faced a short, stocky man chewing on the stub of a cigar, the same man who sat behind Ahmed every day of the trial.

She jerked her shoulder away.

"Let me give you some free advice," he whispered, although there was nobody else around. "Don't mess with that man in there. Do exactly what you promised. And if you want to survive, your man on the jury better be able to deliver. Get the defense verdict and get out of town. And that agreement in the envelope? It isn't worth the paper it's written on."

She eyed him warily. *Is this a setup? Is he here at Ahmed's instructions?* "What are you talking about?"

The stocky man didn't answer. He pulled his hood up on his Windbreaker and headed down the sidewalk, disappearing into the night.

This was getting too weird. She felt lightheaded and vulnerable. She wanted to sit, but there was no seat near her. She waited in the biting wind for what seemed like an eternity before the valet arrived with her car and helped her in the driver's door. He handed her a piece of paper, then waited, expecting a tip, but she was too preoccupied to catch his hints. When he reluctantly shut the door, she wasted no time in hitting the gas and putting some distance between her and the Marriott.

She turned on the dome light and read the note as she drove. One eye on the road, one eye on the disconcerting note in her trembling right hand.

The rain continued to come in torrents as she headed west on I-264. The wind was so strong she could feel it pushing her car sideways. This time, she was in no hurry. She flicked off the light in order to concentrate on the road and think her thoughts in darkness. As she drove, she wiggled out of her fleece and turned up the heater. At least her jeans and pullover wool sweater were still partially dry. The radio blared, but she didn't hear it. She stayed in the right lane, doing no more than the speed limit, and still she had a hard time seeing the lines on the road. The wipers, beating furiously, mesmerized her.

She shuddered from either the cold or the thought of Ahmed, filled with bile, staring her down. She now had a bounty on her head. One hundred million dollars. Her death grip on the steering wheel turned her knuckles white. *Relax,* she told herself. *The worst is over.*

Then why am I shaking? Why am I starting to cry?

C'mon girl, get a grip! She willed herself to relax, to take one hand off the wheel, to stop grinding her teeth. With her free hand, as an act of studied nonchalance, she flipped her wet hair out of her face and over her shoulder.

The headlights from the vehicle behind reflected off the mirror and illuminated her silhouette—a model's face and a long thin neck—framed by the sheen of her windblown and rain-soaked long auburn hair.

43

LESLIE DIDN'T KNOW HOW LONG the vehicle had been there, but she suddenly realized she was being followed. The headlights were elevated—it must be a truck or SUV of some sort. She slowed to give the tailgater a chance to pass. The lights, however, grew closer. She began to panic.

She put both hands back on the steering wheel, resumed her iron grip, and started gradually increasing her speed to see if the tailgater would drop off. But the tailgater maintained the distance, as if attached to her car by a tow bar. The interstate suddenly seemed deserted, and she sensed real danger. She picked up more speed. The tailgater followed suit. She hydroplaned and regained control. The vehicle behind her was still there.

The tailgater flashed his headlights and laid on the horn. Leslie's hands were frozen on the wheel. She was in the left lane, passing what few vehicles were braving the night. Still the tailgater stayed glued to her bumper. She glanced down quickly at the odometer. Eighty-four miles per hour in the pouring rain. *Where are the police when you need them?*

Her cell phone rang, and her heart raced. *Who's calling me now? Who's chasing me? Should I answer?* Her thoughts became jumbled, and her fears fed on themselves. *Must settle down. Maybe it's O'Malley. If they wanted to kill me, they wouldn't have waited for me to get on the interstate.*

Answer the phone!

"Hello," she managed, in a feeble voice.

"It's me. Brad. Behind you," he shouted into his phone. "Slow down and pull over."

Relief surged through her body, like a death-row inmate with an eleventh-hour reprieve.

"Okay," she said and hung up.

Thank God. She slowed the vehicle and started looking for a shoulder.

And then a new anxiety attack started. *How did he get there? What does he know?*

What will I tell him?

She found a good spot, the best that could be hoped for in the driving rain, and pulled over. Her car came to a skidding halt in a wet, grassy spot several feet off the road. She stayed in the driver's seat with the door locked, staring back into the headlights of the vehicle behind her.

It looked like Brad's Jeep, but she couldn't be sure. She could make out only the shadow of a driver. There was no one visible on the passenger side.

She saw a figure open the driver's door and step out into the wind and rain. She put the car in gear, ready to leave in a hurry. Cars flew by, casting long shadows off the silhouette moving toward her. The walk, the build, the posture, the way he carried himself—it was all Brad!

She exhaled and pried her hands off the wheel. She hadn't realized she'd been holding her breath. She put the car in park and jumped out, without even putting on her fleece, and started toward him. They met between the two vehicles, with the glare of the headlights in her eyes, the sound of cars rushing by on the interstate, the rain pelting them, and the wind blasting them. They stood there for a split second, her hair dripping wet and hanging in her face, her sweater quickly soaking through. She watched the rain pouring off his chin and onto his Windbreaker.

He was the most beautiful sight she had ever seen.

She had rehearsed in her mind over and over what she would say if she ever got caught. How she would act. How he would respond. But now that the moment was here, all those strategies seemed useless, lost deep in the gaze of his confused and hurting pale blue eyes.

◁▷

He was angry, bitterly disappointed, and drenched.

"Brad, I'm so glad it's you." She started toward him, but he took a step back.

He shook his head. Slowly at first, then with more determination. He held up a palm to stop her approach.

"It was you, wasn't it?" he shouted over the sound of the storm and the traffic. "It was you all along. Sleeping with the enemy. I saw you outside the Marriott tonight . . . meeting with Ahmed's investigator!" He was yelling now, emphasizing every syllable, hands gesturing wildly in frustration. He gave her no chance to answer. "You sold us out! *Sold* . . . us out."

"No!" she yelled in response. "What're you talking about? Let me explain ..." She reached out to grab Brad by the shoulders to calm him down and get his attention. Her eyes were pleading for a chance to be heard.

Brad brushed her aside and continued his tirade. "I *have* listened to you. I've listened to you through this whole case." He paused, stuttering for the right words. "You ... Leslie ... I saw you with my own eyes ... *my own eyes*! There's no explaining that."

"What were you doing there?" She looked astonished. Then, "Brad, you've got to ... to trust me—" She began inching slowly toward him as he backed up to the hood of his car, shaking his head. He thrust his hands deep into his pockets. He didn't dare reach out for her, knowing that the magic of her touch would melt his defenses and transform his anger to forgiveness.

"You want to talk about trust!" he yelled. "Let's talk about trust. I trusted you with everything—my feelings, my case—and what happened to that trust?" Now they were face-to-face, his muscles tensed, the rain pouring down his face.

"Brad, I can explain everything. . . . Just give me a chance," she pleaded.

Brad wanted desperately to reach out and hold her, to draw her to himself and tell her that it would be okay. But he couldn't let himself do it. He shook his head as words betrayed him. She was looking at him now, beckoning with her eyes. He could barely meet her gaze, but he forced himself to look into those sad blue eyes, beautiful even with the mascara streaking down her cheeks, the eyelashes matted together. And despite everything she had done—all the lies and deceptions—at this moment, he felt nothing but pity.

He allowed her to take another step toward him, then another, to wrap her arms around his neck, to put her head on his shoulder. Slowly, almost uncontrollably, he pulled his hands from his pockets and squeezed Leslie to himself. And he wondered what in the world he was doing.

"O'Malley and I ate dinner together at the Marriott," Leslie said. "If you don't believe me, just call him. We were going on a hunch ... wanted to see if anybody we knew would be stopping by Ahmed's hotel tonight. When I left ... this guy you saw—the one who's with Ahmed—came up to me and basically threatened me. . . ."

He wanted to believe the fairy tale; the death of his dream was just so painful. But the same instincts and suspicions that caused him—literally propelled him—to follow her in the first place, would not allow him to believe her now. He had waited out in front of the Marriott, parked down the street, and watched the front door. She had been inside for no more than ten or fifteen minutes, certainly not long enough for dinner. And Brad had never seen O'Malley, either coming or going.

"I'm sorry for being so paranoid, Leslie," he said calmly as he stared into the distance. "I guess the pressure of this case is just starting to get to me." He gave her a reassuring squeeze.

He would definitely call O'Malley. As soon as he pried himself loose from this woman he could no longer trust.

◁▷

Leslie dialed O'Malley's number the moment she pulled away from her road-side rendezvous.

"Hello, beautiful," O'Malley answered.

"I just had a close call with Brad," she said, then explained that she would need O'Malley to back her story about dinner at the Marriott.

"No problem, Leslie. Now tell me about the meeting with Ahmed."

For the next few minutes, she recounted every detail of her meeting with Ahmed. But she decided not to say anything about her brief encounter with Ahmed's investigator.

"Perfect," O'Malley responded. "So the money hits the accounts some-time tomorrow morning?"

"So he says."

"Once I confirm, I'll pass the word to our juror. You sure we shouldn't have held out for two mil?"

She paused. He sounded disappointed. "I don't know. I guess I just got a little spooked."

"Don't sweat it, babe. A million and a half is still a lot of money."

There was a small beep on the phone. "Brad's calling," O'Malley said. "Gotta run. See you tomorrow."

"Okay," she said. "Don't forget the tickets."

◁▷

Barnes watched Ahmed digest the words of Leslie's phone call, then turn toward him. "Wire a million five to this account tomorrow at 8 a.m." He handed Barnes a sheet of wiring instructions. "But I've got a bad feeling about this other trust account; there's something we're missing. . . ."

Ahmed stopped midsentence; his eyes focused on something a world away. "We never technically agreed on a time deadline for the trust account, as long as it's there before the jury starts deliberating. Don't wire the money until after closing arguments are completed. If everything still looks good at that point, then follow these instructions." He gave Barnes the second sheet with wiring instructions for a hundred million dollars.

"You might not need to wire the money at all," Barnes suggested.

Ahmed raised an eyebrow. "Why's that?"

"I haven't played out my full hand on juror four yet. You know we've had our man paying juror four, pretending to be working for Carson . . ."

"Of course. It's why he's been sending them such negative body language. Mr. Stein doesn't like getting blackmailed."

"Well," Barnes explained, barely containing his enthusiasm, "yesterday in court, I planted some compromising photos of Stein in the back of a deposition transcript that Carson's paralegal left sitting around. They cart those things to court every day and religiously unload them on their counsel table. I'm sure they'll have them for the closing arguments."

Barnes looked straight at Ahmed, studying the man for even the smallest sign of approval. "When Strobel introduces the photos of juror four in the restaurant being bribed, I'm going to go put my arm around one of those marshals and tell him that I just saw the Moreno woman stuff something like photos in the back of one of their deposition transcripts. When the marshals check, if the judge lets them, they'll have proof that it was Moreno and Carson bribing juror four. And then . . . well, the fireworks should be interesting."

Ahmed thought about this for a moment; then his lips slowly curled into a wicked little smile. "Moreno, huh."

"Moreno."

"Perfect."

Barnes returned the smile, watched Ahmed turn serious again, and endured a long silence, the only sound coming from the speaker in the middle of the table as it captured the music from Leslie's car radio.

"One more thing," Ahmed said. "Find out where Connors and O'Malley plan on going tomorrow. Under the present circumstances, I think it would be best if I terminated them myself."

Barnes tried to take this news as calmly as possible, cognizant of the fact that Ahmed was watching him for any hint of a reaction.

◁▷

Pastor Jacob Bailey and the faithful members of Chesapeake Community Church filed out of Sarah's house and headed home. They had prayed for Brad and his closing argument. They had prayed for wisdom for the jury and the judge. They had prayed for safety for the Riyadh church. And they had prayed for patience and strength for Sarah.

At Sarah's suggestion, they even prayed for Ahmed, Mack Strobel, and the rest of the defense trial team. They specifically asked that Sarah might be a testimony to those men, causing them to accept Christ as their Savior.

Bella had joined the prayer meeting and lifted up some passionate prayers of her own, though she couldn't quite bring herself to pray for Ahmed or Strobel. The others enjoyed listening to Bella pray, since she didn't use the platitudes and Christianese everyone else seemed to fall into. Instead, Bella prayed the street-savvy prayer of a Brooklyn girl—direct, bold, and to the point. She didn't hesitate to share everything on her heart. She was a breath of fresh air to the others, who sometimes prayed to God but cared more about the Christians who were listening than the audience of one in heaven.

After an appropriate season of prayer, the church members had enjoyed sharing a potluck dinner. Everyone had brought a favorite recipe, at least half of which fell into the category of sweet desserts. Bella especially liked this part; clearly she was born to be a church member. She would probably have her rough edges from here to eternity, but God was hard at work on her temper and judgmental tendencies. What a difference a prayer made!

By 10:30 the last prayer warriors left, and Sarah began getting ready for bed. When she heard the doorbell ring, she assumed somebody had left behind a dish, a Bible, or some other item of value. She was already in her baggy flannel pajamas and anxious to get into bed; tomorrow was a big day. She hoped it was not someone with a confidential crisis, circling back after the other church members had all left.

She was too tired tonight to bear even one more burden. She padded to the door hoping she could dispose of this caller quickly and feeling a little guilty for even thinking that way.

She opened the door and stood there . . . blinked twice . . . *Who in the world?*

She was staring at the drenched and frowning face of a middle-aged woman she had never met before.

"I'm assistant district attorney Angela Bennett," the woman said, flashing an ID. "And I think we'd better talk."

44

BRAD DRAGGED HIMSELF OUT of bed at 5:30 Monday morning and decided to skip his morning run. He still had some major work to do on the most important closing argument he had ever delivered. And he had no energy.

He had spent the night trying to sort out his feelings. He stared at the ceiling and watched infomercials on television. He was on the raw emotional edge all night—too tired to get out of bed and work on his closing but too heartbroken to sleep.

O'Malley had confirmed Leslie's story, but Brad still had his suspicions. *Is O'Malley in on this too?*

It was all impossible to believe.

He shuffled to the kitchen, fixed coffee, and set up shop at the kitchen table. He scribbled some notes, reviewed a few trial court transcripts, and thought some more about Leslie. The night's events had drained all his energy and destroyed his enthusiasm for the case. The whole thing was like a hall of mirrors. *Who's working for whom?*

Brad resisted the urge to crawl back into bed, pull the sheets over his head, and let the world turn without him. Despite his misgivings, today he would be on center stage in the wild and unpredictable drama of the *Reed* case, and the whole world would be watching.

◁▷

It seemed that the whole world had indeed shown up and set up camp outside the courthouse on Granby Street. The prior night's storm had left a brisk and sunny fall day in its wake. The weathercasters predicted a high of nearly sixty under clear skies. And the protesters, attention seekers, rabble-rousers, and hangers-on were taking full advantage of the good weather and the armada of reporters in order to shine a national spotlight on their favorite cause.

Just as the man in the yellow chicken suit predicted, the scene outside the courthouse resembled a cross between a sidewalk bazaar, a political rally, and a church picnic. There were T-shirts, coffee cups, and other trinkets for sale, all containing cute slogans commemorating the latest trial of the century. If you were a supporter of Sarah Reed, you could get a shirt that read, "Pray for the Persecuted" or a shirt listing the great martyrs of the faith, including the name of Charles Reed. If you supported the defendants, there were shirts reading, "Reed Versus Aberijan: The Witch Hunt Continues" or "The Inquisition: It Isn't Just for Europeans Anymore."

Since the man in the chicken suit was a natural enemy of fundamentalist Christians, he had favored the defendants at the start of the trial. But as the days wore on, his allegiance had gradually shifted to Sarah Reed. He was impressed by the simplicity of Sarah and her trial team. In the early days of trial, they walked through the protesters, carrying their own briefcases and exhibits, while the defense team showed up in limos and didn't get their hands dirty.

The man in the chicken suit had witnessed Brad dump his box of documents on the courthouse steps and handle it graciously. The man had also witnessed in horror the attack on Brad and Nikki and their close escape. As the days passed, he had grown tired of the smug looks on the faces of Ahmed, Mack Strobel, and the others on the defense team as they exited their fancy vehicles surrounded by security guards. It was no single thing, but all of these events taken together, at least in the mind of the chicken man, created this unnatural alliance between this protester and the team representing Sarah Reed. If the opportunity arose on this last day of trial, he would prove his new allegiance.

◁▷

At precisely 8:55, having traveled directly from home, Brad entered the packed courtroom. He was wearing his closing argument suit, a black Armani number with a subtle windowpane pattern, custom-made for Brad—at a cost of more than seven hundred bucks—after a big verdict a few years back. The suit only saw the light of day for closing arguments, and in the last two years, the suit had only lost twice.

Both those losses, of course, occurred before Brad purchased the lucky Bruno Magli shoes and monogrammed shirt with gold cufflinks—fourteen karat—as well as the iridescent silk tie that mesmerized juries with its dark hues of purple, navy blue, and mauve that subtly changed colors as it reflected light. The combination of suit, shirt, shoes, and tie had proven unbeatable. In every other case, when he had put on these threads, he felt empowered— ready to argue the stars down.

But this morning, the clothes could not make the man. The suit hung on him like a scarecrow's would. His lean body had shed nearly ten pounds during the hectic weeks of the trial. His chiseled face looked drawn and gaunt. Dark circles surrounded his eyes. He looked, in the words of Bella, "like death on a bad day."

He walked down the aisle feeling tired, confused, and alone. His head was here—his argument might even be compelling—but he had left his heart by the side of the road last night. Betrayal did that to a person. He could muster no *passion*. He was on automatic, and Sarah's case would rise or fall on the mechanical closing argument of a lawyer who felt like a robot.

To Brad's relief, Leslie was not seated at counsel table. He glanced quickly around the courtroom—there was no sign of her anywhere. But Nikki, Bella, and Sarah were all huddled together as he approached, anxiety etched on their faces.

"Where have you been?" Sarah asked.

"We've got to talk for a moment," Brad said.

"I know," Sarah responded. She pulled Brad aside, away from Nikki and Bella.

For the next few minutes, she talked and Brad listened. She first apologized for what she was about to do, then reminded Brad that she held the trump card. Either Brad would carry out the strategies she was suggesting or she would ask him to step down as counsel and she would do it herself. She was dead serious and unwavering. She was a different Sarah from the one Brad had grown to admire.

First, she demanded that Brad argue for the chance to present one more witness based on newly discovered evidence. In fact, Sarah had a typed copy of the argument she wanted Brad to make, and he was to deliver it word for word. He just stared at her, not even looking down at the paper, as if she had lost her mind. Second, she wanted Brad to inform the court that Leslie had agreed to withdraw as co-counsel effective immediately. This one Brad had no trouble accepting. Third, if the court accepted Brad's argument and allowed him to call a final witness, Sarah would provide a written proffer of the testimony that had been drafted by assistant district attorney Angela

Bennett. Sarah turned and nodded toward a woman seated in the second row. Bennett rose and started walking toward them.

Brad had heard enough. "Sarah, this is crazy. There're things you don't know . . ."

"All rise," the court clerk commanded as Judge Cynthia Baker-Kline stormed onto the bench.

"Do it," Sarah whispered. "Please."

Brad looked at the paper in his hand, then at Sarah's pleading eyes. By now Bennett was next to them, and she shoved another paper into Brad's hands.

"Read it," she said.

"Counsel," Ichabod said sharply, "you might want to take your seat."

Brad hustled to his seat and quickly skimmed Sarah's instructions.

"Good morning, ladies and gentlemen," Ichabod said to the crowded courtroom. "Before we bring the jury in for closing arguments, are there any matters that merit our attention?"

"I have one," Strobel announced.

Brad rose, still uncertain as to whether he should do this. He was only halfway through the written argument he was supposed to deliver. A glance at Sarah convinced him, and he declared, "I have one as well."

Ichabod blew out a quick and irritated breath. "Then let's start with counsel for plaintiff. But let me tell you gentlemen right now, I'm not inclined to delay these closing arguments for one minute. We've got a jury waiting. So this better be good."

Brad walked slowly, tentatively, to the podium, carrying Sarah's typed document with him. He placed it on the podium, stared at the paper, then looked over his shoulder one last time at Sarah. She waved her hand in small, discreet circles, egging him on. He shook his head in resignation.

"First, Your Honor, I need to inform the court that Ms. Leslie Connors has withdrawn as co-counsel of record, effective immediately."

Ichabod let out a sigh. "On what grounds?"

"I'm not at liberty to say, Judge."

Judge Baker-Kline made a perturbed face. "Okay, what else."

Brad began reading the argument in front of him, his voice flat and emotionless. "Your Honor, during our case I promised the court that we would present compelling evidence implicating Saudi Arabia in the conduct of Mr. Aberijan and the Muttawa. I realize that this is the eleventh hour. But this weekend, we became aware of new evidence that this court must hear before deciding this case, if the court is truly interested in a search for truth. We ask for leave of the court to call one additional witness and present approximately one hour of testimony from that witness."

The lines on Ichabod's face deepened in disapproval. The gallery, who had come to hear the drama of the closing arguments, began to murmur its disapproval.

Nevertheless, Brad continued. "Knowing that this is an extraordinary request, and that the testimony would have to be extraordinary in nature to merit this court's indulgence, we have a one-page summary of the testimony we would like to submit to the court as a proffer." Brad held up Angela Bennett's proffer. He had been able to skim only the first few lines.

Ichabod sat there, chin on her hand, sending every signal possible that she was not the least bit impressed with this melodramatic last-minute request. "No way, Counsel. I told you last week that we would start closing arguments this morning. Now you want to try some type of desperate 'Hail Mary' maneuver?" She leaned forward on the bench and practically spit the words out. "Not in my court, Counsel."

Brad's heart wasn't in this request, but Ichabod's cavalier dismissal angered him. She had treated him with such utter disdain through the whole trial, and he was at the end of his emotional rope. *Doesn't this request at least merit some consideration? What would it hurt to take five minutes and read the proffer?* His competitive juices were engaged, and he couldn't resist taking a few swings on the way down.

"Does the court intend to dismiss my request without even reviewing the proffer?" Brad asked. "Is keeping to the court's sacred schedule more important than a witness who can shed light on the search for truth?"

"Counsel, you're treading on very thin ice here," Ichabod replied impatiently. "I have ruled."

He glanced again over his shoulder, this time locking eyes with Bennett, seated in the first row, immediately behind the counsel table. She nodded her head ever so slightly, and Brad turned to face the judge.

"I don't understand why the court insists on punishing my client because of a personality conflict between the court and me," he said fuming. "I don't understand why the court, after a three-week trial, will not take five minutes to read a summary of what might be the most important evidence in the case. Is the court interested in truth, or is the court interested in revenge?"

Strobel was on his feet now, looking perplexed and agitated. "I object.

The plaintiff rested her case on Saturday. This is *highly* irregular and *highly* improper. I've been practicing law for thirty-eight years and have never seen such an unethical and desperate move by—"

"Don't lecture me on ethics," Brad shot back.

"Counsel, I don't interrupt you when you're talking—" Strobel countered.

"That's because I don't make hypocritical accusations—"

"Order!" Ichabod barked as she banged her gavel. The courtroom fell silent. Brad stared straight ahead. Strobel stared at Brad. "You two sound like children," she lectured. "And I'm tired of these outbursts in my court!"

"I apologize, Your Honor," Brad said.

"As do I," Strobel echoed.

◁▷

Judge Cynthia Baker-Kline paused. She wanted to slap Brad Carson down for making such a scene. She wanted to rip up his one-page proffer into tiny little pieces without even reading it. She wanted to hold him in contempt. She wanted to make him suffer.

But she was no fool. She remembered the last time he was about to lose a case in her court. She remembered how he had goaded her into losing her temper and sending him to jail. She remembered the embarrassing appeal he planned to file based on her alleged bias and failure to maintain decorum. Even though she had forced Carson's client to accept a plea bargain, he had tarnished her reputation in the process. She would not allow it to happen again.

If everything went according to plan, she was on her way to the Fourth Circuit Court of Appeals. She could not let an arrogant con man like Brad Carson stand in her way.

It was time for a little reverse psychology.

She was sure the testimony he wanted to present was of minimal importance. He was probably banking on the fact that she would not consider the proffer. Then he could argue judicial bias on appeal.

Not this time, she decided. *I refuse to throw you into that briar patch.*

"Counsel," she said in measured tones, "present Mr. Strobel with your one-page proffer and hand the original to the court. We will stand in recess for five minutes while I consider whether I should allow this witness to testify." She banged her gavel, accepted the one-page summary of the proposed testimony, and left the bench.

◁ ▷

The courtroom broke into bedlam as soon as Judge Baker-Kline made her exit. Dozens of reporters surrounded Brad and fired questions about the proffered testimony. Sarah bowed her head to say a word of thanks.

Strobel and his legal team huddled around the document. After a few minutes, Strobel slid the photographs and evidence gathered on juror number four into his briefcase.

Just a brief glance at the document convinced Strobel that he would no longer be needing those photos. The trial of the century had just taken a sudden and irrevocable turn.

◁ ▷

Things were not going at all according to the perfectly laid plans of Frederick Barnes. All the hours of research and planning, of painstaking investigative work, of operatives following precise orders and carrying out detailed stings and counterstings—all for naught. Barnes felt sick.

He glanced at the document handed to Strobel and had the sinking feeling that the photos of juror four would never see the light of day. It was such a pity; it would have been the perfect plan.

What fun, what sheer genius it would have been to dupe the street-savvy paralegal who had already caused so much trouble. But now Barnes's cleverly planned fireworks would never explode. With this proffered testimony, everything had changed. Juror four was the least of their worries.

There was only one thing left to do.

◁ ▷

In the turmoil, only Nikki noticed that Ahmed Aberijan leaned over the rail separating defense counsel from the gallery and said a few words into the ear of the short and stocky investigator who had handed her the deposition at the close of court Saturday. Ahmed then joined the man as the pair headed for the back door of the courtroom.

Nikki glanced over Brad's shoulder as he looked through the proffer. She let out a soft, low whistle and said to nobody in particular, "No wonder he left."

She grabbed Bella, whispered a few things in her ear, then ran out the back doors of the courtroom to follow Ahmed. Bella in turn found Rasheed

Berjein in the second row of the spectator section. She pulled on his arm, and he followed Bella out of the courtroom, just a few seconds behind Nikki.

◁▷

In the downstairs lobby, Frederick Barnes and Ahmed Aberijan impatiently waited to retrieve their firearms from the marshals who manned the metal detectors. As was their daily habit, the marshals had taken the guns, tagged them, and placed them in a locker to be reclaimed at the end of the day.

But now, as Ahmed and Barnes tried to leave the court building, the marshals were busy checking a long line of persons entering the court through the metal detectors. So the two men waited. And waited. And waited.

Nikki stepped off the elevator and made herself inconspicuous on the other side of the lobby, keeping a close eye on Barnes and Ahmed.

"Gentlemen," an exasperated Barnes said, "we are severely pressed for time. Here are our tags. You've got our weapons in your lockers, and we need them as we leave."

"Sir," one of the harried marshals said, "we'll be with you as soon as we can. Can't you see we've got a lot of people to process?"

"I don't care how many people are lined up to get into this place," Barnes said. "We're entitled to get out." He gritted his teeth. "Now, *get us our guns.*"

"That attitude just earned you an extra five minutes," the marshal replied. "We give the orders, not you."

Barnes looked at Ahmed and shook his head in disgust. "You wait here for the guns," Barnes said. "I'll get the car and bring it out front."

Barnes left the courthouse, cut through the protesters, and headed north on Granby Street to where he had parked. Nikki exited a few seconds later, cut through the protesters, and headed south on Granby Street two blocks to get her car. She looked over her shoulder and saw the stocky man break into a jog. Nikki kicked off her heels and broke into a run of her own.

The timing was perfect. Ahmed received his Glock from the marshal just as Barnes pulled in front of the courthouse in his black Lincoln Continental. The marshal refused to turn loose Barnes's Smith and Wesson unless Barnes himself presented the claim slip. Ahmed gave the marshal some severe grief in nearly flawless English, then decided it wasn't worth the hassle. Barnes could get his weapon later.

The police cleared a path through the demonstrators as Ahmed exited

380 || DIRECTED VERDICT

the courthouse and entered the backseat of the Lincoln. His presence on Granby Street created quite a furor, as some of the protesters broke out in cheers and others hurled insults.

As Ahmed climbed into the vehicle, the man in the yellow chicken suit saw his chance for glory. He ditched his sign, slipped through the police lines, jumped up onto the hood of the Continental, and started shouting incoherently. In his mind's eye, it was a heroic move akin to Boris Yeltsin's mounting the Russian tank during the Moscow coup.

To the police, he was just another fruitcake who needed to be arrested.

Barnes blew his horn furiously, but the chicken kept jumping around on the hood. The police mounted the fenders, grabbed the man by the feathers, and pulled him, sliding, onto the pavement. They cuffed him, read him his rights, and dragged him kicking and screaming into a nearby squad car. They finally cleared a lane, and the Continental sped south on Granby, free at last from the circus in front of the courthouse.

The delay in the Continental's departure had allowed Nikki to reach her Sebring and position her car one block south of the mob that had delayed Barnes. As the Continental flew by in the opposite direction, Nikki pulled a quick three-point turn, holding up traffic and setting off a chorus of horns, then headed out in pursuit of Barnes.

Barnes had already placed several hundred feet and more than a few cars between his vehicle and Nikki's. But Nikki was determined and kept him in sight. The pursuit carried them through the busy side streets of Norfolk and then racing out of the city on I-264. As she drove, Nikki wondered where Barnes was headed and what in the world she would do if she actually caught him. But as always, she would take it one step at a time, and for now her only goal was to keep him in sight and not let him get away.

◁▷

Barnes called his firm in D.C. from his cell phone. "Lease a private jet immediately," he ordered. He thought for a moment. If he guessed right, the Norfolk airport would be crawling with federal agents within the hour. He would try a private municipal airport in Hampton. Nobody would expect that. "Lease it from the Hampton Municipal Airport. We'll be there in thirty minutes. File a flight plan for touchdown at Reagan National and then on to Riyadh, Saudi Arabia. We must take off immediately. We'll work out clearances for the other end once we're in the air. Two passengers. I don't care what it costs."

He ended his first call and immediately made a second. "Cancel the money wire," he said. "Everything's changed."

He had about thirty miles of interstate to cover to get to the airport, including a trip through the Hampton Roads Bridge Tunnel. It was risky. But he knew the attorneys would be squabbling in court for at least thirty minutes before Judge Baker-Kline even knew what was happening. It would be another hour before she could order any type of bench warrant. By then, Aberijan would be in the air and on his way outside the jurisdictional limits of the United States, far away from the reach of the judge and her federal court marshals.

But first Barnes had to shake Brad Carson's pesky paralegal. He kept the accelerator against the floor, intent on burying the speedometer needle, and flew by the other vehicles on the interstate. He would simply outrun Moreno. And if that didn't work, he would pull over and let her catch up. He would drag her into their vehicle, and Ahmed would put a gun to her head and end it. He knew that nothing would give the Saudi more pleasure than to extinguish the life of a woman who had already caused him so much grief.

45

JUDGE CYNTHIA BAKER-KLINE TOOK her perch on the bench in the hushed courtroom. She held the one-page proffer in her left hand and peered down over her long nose and reading glasses at Brad Carson. "Mr. Carson, there are very serious accusations contained in this document. The court does not take these allegations lightly."

The proposed testimony had stunned Brad just as much as it had Ichabod. He was just now getting his bearings and thinking straight. He still didn't understand all the implications. But he was in too far to turn back now.

"And we do not make them lightly," he answered.

"I'm going to allow the testimony, Mr. Carson," Ichabod ruled, her face wrinkled into sternness. "But if these accusations turn out to be unfounded, if this is just another gimmick, then I will personally petition the state bar to revoke your license. Is that clear?"

"Crystal clear, Your Honor."

Brad waited for the jury to return to their seats. He stood tall and straight, facing the rear of the courtroom. He looked down at Sarah one last time.

"She cares about you," Sarah whispered. "Trust her."

"The plaintiff calls Leslie Connors as our next witness," Brad announced.

A marshal disappeared into the hallway and a few seconds later opened the rear door of the courtroom. Leslie walked elegantly down the aisle, her head held high, her perfect lines gracing the courtroom. She avoided looking at Brad as she walked past him and stopped in the well of the court, raised her hand, and took the oath. She was dressed in a conservative white blouse, a black pin-striped skirt that hovered just above the knees, and a matching vest. Her auburn hair was pulled back and braided. Dark blue makeup accentuated her deep-set sky blue eyes.

How could the men on the jury not listen to *her*?

She took the stand with an unmistakable air of dignity. Only the redness of her eyes and the slight puffiness surrounding them betrayed the fact that this witness had probably not slept much the prior night.

"Please state your name for the record."

"Leslie Connors."

"Were you formerly co-counsel for the plaintiff in this case?"

"Yes."

"When did you withdraw from that role?"

"This morning."

Brad felt like he was in a dream; this moment was so surreal. He was starting the examination of his own co-counsel, a woman he had dated, and he didn't have the foggiest idea where this was ultimately headed. He was no longer in control, but at the mercy of a woman who had double-crossed him just last night. Still, the situation felt right.

There had been a flicker of hope in his subconscious the night before, a thought he didn't dare acknowledge, a spark that had now become a flame. Despite what he saw, could he still trust her?

At present, he had no choice.

"Are you testifying today under a grant of immunity?" Brad asked. He had picked up that much from reading the proffer.

"Yes."

"Will you tell the court how that came about?"

"Would you like me to start at the beginning?" Leslie asked.

"Please," Brad said. It was one of the best ideas he had heard in days.

◁▷

Nikki flew down the interstate, trying her best to keep pace with Barnes but dropping farther behind every minute. He was still barely in sight, now headed west on I-64 toward the Norfolk airport. She hoped the police would see the speeding vehicles and pull them over. She slowed ever so slightly and took one hand off the wheel to reach for her cell phone. She used the speed dial to reach Bella.

"Aberijan is heading west on 64. The airport's the next exit. I've barely got him in sight."

"We're not too far behind you," Bella said. "I'm pushing my Honda as fast as it'll go. Rasheed is with me, and the old boy looks like he's in shock."

"Look out!" Nikki heard Bella scream, apparently to some other driver. Nikki envisioned poor Rasheed, white knuckles clutching the dashboard, wondering what he had gotten himself into.

"Why don't you call the police?" Nikki heard Bella yell into the car phone.

"And tell them what?!" Nikki asked. "That they should pick up this visiting foreign dignitary for speeding? What about diplomatic immunity? The police won't get involved."

"Then why are *we* chasing him?" Bella asked. "What are *we* going to do?"

"I'm not sure," Nikki admitted. "I just know that if he leaves the country, we'll never see him again, but if . . . Bella! He went by the airport exit! He's heading for the tunnel!"

"Wha—" Then Nikki heard the sound of Bella's cell phone hitting the floor. She heard muffled shouts from Bella and Rasheed, but she heard no squealing of tires or crunching of metal.

She hit the End Call button and focused on the traffic she was flying by.

"Then why are we *chasing him?"* Bella had asked. *"What are* we *going to do?"*

In truth, Nikki had no idea what she would do if she caught Ahmed, but in the deepest depths of her subconscious, she knew exactly *why* she was chasing him. And now, for a fleeting moment, as the cars on I-64 became a blur, she allowed those subconscious thoughts to bubble to the surface—she allowed herself to admit it, to own the reason she was doing this. And she knew in that same instant that there could be no turning back.

Ahmed was no different from her father. Abusers prey on the innocent until they meet resistance; then they flee. Nikki had never tried to withstand her father when he beat on her mom . . . couldn't have stopped him if she tried . . . so she just turned up the volume of the music in her bedroom to drown him out. Then one day he up and left. Just like that. And she let him go . . . happy to rid their family of the beast.

But she had never confronted him, and nobody had ever held him accountable for the scars he had created. Sure, she ignored him; she never spoke to him again. That would hurt him, she told herself. That would pay him back.

Who was she kidding?

Years of abuse, and he just walked away! And right now he's probably doing it again to someone else. Years of hating myself because I never took him on.

Abusers prey on the innocent; then they run. Gone forever. Scot-free.

Not this time, she told herself.

The Sebring was now doing ninety-eight. She was gaining on them.

◁ ▷

"It all began this past summer," Leslie recounted, "when I returned from Europe to work full-time on this case. The first thing I learned was that I had missed a deadline for objecting to interrogatories—written questions that Sarah Reed had to answer under oath—and that Mr. Strobel was trying to use that mistake to win the case on a technicality."

"How was he trying to do that?" Brad asked. He remembered full well the tactics of Strobel, but he wanted to make sure the jury understood.

"Well, one of the interrogatories they sent to us asked Sarah to identify all the members of the churches in Saudi Arabia whom she ever worshiped with. Sarah knew that if she did that, they would be in danger—"

"Objection. She can't testify about what Sarah Reed knew or didn't know," Strobel said.

"Sustained," Ichabod ruled.

"Anyway," Leslie continued, without flinching, "I knew that we would not provide those names under any circumstances for fear of what might happen to those persons. So when we missed the deadline for objecting to the interrogatory, Mr. Strobel filed a motion asking this court to either make us answer that question or dismiss the case against us."

Brad was amazed at Leslie's apparent composure. Her voice and gaze were steady, hardly betraying the incredible pressure she was under. But she could not entirely fool Brad. He noticed the small red blotches on her neck, a sure sign she had scratched nervously in the hallway before she took the stand.

"How did that lead to a meeting with Mr. Aberijan?"

"It was at that point that I realized the defendants were not interested in justice, only about winning this case, and they would do anything to make it happen." She turned to the jury.

"Objection," Strobel shouted. "She's got no right to mischaracterize our conduct like that."

"Mr. Strobel, sit down and let the witness testify," Ichabod said curtly. "You can cross-examine her later."

Strobel sat down hard and dropped his pen noisily on the table. Ichabod shot him a look but said nothing.

"At that point," Leslie continued, unflustered by the distraction, "I decided that two could play this game. I couldn't bear to lose this case knowing that Mr. Aberijan had killed Sarah Reed's husband. I lost my own husband not so long ago to cancer, and I guess I became personally involved in Sarah's quest for justice. And I began to believe the system could not deliver justice on its own; it needed help. To Mr. Strobel, it seemed that justice was just a game, and I was not about to let him beat us at the game and deny my client the justice she deserved."

Strobel stood to object.

"Overruled," Ichabod said before he could speak.

"So I set up my own little sting operation," Leslie said. "I knew Aberijan would deny what he did until the end, so I decided to set a trap and obtain a confession."

"Why didn't you tell me?" Brad asked.

For the first time Leslie diverted her gaze from Brad and the jury. A pained expression crossed her face, her shoulders slumped, and she compressed her lips. When she spoke, her words came out softly, in the manner of a confessional.

"Because I knew you played so much by the book that you would never have allowed it. And by the time I was ready to come to you . . . wanted to come to you . . . I was prohibited by my immunity deal from doing that. There was so much at stake—this case, my future, everything really. . . ."

It was starting to make sense to Brad, but the sting of her betrayal lingered. Maybe she wasn't working *against* him on the case, but she was still going behind his back. She didn't trust him; it was as simple as that.

He could barely bring himself to ask the next question. It was of no legal significance, but he simply had to know. "Would you do it the same way again?"

Leslie hesitated and seemed to shrink back from the question. "Never," she said in a barely audible tone. "Your unshakable faith in the system and Sarah's unshakable faith in doing the right thing have impacted me in ways you'll never know. I eventually realized that the only thing that separates the good guys from the bad guys is that we're not willing to bend the rules to obtain justice."

Brad let out an audible sigh.

He now had a million other questions swirling through his mind. But first he needed to nail down the basics. Leslie was testifying under a grant of immunity. A good lawyer always put the details of those deals on the table first.

"Did you eventually negotiate with the authorities?" he asked.

"I approached Angela Bennett in the U.S. attorney's office," Leslie said. "She agreed to grant me immunity and agreed I could testify in this case before any arrests would be made." At this critical moment in her testimony, Leslie paused ever so slightly to let the tension build. She turned to face the jury squarely. "In return, I agreed not to talk to anyone else about this plan, except for a gentleman named Patrick O'Malley, who already knew, and I agreed to help obtain substantive evidence against Mr. Aberijan for obstruction of justice, witness intimidation, jury tampering, and conspiracy to commit murder."

This shocking list of accusations set off a wave of activity in the court-room, ranging from gasps to a general buzz of excitement. Mack Strobel stood and asked to approach the bench. Even Brad rocked back on his heels in disbelief.

◁▷

"Approach," Judge Cynthia Baker-Kline said.

Baker-Kline had a feeling during Leslie's testimony that something in the courtroom was different; something was out of place. Now, as she quickly surveyed the courtroom, her eyes came to rest on the first row of the specta-tor section, and she realized what it was. There, for the first time the entire trial, sat ADA Angela Bennett. And on the defendants' side of the court-room, though the lawyers were all sitting in their proper places—mouths now hanging open—Ahmed Aberijan had vanished.

"Ms. Bennett, you too," Baker-Kline commanded.

"Mr. Strobel," the judge said as she glowered at the defense lawyer over her wire rims, "I'm sure you've got a hundred and two objections, and we'll deal with those later. Right now, I need to know why Mr. Aberijan is not with us in court."

Mack Strobel looked at her and clenched his jaw. "I do not know where Mr. Aberijan is or why he is not here," he said tersely. "Further, even if I did know where he was, I would not be at liberty to say since he is my client and any information I have about his whereabouts would be protected by the attorney-client privilege."

Baker-Kline turned from Strobel to Bennett. "Is this true—this testi-mony about a deal to obtain evidence against Aberijan?"

"Yes."

388 || DIRECTED VERDICT

"Jury tampering? Obstruction of justice?"

"Yes."

"Conspiracy to commit murder?"

"Yes."

"Thank you," the judge said. "You may return to your seats." She waited calmly for the lawyers to take their places. "We will continue with testimony from Ms. Connors. But before we do, there is another urgent matter that we should tend to. Based on a sidebar with counsel of record and Ms. Bennett, I am hereby issuing a bench warrant for Mr. Aberijan to be brought into this courtroom to answer potential contempt charges along with other matters."

She turned to the marshals. "I want him brought before this court immediately, and I want you to begin by contacting the Norfolk airport and alerting officials there to check all outgoing international flights—including private charter flights."

The judge then turned to Brad, who had taken his place behind the podium. "You may now resume your examination," she said in the calmest tone imaginable.

◁▷

Clarence lumbered from the courtroom and went straight for the pay phones. The other marshals could call the Norfolk airport. He would call Bella Harper.

46

THE OBJECT OF THE U.S. MARSHALS' manhunt cursed the traffic as his vehicle approached the Hampton Roads Bridge Tunnel. Barnes kept his expletives to himself. They had entered the span of the bridge that snaked out over the Elizabeth River inlet of the Chesapeake Bay separating Norfolk from Hampton. The cars, SUVs, and trucks lined up bumper-to-bumper, barely inching along, as far as Barnes could see.

The bridge accommodated two lanes in each direction, with separate spans for the northbound and southbound traffic. There were small shoulders between the outside edges of the two lanes heading northbound and three-foot-high, two-foot-wide concrete abutments on each side of the bridge. The span hovered about thirty feet above the water when the river was at high tide, and it was undergirded at regular intervals by bundles of huge concrete pillars that supported the road surface and ran deep into the river bottom below. The bridge spanned about two miles of the river, then disappeared into a tunnel that took it below the river's surface. If Barnes and Ahmed could make it to the other side of the tunnel, they would be in Hampton and well on their way to the waiting jet.

"Do something, you fool!" the Saudi shouted from the backseat of the Lincoln. "We're losing valuable time."

Spurred by Ahmed's anger, Barnes turned on his flashers and rolled down his window. He moved from the left lane partially onto the left shoulder, but the big Lincoln could not maneuver past the car ahead, and so it straddled the yellow line marking the outside of the left lane. He pulled the vehicle as close to the concrete abutments as he dared, yelled out his window, and blew his horn. Slowly the drivers in front of him pulled partly into the right lane, allowing him to pass on the shoulder of the roadway.

◁ ▷

Less than a half mile back, Nikki mimicked Barnes's driving strategy and gained the right shoulder of the roadway. The narrow frame on her Sebring made it much easier to get by, and she had a good alibi. She stuffed a pair of sweatpants and a T-shirt from her gym bag inside her blouse. She then hit the flashers, leaned on the horn, and yelled that she was on her way to the hospital.

"My water broke! . . . Thank you! . . . I've got to get to the hospital! . . . Baby! . . . Thanks!" The cars parted like the Red Sea, as she advanced up the right-hand shoulder.

Her phone rang. "What?" she yelled. This was no time for a call. She had Barnes in sight no more than fifteen car lengths ahead.

"Ichabod issued a bench warrant for Ahmed," Bella yelled into the phone. "Don't let him get away."

"I won't; he's within sight. . . . Excuse me, sir—got to get to the hospital! Thanks, so much. . . . How far back are you? . . . Hey! Get out of the way! I'm going to the hospital. . . . Hurry up, Bella. . . ."

Nikki needed a break and found one just a few hundred yards from the tunnel. Barnes was wedged behind a pickup truck, and the two bubbas inside looked like they had no intention of letting him by. Barnes leaned out the driver's window and yelled at them over his hood, commanding them to move out of the way because he was on official government business.

The bubbas gestured and moved farther onto the shoulder to block the path of the Lincoln. The bigger of the bubbas even got out of the truck, stood on the shoulder, and asked Barnes if he wanted a piece of that action. Barnes continued to yell at the man but stayed in his car.

On the opposite shoulder, Nikki glided past the Lincoln and the pickup.

Suddenly the traffic began to pick up speed. Nikki glanced over her shoulder to see that the pickup was moving and that the Lincoln was cruising along behind. Traffic was only rolling at about fifteen miles an hour, but Nikki knew the fickle nature of the tunnel snarls and estimated that in no time the vehicles could be moving at close to normal speeds.

If Barnes and Ahmed made it to the other side of the tunnel, they could not be contained. Several quick exits led to hundreds of roads, and Nikki was sure she would never see them again. They had to be stopped now.

She pulled her Sebring squarely into the right lane of traffic. There traffic moved at about twenty miles an hour. She was about four car lengths in front of the pickup and the Lincoln, which were moving slightly faster in the left-hand lane. Nikki said a quick prayer for forgiveness, then made her move.

She cranked the wheel hard left, broadsiding the car next to her and wedging him at an angle into the concrete abutment at the left-hand edge of the road surface. Then she swerved hard to her right, forcing her car perpendicular to the traffic, turning straight toward the concrete abutment on the right side of the road. She slammed on her brakes.

In the very next instant, a millisecond of time, she felt the jolt of her own sudden stop, her head jerked about like a rag doll. She heard the sound of crunching metal and broken headlights, the squeal of tires, and the blaring of horns. She braced herself to be hit broadside. The second collision, however, never came. The cars behind her miraculously came to a stop just short of her Sebring.

Nikki jumped out of the car and surveyed the damage she had caused. The car she had forced into the abutment had been hit in the rear by another at a low speed. That fender bender, coupled with her car angled across the right shoulder and right lane, brought traffic to a complete stop. There was no room for even one lane to get through. The occupants of the other cars appeared to be fine. For a split second, Nikki flushed with pride at her accomplishment.

Her pride quickly gave way to fear. Barnes and Ahmed came sprinting toward her, Ahmed wielding a large black pistol. Other drivers also alighted from their cars and were now yelling at Nikki. In the chaos, Ahmed ran ever closer, then crouched.

Nikki moved toward the concrete abutment behind her Sebring. She pointed at Barnes and Ahmed. "They're trying to kill me!" she yelled as she backed toward the edge of the bridge.

As Ahmed crouched, he extended both arms, steadily taking aim. He was no more than fifty feet away. The barrel of the gun looked huge. She could dive behind her vehicle, but if she hit the ground, Barnes would be on top of her in a second.

She felt the concrete behind her, turned, placed both her hands on the abutment. She heard Barnes yell "Stop!" as he closed on her.

Nikki glanced in fright at the choppy water below, then thought about the gun. She took a deep breath and swung her legs out to the side, jumping over the top of the abutment and pushing off with both hands. She brought her legs together so that she would knife into the water.

She held her breath and prepared herself to plummet through thirty-three feet of air. As she closed her eyes, she heard the pop of Ahmed's gun.

◁▷

"Let's go back to the beginning," Brad suggested. "Why don't you explain the circumstances leading to your first contact with Mr. Aberijan on this case."

Leslie looked at the back wall, collecting her thoughts, then turned to Brad. "The day that I learned Mr. Strobel was trying to have this case dismissed on a technicality, I had a long talk with Sarah. I remember that I was filled with anger about what the defendants were doing, but she was so forgiving and accepting. She told me that she harbored no hatred toward either Mr. Aberijan or Mr. Strobel. She said that hate only consumes the person who hates."

She looked admiringly toward Sarah and continued. "The night after we had that conversation, I couldn't sleep and could only think about losing my own husband and about Sarah's loss. That night I decided to take matters into my own hands."

"What did you do?"

"I had been working on a document called 'Preliminary Game Plan for *Reed v. Saudi Arabia.*' It had lists of witnesses, exhibits—those types of things. Frankly, it was all the kind of stuff that the defendants would be entitled to obtain through the normal discovery processes, but I knew that Mr. Aberijan wouldn't know that. So I took that document and edited out any confidential stuff I didn't want the other side to see, like the fact that we would be calling Rasheed Berjein as a witness, and I mailed a sanitized version to Mr. Aberijan along with a letter demanding fifty-thousand U.S. dollars and containing wiring instructions for a Cayman Island bank account."

"Did Mr. Aberijan know who you were at this time?"

"I don't think so. The letter was anonymous."

"Okay," a curious Brad said. "When did you contact Mr. Aberijan a second time?"

"The second time was after I met with and prepared a potential expert witness for us named Alfred Lloyd Worthington—"

"I should have known," Brad mumbled.

"What was that, Counsel?" Ichabod asked. She was leaning forward now, her scribble pad sitting untouched in front of her.

"Nothing, Your Honor."

Leslie continued. "Mr. Worthington was a Washington lobbyist and former congressman who served on the House Foreign Relations Committee. He was going to testify about how the nation of Saudi Arabia sanctioned the actions of their religious police, the Muttawa."

"Your Honor, this is ridiculous," Strobel interjected. "They did not call Worthington to testify. They should not be allowed to put in his testimony by proxy through this witness."

"I agree," Ichabod said. "Ms. Connors, refrain from discussing the proposed testimony of Mr. Worthington."

"Yes, Your Honor," Leslie said, without missing a beat. "In the course of preparing him for his testimony, I learned that Mr. Worthington had pleaded 'no contest' to a misdemeanor charge that resulted from beating his wife. I was not about to put a wife beater on the stand as an expert in a case alleging police abuse by Mr. Aberijan. I also believed that the defendants would uncover this information too, so I decided to use Mr. Worthington's testimony as my second piece of bait."

"Then how did you think we were going to make that part of our case?" Brad's frustration was beginning to show. He didn't like hearing his expert witnesses referred to as "bait."

"I knew," Leslie said, "that if this sting worked, we wouldn't need Worthington. And if it didn't work, all the Worthingtons in the world couldn't help us. I knew it was a huge gamble, but it seemed like a chance I had to take."

No it wasn't, he wanted to say. *You didn't need to resort to this to win this case.* But he would admonish her later.

"How did you use Worthington's testimony as bait?" Brad asked, getting back on track.

"I sent a second anonymous letter that explained that Worthington had an Achilles heel that could be exploited. I basically told Mr. Aberijan about the no-contest plea of Worthington in Alexandria General District Court. I told him that information would cost one hundred thousand dollars."

Brad could feel the heat rising on his neck. It was a wonder he had any case left at all. "What happened at Worthington's deposition?" he asked.

"Mr. Strobel asked him a few questions about whether he had ever abused his wife, and Worthington withdrew as an expert," Leslie summarized.

Judge Baker-Kline eyeballed Strobel. She was not content to let this go. "Do you have any information to suggest that Mr. Strobel was part of this conspiracy?" she asked Leslie.

Leslie looked hard at Strobel and then furrowed her brow as she considered her answer. The man's reputation hung in the balance, and Brad could sense that Leslie was wavering. If the shoe were on the other foot, Strobel would hang them out to dry in a heartbeat. What did Leslie know? And what would she tell?

"No, none at all," she said at last.

Other than a slight relaxation of his shoulders, there was no visible reaction from Mack Strobel.

"What happened next?" A safe question to ask, as Brad had no idea where the witness was heading.

"I decided it was time to bring Mr. Aberijan to the trap," Leslie answered coldly.

"How did you do that?"

"Well, I figured the best place to meet a man as dangerous as Mr. Aberijan would be a public place with lots of police officers. So I picked General District Court in Norfolk. I sent him a letter and told him to meet me there alone on a certain date. I told him to bring some transmitters so I could bug our office."

"You did what?" asked an astonished Brad, eyebrows raised in disbelief.

"You'll remember that after the Worthington incident, we were all paranoid and decided we would not use our office phones for any confidential communications. We hired a private investigator, Patrick O'Malley, to check for listening devices. He would come by the office and do that every morning. I believed that I needed something to cement Mr. Aberijan's trust so that he wouldn't think he was being set up. I knew that if I placed some bugs on our office phone lines, he wouldn't hear anything more than harmless information. I also knew that he would no longer have any suspicions about a setup. And finally, I knew that I could simply reattach the transmitters every morning after O'Malley left and take them off every night."

"I thought you said O'Malley already knew."

"Now you're getting ahead of the story."

"Then tell us what happened at this meeting."

"We had a very short conversation. When I invited Mr. Aberijan to the meeting, I told him that I had a plan for knocking out our best remaining expert, Dr. Nancy Shelhorse. I told him the price would be one hundred thousand dollars. At the meeting, he delivered three shortwave radio transmitters. He told me he actually thought it was a bad idea. I think his words were something like, 'Do you really think these are necessary?' But I assured him I knew what I was doing, then left."

Brad was having a hard time believing what he was hearing. From the moment he saw Leslie at the Marriott the prior night, he assumed that she had been responsible for keeping Shelhorse out of the case. But he allowed himself to hope otherwise. Now the reality of it was sinking in, and he was numb.

"But you still didn't talk to me about this."

"I started getting nervous, realizing I was in way over my head. I was playing an awkward game of espionage with a cold-blooded killer. A part of me desperately wanted to tell you everything that was happening, but it was more important for me to protect you and keep you out of this nightmare I had created." Leslie bit her lower lip and paused. "I didn't want to lose you."

Brad looked down at the podium. He felt uncomfortable discussing such a private matter in open court. He admonished himself to stick to the facts, make it easier on Leslie.

"What happened next?"

"I needed more proof before I could go to the authorities," she said, regaining the cool professionalism that had characterized her testimony thus far. "But my plans started to unravel on the third day of trial."

"What do you mean?"

"Mr. Aberijan approached me in the elevator and handed me a note. In it, he demanded details about my plan to deal with Shelhorse. He also demanded a meeting for that Friday at 8:30 a.m. in Norfolk General District Court. He wanted the transmitters back.

"His boldness scared me, but the note gave me what I needed to go to the district attorney. The problem was that I needed to get back to the office before everyone else after court that day in order to retrieve the transmitters.

"When I returned to the office, Patrick O'Malley was there. Instead of his customary inspection that morning, he had conducted his search just a few minutes prior to my arrival that afternoon. Of course, he had found the three devices I was using."

"What did you do?" Brad asked. He was still having a hard time believing his old friend O'Malley was in on this.

"I took Mr. O'Malley into the conference room and told him everything. He agreed to hold it in confidence and help me if I promised to go to the authorities the next day. He became a partner in my sting operation."

"Did you go to the authorities?"

"Yes. The next day, Mr. O'Malley and I went to see Ms. Bennett. She agreed to grant me immunity and let me testify in this case before she had Mr. Aberijan arrested. But it was conditioned on catching Mr. Aberijan with some hard evidence and also on not talking about this operation with anybody else." Leslie paused and gave Bennett a look; then she turned back to Brad. "Including you."

Brad was not surprised. Bennett had never liked him much.

"What happened when you met Mr. Aberijan this second time?"

"I went to the meeting with Mr. Aberijan," Leslie explained, "knowing that he was somehow scanning me for bugs. But I also knew that I would be returning the three transmitters he had originally given me. Mr. O'Malley found a way to tap into the frequency of Mr. Aberijan's shortwave transmitters. So Mr. O'Malley stationed himself outside the courthouse, listened to our conversation, and taped every word."

"What happened?"

"Mr. Aberijan accused me of wearing a wire. I simply gave him the three transmitters. He was very rough with me. He grabbed my arm and jerked me around. He demanded to know the plan for waylaying Shelhorse."

"What did you tell him?"

Leslie paused. There was not the slightest stirring in the courtroom. "I told him I could buy one of the jurors," she said.

Brad looked to the jury box in time to see juror four turn ashen.

"And what was his response?" Brad asked reluctantly. He was no longer sure he wanted to know. Things were growing more bizarre by the minute.

"He wanted to know which juror," Leslie said. "He said that they already owned one."

"I object," Strobel announced, no longer able to contain himself. "This is blatant hearsay."

"No it's not," Brad countered. "It's an admission of a party opponent. Besides, it's all on tape. I'll have some equipment brought in here and play the tape if I have to."

"There's no need for that at this point," Ichabod said. She seemed anxious to hear the rest of this testimony. "We'll play the tape later. But this witness is entitled to testify from memory about this conversation and the resulting admissions of a party opponent. Objection overruled."

"May I continue?" Leslie asked.

"Proceed," the judge granted.

It seemed to Brad that Ichabod was displaying the slightest hint of a growing respect for this witness. Maybe she liked her bold search for the truth. Maybe she liked the fact that Leslie had done all this behind Brad's back. Maybe she just liked the scenario of a resourceful young woman outfoxing an experienced and powerful man. But whatever was causing her change in mood, Ichabod was plainly fascinated with this testimony.

"Mr. Aberijan told me that they already owned a juror. So he asked me which one I was dealing with to make sure it wasn't the same one."

"To make sure the record is clear," Brad said. "Had you actually talked to any jurors up to this point in time or have you talked to any jurors since?" He held his breath.

"No," Leslie said.

Brad exhaled. "What did you say to Mr. Aberijan?"

"I knew I had to make a quick guess." Leslie turned slightly in her seat and faced the jury head-on. Most of the jurors crossed their arms and gave her a stern look. "Based on blatant body language during the trial, I assumed that juror number four was firmly on their side. So I would not name him. Frankly, I assumed that he was the one Ahmed already 'owned.'" She leveled an accusatory gaze at the pale face of Zeke Stein. He had his arms crossed and stared right back.

"The one juror that had been impossible to read throughout the trial—the one who just sat stoically and impassively through everything—was juror number six. I concluded that if I had noticed, Mr. Aberijan must have noticed too. So it would be believable if I picked juror number six, so long as he wasn't actually on the take already. That's what I guessed. And Ahmed accepted it."

She turned directly to juror number six. "I'm sorry, sir," she said.

Juror six nodded his head ever so slightly, his expression never changing.

Strobel rocketed to his feet. "Objection," he roared. "That is highly improper, and I move for a mistrial."

"Objection sustained," Ichabod said. "Please disregard Ms. Connors's apology. As for the mistrial, I can see why you would want one, but you're not entitled to one."

Something suddenly dawned on Brad.

"Ms. Connors, how did you communicate with Mr. Aberijan on these occasions? I am under the impression that he does not understand a word of English."

Leslie smiled for the first time since taking the stand. "I thought you'd never ask," she said. "The man speaks almost perfect English. You'll hear it yourself on the tape."

"What else will we hear on the tape?" Brad asked.

"Two other things of importance," Leslie noted calmly. "The first is my reference to a trust document for an account in a Swiss bank. I called this my life insurance policy, but it was really a means to show that Mr. Aberijan was not acting alone. I asked that one hundred million be deposited in a Swiss bank account subject to the terms of a trust agreement that was to be signed by a high-ranking Saudi official other than Mr. Aberijan. The trust document would state that if I died, the executor appointed in my will would investigate my death. If he concluded that I was murdered, the one hundred million would go to Sarah Reed and her children. If he concluded that I died of natural causes, the one hundred million would revert to the nation of Saudi Arabia."

"Amazing," Brad said without thinking. *It truly was a brilliant idea.* "And was this trust agreement ever signed?" he asked.

"Yes. It was delivered to me at the last meeting that I had with Mr. Aberijan, which occurred just last night. Mr. O'Malley should be bringing a copy of it to court in a few minutes. He'll also have a fax showing the balance of the Swiss account with a deposit this morning of one hundred million dollars."

Brad allowed a small smile to crease his lips. *This girl thinks of everything.*

"And the second item of interest?"

"After I left the meeting, Mr. Aberijan had possession of the transmitters, and they were, of course, still transmitting. After he left the courtroom, he called another gentleman and ordered this gentleman to find out who the executor of my will was." She tilted her head sideways as she looked at Brad. *Are you ready for this?* she asked with her eyes.

He nodded.

"You will hear Ahmed Aberijan order the murder of both me and my executor within one day after this jury returns a verdict."

A collective gasp filled the courtroom. Reporters, no longer able to contain themselves, scurried for the doors. The remaining spectators all talked at once, and Ichabod had trouble restoring order as she furiously banged her gavel.

"We need some equipment in here to listen to that tape," she barked to her bailiff. *"Now!"*

◁ ▷

In the excitement swirling around him, Mack Strobel was largely ignored. All of his years of experience had never prepared him for this. He had rapidly absorbed one shocking revelation after another. And now he was about to listen to his client admit to jury tampering and order two murders, all on tape. Any other lawyer would have been packing his bags. But not Mack Strobel. His expression never changed.

"This old dog still has one more trick," he mumbled to himself.

But it would be hard to argue with a tape.

47

NIKKI MORENO HEARD the shot but felt nothing except the exhilaration of her free fall. She had no time to be thankful. In the next instant, she was knifing through the murky depths of the Elizabeth River. The icy water stabbed at her like a million needles and sucked her breath away.

She descended into the depths for what seemed like an eternity; then she gained the presence of mind to flail her arms and legs to reach the surface. She kicked and pulled, kicked and pulled, but still the water overhead was black. Her breath was gone, but she kicked and climbed some more.

Finally . . . the surface.

She sprang out of the waters gasping for breath, constricted by the cold. She quickly looked up, just in time to see Barnes leaning over the concrete abutment. He was joined by Ahmed, whose gun was pointed at her. She filled her lungs and dove under the water.

The bullet made a short hissing sound as it entered the water. It must have been inches from her head. She had not had a chance to collect much air in her lungs, but she forced herself deeper and began frog kicking toward the concrete pillars under the bridge. If she could just get to the pillars and slide to the side opposite the men, perhaps she would live.

Her lungs gave out before she felt the pillars. Nikki surfaced quickly, gagging on the salt water, and looked up. Ahmed was almost directly overhead and had anticipated her move. He aimed his gun straight at her head and flashed a wicked smile.

◁▷

Rasheed and Bella were caught in the snarl of the traffic jam. Like the others, they had tried to sneak forward on the shoulders of the roadway, but they had not had much success. Bella began pounding on the steering wheel in frustration. Rasheed looked at her, peered ahead at the traffic, pointed to himself, then pointed ahead on the bridge. He jumped out of the car and sprinted past the stopped traffic.

Bella called after him, but Rasheed never turned around. She almost cursed and bit her tongue instead. She said a quick prayer, turned on her flashers, grabbed her pistol from her purse, rolled out of the vehicle, and lumbered after Rasheed.

◁▷

Rasheed heard the horns blowing as he ran. He heard shouts in the distance between Barnes and the men in the pickup truck. A few seconds later, he heard the smashing of metal and the breaking of glass. He saw the havoc caused by Nikki's kamikaze maneuver. As he approached the scene, he witnessed Barnes and Ahmed getting out of their car and running toward Nikki. He saw Barnes run ahead and Ahmed crouch. Then he saw Nikki jump.

When they saw Ahmed fire, gawking motorists ducked in their vehicles or jumped behind them for cover. Ahmed ran to the edge of the bridge and leaned over the concrete wall. Barnes stood next to him, also looking over the edge and searching the waters. As he ran, Rasheed saw Ahmed aim and fire a shot at the water below.

A few more steps and Rasheed was rounding the back of Nikki's car, just a few feet from Barnes and Ahmed. The director of the Muttawa raised his gun again and took aim. Rasheed launched himself into a flying tackle, landing his shoulder squarely against Ahmed's broad back. Rasheed's body slammed against the bigger man, jarring lose the gun, sending it tumbling toward Nikki in the river below. The blow also jolted Ahmed and hammered his body against the concrete abutment. Both men fell hard, in a pile, onto the pavement with arms, legs, and torsos intertwined.

◁▷

Ahmed shook Rasheed loose and staggered to his feet. Rasheed got halfway up, still bent at the waist, one hand on his knee. Ahmed stepped toward the smaller man and pounded a vicious forearm into Rasheed's face, knocking him onto his back. Ahmed spit at Rasheed, then turned around to look back over the edge of the bridge.

Nikki was nowhere in sight.

He stared at the water, waiting for her to surface. But there was no sign of her in the water.

Ahmed turned back to Rasheed, who was lying on his back on the pavement, trying to rise, and shaking his head to clear the dizziness. Ahmed stepped forward, practically frothing at the mouth. A powerful kick squarely on Rasheed's jaw would snap the man's neck like a twig.

Other motorists still kept their distance. Barnes stood back as well. He knew there was no way to stop the Right Hand of Mohammed.

"Beg," Ahmed sneered, as he towered over Rasheed. He repeated the command in Arabic.

He waited as Rasheed looked up at him. But this time, there was no fear in Rasheed's eyes. Only contempt.

"Never," Rasheed replied softly in Arabic.

"Beg!" Ahmed screamed, determined to smell the fear before he killed. "Beg like a dog!"

Rasheed stared back in determined silence.

Ahmed flexed every muscle and drew back his powerful leg.

◁▷

"Don't move!" Bella yelled in a shrill, breathless voice. She was still several feet away, huffing and puffing, but she clutched the small Beretta pistol in her hand and pointed it squarely at Ahmed. In all her excitement, she couldn't remember if she had correctly released the safety.

Ahmed relaxed his leg and turned a contemptuous look on Bella. He stared for a second, sizing up the woman, and began to walk slowly toward her. Her hands shook as she tried to remember the shooting lessons she had taken so long ago.

"One more step and I'll blow you away!" she screamed. It was meant to sound tough, but it came out more as a squeal than a command.

Ahmed continued to advance.

"I mean it!" she yelled.

He was less than twenty feet away. A few more steps and he could lunge at her.

She decided to scare him by firing at his feet. Show him that she meant business. She aimed, closed her eyes, and squeezed the trigger.

She also jerked her arm up at the last second.

Bella heard the smack of the bullet, the tearing of flesh, the cracking of bone, and a full-throated yell. She opened her eyes to see Ahmed's right knee buckle. She watched in horror as blood poured through his pant leg and flowed onto the pavement.

She swung the gun toward Barnes, who took a few giant steps back and never took his eyes off Bella. Then her hands began shaking uncontrollably, and she dropped the gun. She collapsed into a heap and sobbed.

◁ ▷

Rasheed was still woozy but had the presence of mind to grab Bella's gun. He motioned with it for Barnes to stand next to his wounded partner. Then, with the small but lethal Beretta still aimed at the two men, Rasheed slowly circled around them and shuffled over to the edge of the bridge.

While watching his new prisoners, Rasheed leaned slightly out over the concrete abutment and yelled down to the water below.

"Everything is fine!" he screamed in Arabic.

◁ ▷

In the next second, Nikki poked her head out from behind one of the concrete pillars.

"Everything is fine!" she yelled back in Arabic as she looked in disbelief at the smiling face of Rasheed above. Her lips were going numb as she shivered in the water, but she could hold on for a while longer. She now had hope.

And she could hear the beautiful sound of sirens wailing in the distance.

◁ ▷

Ichabod and the jurors barely moved as they listened to Ahmed boast on tape, in perfect English, about the juror he "owned." They heard him discuss the terms of payment for knocking Nancy Shelhorse out of the case and for buying a defense verdict. And they stared at the tape player in disbelief, straining to hear Ahmed, as he ordered the murders of Leslie and her executor. It was hard to make out all the words, but a discriminating listener could clearly hear Ahmed pronounce the death sentences.

Ichabod had Brad rewind the tape and replay it three times. The recording changed many things for Brad. He could hear the trembling in Leslie's voice as she tried to act brave in front of Ahmed. He could hear the business-as-usual tone of Ahmed as he ordered the murders. It drove home to him, for the first time, how much Leslie had risked. His thoughts were no longer about *himself*—*why didn't she tell* me? *Why did she lie to* me? His thoughts turned to *her*—the danger *she* was in. The pressure *she* was under. The brilliance of *her* plan.

When he finished playing it the third time, Brad moved the tape into evidence, and Exhibit Number 63 became an official part of the case.

Leslie explained how she and O'Malley prevented Shelhorse's testimony. It was O'Malley, she said, who sent the e-mail from Nikki's computer. And it was O'Malley who deleted a telephone message left by Shelhorse later that day.

With the jury still intently focused on his witness, Brad directed her attention to the prior night and her meeting with Ahmed. He had Leslie describe the meeting and how she had finally obtained the trust agreement signed by the Saudi minister of public safety. Leslie told the jury about her bizarre encounter with Frederick Barnes outside the Marriott.

"What happened after Mr. Barnes left?"

"The valet brought my car around. He slipped me a note when he opened my door."

"From whom?"

"Mr. O'Malley. The note said that listening devices had been placed inside my car and cell phone while I was meeting with Ahmed. The note said to be careful about what I said." She paused, her lips forming a thin and worried line. The events of last night seemed to pain her the most. "When I talked to Mr. O'Malley later that night on the phone, we both made it seem like we were really going to buy a defense verdict, then leave town."

Brad paused for a moment and pondered his next question. Part of him wanted to drag her through last night's confrontation again, ask her to explain one more time why she lied to him, make her realize how much it had hurt him. But another part of him, the part that saw her nervousness under the mask of cool, the part that noticed the red blotches on her neck, the part that *loved* her, wanted to spare her any more pain. She had been through enough. She had done it for him, for the case.

It was no contest.

"Let me direct your attention away from the events of last night," Brad resumed, "and to the issue of the trust agreement."

He carefully studied Leslie's reaction, but instead of relief washing over her face as Brad expected, he watched her countenance fall, the blood instantly draining from her face. It was the same look Brad had seen on the first day of trial, when Leslie told him they had drawn Ichabod as their judge.

◁ ▷

Leslie happened to be looking toward the back of the courtroom when O'Malley entered. A quick shake of his head told her everything she needed to know. It was O'Malley's job to get a faxed copy of the Swiss account showing the hundred-million-dollar deposit. His dejected look, one Leslie had never seen on his face before, made it obvious that he had failed.

All this work down the tubes. The planning. The risk. Jeopardizing my relationship with Brad. All for naught if I can't prove the money is in the account. What will prevent Strobel from arguing that Ahmed forged the signature and acted alone? The nation of Saudi Arabia will be off the hook.

God, cut me a break. Just once. For Sarah's sake.

O'Malley walked down the aisle, whispered a few words in Brad's ear, then handed Brad two documents. As she watched, the private investigator glumly took a seat in the front row.

Brad placed exhibit stickers on the documents, then looked up at Leslie. She expected panic on his face but saw none. Not even a hint of disappointment. Leslie had seen this look before—the moot court tournament. *Trust me,* he was saying. *Gladly,* she smiled back.

"I'd like to hand you two documents marked for identification," Brad said. "The first is a signed trust agreement; the second is a faxed bank statement showing the balance in a Swiss bank account subject to the trust agreement."

Mack Strobel jumped to his feet. Brad's eyes twinkled. "Objection," he roared. "How can this witness possibly authenticate these documents that were just now handed to Mr. Carson. He hasn't even established if she's seen them before."

Brad spread his palms in protest. "That's because I haven't had a chance."

Judge Baker-Kline looked over her glasses at Leslie. "Didn't you say Mr. Aberijan gave you the signed trust agreement last night?"

"Yes, ma'am."

"And this account balance, have you ever seen that before?"

Leslie paused and sighed. For effect. "No, Your Honor," she replied gloomily. "I haven't."

"Then I'll sustain the objection as to the account balance statement and overrule the objection on the signed trust agreement."

"But, Your Honor—," Brad protested.

Has he lost his mind? Leslie wondered.

"Mr. Carson," Ichabod cut him off, "I've ruled."

Brad frowned. "Yes, Your Honor. After the introduction of this exhibit, I'll pass the witness."

◁▷

Brad handed the signed trust agreement to the court clerk. He took his seat and placed the bank account statement, showing that not a dime had reached the Swiss trust account, onto the table in front of him. He casually placed a legal pad on top of it.

Mack Strobel, always the consummate showman, rose slowly and furrowed his brow. He took on a pained expression, as if he had a grave announcement to make about a matter that troubled him greatly.

"Before I begin my cross-examination, I have a motion to make." He shuffled some papers, then looked up at Ichabod. "From the outset of the case, I have doubted whether I could fairly represent both Mr. Aberijan personally and the nation of Saudi Arabia without generating a serious conflict of interest. I warned Mr. Aberijan about this at our very first meeting."

He paused for effect, and Brad rolled his eyes, hoping one of the jurors was watching.

"It has now become clear that I can no longer represent both defendants. I therefore request leave of the court to withdraw as counsel of record for Mr. Aberijan because of an unavoidable conflict of interest. From this point on, I can represent only the nation of Saudi Arabia."

"I can understand why you would want to withdraw as counsel for Mr. Aberijan," Ichabod commented. "And since he is not here to object, your motion is granted. But it does not mean that this trial will be delayed even one minute so that he can get a new lawyer. Is that clear, Mr. Strobel?"

"Yes, Your Honor, and thank you for your indulgence," Strobel responded. Then he took his place behind the podium and turned to Leslie.

"Did you ever speak with the Saudi Arabian minister of public safety about this case?"

"No."

"Or anyone else from Saudi Arabia for that matter, other than Mr. Aberijan?"

"Yes, I spoke to Mr. el Khamin."

"Anyone other than Mr. el Khamin? What I mean is, did you ever speak with officials from the Saudi Arabian government?"

"No."

"And have you even seen an authentic signature of the minister of public safety, to compare with the purported signature on the document provided by Mr. Aberijan?"

"No."

Strobel nodded solemnly, as if he had just elicited a stunning admission.

"Then isn't it possible that the same Ahmed Aberijan whom we just heard on the tape casually order the deaths of two people and talk about bribing jurors, isn't it just possible that this deceitful man might have forged the signature of the minister of public safety? Couldn't this all just be a fraud perpetrated by Mr. Aberijan himself, with absolutely no authority or sanction from the Saudi government?"

It doesn't take Strobel long to turn on a former client, Brad thought.

"No, I don't believe that's possible," Leslie said confidently.

"Not even *possible*?" Strobel asked, emphasizing the last word and raising his eyebrows. "Why not?"

"Because I didn't believe then, and I don't believe now," Leslie answered coolly, "that Mr. Aberijan had access to a hundred million dollars of his own. I believe that Mr. Aberijan's higher-ups are very much aware of what he did to Charles Reed and very much involved in this case. Where else could money for this trust account come from? Your client, the nation of Saudi Arabia, is every bit as much to blame as Mr. Aberijan."

"But you have no proof that any money is sitting in that Swiss account. Do you, Ms. Connors?"

Brad couldn't help but flinch. He noticed Leslie quickly scratch at the base of her neck. Then calmly, precisely, she steadied her gaze. "Mr. O'Malley is sitting right there in the first row, sir. Why don't you call him to the stand and ask him?"

Beautiful.

Brad glanced at Strobel and, for the first time in the case, saw something other than confidence in the man's eyes. Strobel had been hit with so much, so fast, that he never saw that answer coming. It was a rookie error, asking a question like that. Now Brad could tell that Strobel was instantly recalculating the case, assessing the danger of this witness, forming the desire to get done with this cross-examination quickly and gracefully—before more damage could be done.

"And even though you never talked to anyone, never met anyone, and never communicated with anyone from the nation of Saudi Arabia about this case, except for Mr. Aberijan himself, you somehow think that the nation of Saudi Arabia is responsible for Mr. Aberijan's conduct?"

"That's absolutely right," Leslie said.

"Then if *that's* plaintiff's case," Strobel noted derisively, "I renew my motion for a directed verdict on behalf of the nation of Saudi Arabia. The plaintiff has no proof whatsoever that Mr. Aberijan did not simply forge the signature of a Saudi official and embezzle the money for the trust account himself."

Before Brad could speak in opposition, Ichabod responded. "Isn't that a motion that should be more properly considered outside the presence of the jury?"

"Absolutely, Your Honor," Strobel replied.

"Then the witness may step down. Bailiff, please excuse the jury for a few moments so I can announce my ruling," she ordered.

Leslie breathed a huge sigh of relief, held her head high, and stepped down from the witness box. As she walked past the counsel table, most eyes in the courtroom were on the jury members, particularly juror number four, as they shuffled out of the box. Brad took advantage of this momentary distraction and grabbed Leslie's hand as she passed. He pulled her next to him and whispered in her ear.

"Does the witness have plans for this evening?" he asked.

Leslie placed a hand on his shoulder and whispered, "Spending time with my former co-counsel, if he'll let me."

She pulled back, but her look lingered. He winked, and she nodded, then thrust her chin out and walked elegantly down the aisle, taking a seat in the back of the courtroom.

◁▷

Within minutes, the jury had exited, and all eyes turned to Judge Cynthia Baker-Kline.

"Do you have any evidence of your own, Mr. Strobel, any live witnesses or documentary evidence that would suggest this trust agreement signature is a fraud?" she asked.

"Not at this time," Strobel answered. "But if we could have a twenty-four-hour continuance—"

"Nonsense," Baker-Kline interrupted. "We've been doing nothing but continuing and delaying this case since we started. Either put up or shut up." She knew her comment was rude, almost childish. But she had heard enough about continuances and delays. She glanced toward Brad Carson, who had folded his arms and leaned back in his chair, apparently enjoying the sight of somebody else getting chewed out for a change.

"Mr. Carson," the judge snarled. Brad practically jumped out of his seat. "Do you have a motion to make?"

"Um, yes, Your Honor," he stuttered, obviously unaware of what she meant. Then a look of recognition gleamed in his eyes, followed by a look of skepticism and a look of hope. It was almost as if he didn't trust her, or couldn't believe what he thought he was hearing.

Finally, he cleared his throat. "We also move for a directed verdict, but in favor of the plaintiff, not the defendant."

"Thank you, Counsel," Baker-Kline said. "You may both be seated."

The judge intended to savor this moment of high drama in the courtroom as she considered her ruling. She jotted a few notes down on her legal pad—*2 percent milk, English muffins, laundry detergent, chips*—keenly aware that every eye was watching every scratch of her pen.

She thought about Win Mackenzie, smugly perched in the front row, convinced that she would never do anything to jeopardize her chances for an appellate court nomination. She allowed herself to dwell just briefly on the years of hard work—the drug cases, the asbestos cases, the pure junk that marched through her courtroom every day. How sweet it would be to sit on the court of appeals and hear only the interesting cases being argued by top-flight lawyers. One step below the Supremes!

She glanced up from her scribbling and looked straight into the eyes of Win Mackenzie. Confident eyes. Presumptuous eyes. He knew how badly she wanted it.

"Gentlemen, I have never, in all my years on the bench, seen a case where both sides showed such little respect for the judicial system." She knew vintage scolding was her strong suit. "Plaintiff's counsel has tried every trick in the book to goad me into losing my composure so he can have a mistrial. At the same time, his co-counsel has breached the professional rules of responsibility for lawyers and recorded a conversation with an adverse party in the case. Her conduct was clever, and her plan was bold, but it hardly comported with model conduct for an officer of the court."

Baker-Kline glared at Brad. She looked for Leslie and spotted her in the back. Leslie's face was bright red.

"On the other hand, her plan did shine much light on some of the most reprehensible conduct I have ever witnessed in all my years on the bench. Suffice it to say there is clear and convincing evidence that the defendant will do whatever it takes to win, including bribing jurors and intimidating witnesses."

Baker-Kline paused again for effect and watched as Leslie's face regained some of its natural color.

"After what I have heard today, I can only conclude that this jury panel is so tainted, including at least one member who has been bribed, and possibly more, that the panel itself is of no further use in this case. If I allowed this jury to decide the case, their verdict would surely get reversed on appeal, and we would all be right back here all over again.

"But fortunately, we have available a procedural mechanism called a directed verdict. Any trial judge may dismiss a jury and decide the case herself if she is convinced that no reasonable jury could ever render a verdict different from the one she is prepared to render. After hearing the testimony of Ms. Connors, whom I find to be very credible—" another glance at Leslie, this time accompanied by the slightest hint of a smile—"and after hearing the recording of Mr. Aberijan, and after considering the signed trust agreement introduced into evidence, I have concluded that a reasonable jury could only decide this case one way."

The judge stared sternly at Brad Carson through the glasses perched on the end of her long nose. She knew she was about to make him a multi-millionaire, and she hated every second of it. But she also thought about Sarah Reed and her children. And she thought about her own immense and growing disdain for Ahmed Aberijan. And she knew in her heart that justice demanded this verdict.

She shifted her gaze to Winsted Mackenzie. Her one satisfaction would be watching the look on his face as she forfeited her career for the sake of justice.

"Accordingly, I am hereby *denying* defendant's motion for a directed verdict and *granting* plaintiff's motion for a directed verdict against both Mr. Aberijan *and* the nation of Saudi Arabia."

Mackenzie's head shot back, his eyes wide.

"I am setting the damages at nine hundred thousand dollars for compensatory damages and *fifty million* in punitive damages."

◁ ▷

Brad could not breathe; the ruling sucked the air right out of him. He was not alone. For a fleeting moment, the courtroom was dead silent, *stunned* by a judge who had taken justice into her own hands, dispensed with closing arguments and jury deliberations, and brought this case to a swift and merciful close. The words sunk in. Brad caught his breath.

And pandemonium broke lose.

Sarah reached over and hugged Brad's neck. Reporters rushed for the exit. Excited spectators raised a clamor, struggling to be heard. And the defense team slumped back in their chairs, unable even to scribble the enormous number on their legal pads. All the while, as the noise crescendoed, Ichabod furiously banged her gavel.

After a few minutes, the noise abated on its own. The judge took advantage of the lull to issue her last speech.

"I have issued a bench warrant for Mr. Aberijan. When he is found, assuming that he has not escaped this country's jurisdiction, I want him brought back into *my court* to personally answer to *me*. I expect the assistant district attorney will also be issuing indictments against him. Because those indictments arise out of this trial, I am assigning Mr. Aberijan's criminal case to my docket so that I can preside over that matter as well. Is that clear, Ms. Bennett?"

Bennett stood and assured the court that she understood.

"Good," Ichabod said. "And one more thing, Ms. Bennett."

"Yes, Your Honor?"

"I had better have indictments on my docket within a week for any jury members who accepted a bribe or violated their oath in any way. Is that also clear?"

"We've already issued subpoenas for every juror's bank records, Your Honor."

"Very well."

It was a well-known tradition in the Eastern District of Virginia federal court for the judges to conclude cases by telling the lawyers, in front of their clients, what kind of service they had provided to their clients. Even Ichabod was duty bound by this tradition. She turned first to Mack Strobel.

"Mr. Strobel, as usual, you have tried an exemplary case. I have no reason to believe that you were engaged in or responsible for any of your former client's misconduct. You were thrown some curves in this case that no one could have foreseen, and you handled them with tact and diplomacy. If, God forbid, I am ever in need of legal services for a high-stakes trial, I think I would give you a call."

"Thank you, Your Honor," a pale Mack Strobel replied. Brad could barely hear his baritone voice.

"And, Mr. Carson," she said, turning to Brad. "While I do not sanction your occasional theatrics and unorthodox conduct in the courtroom, I will say that you are an effective advocate and a tenacious trial lawyer. Congratulations."

It was a backhanded compliment, and Brad knew it was the best he could ever hope for from her. It didn't bother him. He knew it was unprofessional, but he couldn't wipe a silly grin off his face. He had been wearing it since Ichabod announced her verdict.

"Thank you, Your Honor," he said sincerely. Fifty million could change his mind about someone in a hurry. "And I want to thank the court for handling this difficult case fairly and evenhandedly in the midst of some very tense moments."

Ichabod looked down again at Brad, one last time, over her annoying wire-rimmed glasses. She gave him the familiar scowl. "That's kind of you, Mr. Carson, but also easy to say when you've just won a big case. I would love to hear that same kind of comment from you sometime after you have just lost a case in my court."

Brad's grin disappeared.

He wanted to respond in the worst kind of way. Her comment was unfair and untrue. He got along with fair-minded judges, he would tell her, but not with tyrants. She needed to learn how to take a compliment, he would tell her, because with her personality, they would be few and far between. He had a million things to tell her, but he bit his tongue and said nothing. After all, this was federal court, and Brad knew the unwritten rules. One of them was that a federal court judge always has the last word.

"Case adjourned," Ichabod said, striking her gavel.

EPILOGUE

BRAD'S TEAM MEMBERS accomplished little in the days immediately following the directed verdict. They were too busy granting interviews, basking in the limelight, and dreaming about ways to spend their money. Not until Friday of that week did the office return to any semblance of normalcy. Even Bella, always the workhorse, found it hard to get motivated.

She arrived at the office at 9:15 and was not surprised to be the first one there. She turned on the lights, made some coffee, and resisted the urge to grab a smoke. It was her third day of trying to quit. The prior two had ended in glorious flameouts right after lunch.

She settled in at the front desk and let the phone ring while she finished an intriguing novel about a dreamy hunk named Brandon. She didn't feel the least bit guilty. Brad had told everyone to take the week off.

At 10:30, Nikki waltzed through the door and acted surprised to see Bella. "Couldn't stay away." She shrugged.

"Me either," Bella said. She held up a check. "The Johnson money came in today."

"Better check to make sure it doesn't have an extra million bucks," Nikki said on her way through the reception area. "I'd get fired for sure then."

Bella felt the heat rising in her cheeks. Typical Nikki. You try to be nice; you get rewarded with sarcasm. She would tell Nikki a thing or two. She stood, scowled . . . then sat back down and started counting. She made it to ten, then twenty . . . fifty . . . a hundred. She could feel herself calming down.

She needed a Camel. She stood again, her body screaming for a quick trip to the kitchen.

It would calm my nerves. I could finish the book. Nikki isn't going anywhere.

Instead, she turned down the hallway and headed for Nikki's office. She stood in the doorway and waited for her to look up.

413

"Um . . ." Bella rubbed her hands together. She had practiced this speech so many times. *How does it start again?*

"What's up?" Nikki asked. It was more of a "why don't you hurry up and say what's on your mind" tone than it was a question.

"Well," Bella said, looking at her hands, "I've tried t-to . . . um, come down and say this about a hundred times in the last few weeks, b-but I . . . I dunno . . ."

Nikki put down her pen and gave Bella her undivided attention. "Tried to say what?"

Okay. There's no easy way to do this. Just blurt it out. "I'm sorry, Nikki." She looked up and saw the blank look on Nikki's face. "That's it. . . . I've just been meaning to apologize for the way . . . for the way I've treated you . . ." She paused and shrugged. *This is really starting to seem like a dumb idea, even if it was Sarah's.* "From day one."

That was it. Her whole speech. She glanced again at Nikki, expecting . . . well, truthfully, she didn't know what to expect.

"Don't worry about it." Nikki shrugged.

That's all! No "Gee, I'm sorry too." No "Man, that's really big of you, Bella." No "Great, let's be friends now." Just a simple "Don't worry about it" and a blank stare. After all I put myself through, that's the best she can offer?

A crestfallen Bella turned to walk out the door. There was no sense pushing this any further. She had tried, given it her best. Some things just weren't meant to be. She would tell Sarah that confession and reconciliation were highly overrated.

"Wait," Nikki called. Bella turned back around and saw Nikki coming out from behind her desk. "Can you give me a hand for a minute?"

"Huh?"

Nikki pointed to the pictures hanging on her wall. "You know . . . getting rid of these things. It's starting to feel like an aquarium in here."

◁▷

It was Brad's idea to celebrate at the Lynnhaven Mariner. He would never forget the first time he and Leslie came to this place. It seemed like an eternity ago. She had charmed him with her beauty and poise. He had regaled her with his stories of the law. And this was the spot where the *Reed* case was born, where Brad and Leslie decided to make new law.

But that was months earlier, and their naive idealism about the case had been shattered by the emotional scars of battle. The beautiful spring day on which they had launched their plan had yielded to this cold and drizzly November day that forced them to enjoy lunch inside rather than on the deck.

It was Sunday afternoon, six days after the directed verdict. The fickle media attention, so white-hot intense in the days immediately following the latest trial of the century, had moved on to more important matters.

Ahmed and Barnes were in custody. Leslie was preparing to go back to school in January and finish her degree. Brad and Sarah were now household names.

Brad had grabbed the brass ring, won his case of national import, and realized that there was no lasting satisfaction in such an accomplishment. One week later, the interviews were over, and the ecstasy was gone. Only the relationships remained. From Leslie, he was learning each day to treasure a woman who understood him and accepted him for who he was. From Sarah, he had witnessed the strength of a personal relationship with God, through His Son, Jesus Christ. Brad wasn't ready to jump yet; all of this religious stuff was still very new to him. But he could not deny the comfort and contentment that both Sarah and Bella had found in their faith. He had heard Bella speak of her conversion experience. He had seen her change. And now he wondered if it could happen to him.

It was, to Brad's way of thinking, an intensely private matter, and one he was not yet ready to discuss even with Leslie. Right now, as they finished their seafood feast, he had things of a more immediate concern on his agenda.

"So what are your plans now?" He was playing with the cheesecake Leslie had forced him to order. She seemed determined to make him regain ten pounds in one week. But as usual, she had skipped dessert herself and was nursing a cappuccino.

"I guess going back to school will seem pretty tame after this," she said, playing with her drink. "But it'd be nice to actually have a law license if I intend to practice law."

"What's our future, Leslie?" he asked bluntly, embarrassed at himself even as the question crossed his lips. "What about us?"

Leslie paused before responding, and Brad looked down at his plate, pushing his cheesecake around with a fork. He loved her so much he was afraid to hear the answer.

"I could use a good tutor, if that's what you mean," Leslie quipped.

"Especially in my legal ethics class. As you know, that's not exactly my strong suit."

Brad put down his fork and looked into her beautiful blue eyes. He reached out his hand without speaking, and she placed hers in it.

"I'm serious, Leslie," he was almost pleading. "We've been great together, but was it all the result of the pressure and the case, or is there something special between us? something we can build on?"

He hesitated. Was it too much too fast? Would he scare her away and ruin the only part of his life that really mattered? His instincts told him to go for it. Now was the time. He would never forgive himself if he didn't.

"I love you, Leslie Connors," he said softly. "And I'll move heaven and earth to make it work for us." He squeezed her hand, held his breath, and waited.

She stared at their hands. "I promised myself after Bill died that I would never again love another man like I loved him. I thought it would be disloyal—" she stopped, blinked a few times, then continued—"and it hurt so much when I lost him." She looked up at Brad with glistening eyes. The world around them came to a stop.

"Then you came along and had the audacity to sweep me off my feet." A small smile. "I fought it as hard as I could, for as long as I could. But something about you and about this case—"

"Sir," said their smiling young waitress with the bleached-blonde hair, oblivious to the moment she was destroying, "I have some good news for you."

Brad didn't take his eyes from Leslie. He totally ignored the waitress, pretending she didn't exist. But Leslie cut her gaze away from Brad and up at the perky intruder.

"That's great," Leslie said, flashing her easy, sparkling smile. She brushed a tear from her eye with her free hand. "We're always in the market for some good news."

"That man in the corner has taken care of your bill," the proud waitress said and, to Brad's surprise, pointed to a smiling Mack Strobel, who sat with some men Brad did not recognize. He gave them a quick wave.

"That man?" Leslie said incredulously. "Are you sure?"

"Yes, ma'am," the blonde said. "He said to tell you it was the least he could do."

"Wow," Leslie said. She and Brad unclasped their hands, and both nodded back at their nemesis.

"Did he take care of your tip too?" Brad asked the waitress, who was still conspicuously hanging around.

"Oh yes, sir," she replied enthusiastically. "He sure did."

Brad felt the need to thank Strobel. Leslie followed at his shoulder.

Mack stood and offered his hand. His eyes were glazed, and he had a smile pasted on his lips.

"Bradley!" he said warmly and loudly.

Brad winced but was determined to be gracious. "Thanks for lunch, Mack. You didn't have to do that."

Strobel released Brad's hand and extended the same courtesy to Leslie. "As I told your waitress, it's the least I can do," Mack said, smiling. "You've already helped me have one of my best billable years ever, and I haven't even started on my appeal yet."

Strobel was talking loud enough that several of the patrons stopped eating and began staring.

"You can chase those old rabbits by my door anytime you want," Mack continued. "In fact, you keep bringing me juicy cases like that one, I might have my firm take out keyman insurance on you. It's plaintiff's lawyers like you who keep old hacks like me in business."

Brad grinned and tilted his head. He didn't quite know what to make of the old man.

"You tried a great case," Brad said.

"As did you, young man," Strobel said loudly. "I just try to give my clients their money's worth."

"They got every penny's worth from you," Brad replied earnestly.

Strobel turned to Leslie. "And as for you, when you get out of William and Mary and want to start a real international law practice, I've got an office right next to mine with your name on it."

Leslie narrowed her eyes, and Brad sensed that she was ready to tell him what she thought of that offer. But Strobel didn't pause long enough to give her the chance.

"I know the fringe benefits might not be as good as Carson & Associates," he continued with a wink, "but at least you wouldn't have to worry about any antinepotism policy."

He slapped Brad on the back. Brad wondered how many drinks Strobel had knocked down at lunch.

"I'll keep that in mind," Leslie said without conviction.

"Do that." Strobel grinned. He was rocking back and forth, barely maintaining his balance.

"Well," Brad said as he started to move away, realizing how little he had in common with Mack, "gotta run. Take care of yourself. And much as it helps your billable hours, I hope I don't see you in court again any time soon. There are much easier defense lawyers out there."

"I'll take that as a compliment." Strobel grinned. "And you probably won't be seeing me in court for a while anyway. I'll be spending the next few months jousting with the district attorney. Can you believe, after everything that happened, Aberijan retained me to handle his criminal case?"

"And you took it?" Leslie cried, wide-eyed in utter disbelief.

"It was all part of the master plan," Strobel said, grabbing the back of the chair and steadying himself. "All in a day's work. He pays the retainer. I take the case. And I think we've got a pretty good argument on entrapment."

Brad noticed the blood rising in Leslie's face. He grabbed her gently by the arm and steered her away.

"And we wonder why lawyers have a bad name," Leslie murmured under her breath as they headed toward the coatrack.

Brad enjoyed helping her into her overcoat and kept his arm around her shoulder as they walked toward the door. Like a refined gentleman, he held the door open for her and for another couple on their way in. The cold November wind blasted his face as he stepped outside. He used it as an excuse to pull Leslie close.

They walked around the corner of the building to where Brad had parked his Jeep. Leslie seemed agitated by Strobel's comments.

"Entrapment?" she asked.

"Fat chance," Brad replied confidently. "Entrapment only works if the government entices you into doing something you wouldn't otherwise do. And since Aberijan had already bribed a juror before you ever dealt with him, how could he make that argument? Plus, nobody enticed Aberijan to order a hit on you and O'Malley. He did that entirely on his own."

"What about the appeal of the civil case?" Leslie asked. "Does he stand a chance?"

"I don't think so," Brad replied without hesitation. "You were a pretty convincing witness with some pretty damaging evidence. He may delay it for a while, but he'll pay. And we can afford to wait now that we have the settlement check from Johnson. In the meantime, the phones are ringing off the hook with new clients. It's nice being famous."

Leslie put her arm around his waist. Brad's confidence seemed to reassure her and put her mind at ease.

But his mind was not, and it had nothing to do with the case. It had taken all his nerve, but he had said it. He had shared his feelings, told her that he loved her, and waited to hear her say it in return. Then the moment was lost to Mack Strobel, almost as if Strobel had planned the whole frustrating thing.

"Brad!" she yelled and pointed toward his Jeep. He jerked his head up just in time to see it on the business end of a tow truck heading out of the parking lot and onto the highway.

Brad sprinted across the parking lot to catch the driver before he made the turn.

"Hey!" he yelled and ran faster. The tow truck was waiting for a break in traffic, and Brad had about fifty yards to go. "Hey! That's my car! It's a mistake! I'm a lawyer! I'll sue!"

Brad caught the eyes of the tow truck driver as he looked in his mirror, then back to the highway. Brad was sprinting hard, closing on the truck. Ten yards to go . . . a small break in traffic . . . a spinning of truck tires on loose gravel . . . rocks and sand kicking up toward Brad . . . and the tow truck was on his way.

Another day, another repo.

"Ugh!" Brad threw his hands up, then leaned forward on his knees, catching his breath.

"This stinks!" he yelled in frustration. He kicked at the gravel. He had been looking forward to spending the day with Leslie: a romantic drive across the Chesapeake Bay Bridge Tunnel and some time together on the secluded eastern shore. *And now this.* Stuck in a parking lot with no wheels, and a hard northeastern wind blowing in a storm.

Leslie walked toward him, smiling. "Maybe we should call Bella," she teased.

"I'm calling a cab," he said. He started walking around Leslie, who had stationed herself between him and the restaurant. "And since my cell phone's in the Jeep, I've got to do it from a lousy pay phone."

As a frustrated Brad walked by, Leslie grabbed his arm, pulled him toward her, stood on her toes, and attacked him with a kiss. He closed his eyes and forgot about the weather, the Jeep, Strobel, and the pay phone. For the first time since they met, he could now focus entirely on Leslie, freed from the pressures of the case, untold secrets, and unspoken feelings. Freed from wondering whether she felt the same way he did.

And when their lips finally parted, they still embraced, her head on his shoulder, his arms gently and tenderly holding her close. They stood there in silence for a moment; then she turned her head and whispered softly and confidently in his ear.

"I love you too, Brad Carson."

ALSO BY RANDY SINGER

Fiction

Directed Verdict

Irreparable Harm

Dying Declaration

Self Incrimination

The Judge Who Stole Christmas

The Judge
previously published as The Cross
Examination of Oliver Finney

False Witness

By Reason of Insanity

The Justice Game

Fatal Convictions

The Last Plea Bargain

Nonfiction

Live Your Passion, Tell Your Story, Change Your World

Made to Count

The Cross Examination of Jesus Christ

www.randysinger.net

CP0232

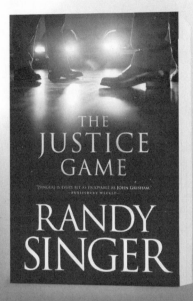

RACHEL CRAWFORD CLOSED her eyes while the show's makeup artist, a spunky woman named Carmen, did a quick touch-up.

"The sun looks good on you," Carmen said. "The Diva's shake 'n bake turns her orange."

"The Diva" was WDXR prime-time anchor Lisa Roberts. She treated the staff like dirt and was easy to hate. Five-ten with long, skinny legs, Lisa always complained about how much weight the camera added to her figure. Her chair had to be adjusted higher than everyone else's; the camera always had to be positioned to capture her left side (exposing a mole on her left cheek that she considered sexy); and her water had to be cold with just the right amount of ice.

"Maybe my next report will be on tanning beds," Rachel said. Carmen removed the makeup cape, and Rachel checked herself out in the mirror. She was no Lisa. A little shorter, heavier, with more of a girl-next-door look. But Rachel had one thing Lisa didn't; it was the reason for her glow.

"I hear tanning beds cause cancer," Carmen said, perking up with the thought. "Not just skin cancer, either—liver, thyroid, all kinds of nasty stuff."

Rachel did a subtle sideways twist, so casual that Carmen didn't notice. The blouse Rachel wore fit loose—not so loose as to be obvious, but just loose enough. She would have a few more weeks before her secret was out.

As a new reporter for the WDXR "I-team," Rachel had been working on a piece about the effect of cell phones on pregnant women. In two weeks, she would break her own exciting news on air as part of that piece. For at least one night, Lisa wouldn't be the center of attention.

"Thanks, Carmen," Rachel said. She scooped up her pad and water bottle and headed toward the door. "This water's way too warm," she said, mocking Lisa's perfect diction.

Carmen cackled. "Plus, it goes straight to my hips." She cocked her chin in the air as she gave Rachel a dismissive little shake of the head.

Rachel smiled and left the makeup room, settling into investigative reporter mode. Most of tonight's report was already on tape. Things had gone well during the 5 p.m. newscast. What could possibly go wrong at six?

She loved her job. But she loved the thought of being a mother even more. She wanted to do both—part-time I-team reporter and full-time mom. But that was a conversation for another day.

◁▷

Rachel fiddled with her earpiece, listening to the show's producer give Lisa Roberts and Manuel Sanchez instructions about the next few segments. Rachel sat up as straight as possible, though she would still be a few inches shorter than Lisa, and she smiled at the camera. The show's producer started the countdown. Lisa didn't change her scowl until the man said zero, triggering a magical transformation from spoiled diva to devoted and caring newswoman.

"Over three thousand international college students come to Virginia Beach each summer to work in the resort city," Lisa said, reading the prompter. "An unlucky few end up being victims of a sinister human-trafficking industry. I-team reporter Rachel Crawford has the details."

Lisa held her pose as they transitioned to the I-team tape. She might be hard to stomach, but she was a pro. Her cover girl looks and unshakable poise would soon carry Lisa beyond the Norfolk market, away from the place she scornfully referred to as a "dead end Navy town," the only place that Rachel could ever imagine calling home.

Rachel watched the report for about the fortieth time and allowed herself a brief moment of pride. The segment started with a few shots of The Surf, a popular Virginia Beach hangout, with a voiceover from Rachel about the way international student workers helped keep the place afloat. They had video of two female Eastern European students tending bar, waiting tables, even taking out the trash. The camera angles had been carefully selected so the viewers could never quite get a good look at the students' faces. The tape cut to Rachel, standing in front of the bar, a serious tilt to her head.

"But a few of these girls, who talked to WDXR under condition of anonymity, said there was a dark side to their summer at the Beach. . . ."

The next shot featured Rachel interviewing one of the students. The editors had blocked out the student's face and digitally altered her voice.

She talked about the owner of The Surf—Larry Jamison—the man who had promised the students jobs and paid for the girls to come to America.

"If you didn't become one of Larry's girls, you could never get out of debt, no matter how hard you worked. Plus, there were threats. . . ."

As Rachel explained the scam, a Web page appeared on-screen. The girl's images were distorted, but it was obviously a porn site, one that Rachel had traced back to Larry Jamison.

"We asked Mr. Jamison about these charges," Rachel said on the tape. "He refused to be interviewed for this report."

In a few seconds, they would be live again. Rachel checked her earpiece and turned toward Lisa. She heard a pop that startled her—it might have been a few pops—something like firecrackers, coming from the other side of the studio's soundproof door. She glanced at the doors but nobody else seemed bothered by it.

"Five seconds," said a voice in her ear. "Four, three, two, one . . ."

A cameraman pointed to Lisa and she turned toward Rachel. "Those girls you interviewed seemed so vulnerable. Did they understand they could press charges against this guy?"

Out of the corner of her eye, Rachel noticed a flash of commotion at the back of the studio. Like a pro, she stayed focused on Lisa, explaining why the girls were not willing to come forward.

"Hey!" someone yelled. "He's got a gun!"

Shots rang out as Rachel swiveled toward the voices, blinded by the bright lights bearing down on her. She heard more shots, screams of panic and pain—pandemonium in the studio.

"Get down!" someone shouted.

There was cursing and a third barrage of shots as Rachel dove to the floor, crawling quickly behind the anchor desk—a fancy acrylic fixture that certainly wouldn't stop a bullet. In the chaos, she looked over to see Lisa, wide-eyed with fear, her fist to her mouth, a silent sob.

For a moment, everything was still.